"SEGUNDO . . . BASTARD!"

Jessica's curse pulled him back from the brink and sealed her own fate. His hard body crushing hers, Duncan caught her parted lips in a fierce, punishing kiss. Her reaction was like a small explosion beneath him.

Pushing against his torso with her hands, Jessica writhed and bucked her slender body in an attempt to dislodge him. Her frantic movements succeeded only in inflaming his already aroused body.

With slow, infinite care, Duncan made sweet love to Jessica's mouth. Her breathing quickened and, as she had before, for one beautiful instant her lips responded to the allure of his adoring mouth. When the instant ended, he raised his head to stare into her confusion-clouded eyes.

"I will have you, Jessie," he whispered, watching emotions flicker in her eyes. "Someday soon, I will have all of you, *querida*, naked and clinging to me."

"I'll die first," she snapped.

"No, love," he murmured with a wickedly seductive smile. "You will die during, over and over again."

Silver Thunder

JOAN HOHL

Silver Thunder

A Dell Book

Published by
Dell Publishing
a division of
Bantam Doubleday Dell Publishing Group, Inc.
666 Fifth Avenue
New York, New York 10103

ISBN: 0-440-21236-7

Printed in the United States of America

Published simultaneously in Canada

September 1992

10 9 8 7 6 5 4 3 2 1

OPM

Special Acknowledgments

Thanks and gratitude to my niece, Vicki Reitenauer, for her patience and help while assisting me with the research for the work.

and to

Charlou Dolan, for her untiring willingness to scour used book stores for additional research material.

Thanks much, ladies

In loving memory of my mother
Edith

I miss you, Mom

Prologue

Wyoming, August 1892

They called him Segundo.

To the ten carefully selected drovers and the ranchers and townspeople they had encountered along the grueling trail between Texas and Wyoming, the tall, unsmiling, dark-skinned man in charge of the cattle drive was known only as Segundo—the man second in command to the unknown owner of the Circle-F spread in Wyoming. To a man, the hired hands believed him to be Mexican. He had the carriage and imperious appearance of an aristocratic Spanish grandee.

In truth, the man called Segundo was neither Mexican nor Spanish. Rather he was a combination, a 50 percent mixture of Scot and English and 50 percent pure American Shoshone Indian. But, for a time, it suited Duncan Frazer's purposes to play a role.

His gaze riveted to the distant mountain range, Duncan arched his back and shifted position in the saddle. Every muscle in his body ached in protest against months spent on the back of a horse. He was bone tired and skin-deep dirty. His eyes and teeth felt gritty from the five-month accumulation of trail dust. His clothing and skin were coated with a sickly gray tinge. The closest he had come to a bath since mid-March was during the rainstorms that had plagued them at too-frequent intervals and the soakings they'd received while fording rivers and streams swollen with spring rain.

At that moment, Duncan longed for nothing more than a hot, all-over bath, a decent meal—that did not consist mainly of beans—and a real bed, warmed by a willing woman. But, though the rigors of the long drive were over, his destination reached, there was still work for him to do. And, although he was firm in his determination to have the bath, the meal, and the bed, the release afforded by a woman would have to wait. Regardless how willing, not just any woman would do for Duncan Frazer—the Earl of Rayburne. He was horny as hell, but he was also as particular.

Puffy white clouds diffused the afternoon sunlight, casting shadows on the jagged mountains. A tightness clutched at Duncan's throat. The Wind River range— the memory of those majestic mountains had in turn tormented and sustained him for over twenty years.

Not a day had elapsed during those years when he hadn't yearned for the sight of them.

Memories flowed through his mind, happy, painful, bittersweet. A faraway look crept into his eyes.

Since he had heard the recitation repeatedly during the long winter nights of his childhood, Duncan knew by heart the story of his father's sojourn from his home in Scotland to the American shores. His discomfort, the unrelenting rays from the summer sun, the vista spread out in front of him, the very present dissolved. The past rushed to the fore. In his mind, Duncan could hear the echo of his father's voice, recounting the tale of his journey and the subsequent capture of his heart and loyalty by the land and a woman of it.

Malcolm Frazer stared entranced at the jagged, snow-crowned mountains in the distance. He felt a stirring inside, a strange sense of beckoning, not unlike a hungry yearning. The odd sensation had begun before he and his guide, an old mountain man who went by the name of Beaver, departed the wagon train to strike out on their own.

Parting from the friends and companions he had made during the arduous journey from Independence to where they would cross the Continental Divide at South Pass had not been easy for Malcolm. Nor had it originally been his intention.

Wealthy and footloose, the second son of Laird Frazer, the Earl of Rayburne, Malcolm had wandered throughout Europe, Asia, and the Far East for over ten years before setting out from his home in the highlands of Scotland to investigate America.

After spending some interesting months in the bustling cities of Boston, New York, and Philadelphia, Malcolm had circumvented the disheartening scenes of dissension between the Northern and Southern states and made his way to Independence, Missouri, eager to see and experience the raw West he had read and heard so much about. He was not alone in his quest to see the vast expanse of country beyond the wide river called the Mississippi.

The year-old war that was rending the fabric of the Union had affected great numbers of people who were not directly involved in the battle. Hordes of citizens and foreigners alike converged on Independence, the gateway to the sprawling Great Plains and the land of plenty and promise west of the Rocky Mountains.

In Independence, Malcolm had hired Beaver, who in turn had signed them on with a wagon train that was preparing to head for California, via the Oregon Trail.

In contrast to the majority of his fellow travelers, funding the proposed journey posed no problem for Malcolm. But, although he had traveled extensively, he was new to this concept of emigration and had scant knowledge of what it entailed. Being a realist, Malcolm put his faith and financial resources in the experienced hands of his guide.

The grizzled Beaver began with his employer. In short order, Malcolm found his elegant, London-tailored attire exchanged for durable homespun clothing, his jaunty silk top hat usurped by a soft, wide-brimmed planter's hat, and his stylish ankle boots replaced by tough leather knee-high boots. When the metamorphosis was complete, Malcolm looked similar to every other man on the frontier. Similar, but not alike. There was a definite difference that set him apart from other men.

The mingled blood of Scottish kings and British aristocracy flowed in Malcolm's veins. He was taller than average and leanly muscled. His features were a combination of chiseled Celtic and patrician English. His thick hair gleamed like a flame in the sunlight. Intelligence sharpened his clear green eyes. His hands were broad, his fingers long and slender, but his palms were not those of a dilettante. Malcolm had never considered himself above turning his hand to manual labor. In the spring of 1862, Malcolm was thirty-one years old, physically strong, and curious about the world he inhabited. He enjoyed the company of his fellow men and it showed, in his actions and manner.

With the job of outfitting his employer finished, the taciturn Beaver turned to the business of outfitting their wagon. Malcolm was engrossed by the entire process. Also true to his heritage of thriftiness, he duly noted each and every expenditure.

When Beaver declared them as ready and prepared as possible for the trek, the wagon was loaded with the guide's idea of the bare necessities: 365 pounds of bacon; 40 pounds of coffee; 80 pounds of sugar; 100 pounds each of lard and beans; 70 pounds of dried peaches and apples; 15 pounds of salt, plus items such as ground corn, vinegar, pepper, and an assortment of medicines. In addition to the staples, Beaver included a milk cow and four sheep. The total cost of Malcolm's clothing and the supplies came to just over 200 American dollars.

The wagon train pulled out of Independence on May 1, 1862. Malcolm was transfixed by the scene. Since their wagon was located midway in the train, he had time to indulge his fascination with the activity. Noise was a constant, a rising clamor of voices, the bellows of animals, the creaking and groaning of wheels and axles. Dust rose in ever-blossoming billows, marking the passage of each separate unit of pilgrims.

The experience was confusing as well as edifying for Malcolm. Having sailed a good many of the seas and oceans of the world, he was not unseasoned. He had crossed the Sahara by means of camel caravan and had stalked the tigers of India from the back of an elephant. But never had he experienced anything quite like this nearly mile-long unwinding train of humanity. Malcolm found the sights and scents, and even the noise and the stench of the process both riveting and exciting.

Once the train was strung out and moving, the excitement was quick to dissipate. The wagon train advanced at a crawling pace, which posed a daily test to Malcolm's patience. The initial part of the journey was uneventful, if uncomfortable. Day-to-day conditions were at best harsh, at worse discouraging. The daily rations of food were unappetizing, unless wild game was available, then it was merely tasteless. Yet the privation didn't bother Malcolm. He had shared countless meals around as many campfires, never venturing to inquire precisely what any particular concoction consisted of, and lived to laugh about it afterward. For Malcolm, it was the experience that counted, the living of it.

Once the train headed into the land just beginning to be known as the Wyoming Territory, the going grew more difficult.

Following the deep wagon ruts cut into the earth by

twenty years of the ever-westward movement of the trains that had preceded them, the lumbering wagons forged onward. But the price of future promise was high, exacted in physical discomfort and emotional trauma.

Children and adults became ill; many died, most frequently the women and their young. The dead were buried along the trail, often with no marker left at all to note their passage. Weariness became the pervasive ailment suffered by every member of the train. Friendships were formed, companionship the means to normality in a world reduced to the extreme fluctuations of temperatures of stifling hot days and chilling cold nights, of wrenching sickness and unbelievable hardship.

Through it all, Malcolm was filled with admiration for the sheer tenacity of his fellow travelers. They suffered, they complained, at times they wept, openly and unashamed, but they maintained, they persevered with grim determination. They were headed toward tomorrow, and, come hell or high water, they were going to make it.

With respect for the irrepressible Americans growing within him, Malcolm shared their deep sorrows and small joys, and rejoiced with them at the passing of each milestone along the trail. After a brief rest at Fort Laramie, there were the sheltering cliffs at Register Cliff, along the banks of the North Platte River. Then the drive was on to reach the 193-foot-high landmark of Independence Rock by July 4, where traditionally emigrants rested and celebrated beneath its shadow. From Independence Rock they moved on to Devil's Gate, along the Sweetwater River. With the Gate behind them, the push was on to South Pass and the Continental Divide. After the Divide, the trail led to Fort Bridger and the golden West.

From the outset, Malcolm had had every intention of trekking the length of the route to California. But his intentions wavered as the train drew nearer to South Pass. He felt a strange, compelling allure of the distant mountains, an allure he had never before in his life experienced. The silent siren song ensnared him. No amount of applied reasoning could gainsay the enticing summons from the mountains.

Unable to resist, Malcolm obeyed the mute call. Taking his leave of the friends he had made, he and Beaver struck out on their own when the train pulled out of South Pass after a brief rest stop.

Beaver spotted the Indians on the second day out. Eyes narrowed against the glare of the August sunshine, the old mountain man stared into the distance, studying the approach of the mounted natives.

It was not a large band, but they came toward the solitary wagon with purposeful intent. Watching them draw near, Malcolm felt a mixture of anticipation and apprehension. While he was eager to see one of the native Americans up close, he had heard some blood-curdling tales about the savage practices of some of the Plains Indians, and the idea of parting company with his full head of red hair, along with a portion of his scalp, sent a thrill of unadulterated fear into his heart.

"It's all right," Beaver murmured, when the band was close enough for identification. "They're Shoshone. More'n likely from Washakie's camp."

Malcolm received the information with a quiet sigh of relief. Along with the tales he had heard of savagery, he had also heard of the friend of the white man, the powerful warrior Washakie, chief of the Shoshone tribe.

Anticipation sank into disappointment inside Malcolm when the small band drew to a halt several feet away from where Beaver sat astride his horse beside the wagon. In truth there was little resemblance between the rag-tail group and the noble savages he had expected to encounter.

Their black hair was lank and greasy and hung straight and straggly to their shoulders. Their clothing was a mish-mash of buckskin and white men's cotton, and none too clean. Some were half naked. They might even have appeared pitiful or comical to the casual observer—until the observer looked into their faces, and their eyes. There was nothing pitiful or comical there. Their features were etched with arrogance; the depths of their dark eyes burned with fierce pride.

Possessing a fair share of both arrogance and pride of race himself, Malcolm felt an immediate shift in feelings. His disappointment changed into a deep sense of affinity, renewing his eagerness to meet and mingle with these people.

Beaver spoke to the small group in a low, harsh-sounding language. One of the group, a young, steely-eyed stalwart, responded.

"What did he say?" Malcolm asked in a murmured aside.

"Wants to know if we're lost," Beaver muttered. He raised his voice a notch to reply to the brave, then translated for Malcolm. "I told him we're not lost, but left our train because we like the look of their land."

There ensued a garbled, animated discussion among the six members of the group. Then the man who had spoken before walked his horse closer to Beaver. Head held high, he rattled off what sounded to Malcolm like instructions.

Malcolm's spirits plummeted. "Are they refusing us passage?" he asked, switching his gaze from the brave to Beaver.

"Nah." Turning his head, Beaver spat a stream of dark juice from the wad of tobacco wedged in the corner of his cheek. "Just the opposite. They're offering us their protection, in accordance with the wishes of their chief." The guide gave one of his rare, crooked smiles. "I figured as much, seeing as how their chief is Washakie."

"Washakie!" Malcolm exclaimed, staring expectantly at the guide. "You know him?"

"Never had the pleasure." Beaver grunted. "But I know of him. Washakie has been friendly with whites for over twenty years, starting with the beaver trappers in the late thirties or early forties. Even learned to speak English. Old Jim Bridger's married to one of the chief's daughters."

Sudden excitement was a living entity inside Malcolm. He had come to America to experience all it had to offer. What better way to experience the raw West than to meet and converse with this chief who was a friend of the white man?

"Could we meet with him?" Malcolm asked in a tone of suppressed excitement. "Speak with him?"

"Don't see why not." Shrugging, Beaver once again addressed the spokesman of the group.

His face expressionless, the young man turned to relay the request to the other braves. There was a brief discussion among the men, and then the spokesman turned to respond to Beaver.

Malcolm was unaware that he was holding his breath until it eased from his chest in a long sigh when Beaver gave a sharp nod of his head and said, "They'll escort us to the camp."

The Shoshone encampment was anything but prepossessing, but Malcolm was neither discouraged nor disappointed by the crude conditions under which the Indians lived. He had dwelt for over a year with a nomadic tribe in Arabia. To Malcolm's way of thinking, the tepee lodges of the Shoshone differed little from the tents of the nomads.

The Shoshone chief was impressive, not so much in appearance as in the determined set of his features and the steely look of his eyes. His leathery, copper-tinged, scarred face was framed by long straight gray hair, which he wore in thong-bound tails on either side of his head. There was nothing to distinguish him from the other men in the tribe, and yet Malcolm correctly identified him on sight.

After Beaver introduced himself and Malcolm, Washakie invited them into his lodge then, in halting English, made them welcome to the camp, for as long as they wished to bide. When Malcolm professed a desire to remain with the tribe for a week, the chief ordered a tepee erected for his guests.

In the end, Malcolm stayed in the camp for over a month. The reason for his extended visit was his fascination with a small, slender member of the tribe. Though there was no similarity in facial appearance, she reminded him of the young woman who had warmed his sleeping mat during the final week of his sojourn in the Sahara with a Berber-speaking group of Tuaregs.

Her hair was long, black as a starless night, and her name was First Star, because the first thing her mother had seen after giving birth was the first star of evening. The daughter of a lesser chieftain, First Star was gentle and delicate, her dusky skin as soft as her doelike brown eyes. To Malcolm, she was the most beautiful creature alive. In her shy, hesitant way, First Star let it be known that she reciprocated Malcolm's tender feelings.

With Washakie's blessing, Malcolm took First Star to wife at the end of his month-long visit. Then, along with his wife, Beaver, and First Star's brother, a tall, handsome young man named Chill Wind Blowing, and his wife, Inga, a strapping blond Scandinavian he had rescued from an Arapaho raiding party, Malcolm left the encampment late in September to settle on the eastern fringes of the Shoshone hunting grounds of the Wind River valley. Not long after they were on the land Malcolm claimed as his own, he christened his wife Mary, after his beloved mother.

Fortune smiled on them during the month of October, for other than a few days of cool temperatures, the weather remained sunny and mild. Living in hastily erected tepees, and following Beaver's directions, they built three earth-covered dugout dwellings. The living quarters were crude but secure against the harshness of the approaching winter. They were the first structures on what was to become the sprawling spread Malcolm named the Circle-F ranch.

During a raging blizzard in late January '63, Malcolm made Mary-First Star his legal wife under the law of his adopted country. They said their vows before a dour circuit preacher, who had taken shelter with them against the brutal storm. Their son was born premature but fully developed and healthy three months later.

Like his mother, the baby's skin was a dusky hue and his hair was dark, though shot through with strands of deepest red. His eyes were a startling combination of his mother's brown and his father's green, emerging in a bright turquoise flecked with amber, framed by long black lashes.

Malcolm named the boy Duncan in honor of a distant ancestor, Duncan I. That first Duncan had been king of the Scots. In 1040 he'd been murdered by Macbeth, who in turn was killed by Duncan's son, Malcolm III. Malcolm later married an English princess, bringing English blood, customs, and titles into the family.

Duncan's Shoshone grandfather named him Stone Eyes.

Malcolm spent the winter formulating his plans for the future. He intended to ranch but, as he possessed neither herd nor experience, his first order of business in the spring was to acquire both. Setting his plans into motion, and with Beaver again acting as advisor and guide, Malcolm left for Texas on a cattle-buying trip two weeks after his son's birth, leaving the infant and his mother in the care and protection of her brother and their people.

The biting winds of late fall were sweeping the plains by the time Malcolm returned, but the long, grinding trip had proved fruitful. Along with an experienced ranch foreman and five cowboys, Malcolm brought back with him a thousand head of tough Texas longhorns. But he came back without Beaver, who had decided to explore the wilds of West Texas.

Content with his place in his wife's affection and in his position of right-hand man to Malcolm, Chill Wind Blowing took the name David Robertson. Two years after Duncan's birth, Inga was delivered of a son. The boy's sharply defined features were a combination of his Shoshone and Scandinavian parents, but in coloring he favored his mother. He had a golden-copper skin tone and light brown hair and eyes. With David-Chill Wind's approval she named him Eric, in memory of her father, who had been killed during the Arapaho raid on their wagon train.

Eric's Shoshone grandfather called him Soft Eyes.

As Duncan and Eric grew from infants to toddlers and then young boys, the ranch and surrounding area grew along with them. By the spring of Duncan's seventh year the town of South Pass boasted some four thousand citizens, and another, smaller town had sprung up closer to the Circle-F ranch—which by then had grown to encompass over 40,000 acres.

The small, unattractive town of a mere couple hundred residents was called Sandy Rush, by dint of the fact that it had been built along the banks of a stream that either ran shallow, revealing a sandy bottom, or rushed with water, depending on the season and the prevailing weather conditions.

Although the dirt-covered dugout had long since been replaced by the two-story ranch house Malcolm and David built during their second summer on the land, life on the plains was not easy for young Duncan and Eric. Except for the young couple who had settled down to ranching on the land bordering Malcolm's after

Wyoming became a territory, all the good citizens of
Sandy Rush, and the neighboring ranchers and farmers,
ostracized the Frazer family, their relatives, and employees. Motivated by fear and prejudice, they resented the presence of Mary-First Star, her brother
David-Chill Wind, Inga, and the children of the two
couples.

From the time they started school in the crude, one-
room school house outside Sandy Rush, Duncan and
Eric had engaged in numerous fistfights with other
boys their own age and much older over being called
savage half-breeds. Shunned and ridiculed by the
"whites," their only social interaction was with the
neighboring couple, Ben and Emily Randall.

Tall for his age, with the sharp Celtic features and
strong, rangy frame of his father, Duncan was ever protective of the Randalls' four-year-old son, Parker, and
enthralled by their eighteen-month-old, platinum-
haired daughter, Jessica. As in everything else, Eric
shared his cousin's protective feelings toward the Randall children.

But if life was not always easy, it had its compensa-
tions. There were times of great joy and laughter in the
Frazer homestead. Mary-First Star bloomed in the radi-
ance of love showered upon her by her husband and
son. Having learned of the cruelty as well as the good-
ness inherit in human nature, Malcolm was content to
be content.

If not perfect, life was good. Once more, with David-
Chill Wind's assistance, Malcolm set to work, erecting a
large, permanent residence for what he hoped was his
growing family. But his hopes were dashed soon after
the house was completed when Mary-First Star suc-

cumbed to influenza late in the winter of 1872. His
sense of contentment shattered, made bitter by the
cold, uncaring attitude of the townsfolk and most of his
neighbors, and inconsolable over the loss of his beloved
wife, Malcolm rejected his adopted country.

In the spring of 1872, almost ten years to the day of
his original departure west from Independence, Missouri, Malcolm, vowing never to return to America, departed with his son for his birthplace in the highlands
of Scotland, leaving the management of the Circle-F in
the capable hands of his brother-in-law, David-Chill
Wind.

As the wagon loaded with their personal possessions
lumbered away from the ranch buildings, young
Duncan twisted around on the hard wooden seat to
stare with longing at the jagged spires of the distant
mountains. The last words he spoke to his seven-year-
old cousin were:

"Take care of Parker and our baby."

1

He was home.

Memory shifted, receded, leaving a backwash illuminating one tiny reverberation.

"Take care of our baby."

A gentle, reminiscent smile softened the hard line of Duncan's mouth. Our baby. A chuckle rumbled deep in his throat. Twenty years had passed since he had charged his young cousin with the care of a toddler. Their baby was no longer a child.

What was she like now at . . . nearly twenty-two? Duncan wondered, recalling the scant tidbits of infor-

mation sent to him over the years in letters and the
ranch reports from his uncle David and his cousin.

In actual fact, Duncan knew very little about the
child he had adored, other than that she had been sent
away somewhere to school at the age of fifteen and that
she loved her home territory with a passion. He empathized with her feelings for the land, because he harbored the same passion.

Home. God, it was beautiful.

Narrowing his eyes against the glare from the westering sun, Duncan swept the area with an encompassing
look. Anticipation tingled the length of his spine, banishing the weariness of months of arduous labor. The
mountains were still there, still the same. The valleys,
rivers, and streams were all where he remembered
them to be, exactly where they had all lived, inside the
secret longing place in his mind. With a smile, Duncan
repressed an urge to shout his feelings of elation aloud,
just to hear the echo roll back to him from the mountains.

Flipping its long black mane, the big dun beneath
him danced with restless energy along the crest of the
sloping hill rising behind the town of Sandy Rush.
Jolted from introspective meandering, Duncan redi-
rected his gaze. The sight of the scraggly assortment of
clapboard buildings brought a faint bittersweet smile to
his thin, trail-dried lips and another surge of sharp-
edged memories to his mind.

Tightening the reins he held in one hand and applying pressure with his thighs, Duncan controlled the animal with absent expertise, while his gaze skimmed the
rundown structures on either side of the town's central
dirt street. Except for a few minor additions, Sandy

Rush had changed little in twenty years, and he had a gut feeling that its residents had matched it in both progress and enlightenment. Duncan would have wagered his inheritance that the good citizens of Sandy Rush were still as narrow-minded and prejudicial as they had been the last time he'd been there.

A blur of movement and a puff of dust caught his attention. Dismissing the town, Duncan shifted his gaze. Through eyes still narrowed in defense against the summer sun, he watched the approach of a solitary rider. Recognition eased the tension gathering in his body as the horseman drew near enough to identify. Duncan had not seen his cousin in twenty years, yet he'd have known him anywhere.

There was a slight similarity, a family resemblance, between the two men, in so far as they were both tall, broad-shouldered, slim-waisted, and sharp-featured. There the resemblance ended. In comparison to Duncan's darkness, his cousin's skin had a light copper hue. His eyes and hair were a soft brown, opposed to Duncan's gold-flecked turquoise eyes and black hair, shot through with streaks of dark red.

The rider brought his horse to a stop a few feet away from Duncan's mount. The two men stared with solemn interest at each other. Then in a soft, cultured voice, Duncan greeted his cousin in the guttural Shoshone tongue.

"I'm surprised you remember the language, Stone Eyes," the man said, extending his hand. "I seldom use it myself."

A half-smile relieved the tension lines bracketing Duncan's mouth. "I have forgotten nothing, Soft Eyes," he replied, grasping his cousin's hand.

The physical contact sparked a flood of childhood memories. Inside his mind, he and his cousin were boys once more, tramping through waist-high snow to the chill one-room schoolhouse, where neither one of them were ever welcomed. He was a youth again, reveling in the freedom he had felt while sweating beside his cousin as they learned the ropes of ranching from the cowboys, and when galloping his pony alongside his cousin's during their summer visits to the Shoshone reservation. He could feel again the warmth of the fire-place in his home, and the deeper warmth of his mother's and father's love as, without showing favorit-ism, Malcolm enriched his and his nephew's education from his own worldwide gathered store of knowledge and Mary-First Star instructed them in Shoshone lore. The strength of the childhood remembrances hurt and soothed at the same time. Duncan could see his remi-niscences reflected in the depths of his cousin's mem-ory-clouded brown eyes.

"How are you, Eric?"

"It's been a long time, Duncan." Eric's fingers tight-ened in memory and welcome for an instant, and then he released his grip and shrugged. "I'm fair to mid-dlin'," he drawled. "How about you?"

"Tired, but otherwise fine." Smiling from the pure pleasure of seeing his cousin again, and because he sounded exactly like every one of his hired hands, Duncan asked after his aunt and uncle. "And your mother and father?"

"Mother is . . . Mother," Eric said, as if that ex-plained everything, which to Duncan, it did. "But my father is mad at life for crippling him with the arthritis that forced his retirement." He sighed, then brightened. "But he's feeling a whole lot easier now that you're here."

The emotional homecoming moment was over. Duncan frowned. "The situation worsening?"

"A mite." Eric canted his head to indicate the town at the base of the hill. "There are some hard-eyed strangers taking up space at the bar in the Sawdust."

Shifting around, Duncan stared at a building midway along the three-block-street bearing the unoriginal name of Main. The Sawdust Saloon had been there when he was a boy. "Trouble coming to a boil?" he asked.

" 'Fraid so."

"Any idea who's stirring the pot?"

"Yeah." Eric's smile was grim. "Dad and I were buffaloed for a spell about the hit-and-run rustling, but some things have come to light since I wrote to you last."

"What things?"

"Oh, things like small ranchers and farmers being harassed and pressured to sell out, and like one big rancher—a friend—losing a sizable number of cows after his daughter turned down a proposal of marriage."

Duncan's eyes narrowed. "The rancher being rustled is Ben Randall?"

Eric nodded.

"Jessica?"

Again Eric answered with a nod.

Duncan had another memory flash, this one of the last time he had seen the girl. He had been a tall, awkward nine-year-old. He and his father had gone to the Randall ranch for a farewell visit. The Randalls' daughter had been little more than a baby, with big gray eyes as soft looking as a kitten's fur and a cap of silky hair the amazing color of shimmering silver. Tiny and delicate, she was just beginning to master dashing about like a young filly without crashing into people and furniture. When Duncan entered the sparsely furnished but welcoming kitchen, the child had squealed with delight. Tripping in her excitement, she had flung herself against his thin, gangly body. He could still recall the sweet baby smell of her.

"But Jessica's just a child," he said in protest, reacting to the memory rather than reality.

"Like I said, it's been a long time, Duncan," Eric said in chiding tones. "Jessica's all grown up now."

For a moment Duncan felt a pang of regret, a grieving for the beautiful child he had loved so very much. "Yes, of course." A sad smile flickered over his lips. "And she does not wish to marry this man?"

Eric made a face. "From all indications, Jessica doesn't want to marry any man. Hell, there are those who believe she thinks she is a man, the way she dresses and acts. And she is getting a little long in the tooth, you know." He grinned. "She's almost twenty-two."

Setting aside the intriguing information of her apparently unusual way of life for future examination, Duncan returned to the subject under discussion. "Who is this man you believe is causing things to happen?"

Eric's grin curved into a grimace. "His name is Josiah Metcalf, but he goes by Josh. Turned up here a little over a year ago from Chicago. He's a good-lookin' dude about forty or so, and from all indications, he wants land and power and Ben Randall's daughter."

"And you believe Metcalf is paying wages to the hard-eyed strangers?"

"Couldn't prove it," Eric said. "But I'd bet my best cow pony on it."

Exhaling, Duncan shifted his weight in the saddle. "You wrote in your letter that you were afraid of a situation similar to the Johnson County war. What happened in Johnson County? I have never heard of that war."

"I'm not surprised." Eric shrugged. "It wasn't much of a war and hardly lasted a week. Weren't any real winners or losers either. What it boiled down to was the big ranchers against the homesteaders and small ranchers, who were supposedly building their own small herds with running irons, and—"

"Running irons?" Duncan interrupted.

"It's a tool used to alter cattle brands," Eric explained. "Anyway," he continued, "I heard tell that the big boys got together and collected a war chest of over one hundred thousand dollars to hire an army of gunslingers, ex-marshals, and hard cases. Had a list of twenty or thirty names of men to be eliminated. The farmers and cowboys had formed their own army of some two hundred strong, led by a local sheriff named Red Angus. There were a few skirmishes, then the war was ended by the arrival of three troops of soldiers from Fort McKinney."

"And you suspected the same thing was happening here?" Duncan asked.

"For a while." Eric's smile was sardonic. "Dad and I thought we were being excluded from the big ranchers' plans for the same reason we've been left out of everything else."

"Your Shoshone blood?"

"Correct." Eric moved his shoulders, as if shrugging off years of being ostracized. "But then I talked to Ben about it and he assured me there was no plan to force the farmers and small ranchers to sell out."

"Hmm." Duncan was quiet a moment, digesting the information. When he spoke again, his tone betrayed confusion. "But you also mentioned in your letter that we had had fences cut and were losing cattle, and that you believed the farmers and small ranchers were making free with our stock." He raised his dark brows in question. "But now you have changed your mind and believe the rustling was instigated by Metcalf and not the farmers and small ranchers?"

"Basically, yes." Eric shrugged. "Oh, we all know that the farmers have free beef on their tables occasionally and that the small ranchers increase their herds with a running iron now and again. It's a fact of life out here. So long as the number of beefs gone missing is low, we deal with it ourselves, without involving the law. I wouldn't have bothered you with such a piddlin' piece of information. But the reason I wrote to you was because I was worried about the situation turning into another Johnson County mess, and I thought you, being the owner of the Circle-F, should know."

"I see." Beginning to feel that his saddle was made out of lead instead of leather, Duncan shifted his butt once more. "But, even though the situation is not as you originally thought, you still believe there is trouble brewing here?"

Eric jerked his head in the direction of Sandy Rush. "With those toughs in town? Oh, yeah, I'd say we've trouble brewing aplenty. Metcalf is up to something. The days of the cattle kings are gone—due to many reasons. If you recollect, the blizzards of eighty-six and eighty-seven destroyed about three-quarters of the stock on the plains . . . wiped out some of the big boys who'd overextended themselves." He paused, but continued after Duncan indicated recall with a nod. "Then, with the arrival of more and more settlers, there was less and less open grazing range. There are still the large ranchers, like us and Ben Randall and a bunch of others, but it's getting a mite too crowded around here for the old style of free-wheeling, law-unto-themselves cattle barons. And yet Metcalf is buying up property as fast as he can force someone into selling. I can't help but wonder what in hell he's up to."

"Very well." Duncan again gave a brief nod of his head. "Then the trouble I went to arranging the cattle drive from San Antonio was not a waste of my time."

They had been sitting a long time, and now Eric began to squirm in the saddle. "How'd the drive go?"

Duncan's smile was wry. "Since I have no previous experience with which to compare it, I can give you no more than my own personal opinion."

Eric's lips twitched at the underlying disgust in his cousin's tone. "And that is?"

"It was a son of a bitch."

The sound of Eric's explosive laughter floated on the hot afternoon air. "I've never heard of one that wasn't," he said, his laughter subsiding. "How big was the herd?"

"I started out with a thousand head—good purebred stock." Duncan smiled with grim acceptance. "They cost me a small fortune."

Eric nodded. "They would. But you could see some return on your investment, if you're so inclined."

"Indeed?" Duncan raised his brows.

"Yes. I told Ben about the herd. He said he'd like to buy a couple hundred head, if we're willing to sell."

"Did you tell him I was coming with the cattle?" Duncan's voice was sharp.

"No," Eric answered at once, shaking his head. "I kinda figured that if you'd wanted everybody to know you were coming, you'd've come on ahead of the herd."

"You figured correctly. I prefer to keep my identity a secret, at least for the time being."

"I understand." Eric smiled. "Folks tend to talk more freely to the hired help than to the owners. Right?"

"Precisely," Duncan concurred. "As to Ben, he can have half of the cattle that are left." His smile was wry. "I'll deliver them myself, tomorrow." His smile deepened. "I just might apply to Ben for employment."

"Be good cover for you," Eric agreed. "How many head did you lose along the trail?"

"Not quite two hundred."

Eric looked surprised. "Then it wasn't too bad. Hell, I've heard of outfits that lost almost half of what they started out with, and still considered the trip a success."

"Yes, I recall hearing the cattle drive stories when we were boys," Duncan said. "But I had assumed there had been some advances made over the last twenty years."

"There have been but, hell, Duncan, moving cattle from one place to another is still moving cattle from one place to another." Eric's tone and shrug were philosophical. "Which reminds me," he went on, shifting his eyes to glance around the terrain. "Where did you leave the herd?"

"A few miles to the south." A frown tugging at his brows, Duncan indicated the direction with a slight head motion. "The man I sent to the ranch didn't tell you?"

"No." Eric shook his head. "All he said was that you'd be here, waiting for me." A grin split his face, revealing strong white teeth and the youthful companion he had once been. "And, damn, here you are, home at last."

"Yes," Duncan murmured, raising narrowed eyes to the mountains cast in dark relief against the red glare of the setting sun. "Home at last." Though still a murmur, his voice took on a hint of steel. "And this time I think I'll stay."

"Stay!" Eric's expression mirrored delighted surprise as well as astonishment. "But what about Scotland, your family and your responsibilities?"

Duncan's shrug was both elegant and eloquent. "Since I have spent a rather brief amount of time in Scotland over the last twenty years, I can hardly call it home. In consequence, I barely know my Scottish family."

"But you have a stepmother and a half-sister," Eric said. "What about them?"

"My stepmother, Deirdre, is a charming lady but, as she is also unaccustomed to having me around, she is quite capable of handling all of the estate responsibilities. But I will miss my half-sister." A tender smile played over his mouth. "Heather is fifteen now, and she is growing into a lovely young woman." He shrugged again. "Perhaps I'll send for her, bring her here for a visit."

"Dad always said you'd come home someday."

Duncan's laughter was shadowed by memory. "Your father knew me almost as well as my own mother." His gaze skimmed the darkening landscape. "David-Chill Wind understood how deep my feelings were for my home and this land."

"Yeah." Eric's glance tracked Duncan's. "It's in our Shoshone blood—this feeling for the land."

"Yes." Duncan was quiet a moment, absorbing the feeling of being in the land of his mother's people. Throughout all the years of wandering the world with his father before his death the previous year, Duncan had been aware of an ache inside, an emptiness. In a secret spot, deep inside his mind, he had nurtured the memory of this vast land, warming the cold, lonely places with reflections of hot summer sunlight bathing the earth, holding close to the silent promise of some-day, some way.

Now the ache was soothed, the emptiness filled. Duncan Frazer was home, in the place where he had always known he belonged. An expression of fierce pos-sessiveness set his aristocratic features into lines of un-relenting determination. "And this time I will not be driven away."

"Good." His countenance reflecting his cousin's fierceness, Eric stared with solemn accord into Duncan's hard-looking eyes. Then he grinned, easing the atmosphere of emotional tension. "By the way, Duncan, I like your hat."

Duncan started then laughed. "Thank you, I pur-chased it in Spain—Andalusia." He touched his fingers to the wide stiff brim of the flat-crowned black hat. "I rather fancy it myself." His smiling lips drew into a forbidding straight line. "By the way, Eric," he mimicked, "I think it would be advantageous to our purposes if you would not call me Duncan for a while."

"Okay," Eric agreed, frowning. "But what do I call you in the meanwhile?"

"I suppose the name my drovers know me by is as good as any other," Duncan replied.

"And what is that?"

"They call me Segundo."

2

The Randall ranch house was a silent but solid testimony to the enormous amount of money to be made by the careful, thoughtful planning of the ranch owner. The house was large in comparison to the homes of most of Ben Randall's neighbors, but merely average in comparison to the elaborate mansions some of the cattle barons had built.

Constructed of wood and stone, the sprawling house was two stories high and contained eight rooms. A deep veranda, shaded by a sloping shake roof, wrapped around the north- and west-facing sides of the house, affording protection from the harsh winds of winter and the fierce rays of summer sun. The decor was graceful if not opulent, comfortable if not elegant. The house did boast several modern amenities not found in most western homes and establishments.

There was piped water running into the house, not only to the kitchen, but to a private bathroom on the second floor, which contained a large, cast-iron claw-foot bathtub and a flush toilet as well. The luxury of the piped water and the bathroom was a direct result of the influence of the daughter of the house. At her parents' insistence, Jessica Randall had attended an exclusive boarding school in Boston for young ladies of wealthy fathers. When her schooling was completed, Jessica came home a well-educated, sophisticated young woman of nineteen, accustomed to certain luxuries.

The indoor plumbing was installed in the Randall house less than a year after Jessica returned to Wyoming.

Duncan was grateful for Jessica's sojourn to Boston. While wallowing in the hot water, which threatened to spill over the rim of the deep tub, he speculated on the young woman who had been such an enchanting child.

What was she like? he mused, scraping trail dirt from his body with a thick cloth. Given the evidence of the room, so unusual in the West, and the creamy-looking oval bar of lilac-scented soap he'd sniffed at before picking up a larger, coarser bar to take into the tub with him, Duncan concluded that Jessica Randall had grown into a feminine as well as a willful and determined young woman.

How had Eric described her? Duncan didn't need to

rake his memory, for his cousin's assessment rang true in his mind. Dresses and acts like a man, does she?

Interesting. But why does she?

The puzzle of Jessica was even more intriguing to Duncan than the puzzle of the rustling in the area. Deciding he would solve both mysteries, he finished his bath, dressed, then, the scent of her bath soap lingering to tantalize his senses, he sauntered through the rambling building to rejoin his host.

The ranch office was located on the veranda side of the house, next to the dining room. Ben Randall was seated behind a roll-top desk, staring through one of the long narrow windows overlooking the ranch yard. He swiveled around in the spacious wooden chair when Duncan entered the room.

"Feeling better?"

Duncan cast a wry glance over his trail-worn clothing. "Cleaner, at any rate," he answered.

It was midafternoon of the day after his arrival on the Wind River range. At dawn, Duncan and Eric had separated the herd and the men, half to go with Eric to the Circle-F, the other half to be delivered to the B-Bar-R ranch. Ben Randall recognized Duncan almost as fast as Duncan had recognized Eric. Telling the older man that he'd explain later, Duncan murmured a request to keep his true identity a secret. Nodding his understanding, Ben turned the cattle and the men over to his foreman and invited Duncan to ride back with him to the ranch house.

Emily Randall greeted Duncan like the proverbial prodigal son, with hugs and kisses, laughter and even a few tears. She flew around the kitchen preparing a quick but delicious meal for him, then preceded him to the bathroom, where she insisted on running his bath water for him. With a smile twitching the corners of his lips and a gentle firmness, Duncan eased her from the room before she offered to scrub his back.

Now Duncan strolled to the leather-covered chair Ben indicated with a negligent wave. "These clothes weren't the height of fashion to begin with," he said, frowning at the dark trousers as he sat down and stretched out his long legs. "And they weren't improved by being rolled into a bundle and tied behind the saddle."

A grin spread across Ben's sun-weathered face as he examined the younger man. "Wool shirts and pants are regular attire for working cowboys." His expression turned contemplative as he stuck out one foot and examined his own hand-stitched, slanted-heeled boot. "Except for your hat and your boots, you look like just about every other hired hand." He grinned again, revealing crooked, tobacco-stained teeth. "Every other hired hand from Mexico, that is."

Duncan's smile was faint, but his dark eyes glowed with inner amusement. He lowered his gaze to his unadorned, low-heeled, knee-high soft leather black boots. "I have a particular fondness for my hat and these boots." Lifting one foot, he settled it across his other ankle—looking the picture of the elegant, indolent English gentleman.

"You bought them in Mexico?" Ben's raised foot dropped to the carpeted floor with a muted thud.

"No, my friend." Duncan smiled. "I acquired the hat in Spain—Andalusia. The boots are Arabian made —Berber, to be precise."

"Never heard of them." Ben snorted.

"The Arabs or the Berbers?" Duncan arched his eyebrows and grinned. Bathed in the long rays of the westering sun slanting through the windows, his teeth gleamed a brilliant white against the darkness of his skin.

"Berbers." Ben shifted the solid bulk of his stocky body in the confined area of the curved-armed chair. "You've moved around some in the last twenty years, haven't you?"

"Some," Duncan echoed in a dry understatement.

Ben nodded. "Can't help but wonder why your travels never brought you back this way." His shrewd stare probed the hooded depths of Duncan's eyes. "Even with all the shit you had to endure from most folks hereabouts, you loved it here when you were a boy."

"Yes." Breaking eye contact with the older man, Duncan turned to stare through the window at the shadowed spires etched against the vermilion sky. "I still do. My feelings for this land have not altered with time."

"Then . . . why?" Ben shook his shaggy, gray-streaked head in confusion.

Duncan turned to look at Ben. A ghost of a bittersweet smile curved his lips. "My father," he explained. "I could not, would not return as long as he was alive. He traveled with me, you understand." Memory softened the harsh set of his features. "I believe the longest periods of time he spent in Scotland were while he was courting my stepmother, begetting my half-sister, and the years I was away at the university in Edinburgh."

"But Malcolm's been gone almost a year," Ben pointed out in a compassion-roughened voice.

"Yes." Duncan sighed. "I spent the major part of this last year seeing to the estate and all it entailed."

Ben's sober expression gave way to one of astonishment. "By God, that's right! I had forgotten but . . . you're the earl now! Lord Rayburne, isn't it?"

"Yes."

"I remember now," Ben said, frowning in concentration. "Malcolm wrote to me, first about his father's death and then the sudden, unexpected death of his older brother." His bushy eyebrows came together. "I forget his name."

"Robert."

Ben's brows sprang apart. "That's right! That's how David came by the last name of Robertson."

"Correct." Duncan smiled. "Your memory is excellent. It merely needed a slight nudge."

"Well, I'll be pistol-whipped." Ben stared at him in awe. "You're a real goddamned earl! And a Scottish laird, to boot." He ran a wide-eyed glance the length of Duncan's lean, lounging body. "And here you sit in my office, looking like any other goddamned cowboy!"

"Goddamn," Duncan murmured in a dust-dry voice.

Ben laughed; then he frowned. "Well, hell, man, what do I call you? I mean, what's the proper address? My lord? Laird? Lord Rayburne? Or just Rayburne?"

"Segundo."

"Huh?" Ben scowled. "I don't understand. A *segundo* is the Mexican equivalent of our ranch foreman, isn't he?"

Duncan sighed. He had explained all this to his cousin last night, over the usual dinner fare of bacon, beans, pan biscuits, and black coffee strong enough to float a thrown horseshoe. Drawing a breath, he launched into the explanation once again. "Yes, a *segundo* is the second in command to the Mexican *patrón*. My men believe that I was hired out of Mexico by the owner of the Circle-F to head up the cattle drive from Texas to Wyoming. They know me only as the *segundo*."

Ben appeared more confused than enlightened. "But why would they believe that?"

"Because that is what I instructed my man of business in San Antonio to tell them when he hired the cowboys on for the drive up here."

"I see." Still frowning, Ben leaned forward to reach for a humidor perched on top of the desk. He held it out in silent invitation as he selected a long fat cigar for himself.

"No, thank you," Duncan declined the offer. "I prefer my own." Arching the lower half of his body, he dipped his fingers into the straight right front pocket of his pants and withdrew a narrow box. After prying the lid open, he took out a pencil-slim dark cigarillo. "Thank you," he murmured again, placing the cigarillo between his lips and straightening to accept the light Ben flared to life by striking a wood match against the thigh side of his rough pants.

"Spanish?" Ben asked between deep puffs on his cigar.

"Hmm." Duncan nodded. "I acquired the habit for the milder smoke while my father and I were there. I have a standing order now with the tobacconist for them to be shipped to me"—he smiled and flicked one hand to indicate his surroundings—"wherever I happen to be."

They smoked in companionable silence awhile, savoring the bite of strong tobacco. After several minutes, Ben broke the quiet with a question that had obviously been troubling him. "Why did you want your men to believe you were only the second in command and not the actual owner of the Circle-F?"

"Simple." Clamping the cigarillo between his hard teeth, Duncan flashed a wicked-looking grin. "I wanted to come to Wyoming incognito, to have a look around and assess the rustling situation as a disinterested observer."

"Makes sense." Ben grimaced with distaste. "That damned Metcalf is up to no good." He cocked an eyebrow. "Eric tell you about him?"

Before Duncan could reply with other than a brief nod, a light knock sounded on the office door an instant before it was opened. "Here's the coffee you asked for, Ben." Emily swept into the room carrying a large tray, upon which rested a silver coffeepot with matching sugar bowl and creamer and two commonplace white mugs.

Both men moved to assist her. Duncan moved faster than Ben. Saying a quiet "Thank you," he relieved her of the burden and placed it on a nearby table. Her smile soft, her gray eyes misty, Emily stared at him a moment, then she blinked and turned away. At the doorway she paused to give the men a gentle reminder of the passage of time.

"It's almost sundown. Parker and Jessica will be riding into the yard soon." The smile she gave Duncan heightened the beauty of her faintly lined face. "I can't wait to see their expressions when they find out who you are." Chuckling to herself, she stepped through the doorway, only to pause again, her smile curving into a frown, when Duncan issued a soft but sharp command.

"No, Emily."

"No?" Emily looked puzzled. "No . . . what?"

"Parker and Jessica are not to know who I am."

"But, Duncan, why on earth not?" Protesting, Emily stepped back into the room. "The children have talked about you so often. They'll be thrilled by your return."

Though pleased by her assurance, Duncan remained firm. "I'm truly delighted to hear that, Emily, but . . ." Weary of repeating the explanation, he looked to his old friend for help. Ben stepped into the breach without hesitation.

"Duncan simply prefers to keep his true identity a secret for a while, Emily," Ben said in soothing tones. His broad, stubby-fingered hand looking incongruous wrapped around the ornate handle of the silver pot, he poured the steaming coffee into the mugs and arched his bushy eyebrows in question as he looked at Duncan.

"Black, please," Duncan murmured, leaning forward to accept the mug Ben extended to him.

Emily watched the exchange in frowning consternation. "I don't understand," she said, shifting her puzzled gaze from her husband to Duncan. "Why would you want to keep your identity a secret? For what purpose?"

"For the purpose of looking into the reason for the recent rustling incidences in the area." He took a tentative sip of the hot coffee before continuing. "I thought perhaps I could learn more as an outsider, so to speak."

Instead of clearing, Emily's frown deepened. "I can see that you might," she said. "But why keep Parker and Jessica in the dark?" Her voice contained a hint of offense. "They can be trusted with your confidence."

"I'm sure they can, but—"

Ben interrupted. "It's not a question of trust, Emily," he said with controlled patience. "It's a question of numbers, and you know as well as I do that the more people who know Duncan's identity, the fewer his chances of keeping it a secret."

Emily sighed but agreed. "I suppose. But it's not going to be easy. How are you going to explain Duncan's presence here at the ranch?"

Ben scowled. "We hadn't gotten that far yet," he muttered.

Rolling her eyes, Emily cast an exasperated look at the two men. "Well, you'd better come up with something soon. You're running out of time."

"I was thinking of applying to you for employment." Duncan directed his remark at Ben.

"I was thinking along the same lines, but—" Ben broke off to frown.

"But?" Duncan prompted.

"But we're top-heavy with cowboys already," Emily inserted. "Hiring another hand will arouse suspicion."

"And a lot of questions from Parker and Jessica," Ben concluded.

Annoyed at the prospect of having his plans thwarted by the interference of Ben's children, Duncan drank his coffee in frustrated silence. It was to the ultimate benefit of every member of their combined families that he remain incognito, and yet . . .

A slight smile playing over his lips, Duncan stared at Ben. "I have a suggestion."

"Let's hear it."

"If you are, as Emily said, top-heavy with hands, the loss of one of your men would be of no moment." Duncan raised an eyebrow. "Is that correct?"

"Right." Ben grunted.

"But what if your foreman were to suddenly quit . . . or be called away for some vague reason?" Duncan asked in a speculative tone. "Of course, I would continue to pay his wages while he was gone."

Eyes narrowed in thought, Ben nodded. "Might work. But that would mean explaining the situation to him."

Duncan shrugged. "Needs must."

"Not necessarily." The comment startled the men, coming as it did from Emily. Hands planted on her still-slender waist, she confronted her husband. "Weren't you talking about possibly taking a trip to the Flemming *estancia* in Argentina to buy a blooded bull?"

Never slow on the uptake, Ben caught on at once. "By damn, you're right!" He shot a grin at Duncan. "I've been corresponding with George Flemming, the English owner of a huge *estancia* in the pampa in Argentina. Besides running cattle, George raises pureblood bulls, and I've been giving some consideration to going down there to have a look-see at them. Hell, I can just as easily send Frank as go myself."

"Frank being your foreman?" Duncan guessed.

"Yeah." Ben smiled. "And, since both Parker and Jessica know I was thinking about it, it won't arouse their suspicions." He chuckled. "Matter of fact, at one point Jessica suggested that I send Frank instead of making that long trip myself."

"And that way you won't really be lying to the children," Emily chimed in, smiling in satisfaction. "You can honestly tell them that you decided to send Frank to Argentina and that you've hired Duncan as your temporary foreman."

"Not foreman. *Segundo*."

Her smile faded as she looked at Duncan. "*Segundo?*"

"Yes." His reply was adamant.

"But—"

"It's the same thing, Emily," Ben explained. "A *segundo* is the Mexican version of our ranch foreman."

"I know that," she retorted. "What I don't understand is, why *segundo* instead of foreman?"

Duncan's smile was gentle. "Do you call Frank *foreman* or do you call him Frank?"

"Frank, of course, but—"

He silenced her with a flick of his hand. "And is Duncan a common name here?"

Emily frowned, and tried again. "No, but—"

"Then, don't you agree that Parker and Jessica might put their heads together, add one and one, and come up with the correct answer?"

"Oh!" Emily's eyes grew wide. "Oh, my, yes!"

"Yes." Duncan's voice was soft. "Segundo."

"Yes, Segundo," Ben repeated. The desk chair creaked a protest as he heaved his bulk from it to walk to his wife. "And we'd better get used to it. It'll only take one slip of the tongue to give the game away." He raised his hand to touch her shoulder. "Now, would you go see if you can find Frank and send him in to me?"

"Yes, all right." She gave him a vague smile, then murmuring the name like a litany, she turned and left the room.

Ben looked at his new *segundo*. "She won't forget."
He grinned. "Don't be surprised if, the next time you
see her, she treats you more like a stranger than a
friend."

Duncan smiled in understanding. "She's a fine
woman, Ben. I knew it, even as a boy."

"Yes, Emily's the best." Ben's answering smile evi-
denced deep satisfaction. "And Jessica's a lot like her
mother."

At sundown, Ben ushered Duncan onto the veranda
through a narrow door in the corner of his office. The
last lingering rays of sunlight bathed the ranch yard in a
golden haze, softening the rough edges and hard angles
of the ranch buildings.

The Randall progeny rode into the yard side by side,
one looking much like the other from a distance. The
similarity diminished as they drew closer to the house.

From beneath the shading veranda roof and the
shadow of his lowered hat brim, Duncan observed their
approach through narrowed eyes. After running a swift
but encompassing glance over Parker, he transferred
his piercing gaze to Jessica, searching for a lingering
sign of the child he had loved.

The sweet child was gone, absorbed into the slim
but rounded figure of the woman. Even forewarned, his
first reaction to her appearance was one of shocked
astonishment. Like her brother, and every other man,
Jessica was dressed in masculine attire, and all in black,
from the hat that concealed her hair to the boots that
covered her rough trousers to above her ankles. But the
most startling thing to Duncan was the sight of her,
mounted astride a big chestnut gelding.

Her seat in the western saddle was faultless. Her hold on the reins was loose, confident. Her back was ramrod straight and she held her head high, tilted at a proud angle.

The sun at her back robbed her face of color, giving Duncan an impression of skin pale in the extreme. Her features were delicate yet sharply defined. Her small jawline was slightly squared, revealing in its defiant tilt. Her eyebrows were dark, with a natural, gentle arch. He could not see her hair as it was concealed inside her western-style hat, but the darkness of her brows convinced him that the silvery blond of infancy had darkened with maturity.

Duncan was wondering if her eyes were still the enchanting color of quicksilver when Jessica brought her horse to a stop before the veranda and lowered her eyes to stare with haughty disdain down her slim nose at him.

Unrevealed by his motionless stance, his closed expression, an unprecedented thrill of awareness, sensual and antagonistic, ricocheted the length of his body.

He could smell her—not her actual scent of here and now, but the elusive fragrance of spring lilacs. Her imaginary essence set his senses on fire, and though she was dressed in masculine garb, she was all woman, primal and exciting.

He wanted her. It was as basic as that.

In Duncan's eyes, Jessica was the most beautiful and desirable woman he had ever seen. Her effect on him was like a bare-knuckled blow to his head.

It was the most exciting, puzzling, and infuriating sensation Duncan had ever experienced, inducing within him two startling, opposing desires. While part

of him chafed with an urge to administer what he perceived as a much-needed shaking, an equally strong
part of him burned with a driving impulse to pull her
from the back of the big chestnut, tear the offensive
masculine garments off her, then throw her to the
ground and plunge his rigid body into hers.

3

Arrogant bastard!

Seething with barely contained fury, Jessica glared into the remote, unrevealing turquoise eyes of the stranger for a long moment before turning to stare at her father in outraged astonishment, unable to believe he had said what she had heard.

Speechless with anger, she gathered the reins together with trembling fingers and wheeled her horse away from the veranda, her mind a boiling cauldron of questions she was determined to have answered.

Her father said he had hired a temporary replacement for their foreman, Frank. But why? Frank would be gone only for a few months at most. Why had her father thought it necessary to hire a replacement for Frank when he knew full well that both she and Parker were capable of handling the foreman's duties? Didn't her father realize that his action would be viewed as an insult—not only by her and Parker but the cowboys as well? And, compounding the insult, was the man Ben Randall had hired.

Segundo. Not John Anybody, the *segundo*, but merely Segundo, Jessica railed in silent fury. Who was he? Where did he come from? What were his credentials? What did her father know of him, about him?

And who the hell did the man think he was, staring at her, through her, with those strange turquoise eyes?

Still feeling a premonitory, frighteningly sensuous chill from his piercing stare, Jessica shivered. Incensed by her involuntary reaction to the stranger, she muttered a curse, drawing her brother's attention and comment.

"I agree."

Jessica shot a distracted look at him. "What?"

Parker's expression was grim. "You said 'goddamn him,' and I agreed with you." He seemed unaware that they had brought their horses to a stop at the stable, or that Shaky, the short, spindly horse wrangler, stood by waiting for them to dismount. "Who is he?" he asked, echoing her thoughts. "And why did Pa hire him?" His heavy brows, so like their father's, came together in a contemplative frown. "Pa never makes snap decisions, and yet, in the hours we were away from the house, he not only decides to send Frank to Argentina, he hires this . . . this *segundo*." His clear blue eyes, also very like their father's, reflected suspicion. "Something bothers me about this whole business."

"Hmm." Nodding, Jessica plucked the slim, coiled horsewhip from the saddle horn, flipped one leg over the horse, and jumped lightly to the ground. "It seems more than odd that while you and I were riding line, this *segundo* person rode into the position that by rights should be ours."

"Yeah." Dismounting the more traditional way, Parker grimaced and arched his back to ease muscles cramped by long hours spent in the saddle. "I don't like the smell of this, Sis," he said in a disgruntled mutter. "The whole thing stinks."

"Yes." Her expression set into skeptical lines, Jessica handed the reins to Shaky, pivoted on her boot heel, and strode toward the house. "I have a feeling something is rotten, and not only in Denmark."

Parker made a sour face as he fell into step beside her. "Let me guess . . . Shakespeare, right?"

Jessica thawed enough to reward him with a quick smile. "You're getting pretty good at it," she said, referring to her brother's ongoing attempt to keep up with her better-educated mind.

The look Parker threw at her was bone dry. "I don't know why I even bother."

"It passes the time." Jessica's tone was laconic, her smile sardonic, but her actions telling as she pulled her work-scarred gloves from her hands.

"Yeah, but I reckon I'll have plenty to pass the time with now just trying to figure out what Dad's game is."

His remark wiped the wry smile from Jessica's face. Crushing her gloves in her left hand, she raised her delicate chin in determined defiance and mounted the steps onto the veranda. "I suggest we clear up this mystery at once," she snapped, yanking open the kitchen door.

He was the first thing she saw upon crossing the threshold. The mere sight of the dark, turquoise-eyed stranger set Jessica's teeth on edge. Without the shadowing influence of his hat, his face was revealed in sharp angles and smooth, taut planes. He was handsome, in a harsh yet oddly elegant way. His hair was stick straight, inky black, overlong. Yet, even with its length, it was obvious to Jessica that his hair had been cut, shaped by a master of fashion.

His appearance annoyed her—possibly because the look of him set off warning signals of awareness deep inside her body and her mind. Resentment flared to combat the awareness, drawing forth from the darkest part of her an immediate response of dislike and uncharacteristic antagonism.

He was seated—sprawled—in a chair, looking like he owned the world. Incensed by his superior expression, by his very presence, Jessica was hard put to keep from kicking the chair out from under him.

He spared her the effort. At her entrance, the stranger stood in a move that was both swift and liquid smooth. Standing erect, his impact on her senses was devastating. He was tall, topping Jessica's own five-foot seven-inch frame by a generous six inches, and every one of those raw-boned inches was packed with long, lean muscles sheathed in taut dark-brown skin.

Magnificent.

Jessica immediately rejected the descriptive word that sprang into her mind and steeled herself against the magnetic power radiating from him to her.

"Señorita." His voice was low, appealing, oddly devoid of accent. He didn't smile. He didn't bow. He stared at her with stone-hard eyes glittering with blatant sexual hunger for an instant that seemed to stretch into eternity. Then he shifted his eyes and attention to Parker. *"Señor."*

A reply was expected, called for, demanded. Jessica knew it, and knew also that Parker knew it. Yet they stood, side by side, silent and rebellious.

"Jessica!"

"Parker."

The two voices shattered the crackling silence—Emily's in shocked exclamation, Ben's in angry rebuke.

Parker reacted at once to the sharp reprimand. Stepping forward, he thrust out his hand. "Mr.—eh—" His expression went blank in indecisive confusion.

"Segundo." A hint of a smile feathered his chiseled masculine mouth. "Just . . . Segundo."

"Eh . . ." A frown tugged at Parker's eyebrows. Then his shoulders moved in a careless shrug. "Whatever you say, fella. Segundo it is."

"Gracias." Even as he murmured the word of thanks, the stranger's piercing stare came to rest on Jessica.

Refusing to be intimidated by his knowing, insulting, and wildly exciting visual probe, Jessica stared back at him with cool disdain before deigning to speak, and then only to upbraid him.

"You should be out at the bunkhouse, making yourself known to the cowboys." Though her silvery eyes were sparked by fury, Jessica's voice carried an arctic chill. She did not extend her hand in welcome; she curled the fingers of her right hand tightly around the braided whip handle in an effort to control an urge to strike his handsome face and gripped the gloves in her left hand to keep from flinging them to the floor in challenge.

"Jessica, really!" Exasperation erupted from Emily. "Is that any way to greet a new employee?" Her entire body quivering with emotion, she took her familiar stance of hands gripping her aproned waist. "Apologize at once."

"Sorry, Mother." Jessica offered the apology, but not to the stranger, and every one of them knew it. "But I can't help but wonder why he is here, not only here in the house but here at all, on our land."

Her comment caused an interesting mix of reaction. Emily gasped. Ben became mottled with anger. Parker smirked. The *segundo* stared at her with hooded eyes shimmering with a promise of retribution.

Shaken but undaunted by his silent vow, Jessica faced him and her parents with haughty pride, steeling herself against giving in—either to her parents' disapproval or to her own bafflement concerning her unusual behavior. Jessica was not by nature argumentative or difficult, except on rare occasions. This was one of them. For some incomprehensible reason, she had taken immediate umbrage at the sight of this strange dark man. The fact that her father chose him over both her and her brother angered and deeply hurt her.

"A replacement for Frank is unnecessary and uncalled for." Not giving by as much as an inch, Jessica raised her chin another notch. "You have me and Parker."

An uneasy silence blanketed the room. During it her father looked sheepish, her mother appeared crestfallen, Parker nodded in agreement, and the stranger, damn him, continued to smile in that annoying, superior manner.

"I . . . eh . . ." Ben shifted his feet, as if the physical movement might loosen his tongue. "Goddammit, girl!" He exploded, covering his sense of guilt with impatience. "I'm not so old and feeble that I can't make the decisions around here any more!"

"I didn't say—" Jessica began, only to be cut off by her father's booming voice.

"You didn't have to say it, and by damn, I don't like your attitude, young lady!" Unconsciously mirroring her stance, he jutted his jaw. "This is still my ranch, and I have hired on a temporary foreman, and that's that." He stabbed a blunt finger at her. "And you will behave yourself while he's here. Do you understand me?"

"Ben." Emily's voice held a cautioning note. "Aren't you being a bit harsh . . . considering the situation?"

"No." Riled, Ben shook his head. "You stay out of this, Emily. Jessica's getting just a mite too big for her britches lately. Dammit, she's a woman! Maybe it's time for her to begin acting like a lady, instead of like one of the boys."

"Oh, Ben."

"Dad!"

Ignoring the simultaneous protests from his wife and son, Ben, obviously expelling long-repressed emotions, vented his anger and disappointment, unmindful of the stark expression on his daughter's face. "You've been doing pretty much as you pleased since you came home from that hifalutin' eastern school, and I let you have your way, putting in the bathroom, going along with your plans to install this newfangled electricity, letting you get away with dressing like a man. But I'm pulling in the reins on you now, girl. You will work with the *segundo* without complaint, or you will not work outdoors at all." Red-faced, quivering, he glowered at Jessica. "You will either follow orders or stay inside the house helping your mother—doing the work women are meant to do. Do you understand me?"

Struck speechless by her father's sudden attack, and hurt to the quick, Jessica fought for an inner control, a measure of calm with which to respond to him. Before she found her voice, another was heard.

"*Señor* Randall, perhaps this is not the time for ultimatums." The *segundo* stared at Ben with meaningful intent.

His interference merely abraded Jessica's sense of embarrassment and humiliation. She felt like a fool; she didn't like the feeling. Ignoring the sharp-eyed stranger, she looked at her father.

"I'm sorry if I'm a disappointment to you," she said, despairing the crack of emotion in her voice.

"Oh, Jessica, you're not . . ." Biting her lip, Emily glanced from her daughter to her husband. "Ben, you must tell her you didn't mean—"

"I meant every word!" Ben interrupted her. He shot an adamant look at Segundo. "And now is as good a time as any. Dammit! I will not have my authority questioned." His gaze settled on Jessica. "Do you understand?"

Close to tears, but determined not to reveal weakness in front of the stranger she was beginning to hate as well as resent, Jessica met her father's stare without flinching and said, "Yes, sir."

"Parker?" Ben growled.

Parker snapped to attention. "I never questioned your authority, Pa."

Ben gave a sharp nod of his head. "Emily?"

Though she appeared on the verge of arguing, Emily sighed, sent an apologetic look at Jessica, and gave in. "Whatever you say, Ben."

The high color fading from his cheeks, Ben directed his scowl to Segundo. "Segundo?"

Jessica was both confused and annoyed by the slight smile that curved the stranger's lips.

"You are the boss, *patrón*," he replied in a tone that more than hinted at an inexplicable inner amusement.

To Jessica's amazement, his amusement was reflected by the sudden gleam in her father's eyes. Feeling as if she were missing something of importance, and puzzling over what that something could be, she stared at her father. He actually seemed to be fighting a smile!

"And don't you forget it," Ben replied, lips twitching. "At least for as long as you're here."

Her sense of confusion overriding her anger, Jessica shifted a narrowed glance from Ben to the *segundo*. What was going on here? They were up to something, she decided. But what? Suspicious but stymied for an explanation, she jerked erect when her father barked at her.

"Jessica, go get cleaned up for dinner. You too, Parker," he tacked on as an afterthought. "Oh, and by the way, your mother has invited the *segundo* to take his meals with us while he's working here, which is why he is here, in the house, and not out in the bunkhouse with the men."

His statement sent a resurgence of anger storming

through Jessica. A ranch foreman never took meals in the house with the family! The information had the effect of yet another burr under her personal saddle. Gripping the coiled whip in her hand, Jessica strode across the kitchen and dashed up the back stairway to her bedroom.

Women's work! Grimacing, Jessica slammed the bedroom door behind her. The very idea of spending her day, all of her days, like her mother—cooking, cleaning, washing, tending the kitchen garden—sent an apprehensive shudder through her. Jessica had never made a secret of her opinion of women's work, and it could be summed up in one word.

"Bah!" Jessica spat the word aloud and scowled at her reflection in the standing beveled mirror in the corner. In contrast to her near-masculine appearance in the slouch-brimmed hat and cowboy garb, the room, though Spartan in furnishings, was feminine. As the mirror reflected her outdoor image, the vibrant colors of bedspread, draperies, and carpeting reflected her inner personality.

Jessica was every inch a woman, in every definition of the term—she loved pretty things and clothes, and had a small dressing room full of gowns of every type, which she seldom got the chance to wear since returning from the social activity of Boston to the more reclusive life on the ranch. Jessica simply preferred the freedom of what was considered men's work, opposed to the confining, tedious chores assigned to women by tradition. And she knew that she would run screaming mad should her father deny her the right to ride out with her brother and the other hands and roam free on the land she loved.

It was all his fault. Jessica's silvery eyes glittered from between narrowed lids. That stranger with the Mexican look and name. That . . . that . . .

"Se-gun-do." Spoken aloud, his name had the sibilant sound of a hissed curse.

Damn him! Jessica cursed in silent frustration, flinging the horsewhip into a corner. Damn him, damn him, damn him, she railed, tearing her sweat-stiffened clothes from her overheated, anger-charged body. Damn his smug, superior smile. Damn his tall, angular, whipcord lean, too-attractive body. And damn his all-seeing, all-knowing, beautiful turquoise eyes!

The last item of clothing to go was her battered black hat. As Jessica pulled it from her head, her hair spilled over her shoulders and down her back like liquid silver. After gathering the platinum mass with fumbling fingers, she coiled it to the top of her head, then anchored the knot by pushing long, lethal-looking hairpins into it, wincing in pain as the pin tips scraped her tender scalp.

Who the hell does he think he is? Jessica asked herself, shoving a slender arm into the wide sleeve of her silk wrapper. He's a mere hired hand, no better and perhaps worse than any other hired hand. And a foreigner to boot! she fumed. And how dare he stare at her with those hot, hungry eyes?

The seemingly unrelated question brought with it a memory of those shadowed turquoise eyes, the heated look in their depths, and sent a shocking thrill of sensuous awareness tingling through every inch of her body.

Stunned by the intensity of her reaction to the mere thought of the stranger's dark, erotic gaze, and frightened by a sense of softening warmth flowing into her limbs, Jessica clutched the folds of her wrap close to her throat and took off at a run for the bathroom at the end of the hall.

The bathroom was located directly above the kitchen. Seated on a chair, his legs stretched out in front of him, Duncan looked into the clear blue eyes of the young man seated opposite him and listened to the unmistakable sounds of bathing filtering down to him through the ceiling.

"This your first trip to Wyoming?" Having cleaned up in the wash shed attached to the kitchen, Parker now seemed intent on drawing information from the new foreman.

Duncan heard Parker's question with his intellect; he heard Jessica's splashing noises with his lilac-scented permeated senses.

"No, *señor*, I was in Wyoming before . . . a long time ago." Duncan answered with the truth—if not the complete truth—in a casual, relaxed manner, while inside he was quivering with awareness of the woman in the room above.

Duncan could see her. His inner eye held a vivid image of Jessica, naked and submerged in the large, claw-foot tub he had occupied only a few hours ago. His blood ran hot. His imagination ran riot.

"And you drove a herd up from Texas?"

"*Sí,*" Duncan responded to Parker's continued probing, managing to remain in character, even though his inflamed senses were responding with wild abandon to the erotic visions flashing into his mind. "I was hired in San Antonio to drive the herd up here to the Circle-F ranch."

Duncan possessed an excellent memory for detail, and he judged that, if the bathtub was filled to the lipped edge, the water would come up to just about midchest on Jessica. Was she, he mused, a woman given to the luxury of bubbles in her bath? If so, the floating bubbles would probably caress the water-puckered tips of her breasts.

Speculation aroused an uncomfortable tightening in the lower half of Duncan's body. In a strained move that appeared casual, he sat up straight in the chair and shifted his legs, and the betraying evidence of his discomfort, beneath the plain wooden table.

"Pa told me that Eric was expecting a sizable herd sometime this month," Parker said, getting up to walk to the big black cast-iron cooking stove. He filled two mugs with coffee from the agate pot that was never allowed to empty and carried them back to the table. "You lose many along the way?" He echoed Eric's concern of the previous day as he set one of the mugs on the table in front of Duncan.

"*Gracias,*" Duncan murmured, sipping the steaming brew before answering. "Two hundred or so head."

Inside his own head, Duncan felt sure his temperature must be averaging at least a hundred or so. Was she as pale all over as her hands and face were? A hot shiver shot straight as an arrow from his mind to his manhood. Pale visions tormented his senses, visions of Jessica's nude slender body, her creamy shoulders and arms, the gentle swell of her breasts, the enticing twenty-two-inch curve of her waist, the rounded allure of hips and derriere, her long legs, and her inviting silken thighs. The visions interfered with Duncan's breathing and drew a tight band around his throat.

"Only two hundred?" Parker's voice penetrated the sensuous fog clouding Duncan's mind. "You were lucky."

No, he'd be lucky if he managed to hang onto enough control to keep from jumping out of his chair to dash up the back kitchen stairs, rush into the bathroom, rip off his clothes, and fling himself into the tub with Jessica. The thought brought a faint smile to Duncan's lips and a painful leap into his loins. Gripping the forgotten mug in his hand, he took a bracing gulp of coffee. The hot liquid burned his tongue but did the trick, easing the tightness in his throat enough for him to reply to the younger man's comment.

"I suppose." Although it wasn't much of a response, its very briefness was in keeping with the role Duncan had assumed for himself. Still, he was unsatisfied. He felt disoriented, not at all like his normal, cool, deliberate self.

It was her fault.

Locked onto the cause of his inconvenience, Duncan no longer knew or cared about the activity around him. He noted but was unaffected by Ben's return to the house from the bunkhouse, where he'd gone to talk to his men about the temporary foreman, Emily's movements as she bustled back and forth between the kitchen and the dining room in preparation for the evening meal, or Parker, silent now as he stared into the murky depths of his coffee. Duncan saw but ignored it all.

It was her fault. A woman had created this chaos inside him. And a mere slip of a woman, at that. Anger stirred within, restoring reason to his rattled mind. Never before in his life had Duncan allowed a woman to so arouse his passion that his thought processes were interfered with.

From the time of his initiation into manhood at the age of fourteen, Duncan had enjoyed the favors of a variety of different females, in as many different countries and cultures. He genuinely liked most women and derived satisfaction from giving them pleasure while being pleasured in turn.

This woman, this Jessica Randall, was an exception. Her choice of attire made a challenging statement. The strength of her personality intruded, intrigued, and teased, while outraging his masculine stance. It could not be endured.

Anger shimmered inside Duncan, consuming the raging desires clawing at his body, clearing his senses. Allowing the anger to expand into an icy fury, he stared sightlessly at Parker and made a promise to himself concerning the young Randall's beautiful, proud sister.

He would have her.

Duncan's eyes took on the hard appearance of the stone they resembled. He would have her, possess her, own her, body and soul. Her beauty would belong to him. Her pride would belong to him. Her life would belong to him.

His course set, Duncan relaxed, and even smiled at a remark Emily made in passing. He was in no particular hurry to execute his plans for Emily's daughter.

He was home. He had all the time in the world to bring Jessica to heel.

In the room above the kitchen, Jessica stepped from the large bathtub onto a handmade oval rag rug. The warm water, scented with bubbling bath salts and hand-milled French soap, had had a soothing effect on her nervous system. She was calm, her features composed. Resolution instilled a glow of serenity in her silvery eyes. To all appearances, she would obey her father's dictates. She would work alongside the stranger as she did with the other men, but at her convenience, the usurper would be taught a lesson.

Wrapping her moisture-beaded body in the folds of her robe, Jessica sauntered to her bedroom. Humming to herself, she went through the drill of donning a chemise, drawers, stockings, and flounced petticoats. She even deigned to lace herself into a short corset, just to please her father. A contemplative smile played over her full, soft lips as she slipped into a simple cotton frock and smooth silk slippers.

The day would come when she would please herself, she told her reflection in the mirror as she coiled her hair into a neat figure eight at her nape. And when that day did arrive, Jessica vowed she would make the stranger pay dearly for the embarrassment, humiliation, and sense of hurt injustice she had endured.

Segundo.

Thinking the name brought his image to her cooled mind. Yes, she decided, that arrogant, overbearing, hard-eyed bastard would pay her price.

She would wipe that hot-eyed, smug expression from his damned turquoise eyes. Anticipation lent color to her pale cheeks.

She would grind the *segundo*'s arrogance into dust.

4

Intuition drove Eric from his bed a few hours before dawn. Without pausing to question the goading, urgent inner command, he pulled on his clothes then, carrying his boots, moved in swift silence through the house.

His father was already in the kitchen, waiting for him, a freshly brewed cup of coffee in his gnarled hand.

Eric accepted the proffered cup with a nod of thanks and a wry smile. "You feel it too, huh?"

"Very strong. Something bad is happening," David-Chill Wind muttered. The spaced precision of his words revealed the difficulty he had overcome on being introduced to the English language in his twenty-ninth year. "Out there." He jerked his gray-streaked head. "On our land."

"Yeah, I know." Eric took a deep swallow of the scalding drink, burned his tongue, grimaced, and set the cup on the table. "I'd better get moving."

"Yes." Regret tinged David's tone and shadowed his eyes. "I would ride out with you"—he sighed—"but I would only slow you down."

Eric paused with his hand on the door latch. "I'd like having you by my side, but—" He broke off as his mother, looking like a disheveled Valkyrie in her night robe and bedroom slippers, swept into the room.

"Get going, son," Inga ordered, blessing him with the loving warmth glowing from her blue eyes. "You're needed out there," she said in a resigned tone that spoke of acceptance of her husband's and son's intuitive knowledge.

With a final glance at his father, who stood as straight and proud as his arthritis-ridden spine permitted, Eric nodded and strode from the room.

The night was clear, the terrain a contrast of black shadows and milky white moonlight. The air was crystal, refreshing, cool with the harbinger of approaching fall.

Eric rode through the night following the trail of instinct. He had long since ceased to wonder about his sense of intuition, which had never failed him. He knew certain things. His father said the knowing was part of his heritage, that, like their parents and grandfather before them, Eric and Duncan possessed the deep intuitive senses of the shaman.

Like his mother, Eric accepted without question the mystical sense of knowing.

Eric had been riding for over an hour and was nearing the fenced boundary of the south pasture when he heard the distant, distinctive sound of gunfire. Two of the hands were riding night line, as two of the hands had been riding night line ever since the rustlings started. A different section of line was patrolled each night. Eric knew it was a hit-or-miss method at best. And yet, from the sound of things, it was obvious that the section picked for tonight was a hit.

Kicking his horse into a gallop, he streaked through the night in the direction of the echoing sounds. As he drew closer, his acute hearing identified the reports of four different handguns. As his own men were armed, Eric knew there were at least two interlopers onto the land, and those two were very likely rustlers.

Controlling the horse with his knees and one hand on the reins, Eric slid the long-barreled pistol from the leather holster tied to his thigh. Ready yet cautious about firing at random, he headed for the site of the action.

The south pasture was dotted with trees, some of which had been used instead of fence posts when the wire was being strung. The trees, in full summer leaf, lent more shadows to the scene and afforded a measure of protection to both the Circle-F cowboys and the rustlers. At the same time, the trees made it difficult for Eric to differentiate between the two groups. Holding his fire, he called out in a low, carrying voice.

"Muldoon."

"Over here, Eric!" The response from the seasoned hand came from a stand of trees off to Eric's left. "There are four or five of them, and they've got us pinned."

Veering the horse to a sharp left angle, Eric lay low over the animal's neck and rode hard for the trees. There was an increased rattle of gunfire. Bullets buzzed over his head and into the ground near his mount's hooves, but he made the cover unscathed; one of his men wasn't as lucky.

"Goddamn!" Muldoon cursed in a startled tone of pain the instant Eric flung himself from the back of his horse beneath the protective umbrella of tree branches. "The son of a bitch caught me!" The Irishman's big body hit the ground with a thud.

"Where?" Eric asked, dropping to one knee beside the wounded man.

"Shoulder," Muldoon muttered through teeth gritted in pain. "That's the thanks I get for revealing my position when I called out to you."

Ignoring Muldoon's disgusted comment, Eric flipped his pistol to his left hand and reached out with his right hand to examine the wound. "Keep firing, Randy," he instructed the other cowboy crouched behind a tree trunk.

"Can't see a damned thing," Randy groused, continuing to empty his revolver into the inky pool created by another stand of trees.

"Yeah, but what the hell, neither can they," Muldoon retorted, referring to the rustlers concealed in the shadowed depths of the other trees.

"Quiet." Eric whispered the command as he drew his wet fingers away from the blood-soaked clothing around Muldoon's wound. "It's a flesh wound," he said, diagnosing by touch. "You'll live . . . that is, if any of us do."

"Yeah." Muldoon grunted. "They got us fairly well

pinned down here. Be damned foolish for any one of us to step out of this shade into the moonlight." He took a gasping breath then said in a dry tone, "When are you goin' to make your move, boss?"

Eric didn't respond to the compliment that had the sound of an insult. After wiping the blood from his hands on the grass, lush beneath the sheltering trees, he dug into his pocket for a handkerchief and pressed it to the seeping wound on Muldoon's shoulder. "That'll have to do until we get back," he murmured, standing as he transferred the pistol to his right hand.

A bullet plowed into the ground mere inches from his right foot. Anger and frustration tautened Eric's body. Motionless, frowning, he strained to see a glimmer of movement in the pool of darkness beyond the swath of moonlit terrain.

A move would have to be made—and soon. Gunfire from the rustlers continued to pour like a shower of lethal lead into the stand of trees, zinging above and around them. Eric knew that before long one of the aimlessly discharged bullets would find another target. The rustlers, whoever they were, were not going to get bored and give up the battle. On the other hand, they were every bit as pinned down as Eric and his men.

A damned Mexican standoff, Eric thought, looking around for a means to gain an edge.

The edge came from the east, from the unfenced boundary to the Randall property. And it came in the form of pounding hoofbeats and the rapid-fire peppering of a spitting rifle.

Eric heard an outcry, a babble of cursing voices, then, bent low in their saddles, four riders broke from

the trees in a galloping headlong flight. Within moments the riders were swallowed up by darkness.

It was over—at least for this night.

"Who in hell is that out there?" Randy asked in a
quavery voice, as if afraid their rescuer was some sort of
materialized shade.

"The marines?" Muldoon responded in disgust.

In knowing silence, Eric waited for the rider to approach. A murmur in the Shoshone tongue wafted to
them on the cool air, confirming his expectation. Eric
hadn't forgotten his cousin's instructions. His reply was
as soft, but in Spanish.

"*Gracias*, Segundo."

"Who in hell is Segundo?" Randy demanded.

Struggling to sit up, Muldoon peered at the lone
horseman, bathed in eerie moonlight, as he brought his
mount to a halt just beyond the stand of trees. "Not the
marines," he drawled, grinning up at his employer.

Eric acknowledged the grin with a brief smile. He
liked Muldoon. Not that he disliked the younger, im-
mature Randy. Eric didn't understand the boy, who
lived life on the surface, content to do his work, draw
his wages, and get drunk and laid on his days off. Muldoon was different, and Eric not only understood but
empathized with him.

Some ten years older than the nineteen-year-old
Randy, Muldoon was a big man, with an insatiable lust
for life and for the land that nurtured it. With a full crop
of silky black curls, incisive sapphire blue eyes, and his
fair share of humor-tinged intelligence, he was handsome as sin and twice as appealing. He worked hard
and spoke little—and then usually in a dry drawl that

went directly to the heart of the subject matter, quite like Eric himself.

If Eric could call one man other than Duncan "friend," that man was Sean Muldoon, and Eric knew his friendship was reciprocated by the big, laconic Irishman.

"No, not the marines," Eric said, glancing out at the solitary horseman. "It's the man who headed up the cattle drive from San Antonio. The *segundo*."

"Well, damned if he don't look like an Indian," Randy observed, with more insight than he knew, "sittin' out there so still and quiet."

"Maybe he's waiting to be invited in," Muldoon drawled, grunting as he heaved himself to his feet.

"You have an injured man, *señor*?"

Eric smiled at Duncan's term and tone of respect. "A flesh wound, painful but not too serious."

"I have some knowledge of these things," Duncan said in the same respectful tone. "If he will step out, into the moonlight, I will examine the wound."

Muldoon was noticeably unimpressed and adamant in his refusal. "No, thanks, *amigo*. I'll wait till we get back to the bunkhouse and let Eric examine it . . . he also has some knowledge of these things."

Eric was hard put to hide a smile. The skill he and his father possessed in healing potions—among other things—was well known by all of the Circle-F employees but, of course, there wasn't any way that Muldoon could know that the man called Segundo was as well versed as Eric and David-Chill Wind in Indian lore.

"As you will . . . *amigo*."

A soft chuckle escaped Eric's guard at the underlying note of amusement in Duncan's voice. It appeared that his cousin was enjoying the role he'd created for himself. Scooping up the reins of his ground-tethered horse, Eric walked into the shimmering moonlight.

"By what stroke of fate were you roaming the countryside tonight?" he asked in a tone of voice pitched to reach his men, who were moving around, preparing to leave.

"I was restless," Duncan replied in a like tone. "I couldn't sleep."

"You felt it too, did you?" Eric asked in a murmur. "That uneasy feeling that something was wrong."

"Yes. That feeling—intuition—whatever it is, has always been with me."

Duncan's response came in a whisper, yet Eric heard and understood. Nodding, he raised his voice as his men walked their horses into the moonlight. "The restlessness is likely from being in a strange new place," he said for the men's benefit. "When are you heading back to Texas?"

"Not for a while," Duncan answered in a normal tone. "*Señor* Randall has hired me as his temporary *segundo*."

Unsurprised that his cousin had achieved his purpose, Eric smiled. Unaware of the situation, his men reacted as he would expect to the startling news.

"*Segundo!* What about Frank?" Randy exclaimed. "Ain't he the Randall ramrod no more?"

"Frank's not sick, is he?" Muldoon asked with concern.

"No, *señor*, Frank is not sick." Duncan addressed his reply to Muldoon. He went on to explain the circumstances surrounding his recent employment.

Eric listened with admiration to his cousin's recitation, aware, as he knew Duncan was, that every hand on the Circle-F would know the particulars before sunrise.

"Well, damn, imagine that," Randy said. "Ole Frank goin' on a buying trip to Argentina for the boss. Now, don't that beat all hell from here to Sunday?"

"I'd like to go to Argentina some day," Muldoon said.

"Yeah, some day." Eric laughed. "But right now you'd better hightail it back to the house and have that shoulder tended to." He looked at the other hand. "You might as well pack it in too. I doubt they'll be another rustling attempt tonight." As the men mounted their horses, with a string of colorful curses from Muldoon, Eric turned his attention to Duncan. "Thanks, again . . . Segundo."

"It was nothing." Duncan's voice was little more than a murmur.

"Like hell!" Eric retorted. "They had us pinned and outnumbered. If you hadn't come along . . ."

"You would have thought of something," Duncan finished for him in a dry drawl.

"Likely." Eric laughed. "But the least I can do is offer you a cup of coffee . . . if you want to ride back with us?"

Amusement tugged at Duncan's lips at the cleverness of Eric's ploy. This way Duncan could return to his own home without arousing the suspicions of the men. "*Gracias*, I would enjoy a cup of coffee." His smile was barely discernible in the waning light from the moon.

"Then let's get on with it." Eric stepped into the saddle. "Muldoon's shoulder needs looking after."

*   *   *

The bright moonlight was on the wane, retreating
before the advance of misty-gray predawn, when the
four men rode into the ranch yard. There was the
routine of activity around the stables as the cowboys
saddled their horses in readiness for the working day
before going into the cookhouse for breakfast. The low
murmur of their early-morning voices carried on the
cool air to the four riders.

"You can go right to the house, Segundo," Eric said,
jerking his head at the large ranch house. "My mother
will give you coffee." He started to move on with his
men, then he paused to flash a grin at Duncan over his
shoulder. "Inga . . . her name's Inga."

Since the men kept moving and weren't looking,
Duncan grinned back at him. *"Gracias . . . señor."*

A plethora of emotions thrummed inside Duncan as
he dismounted and tied the reins to the rail near the
veranda steps at the back of the house. Staring at the
rambling structure his father had begun building when
he was still a toddler, Duncan felt a sharp pang of grief
and regret.

Malcolm had planned to live out his life in the house,
and so he had been meticulous about detail and adamant about its size. Hoping for more children, he had
been lavish with the number of rooms. When it was
completed, the year Duncan turned eight, the house
was a sprawling two-story building of Malcolm's own
design, with large fireplaces inside for winter warmth
and a surrounding veranda to provide cooling shade in
the summer.

In contrast to the imposing manor house Malcolm
had grown up in Scotland—which contained sixteen

bedrooms, each with its own garderobe—the ranch house had only six bedrooms, none of which had bathrooms, although the master bedroom did have its own attached dressing room.

Nevertheless, for a home in the American West, the ranch house was an unusual structure, huge in comparison to the boxlike houses more common to the prairie. From its completion, it had proved a surprise to the few strangers who came upon it, either by invitation or happenstance.

Since the two families had lived together in the first house Malcolm and David had built, and since the new house was twice as big as the first, Malcolm saw no reason to change their living arrangements. The original ranch house was turned into a bunkhouse—affording the hired hands a degree of comfort unknown to other cowboys.

A bittersweet smile shadowed Duncan's mouth as his brooding gaze roamed over the house.

Memory teased, replaying happy and sad scenes. He could see his mother's beautiful, composed face, her dark eyes alight with laughter at something his father had either said or done to amuse her. He could feel the pain of rejection he'd suffered on being ridiculed and called a "breed" by his classmates on his first day at school. He could hear the merriment of the two families in celebration of some holiday or special occasion. He could feel the sense of shared anxiety when the threat of disease stalked the animals. He could hear the murmured voices of his mother and his aunt, the stronger tones of his father and uncle, and the more boisterous voices of Eric and himself at play, when they all were confined to the house during the bitter snow-

storms of winter. And he reexperienced the sorrow on
the death of his Shoshone grandfather, the aging but
still proud man who had instructed him and Eric in
Indian lore.

How he loved the house. How he had missed it, the
house and the land it sat so majestically upon. Inside
Duncan's mind the memories and years unwound. His
mother was long gone, at rest on the tree-shaded, grassy
plateau atop the gentle incline beyond the kitchen garden on the other side of the house.

Now his father was gone, at rest in the Frazer family
vault in Scotland.

Duncan was left. The house and land were now his,
his birthright, as were his titles, the estates in England
and Scotland, and the family manor house.

But this, this great rambling edifice in the middle of
nowhere, surrounded by the land overshadowed by the
jagged edged mountains, this was home.

The blood of his ancestors stirring in his veins,
Duncan released his visual greeting from the house,
mounted the steps, and crossed the deep veranda to
the kitchen door. As he raised his hand to knock, the
door was pulled open. Looking much as she had twenty
years ago, Inga stood in the doorway, her eyes bright
with welcome and tears.

"Duncan!" she cried, flinging her arms wide.
"Duncan Frazer, you get in here and give your Aunt
Inga a hug!"

The endearingly familiar command blended with his
memories. How many times had he heard a similar order from his Viking aunt? Too many to count, but he
recalled, too vividly, the last time. She had commanded
him in the same manner on the day he and his father

left the ranch, ordering him down from the wagon for one last hug.

Smiling, Duncan stepped across the threshold and into Inga's crushing, loving embrace.

The years had wrought a difference. On the occasion of that last hug, his face had been pressed to the tall woman's bosom. On this occasion, the top of Inga's head was on a level with the lower part of his face. Taking advantage of the position, Duncan pressed a kiss to her brow.

"I missed you so," she said in a tear-choked voice. "We've all missed you . . . so much."

His hands gentle, Duncan grasped her arms to stare his fill into her care-worn but still lovely face. "I missed you too. All of you." He turned his head to glide a hungry-eyed glance around the kitchen; it looked much the same as it always had, the changes were minimal. "All of this," he murmured as he brought his dark gaze back to hers.

Dashing a work-roughened hand over her eyes, Inga stepped back to rake a sharp-eyed look over his body, as if needing to make sure he was all of a piece. "You belong here," she stated in a simple, matter-of-fact tone. "You are as much a part of this land as the mountains that grew out of it."

"Yes." Duncan nodded.

"So, why didn't you come home sooner?" Inga demanded, her blue eyes flashing with impatience.

Her sharp tone struck a chord in Duncan's memory. How often had he heard that very same concern-sharpened tone when he was a boy. His smile faded. "There were circumstances, Aunt Inga, and you know it."

Sorrow banished the light from her eyes. "Malcolm," she said on a sigh.

"Yes. I could not return while he was alive."

Tears brightened her eyes again. "I know." Sniffing, she turned away, as if ashamed of her show of emotion.

His eyes softened by the love and compassion he felt for her, Duncan moved to stand close to her. "He died loving her, you know," he murmured, placing his hand on her shoulder, "despite the regard he felt for my stepmother."

"I'm not surprised." Inga slid her hand over his. "She was the most gentle, loving woman I ever met. We'll likely all go to our graves loving Mary-First Star."

Feeling a brief but intense stab of loss, Duncan tightened his grasp on Inga's shoulder. The moment was deep with unspeakable insight and emotion, and unbearable for either one to maintain.

"Where is Uncle David?" Duncan asked in a soft voice made rough by the tightness in his throat.

With a determined, final-sounding sniff, Inga turned to give him a faint smile. "He's down at the bunkhouse. Eric felt . . . compelled . . . to ride out a coupla hours ago." Though her voice was brisk, it couldn't conceal the thread of worry woven through it. "And, since he hasn't come back yet, David went to give the men their work instructions for the day."

"Eric is back," Duncan said, smiling in understanding of her sigh of relief. "I rode in with him."

"But how did you . . . where did you . . . ?" Inga broke off to expel a soft laugh. "Dumb question. I must be getting old. You felt the same compulsion, didn't you?"

"Yes."

Inga rolled her eyes. "I should have known. Did Eric go straight to the bunkhouse?"

Duncan answered with a brief nod. "One of his men —Muldoon—was injured. Eric is tending the wound."

"Injured!" Inga exclaimed, starting for the door. "I must go see if there's anything I can—"

"Wait," Duncan interrupted her words with the command and her progress with a hand clamped to her wrist. "It's a flesh wound. Eric and David can handle it."

"But . . ." Inga's blue eyes clouded with indecision.

"Eric told me you would give me a cup of coffee," Duncan cut in, not only to give her something to do, but because he really wanted the hot drink. "I'm hungry too."

The transition from anxiety to purpose was immediate. "Well, why didn't you say so?" Inga demanded, swinging around to rush to the stove. "Sit down, boy," she ordered, motioning to the table with one hand while reaching for the large coffeepot with the other.

Smiling with satisfaction and the warmth of memory aroused by hearing her call him "boy," Duncan walked to the beautifully hand-crafted long table. He was sliding a chair out from beneath it when his cousin and uncle entered the room. The sight of his uncle sliced into Duncan like a slashing blade.

The reality of David-Chill Wind Blowing clashed with the image Duncan had carried for twenty years of the man. In his memory, his uncle was tall, straight, and strong. The man standing before Duncan now was little more than a shadow, a caricature of that younger man. His once-strong hands were gnarled, his straight spine

bent from the ravages of arthritis. The coppery sheen
of his skin was dulled by illness and despair.

"Duncan!" David's depthless dark eyes brightened
with surprise. "Eric did not tell me you were here," he
said, moving forward at a shuffling gait.

Swallowing an outcry of protest against a fate that
would inflict such a painful and crippling disease upon
his once-stalwart uncle, Duncan moved with sure-
footed swiftness, striding to David to enfold him within
a crushing embrace.

The man who had once towered over the boy now
clutched at Duncan's chest. But his voice was strong
and rock-steady as he spoke in his native tongue of his
feelings of joy at having his other "son" returned to
him.

His eyes stinging with a sheen of tears, Duncan
stared over his uncle's gray-streaked head into the sad
eyes of his cousin. Eric's features were set, locked into
place against the feelings running too close to the surface. In visual communication, they commiserated with
each other.

Staring into Eric's compassion-softened eyes,
Duncan held David's frail body close to his own
strength and responded to his welcome greeting in the
Shoshone language.

When at last they broke the embrace, there was no
embarrassment, no strain. A smile of contentment
curved David's lips as he shifted his gaze from his son
to his nephew. "I am proud and grateful for this day."
He tilted his head to look at his wife. "We have two
fine men here, Inga."

Inga's blue eyes were misty and her soft mouth betrayed a tremor. "Yes, Chill Wind Blowing," she mur-

mured, honoring him by using his Shoshone name.
"Two fine men." Then she blinked, twitched her nose,
and said in a forced, brisk tone, "I have three fine,
hungry men, and breakfast will be ready shortly."

Breakfast was a celebration of reunion. Conversation
zinged around the table, most of it beginning with the
phrase: "Do you remember when . . ."

They were finished eating before Duncan recalled
the incident of earlier that morning and the man who
had been injured during the skirmish.

"How is Muldoon?" Duncan asked his uncle.

David winced as he shrugged. "It is a shallow
wound; a scratch. He will quickly heal."

"I don't like it," Eric said, pushing his chair away
from the table. "This was the first time we've had any
gunplay."

Duncan watched his cousin walk to the stove to refill
his cup. "Do you think those rustlers were those men
you were telling me about . . . those hard cases?"

Eric frowned and blew on his steaming coffee. "Hell,
I don't know. Could've been, but it was too dark to see
them, let alone identify any of 'em."

"I think I may have hit one of them." Duncan held
his cup aloft in a silent request for refilling. "I heard an
outcry of pain from one."

"Yeah." Eric absently filled the cup and handed it
back to Duncan. "Maybe I'll take a ride into town this
morning . . . see what I can see."

"Good idea." Nodding, Duncan sipped at the hot
brew. "And I've got to get going." He glanced at the
window, noting the pink blush of morning sunlight.
"Ben will be wondering what became of me."

"You're not staying?" Inga exclaimed.

"No." Duncan murmured, pushing his chair away from the table. "Eric will explain." He drained his cup, set it on the table, then walked to the door. "Thanks for breakfast." He smiled to relieve the concerned expressions of the older couple. "Don't worry, I'll be back." He shifted his gaze to his cousin. "You will let me know what you learn in town?"

"Sure."

"Good." Duncan gave a brief nod, pulled the door open, and flashed a smile. *"Adios . . . amigos."*

Eric's laughter followed him out of the house.

The sun was well above the horizon when Duncan cantered into the Randall ranch yard. Horses whinnied, chickens cackled, milk cows bawled, but there was an absence of human voices. The hands had long since left for the day.

The hands . . . and Jessica.

Jessica.

A tired smile twisted Duncan's lips. Thoughts of the infuriating woman had played at the edges of his mind throughout the night. Thoughts of her had been the original reason for his sleeplessness, hours before the intuitive feeling drove him from his bed to the rustling scene on the Circle-F.

After being there, Duncan wanted more than ever to return to his home. But, before he could do so, there were two priorities that required his attention: the rustling and the woman.

While Duncan regarded the first as an irritating necessity, he contemplated the second with a growing sense of pleasurable relish.

The delicate scent of lilacs wafted through his mind,

bringing a vision of Jessica that heated his blood. With his inner eye, Duncan could see her as she looked when she appeared for supper last night. Though simple, her dress was feminine. It clung to the upper part of her slender form and swished enticingly around her ankles. He was relieved to note that her hair was still the color of liquid silver, and though anchored to the back of her head, it shimmered in the soft glow cast by the globed coal-oil lamps. Her pale skin was flushed from her recent bath. Everything about her appeared soft and gentle. Everything, that is, but her eyes. When she looked at him, Jessica's silvery eyes were hard, and as cold as a midwinter ice storm.

On sight of her, Duncan had experienced a strong recurrence of conflicting desire and antagonism.

The memory brought the sensations flooding back, firing his passion.

Take care of our baby.

Duncan chuckled as he once again recalled the instruction he had given to Eric all those years ago. The haughty young woman he had encountered yesterday was far removed from infancy, far removed from cosseting and caressing—at least of the kind lavished upon a child.

His chuckle grew into a soft but full-throated laugh. He and Jessica would clash; Duncan knew it. The battle lines were drawn. Excitement surged through him, banishing his weariness.

With a light tap of his heels, Duncan nudged his horse toward the stable.

He couldn't wait for their next skirmish.

5

"Now?" Blinking sleepily, the woman pushed her tangled mass of red hair off her face. "It's hardly morning yet." Turning her head on the pillow, she peered at the window. "It's hardly light yet, for God's sake."

Josh Metcalf slid his smooth hand over the woman's full breast. "Yes, now. Who the hell cares if it's light or not?" he retorted, flicking his index finger against the nipple and smiling with excited satisfaction as it sprang to attention. "I've got to get back to Sandy Rush."

"But I'm still half asleep," she protested, shoving her lower lip out in a practiced pout.

"Only from the neck up," Josh retorted, excitement

tingling along his spine as he watched in avid fascination the tightening of the dusky nipple.

The woman yawned in his face. "What's the hurry, anyway?" she mumbled. "What do you have to get back for?"

"Business," Josh said in a harsh tone, which told her it was none of hers. The day hadn't arrived when Josh felt he should explain himself to any woman, let alone a whore.

The woman he knew only as Meg looked more than sleepy. She looked world-weary and bored. She yawned again. "I didn't know there was much business to speak of in Sandy Rush."

Josh frowned and rubbed his manhood against her soft thigh. He didn't want to talk, at least not about business. He was hard, and getting harder by the second, and he wanted nothing so much as he wanted to pump his body into hers.

But Josh had a quirk. He was smart and a realist. He knew that few whores were ever really aroused. They were adept at feigning arousal and climax—as she had in their coupling last night. He didn't resent the deception; he understood it, and that's where his quirk came into play. Josh's excitement rose to fever pitch when he succeeded in genuinely arousing a whore. He had been too horny, too hungry to indulge his quirk last night, but he had awakened before dawn, still horny but more inclined to take his time with her, to bring her body to a fever pitch matching his own passion.

"You don't have to know anything about business, in Sandy Rush or anywhere else," he muttered, lowering his hand to the mound between her thighs. "All you have to know is how to pleasure me." Watching her

eyes, Josh slid two fingers into her body. A scowl
twisted his attractive face. She was dry.

Meg dutifully wiggled her behind, but he could tell
from her expression that she was acting the part of passion. The realization aggravated his patience while
whipping his own passion into a frenzy. Damn the
whore! he raged in silent frustration. Hadn't he told her
he was in a hurry?

Josh needed to get back to that fly speck on earth
called Sandy Rush. His work had been laid out for him
in the terse message contained in the telegram he'd
received late yesterday afternoon. It read: "Decision
firm on spur line. Track work to begin in spring."

Though brief, the information contained in the terse
message sent elation soaring through him. The railroad
company was planning to build a spur line into Sandy
Rush. Josh had until spring to buy up as much land as
possible in and around the town. Come spring, Josh
planned to be a big man in a booming Sandy Rush.

He had set the wheels in motion almost a year ago,
less than a month after overhearing a conversation
about the possibility of the company running a spur
line to a town in Wyoming he had never before heard
of. He had been eavesdropping, of course. In his position of clerk in the railroad office in Chicago, he had not
been privy to decision-making information. He had resigned his position and left two weeks later.

Soon after his arrival in Sandy Rush, Josh had instigated the hit-and-run rustlings, creating what appeared
to be the beginnings of a range war, in an attempt to
scare off at least some of the small farmers and ranchers. So far two of the small landowners had sold out to
him, encouraging him to increase his efforts.

Now, with the telegram confirming that the spur line would be built, Josh knew that the last thing he should be doing was dallying with a woman. He had to return to Sandy Rush to learn the results of last night's raid and to plan his strategy for future attacks.

But this morning, this minute, his quirk was in command, and Josh was determined on making the bitch hot if it took all day. Controlling an urge to rail at her, curse her, he concentrated on the task at hand. He didn't bother raking his mind for words of enticement; he knew Meg had heard them all before. Instead, in silence, he stroked her, caressed her, feasted upon her body until, at last, it betrayed itself with the moisture wetting his fingers. His blood hot, his heart pounding, Josh slipped between Meg's thighs and into her body.

Sheathed at last within Meg's heated softness, Josh lost all control. Giving in to his fiery lust, he thrust his body into hers with relentless determination.

Meg gave a strangled gasp and her eyes grew wide and dark. Josh knew he had hurt her, but he was too far gone to stop himself. Unmindful of her pain, he drove himself toward completion, his body slamming against hers more forcefully with each repeated plunge.

Wide-eyed, Meg endured his piercing blows then, suddenly, she caught fire. Her fingers raked his back, and she met each of his rhythmic plunges with an abandoned upthrust of her ass, driving him wild.

Josh was no longer quite sane. His chest heaving, working his body with ruthless intent, he stared at Meg and saw another visage superimposed on her face.

Jessica. Josh's lips thinned, baring his teeth in a snarl. That cold, haughty bitch wouldn't give him the time of day, let alone her body. Not that he really wanted her;

Josh didn't. To his mind, Jessica wasn't much of a
woman—what with her dressing like a man and doing a
man's work.

No, Josh didn't have designs on Jessica Randall's
body, he desired the land which accompanied that
body with matrimony. The section of land Ben Randall
had apportioned to Jessica in the event of her marriage
was common knowledge in the district . . . and in a
prime location in regard to the railroad spur line into
Sandy Rush.

Josh wanted that section of land and considered marriage to the aloof Jessica worth the sacrifice to acquire
it. But not only had Jessica turned down his proposal,
she had looked down her delicate nose at him as if he
were lower than cow dung.

Seeing Jessica's image imposed on Meg's writhing
body sent Josh's hormones into spasm.

Damn her! In a lustful delirium, Josh increased the
pounding motion of his clamoring body. In his mind, he
was spearing three targets with one shaft. While punishing the haughty Jessica, he was inflicting genuine
pleasure on a whore, and, at the same time, he was
thrilling to the most intense sexual encounter he had
ever experienced.

Meg's outcry pierced the haze clouding his mind.
Her body clenched around him, throbbing with release.
The sensation pushed him over the brink. The tension
snapped. His body exploded, expelling his seed into
the depths of hers.

Spent, Josh collapsed onto Meg's sweat-slickened
body. He was shaking with reaction. His breathing was
harsh and labored. He had never felt better in his life.

Strength and purpose resurged within Josh as the

sense of euphoria dissipated. After levering himself off Meg's depleted body, he crossed the room to the chair on which he had so carefully arranged his clothes last night. As he dressed, Josh could feel Meg's stare monitoring his every move.

Ignoring the woman, Josh smoothed his hair and patted his pockets. He smiled at the feel of the folded telegram inside one pocket and the outline of his derringer in the other. He paused with his hand on the doorknob to glance back at Meg.

"That was pretty good," he said, smiling with satisfaction at the shattered look of her. "We'll have to do it again the next time I'm in South Pass."

"Son of a bitch." Meg muttered the epithet aloud as the door closed behind Josh Metcalf. Anger burned like bitter acid inside her. "Dirty smooth-talking, soft-palmed son of a bitch."

Giving voice to her rage didn't alleviate Meg's feeling of self-disgust. At that moment, she hated Josh Metcalf, but she hated herself more.

The degree of arousal and passion Meg had experienced did not happen often . . . in fact, hardly ever. She prided herself on her immunity to the sexual advances of most men and despised the few who managed to break through her self-control.

Meg didn't merely hate men—she disdained them. She had reasons for her antipathy . . . many reasons.

She had been christened Margaret Mary Shanely by her mother, six years before that overworked and exhausted woman drew her last agonized breath. Yet there were few people who knew her full name. To the residents of South Pass, and to the men she serviced, she was simply Meg—the whore.

Meg had not chosen the profession of prostitution. It had been thrust upon her by the man who had married her widowed mother, not for love or even caring for her, but for the run-down farmhouse and scrap of land she'd inherited on the death of Meg's father. Too lazy to work the land, and a slave to drink, Meg's stepfather had bargained her undeveloped thirteen-year-old body to a drifter in exchange for a few coins and a bottle of whiskey.

If she were to survive to a hundred, Meg knew she would never forget her initiation into womanhood. The man, whose name she never knew, had an unhealthy appetite for premature girls. He had hurt her, in more ways than the usual pain connected to the piercing of the membrane, by taking her again and again, using her body in every sexual way imaginable, and forcing her to perform unspeakable acts with and to him.

But that unknown man had been only the first in a long line of despicable creatures her stepfather had "rented" her to for a bottle or money. In between the faceless men, her stepfather had used her himself.

Alone, frightened, a virtual prisoner in the isolated farmhouse located some miles outside a dying town in Kansas, Meg had little option but to endure a miserable life of deprivation and degradation. There were times when, sick with shame, she prayed for the release of death, yet, strangely, she never considered taking her own life. It was the one mortal sin she would not allow herself to commit.

But Meg did consider committing the sin of taking

her stepfather's life. Her hatred of him was soul deep and mind consuming. She even attempted the act.

Meg reached her breaking point on a sultry night in her sixteenth summer, when her depraved stepfather agreed to allow not just one but two men the use of her body at the same time, on the condition that he be allowed to watch the fun.

When the "fun" was over, Meg lay curled into a ball on the dirt floor, retching from disgust and loathing, all the spark of youth and resiliency apparently beaten out of her.

Observing her through whiskey-clouded eyes, and with a lecherous smirk on his twisting lips, her stepfather made the mistake of mocking her.

"What you got to be snivelin' about, pussy girl?" he taunted in a slurred voice. "You ain't foolin' me none. You had yore fun. I seen ya buckin' away." He bent down to leer into her tear-streaked face; she gagged at the smell of raw rotgut on his putrid breath. "I been watchin' ya of late. You gets hot when they hurt ya, don't ya, pussy girl?"

Had Meg been stronger, they'd have been the last words he ever spoke. As it was he might have wished for death, because while Meg failed to kill her stepfather with the skinning knife she pulled from his belt, the fury behind her blind slash of the blade severed the muscles and tendons just above his knees, crippling him for life.

His screams of pain pounding against her ears, Meg ran from the house, and kept running, whoring to earn sustenance and a place to sleep, all the way to Wyoming. She had earned her way by whoring throughout

the eleven years since that mind-scarring, never-to-be-
forgotten night.

Now, lying on her place of work in the small house
she had bought with the money she earned while flat
on her back, Meg stared at the closed bedroom door
and made a silent promise to herself that Josh Metcalf
would pay for arousing her, thus raking up memories
long suppressed.

Though uneducated, Meg had not accrued the
money to purchase her own small house of pleasure by
being stupid. Nor did she in any way resemble the ro-
manticized western "soiled dove" with loose morals
but a heart of gold. While on the surface Meg was full-
figured and soft, inside she was as tough as tempered
steel, and preferred gold in the form of coin.

Meg was ambitious and had no intentions of remaining where she was. Since the gold had petered out of
the Clarissa Lode mine, South Pass was yet another
dying town in her life. And Meg was through with dying towns. Her goal was to save enough money to set
herself up in business in a discreet, elegant house in
the bigger, more affluent city of Cheyenne, where she
would conduct the transactions for her "ladies" and use
her own bed for sleeping purposes only.

It was because of her future plans that Josh Metcalf
and men of his ilk were allowed to spend the entire
night with Meg. The going rate was much higher for
the occasional customer who desired the whole night in
her bed.

Josh Metcalf had willingly paid her price, but he had
exacted more from her than the sum entitled. As morning filled her narrow bedroom windows, Meg vowed

that some way, someday, Josh would have to pay the difference.

Perhaps, she mused, closing her eyes and yawning, the telegram she'd discovered during the night—while engaged in her usual practice of investigating the contents of a sleeping customer's pockets—could be of use to her. Yes, the telegram plus the knowledge that, while to all appearances Josh Metcalf went unarmed, he carried a small derringer concealed on his person, might prove to be the weapons she could use against the son of a bitch.

As she snuggled into a comfortable position, Meg's soft, full lips curved into a hard, thin line.

6

She was late.

Her expression a study in consternation and disbelief, Jessica absently tucked her shirt into her pants and stared out her bedroom window at the glare of morning sunlight.

She had slept badly, tossing and turning on her bed, while memories of the evening spent in the company of the *segundo* tossed and turned inside her head. Only a few hours before dawn had she drifted into a restless slumber. But her lack of sleep was an unacceptable excuse; she was never late; she never overslept.

Grimacing, Jessica dragged a brush through her tan-

gled hair. Not once since she'd returned home from
school had she missed riding out at dawn with the men.
And now, to miss muster this morning of all morn-
ings . . .

What would they all think? Muttering to herself, Jessica separated her hair into three clumps and braided
them into a single loose plait that hung to the middle of
her back when she tossed it over her shoulder. She
didn't have to question, she knew full well what everyone would think about her failure to present herself for
her father's morning work assignments. They would
think she was closeted in her room, pouting over being
usurped by the stranger.

The *segundo.*

Jessica ground her teeth with impotent fury. Damn
the man. Because of him, she would be perceived as a
sulking female, when in truth everyone on the B-Bar-R
knew that she neither pouted nor sulked when things
didn't go her way.

Impatient with herself, with the situation, Jessica
stamped into her scarred boots, grabbed her hat, gloves,
and horsewhip, and strode from her room.

Her mother was standing at the metal-legged, porcelain kitchen sink, rinsing the breakfast dishes in the
water flowing from the narrow spigot. She turned to
smile at Jessica as she emerged from the enclosed back
stairway.

"Good morning, dear." Not a hint of censure, or
even surprise, colored Emily's pleasant tone. "I imagine you're starving."

"No, I don't have time to eat," Jessica replied,
frowning. "I'm late."

"The ranch won't fall into wrack and ruin because

you're late one morning, Jessica," Emily chided. After drying her hands, she picked up a newly washed cup and walked to the stove. "And you can't work all day on an empty stomach." She filled the cup with strong dark coffee and set it on the table. "Now, drink your coffee and tell me what you want to eat."

"Mother . . ." Jessica began, prepared to argue.

"Jessica," Emily said, in a tone that brooked no argument, "I said, sit down, drink your coffee, and tell me what you want to eat." She planted her hands on her waist in a manner that told her daughter that argument would be useless. When Emily Randall dug her heels in, she was as immovable as the distant Rocky Mountain range.

Sighing in defeat, Jessica scraped a chair away from the table and sat down. "I'm really not very hungry," she said truthfully. "Is there any oatmeal left?"

"Yes, but . . ."

"And a biscuit?" she tacked on, not because she wanted one, but to pacify her mother.

"Well, if you're sure that's all you want." Looking uncertain, Emily hovered between the table and the stove. "The biscuits are cold by now."

"It doesn't matter, Mother, I'm used to cold biscuits. And, yes, I'm positive that will be quite enough to get me through the day without starving," Jessica assured her.

Tamping down her impatience to be gone, Jessica sipped her coffee in silence until Emily set a bowl of hot cereal and a plate of biscuits on the table in front of her.

"Where's Dad?" she asked, eyeing the food with little appetite and less interest.

"In the office," Emily answered, placing a jar of homemade preserves next to the plate of biscuits.

Thinking she'd go to her father for instructions as soon as she'd satisfied her mother's demand that she eat, Jessica picked up her spoon and began making inroads in the oatmeal. She had forced down every last bit of the cereal and was absently slathering preserves on half a biscuit when Ben Randall emerged from his office. He was not alone.

Jessica's muscles clenched around the oatmeal sitting uneasily in her stomach and her fingers tightened around the knife in her hand at the sight of the man trailing her father into the kitchen.

Why wasn't he with the men, where he belonged? She questioned with flashing anger. The *segundo* looked tired, strained . . . and yet far too attractive for her peace of mind. His presence in the room irritated Jessica, while at the same time she felt a rush of excitement wash over her—which abraded her feeling of irritation even more.

His dark eyes were hooded, but not enough to hide the glimmer of interest that sprang into their depths when he saw her seated at the table. Feeling the raw power radiating from his intense gaze, and resenting the tingling effect that gaze had on her senses, Jessica exerted every ounce of control she possessed to casually raise her hand and sink her perfect white teeth into the fluffy biscuit.

"Well, you finally rolled out, I see," Ben said, grinning at Jessica. "I was beginning to think I was going to have to come up to your room and tilt your bed." Not waiting for a reply from her, he switched his attention to his wife. "How about a cup of coffee for me and the *segundo*, Emily?"

"Right away." Emily beamed the smile reserved only for her husband of twenty-six years. "I made it when I heard Jessica moving around upstairs, so it's good and fresh."

It is? Jessica stared into her empty cup; the brew could have been four days old for all she'd noticed.

"Good morning, *señorita*."

His soft voice affected Jessica like a blast of frigid air. Jerking her head up, she stared at him with icy, unconcealed disapproval. "My name is Jessica," she said coldly, disdaining to return his greeting.

"As you wish." The *segundo* smiled, with his lips and eyes, in a manner so blatant with sensual overtones, it sent a thrill of both sexual awareness and sheer fury surging through her bloodstream. "Good morning," he repeated in an even softer voice. "Miss Jessica."

Damn his eyes! Jessica railed, enraged. And damn his wicked smile and suggestive soft voice. But she was caught in a net of her own weaving. She had thrown her name at him like a challenge, and he not only picked it up, he'd tossed it back at her. Unless she was willing to appear both churlish and childish, she was left with little option but to respond to him.

"Good morning," Jessica replied in a curt tone, then in a deliberate act of dismissal, she turned her head to center her attention on her father. "I'm sorry I overslept," she said in a tone of self-condemnation. "I have no excuse for it," she continued, determined she'd rather die of boredom helping her mother with the household chores than admit to having spent the night tossing and turning, bedeviled by thoughts and images and feelings aroused by the new foreman—Segundo.

"No matter." Ben dismissed her tardiness with a negligent wave of his hand. "In fact, I'm glad you're here."

Jessica was at once suspicious and apprehensive. Surely her father wouldn't follow through with his threat to confine her to the house and yard? The idea sent her jerking to her feet. Her chair skidded over the clean linoleum on the floor—linoleum that she had had no hand in scrubbing.

"I . . . er . . . better get to work," she said, edging around the table in the direction of the door. "If you'll tell me where you want me to—"

"Sit down, Jessica." Ben cut her off with a show of impatience. "There's plenty of time, have another cup of coffee. I don't want you joining the men today. I've got another job for you."

Jessica didn't want another cup of coffee; and she felt positive she didn't want to hear what it was he wanted her to do. Nevertheless, averting her eyes from the silent man seating himself next to her, she sat down, accepted the cup her mother handed to her, and watched, tight-lipped, as Emily smiled and placed a cup on the table in front of the *segundo*.

"*Gracias.*"

The soft sound of his voice sliced through Jessica's scattered thoughts. His voice was deep, smooth, appealing, and yet the lack of accent bothered her. She stole a quick glance at him, then as quickly looked away. He was watching her, waiting to hear her response to her father.

The kitchen was like an oven. Jessica felt hot and

sticky. She longed to place the blame for her sudden discomfort on the heat radiating from the large cooking stove, but in truth knew the warmth suffusing her being was a direct response to the molten gleam in the depths of Segundo's eyes. Feeling a need to put distance between them, she had to force herself to remain seated, while trying to look cool and composed. It wasn't easy; in fact, it was damn near impossible.

Jessica groaned in silent frustration. With visions of mounds of dirty laundry rising to terrorize her mind, she asked, "What other job?"

Lowering his solid body onto a chair opposite her, Ben blew on his steaming coffee and took a tentative sip before answering. "I want you to show the *segundo* over the place," he said, nodding at the too-silent man seated too close to her. "You can give him a tour, explain the operation, so he can familiarize himself with the layout. I was going to show him around myself," Ben went on, "but I've got a pile of paperwork on my desk and, since you're here, you can do it."

No! Jessica had to clamp her lips together to keep from expelling the protest in an appalled outcry. Spend the entire day with him? Alone with him? No. She would not do it. He couldn't make her do it. Could he?

Yes, he could . . . and would, Jessica acknowledged, a sinking sensation settling in her stomach as she stared at her father. He didn't need to say any more; his set expression was telling her that she had three choices.

Jessica didn't have to hear her options voiced aloud. She knew what they were. She could help her mother with the household chores, tackle the paperwork on her father's desk, or escort the disturbing stranger around the ranch.

In actual fact, there was another option, even less appealing than the other three.

"Or," Ben went on in a prompting tone when she failed to respond, "you can help your mother write out the party invitations."

Oh, God! Jessica shuddered at the very idea. Sitting for hours drafting party invitations in the elegant script her mother preferred was enough to give her the willies.

"You are giving a party?"

If she had believed for one instant that she could have gotten away with ignoring the *segundo*, Jessica would have done so. But, since he had spoken directly to her, she couldn't ignore him, and knew it.

"Not me, my father."

A short silence ensued, during which Jessica knew everyone was waiting for her to elaborate. When she didn't, her mother rushed into speech to cover the breach of good manners.

"Ben throws a preroundup party at the end of each summer," Emily explained, slanting an exasperated look at Jessica. "It's become something of a local tradition around here."

"I see."

Good for you.

Deciding she had better not press her luck with her father, Jessica kept the sarcastic thought to herself.

"Yeah, I let everyone whoop it up good before tackling the roundup." Ben grinned.

Segundo grinned back at him. "Soften them up for the hard times ahead . . . hmm?"

"Something like that."

"Is there anything I can do to help?" Segundo glanced from Ben to Emily.

"No." Emily shook her head.

"Not just now," Ben clarified. "Be plenty for you to help with closer to the day."

"And when is that?"

"Two weeks." Ben stared at Jessica. "So, what's it going to be? Make up your mind."

Making a choice was not easy. If there was anything Jessica disliked more than household chores, it was the tedious paperwork involved with ranching, and writing formal invitations. On the other hand, she didn't relish the idea of spending the entire day in the exclusive company of the new foreman.

What to do? Bidding for time, Jessica made a pretense of concentrating on the coffee she didn't want. But her father was through with her delaying tactics.

"Jessica?"

Jessica jerked erect at the sharp edge on Ben's voice. Her time had run out; she had to choose. "I . . . er . . ." she began, only to be interrupted by the soft voice of the dark man seated less than a foot from her.

"If Miss Jessica has more important duties elsewhere," he said in an indifferent, thus insulting, tone, "I can wander around on my own."

Resenting him, and the less than respectful emphasis he'd placed on the address, "Miss Jessica," she gritted her teeth and turned to face him, prepared to administer a blistering setdown. But before she could articulate her seething thoughts, her father doused them with a cold command.

"You'll do nothing of the kind, Segundo." Angry

sparks flared in the eyes Ben directed at his daughter. "Jessica, I'm growin' mighty weary of your shilly-shallying here. You will do as you're told. Is that understood?"

Recognizing defeat when it stared her right in the face, Jessica gave in with a sigh and a shrug. "Yes, sir." Avoiding the *segundo's* eyes—which she felt positive were alight with an unholy gleam—Jessica set her cup on the table and pushed back her chair. "I'm ready whenever he is."

"Ready for . . . anything?"

"What?" Angry, frustrated, and distracted by the bitter taste of surrender stinging the back of her throat, Jessica shot a narrowed, sideways glare at the tall man matching his stride to hers as they walked to the stables.

His lips were tilted in a mocking curve; his voice held more than a hint of taunting laughter. "You told your father you were ready whenever I was," Segundo murmured. "I was asking if you were ready for anything . . . Miss Jessica."

Fighting down a sudden and startling surge of excitement, Jessica lifted her chin to an arrogant angle and stared along the length of her elegant nose at him. Looking at him full face was a mistake. He was far too attractive, his expression much too confident for her taste. Jessica knew that if any other man had made that remark, in that same suggestive tone of voice, she'd have verbally ripped him apart without compunction. Yet, coming from him, the remark caused an amazing reaction of tingling anticipation inside her.

The physical sensation was new and unacceptable to

Jessica. It confused her, and that was not to be borne.
Her silver eyes taking on the sheen of clouded ice, she
confronted him with the haughty, superior look that
had quelled numerous would-be suitors . . . on the
East Coast and on the range.

"I can handle anything, any situation, any man might
contrive," she retaliated.

"Indeed?" Challenge glittered in the *segundo*'s eyes;
his teeth flashed white against the darkness of his skin.
"Anything, Miss Jessica?"

Incensed by the effect of his devastating smile on
her senses, Jessica imprudently flung his challenge
back at him. "Yes, anything, Segundo," she hissed.
"Try me."

"Oh, I intend to," he said in a bone-melting whisper,
"in every way imaginable."

For an instant, Jessica was struck speechless,
thoughtless, immovable. Every way imaginable! The
possibilities contained within those three words were
frightening . . . and insidiously arousing. A riot of impressions, erotic and unspeakable, scampered through
her stunned mind, breaking the grip of shock-induced
stillness.

Jessica came to her senses to the realization that she
was standing in the middle of the ranch yard, cold and
shivering beneath the unrelenting rays of the summer
sun. Pride rushed to her rescue, dispersing the chill and
filling the void with the heat of renewed anger and
purpose.

Oh, yes, this man, this . . . Segundo, was long over-
due a come-uppance.

"To your left, to the rear of the house, are the
kitchen gardens," Jessica said in a flat, controlled

monotone. She indicated the area with a flick of her gloved left hand. "Beyond the gardens are the pigpens and chicken coop."

Though his lips twitched with unconcealed amusement, Segundo dutifully turned to survey the gardens, pens, and coop. "I see," he said, then proved his observance by asking "And those buildings behind and off to the side?" He turned to look at her. "I know the one closest to the bunkhouse is the foreman's house, but what are the other three used for?"

"The married hands," Jessica said. "Only two of them are occupied at present. The wives help my mother with the house and yard work."

Segundo's eyebrows arched. "Feudalistic . . . isn't it?"

"Hardly," Jessica snapped. "The women are adequately compensated for their services." Her lips curved into a condescending smile. "Your remark betrays your ignorance about this part of the country."

"In what way?" He didn't appear offended by her smile or scathing tone, but merely interested.

Jessica was more than happy to enlighten him; in fact, she relished the telling. "The women of Wyoming have enjoyed political equality since 1869."

Segundo's reaction to enlightenment was disappointing. Rather than the amazement, or even the surprise, she expected, he appeared blasé.

"Oh, I knew that," he said, shrugging. "Anyone even remotely interested in world events knows that." His eyes took on a taunting gleam. "But, by and of itself, political equality does not make every woman the equal of every man."

Jessica went rigid with anger. There it was again, that

superior, self-satisfied, dominant-male attitude! She
felt compelled to lash out at him, verbally and physically. Instead, recalling her father's instructions, but
promising herself future retribution, she swallowed the
tirade clogging her throat and salved her pride with a
glaring stare and a single comment. "Since that observation comes from a man, I'll consider the source . . .
and ignore it."

"Along with reality?" Segundo's voice held a mocking, indulgent tone.

Jessica was incensed but managed to contain her
fury. "This is neither the time nor the place for a philosophical discussion," she said through her gritted teeth,
in her most patronizing, exclusive-school-educated
tones. "I suggest that we get on with the business at
hand."

The bastard had the gall to laugh! In itself, his laughter was aggravating, but what was even more annoying
to Jessica was the pleasant, nerve-tingling sound of it.
The sound was deep and rich and thoroughly demoralizing.

"By all means." Segundo chuckled, indicating the
stable with a sweep of his arm. "Do let us get on with
it."

Although his phrasing struck her as strange—wasn't
he Spanish?—it was all a piece of everything strange
about him, so Jessica shrugged it off. Lifting her chin,
she spun away from him and strode to the stable. And,
though she couldn't hear him, the prickly sensation at
her nape assured her that the *segundo* was right at her
heels—still laughing.

"I'll need a fresh mount."

A jolt of awareness crashed through Jessica. Though

she had known the *segundo* was close, she hadn't dreamed he was close enough to ruffle the tiny hairs at her nape with his breath. The moist feeling was delicious—Jessica liked the feeling so much, she hated it.

"Shaky, saddle Don Quixote for the *segundo*," she said, stepping away from him, his breath, into the relative safety of the stable.

"Cervantes," Segundo murmured, shadowing her into the shadows. "Am I expected to tilt at windmills as well as ramrod this outfit?"

Once more Jessica was struck by a sense of strangeness. Not only had the *segundo* fallen into the pattern of response set by her brother, he had revealed a certain knowledge of literature. A well-read cowboy? she reflected. If nothing else, this *segundo* was unique.

"The first one you come across," Jessica replied in a dry tone, amused, if against her will, by his remark. He grinned. She felt a stirring of panic. Gathering the reins of the horse the wrangler had saddled and ready for her, she walked the animal from the stable, into the cooling glare of sunlight.

Leading the high-spirited, dancing Don Quixote, Segundo followed her into the yard a few moments later. He ran an appreciative glance over her gleaming quarter horse, then raised his devil-dark eyes to hers.

"Please, don't tell me, let me guess," he said in a soft drawl. "Is the mare's name Dulcinea?"

"Of course not." Struggling against a burst of delighted laughter, Jessica shoved her boot into the stirrup and swung up into the saddle. "Her name is Bath."

"Bath?" Segundo repeated, frowning. "What sort of name is that?"

"A diminutive." Her lips curving into a satisfied

smile, she tapped her heels against the mare's body. As the horse leapt into motion, Jessica called back over her shoulder, "It's short for Bathsheba."

Segundo's bark of laughter mingled with the sun-spangled cloud of dust pluming behind her.

7

Bathsheba, the temptress. The innocent temptress? Apropos Jessica herself?

Amused by the trend of his thoughts, Duncan was content to trail several lengths behind Jessica, contemplating the enticing curves of her body, as well as the possible comparison between the mare's uncommon name and the equally uncommon woman seated so flawlessly astride the animal's back.

Would she ride a man as flawlessly?

The speculation shot directly from Duncan's mind to his manhood. Shifting against the tough leather saddle to relieve the exquisite ache between his legs, he smiled at the erotic images forming beneath his sweat-beaded brow.

Enthralled by the vision of Jessica, crying out soft heated words of encouragement while riding his thrusting body with wild abandon, Duncan was unaware of the terrain, with its summer-dried grasses and sparse stands of trees, their small leaves shivering in the hot breeze. Most especially, he was unaware that she had brought her horse to a stop. He very nearly crashed Don Quixote into Bathsheba.

"Segundo!"

Jessica's sharp, cautioning tone pierced Duncan's bemusement. Gathering his senses, and the reins, he brought his horse to a jarring halt mere inches away from the mare. With a murmured "Pardon," he backed his horse away from hers.

"You were dozing in the saddle," she accused in a scathing tone of voice that contrasted jarringly with her soft murmur in his erotic imaginings.

"I beg to differ," Duncan retorted. "I was not dozing, I was . . . er, distracted."

"You? Beg?" Jessica's arched brows disappeared in the shade cast by her tugged-down hat brim. Her inviting soft lips curved into a wry smile. "I long to see and hear it."

Duncan suddenly found himself in an uncomfortable dilemma. In an uncanny repeat of the feelings he'd experienced less than twenty-four hours ago, a rage of conflicting desires stormed through him. He was once again torn between the necessity to administer a blistering set-down to her and the urgent need to pull her from her saddle, onto his taut thighs, and administer a blistering kiss to her brazen mouth.

By nature, Duncan was a patient man—some might even call him stoic—and yet, this mere slip of a woman possessed the singular ability to rile his deepest emotions and undermine his strength of purpose, and all with the most insipid of barbs.

It was not yet midday and he was already sweating like a draft horse, and not only because of the unrelenting rays from the summer sun. Duncan ached in the very center of his life force, ached with the physical demand to seek relief by burying himself deep within the depths of Jessica's body. While, at the same time, his intellect commanded vindication in the form of putting her in her feminine place.

But, in truth, wouldn't the same result be derived from either act? A smile played at the edges of his lips as the deduction occurred to him.

"I amuse you?" Jessica's irritation was evident.

"Among other things." Duncan's smile grew into a taunting, sensual grin.

"What . . . other things?" Jessica's eyes narrowed. She looked dangerous, and infinitely appealing.

Duncan laughed and raked her rigid figure with a blatant gaze. "Are you sure you want to know?" His dark eyes alight with amusement, he watched her gloved right hand move to the horsewhip looped around the saddle horn, fingers closing on the leather coils.

"You try anything, Segundo," she said in a chilled whisper, "and I'll rip your hide from your back in tiny strips."

Tension shimmered in the hot air surrounding them and leapt with fresh excitement along Duncan's nervous system. He released a measure of that tension with a roar of laughter. "Perhaps you will score the hide from my back in the future, *señorita*," he mocked her. "And with deep passion. But with your fingernails, *querida*, not that leather snake."

"Don't you dare call me darling!" Jessica exclaimed, her silvery eyes taking on a sheen of molten glitter. "And don't you dare insinuate that I . . . I'd . . ." She paused to draw a quick harsh breath. "I wouldn't allow you to touch me . . . ever," she raged. Anger lent a becoming flush to her pale cheeks and visibly quivered the length of her slender form. Feeling her rider's tension, the mare nervously danced closer to Don Quixote. The distance narrowing between them, Jessica glared at him and vowed, "I would die first."

Incensed and bristling, Jessica was like a glorious flame. Duncan couldn't ignore the challenge she presented. He didn't try to ignore it. He didn't pause to reflect. Without thinking, he reached out to grip her waist, dragging her from Bathsheba's back and into his lap. Spooked, the horse whinnied and danced away to a safe distance.

"You . . . you . . ." Jessica sputtered. "What do you think you're doing? Put me down at—" she began, only to have her voice desert her when he gave her an impatient shake.

"Oh, shut up, Jessie," he said in an exasperated command. Raising his right hand, he grasped her by the nape. "Shut up and be still."

"I will not be still!" she railed, struggling against his gentle but firm hold. "And don't call me Jessie!"

Duncan was growing tired of listening to her rant. He was also becoming more aroused by the second from the sensations created by her bottom wriggling against his manhood. Obeying an atavistic instinct, he silenced her in the ancient way by covering her open mouth with his own.

The feel of her lush warm mouth beneath the crushing force of his lips splintered the sensations attacking his loins and sent shards of stimulation rocketing through his body.

Jessica fought him with the strength of outrage and anger. Her gloved fists grazed his face, knocking his hat flying to the ground. Her fingers clutched his hair in an attempt to yank his head back, away from hers.

Duncan reacted to her violence by deepening the kiss and plunging his tongue into the heated sweetness of her mouth. She bit him. In retaliation, he stiffened his tongue and thrust to the portal of her throat.

Jessica made a muffled sound of surprise; her body stiffened with shock, and then she went limp in his arms, as if overcome by his sensual onslaught.

Satisfaction rippling through him, Duncan withdrew his rigid tongue, softening it to lave the tender flesh on the inside of her quivering lower lip. Her distinct flavor caused a hungry clamoring in his senses. To Duncan, Jessica tasted of wild strawberries and potent wine, hot, languorous afternoons, gliding into sultry, frenzied nights. She lay passive in his embrace, and then, for a thrilling instant, he felt a hint of response from her mouth. The sensation tested the bounds of Duncan's control. His passion mounting, his senses flaming, he drank from her mouth like a man dying of thirst.

From deep in Jessica's throat came a shuddering breath carrying a broken whimper. The soft, pitiful sound tore with savage force through the smoky haze of desire veiling Duncan's conscience. Startled and shocked by the very idea that he may have hurt her, regardless of how inadvertently, he released her mouth and loosened his hold on her.

The result of his concern for her was instantaneous, and could have been likened to setting free a snarling, spitting she-devil. Jerking back, away from him, Jessica balled her gloved hand into a fist and drove it into his vulnerable unguarded solar plexus.

"You belly-crawling son of a bitch!" she hissed, flinging herself forward. She hit the ground running, cursing him with a fluency that would have awed the most seasoned cowboy. "Goddamn you! I warned you not to touch me," she yelled, reaching for the whip looped around the saddle horn on her ground-tethered horse. Her fingers groped for the black coils.

"Don't try it, Jessie." Duncan issued the command with harshly drawn breath. With fluid grace, he slid from the saddle. His smarting midsection protested the effort. He acknowledged the discomfort with a sense of surprised admiration; Jessica was a hell of a lot stronger than she appeared to be.

Jessica didn't heed his warning. Grasping the whip handle, she turned to face him, setting free the length of leather with a flick of her wrist. The slender strand writhed along the ground like a long black snake.

The muscles clenched over the tender spot in the pit of Duncan's stomach. Still, with a casual-looking ease, he bent to retrieve his hat before strolling toward her. "I wouldn't if I were you, *querida*," he said softly, gently, deadly. "I will not be flayed," he warned. "Not even by you."

Ignoring his admonition, Jessica flung back her head to glare at him with cool arrogance from cold silver eyes. She had lost her hat when she'd leapt to the ground. Her hair shimmered like rainwater bathed in sunlight. "And, if I were you, I wouldn't take one more step," she advised with icy hauteur.

Her proud stance caused a different kind of clenching inside Duncan. She was magnificent in her defiance. Magnificent and irresistible. He took another step. The whip undulated and gave a sharp crack. The black tip rent the air less than an inch away from his right shoulder.

"Stay back, damn you!" Jessica's wrist flexed. The whip leapt forth like a striking serpent.

Duncan's right arm shot out with blinding speed, a breath faster than the slim weapon. His gloved hand grasped the smooth leather, twining it to draw it into a taut black line between them. Jessica gasped in surprise. Her eyes flew wide with disbelief, but she held onto the whip handle, refusing to admit defeat by letting go.

Duncan couldn't contain the smile teasing his compressed lips. She was going to fight him. He was going to enjoy every second of the battle. Tensing his arm, he jerked it back. The black leather line connecting them quivered, then went slack as Jessica, with a startled yelp, was yanked off her feet and onto her knees on the hard ground.

His eyes gleaming like the stones they resembled, his jaw set with purposeful intent, Duncan approached her in slow, measured steps. As he drew to within a few feet of her, Jessica's eyes flickered, revealing her uncertainty.

"Wha . . . what are you . . . ?" Her voice failed as he closed the gap separating them.

Bending over her, Duncan extended his hand to assist her to her feet. Obviously misinterpreting his intent, Jessica jolted back, landing ignominiously on her rump in the dirt, legs apart, palms pressing the ground, her stiffened arms supporting her rigid torso.

"Oh, Jessie." Sighing, Duncan moved again to help her up. He gently clasped her arm. She shook his hand away with a violent shudder.

"Damn you to the blackest hell!" Her voice quivered with rage. Her eyes flickered with betraying uncertainty. "I warned you not to touch me!"

The intensity of her rebuff ignited a blaze of angry passion inside Duncan. It was too much. Since she would persist in challenging him, he fumed, she had no one to blame but herself when he accepted.

Throwing caution and common sense to the wind, Duncan dropped to his knees onto the earth between her thighs.

"What are you doing?" Jessica moved to scramble back, away from him. "Don't you dare!"

Her movement and warning came too late. Duncan had reached the point of daring anything. Grasping her arms with both hands, he took her to the ground beneath him. Her breath was expelled from her body with a moist *whoosh*. The moistness mingled with the woman scent of her, singeing his lips, invading his mouth, driving him wild with wanting.

"Damnation." Duncan muttered the protest against his loss of control as he lowered his head. The stiff, wide brim of his hat shaded her face. For a moment, he gazed deep into her eyes, still glittering silver defiance. And, for a moment, he teetered on the brink of relenting.

"Segundo . . . bastard!"

Jessica's curse pulled him back from the brink and sealed her own fate. His hard body crushing hers, Duncan caught her parted lips in a fierce, punishing kiss. Her reaction was like a small explosion beneath him.

Pushing against his torso with her hands, Jessica writhed and bucked her slender body in an attempt to dislodge him. Her frantic movements succeeded only in inflaming his already aroused body. Ignoring the blows her fisted hands rained on his chest and shoulders, he arched his hips, stiffened his tongue, then thrust his body against hers and his tongue into her mouth. His hips moving with unmistakable sensuous intent, Duncan demonstrated in parody for her the more intimate act of possession.

He felt more than heard the muffled gasp that swelled in her throat at the instant Jessica went stone-still beneath him. Her very stillness cooled the rage of passion storming through his mind. But, though he withdrew his rapacious tongue, he did not release her mouth. With slow, infinite care, Duncan made sweet love to Jessica's mouth. Her breathing quickened and, as she had before, for one beautiful instant her lips responded to the allure of his adoring mouth. When the instant ended, he raised his head to stare into her confusion-clouded eyes.

"I will have you, Jessie," he whispered, watching emotions flicker in her eyes. "Someday soon, I will have all of you, *querida*, naked and clinging to me."

"I'll die first," she snapped.

"No, love," he murmured, smiling with wicked seduction. "You will die during, over and over again."

Her eyes grew dark as gunmetal, reflecting wariness
—and perhaps just a tinge of anticipation. Then they
flashed with silver fury. "Get off of me, you insuffer-
able peon!" she ordered in tones of variegated ice.

Duncan was quite content resting the hardest part of
his body against the softest part of hers. He wanted
Jessica, in a God-awful way . . . but not like this, in
the harsh sunlight, on the hard ground, all sweaty and
covered with dirt. Duncan was neither ashamed nor
averse to making love in broad daylight, on the ground
in the open, his body sheened with honest sweat. And,
on the spot, he decided that, someday, he would share
a sensuous outdoor experience with Jessica, with the
sun and all of nature as witness to their pleasure.

But not for their first time together. From her reactions and from the secrets he read in her eyes, Duncan
was fairly certain Jessica was innocent to the ways of
men and women. And he determined that her initiation
would take place under cover of embarrassment-con-
cealing darkness.

Swallowing a sigh, Duncan clamped a restraining order on his passion. He could wait . . . at least for a
while.

"Are you suddenly deaf?" Jessica's gritty voice put a
swift end to his introspection. "I told you to haul your
damn carcass off me."

"Tsk, tsk." Duncan clicked his tongue and shook his
head. "Such shocking, unladylike language, Jessie. I
really am quite appalled."

"You're also heavy!" she shouted, shoving against
him with her flattened palms. "Now, move!" She
glared at him. "And don't call me Jessie."

Her demand left him with two options, obey her or

kiss her. Since he wanted very badly to kiss her, Duncan decided he had better obey her. But, on the other hand . . . laughing, he dipped his head and brushed her mouth with his, then levered himself up and off her before she could sputter a protest.

"Your wish is my command . . . Miss Jessica." Standing over her, Duncan smiled into her glittering silver eyes. "May I assist you to rise?" he asked politely, extending his hand.

Ignoring his hand, Jessica scrambled to her feet. Scowling, she brushed at the dust clinging to her shirt and pants. "You may go to—"

"Now, now," Duncan interjected, bending to scoop up her hat. "Well-bred ladies never swear at their lovers."

Jessica's pale cheeks flamed scarlet and she looked to be nearing the point of choking. "Lover!" she screeched, grabbing the hat from him and jamming it on her head. "You . . . you're . . . you are . . . oh! Dammit!" Spinning, she ran to her horse and hoisted her shaking body into the saddle. With a tap of her heels and a yank on the reins, she wheeled the mare around, heading south at a brisk canter.

Laughing aloud at her, Duncan called, "But, Miss Jessica, ma'am, what about my tour of the place?"

"You're the know-it-all *segundo*," she flung over her shoulder. "Find your way around by yourself."

Still laughing, and feeling amazingly good considering he hadn't had any sleep in over twenty-four hours, Duncan strolled to his horse. "Come on, Don Quixote, time for us to amble." Talking softly to the skittish animal, he gathered the reins and stepped into the saddle. "I suppose we've tilted at enough windmills for one day."

He was laughing at her. Even though the *segundo* was some distance behind her, Jessica knew he was laughing at her. She could hear him, with her senses. The deep, beguiling sound tormented her inner ear. The back of her neck tingled. Her nerves jangled. And her mind felt ready to erupt into flames.

Damn him! she cried in silent protest. He'd had no right to look at her the way he had, to touch her, let alone . . . Jessica's thoughts scattered and a thrill skipped the length of her spine and down the back of her thighs.

What was wrong with her? Why was she feeling like this—all quivery and excited inside? She didn't merely dislike the man, she detested him. And yet . . .

Jessica shivered. The wild, intoxicating taste of him was still on her mouth. The potent, arousing feel of him was imprinted on her body.

The south pasture. She thought of the section of land in an uncomfortably desperate way. She needed company, a lot of company, and, from the talk around the supper table last evening, she knew that Parker and a few of the men would be in the south pasture. Her father had asked Parker to take care of the chore of superimposing their B-Bar-R over the Circle-F brand on the cattle that man, that Segundo, had delivered yesterday.

Jessica stole a glance over her shoulder. He was there, keeping well behind her, but there. Beginning to feel stalked, she again nudged the mare to increase her speed, making a flat-out dash for the pasture and her brother.

She arrived just in time for the midday meal break. The men were in a loose group around a small campfire, some sitting cross-legged on the ground, others hunkered down to rest on their haunches, eating the sandwich lunches her mother had prepared for them and swallowing down the dry food with coffee brewed over the open flames.

"Hey, Sis!" Parker hailed her, waving an arm and grinning like a devilish schoolboy. "Where ya been all morning? We coulda used some help here."

"Playing wet nurse." Jessica tossed a disgusted look at the man trailing her into the encampment. "Dad assigned me the privilege of showing him around the spread." After leaping from her horse, she walked to the campfire and the coffeepot.

"So what are you looking so sour about?" Parker frowned. "It beats wrestlin' cows."

Since she had no intention of telling her brother that she had just engaged in wrestling with the *segundo*, Jessica shrugged and kept moving.

The men called bantering remarks to her as she joined their loose circle. Masking her churning emotions, Jessica responded in kind. The B-Bar-R hands were no different from cowboys anywhere. They considered ranching men's work. Well aware of the resistance she was facing, Jessica had pushed herself to the point of exhaustion to gain their respect. Though skeptical when she had joined their ranks on her return home from school, the hands had accepted her presence when she had proved her worth within the first week of working with them. Now she was one of them, although they never forgot that she was the daughter of the house.

"Whadda ya say, Jessica? You gonna do some real work or lolly-gag all day?"

Jessica laughed along with the rest of the men at the gibe from the veteran of the group. At fifty-two, Harley Clouser was the undisputed expert. He had been pushing cows for nearly forty years. If Harley said something was so, it was so.

"I thought I'd goldbrick as long as I could get away with it, Harley." She gave him a genuine smile. "Wouldn't you, if you were me?"

"Sure." Harley showed crooked teeth in a grin. "My daddy din't raise up no fools."

"Neither did mine." Jessica hesitated, then, casting a glance at her brother, added in a teasing tone, "Well . . . the jury's still out on Parker."

Because they took their amusement wherever they could find it, and because they were certain of the mutual affection shared by the siblings, the men responded to her gentle sally with loud guffaws and catcalls.

"Hey, Parker, ya hear that? Jessica sez you're not too bright. What do ya say to that?"

Parker, always willing to ease the day's work with a bit of fun, contorted his lips into an idiot's grin. "Why would she say something like that, anyway? Everybody knows that I'm the smart one in the family."

Jessica rolled her eyes and the men hooted.

"May I share the joke?"

The *segundo*'s soft, drawling voice brought the merriment to an abrupt halt. Without bothering to answer, the men moved as one to return to the task of branding the cattle.

Jessica sipped the strong coffee and eyed the *segundo* over the rim of the tin cup. By their action, the men had made it plain that, as far as they were concerned, the jury was still out on the *segundo*. In exactly the same way she had, the *segundo* would have to earn their acceptance. A feeling of vindication soothed her rattled emotions.

"The coffee's hot."

"Gracias." Segundo ambled to the pot. "I take it I am on trial with the men . . . *sí*?"

"Of course."

"Of course." His voice was bone dry.

"Nothing to take offense about, Segundo." Looking anxious, Parker tried to smooth any feathers that might have been ruffled. "Every new hand must earn approval."

"No offense taken." Segundo took a swallow of the coffee and grimaced. "God, that's awful. I expected no less."

"Than awful coffee?"

A gleam sparked in his eyes at her innocent-sounding barb. "That also, Miss Jessica," he said, gliding that sparkling gaze from her face to her dust-spattered boots. "But, no, I expected no less than having to earn acceptance from the men."

"And can you?" Jessica deflected his probing glance with a doubtful look.

A wry smile kicked up the corners of his mouth. "We shall see, *señorita*. Shan't we?"

His phrasing jarred Jessica's expanding sense of complacency. Never before in her life had she heard a working cowboy use the words shall and shan't. The more commonly heard terms were hafta and won't. What manner of man was he, this Segundo? Suspicion curled through her mind. Who was he? Where was he from? And, more to the point, what was he up to? What did he want?

"Lunch."

Jessica jerked in reaction to the sensation of having her thoughts violated. "What?"

"I was wondering aloud about the prospects of food." Segundo shrugged. "I'm hungry. It has been an active morning." His teeth flashed white in a taunting smile.

Reminded of the activity, Jessica glared at him.

"Sorry, Segundo. You're too late. The food Mother sent along with us is gone." Parker shrugged. "You're going to have to go back to the house to eat."

"So be it." Segundo glanced at Jessica. "Since I gather the tour is over for today, we may as well return."

"You go ahead." Jessica turned away from his mocking eyes. "I'll stay and help finish up here."

"No, you may as well go along with him, Sis," Parker said, to her chagrin. "We're just about done."

Thwarted, Jessica tossed the dregs of her coffee onto the ground and strode to her horse. She didn't want to ride back to the house with Segundo. She didn't want to ride anywhere with him. She didn't want to be in the same county with him. But, even more, she didn't want to appear childish to the men. Gritting her teeth, Jessica mounted Bathsheba.

The ride to the ranch house was made in chilled quiet that was broken only by the breeze soughing through the branches of the occasional trees they rode past.

Certain the *segundo* was still laughing in silence at her, Jessica refused to look at him. She greeted the sight of her home with a sigh of relief and look of pleased surprise. A horse was tied to the veranda rail.

Though the animal was familiar to Jessica, it was not from the Randall remuda. The horse belonged to a neighbor and friend. She frowned.

What was Eric Robertson doing at the B-Bar-R in the middle of a weekday?

8

❦

"Company?"

"Seems like." Good manners demanded Jessica's attention. She hedged by sliding a sidelong glance at him.

Segundo smiled.

Jessica shivered.

Drat the man! The short hairs at her temples and nape were damp from perspiration. Her shirt was plastered to her spine. The hot, dry air was an assault to her throat. He smiles at her, she shivers.

Wonderful.

Jessica smothered a groan, and wondered if she had reason to doubt her sanity.

"Recognize the animal?"

There was no help for it; she would have to attend. "Yes." Jessica turned in the saddle to look him full in the face. "That's Dancer, Eric Robertson's horse. Eric is the ranch manager of the Circle-F." She flicked her hand. "The property bordering ours to the west."

"Hmm."

Hmm? Jessica felt a flare of irritation. What did *Hmm* mean? Did it mean anything? God! She hated enigmatic men. She tossed him a sour look as she brought Bath to a halt at the stable. In her normal way, she kicked her feet free of the stirrups, swung a leg over the animal's head, and leapt to the ground. "Is that 'Hmm' a comment?"

Segundo laughed.

Jessica experienced an uncanny, melting sensation. It began in her legs and worked its way to her head, turning her brain to the consistency of mush.

She hated the feeling even more than she hated enigmatic men. Impatient with him, but more so with herself, she spun on her heels and strode for the house. Every step jolted the seething mass in her head, reactivating scenes and impressions of their tussle in the dust.

Even though Jessica would have thought it impossible, her throat went drier still, while her body became wetter. She needed a drink. She needed a bath. She really needed to be alone, away from Segundo's disruptive influence.

Jessica was forced to settle for the drink.

Emily had just made a pitcher of lemonade for Ben

and Eric. She reached for two glasses as Jessica, followed by the *segundo*, entered the kitchen.

Ben and Eric were seated at the table. Ben frowned
at Jessica's entrance.

"What are you doing back so soon?" He shot a scowling look from his daughter to her dark-visaged shadow.

"Your *segundo* is hungry." Jessica smirked and canted
her head backward to the man behind her.

"We'll soon take care of that." Beaming at the
segundo in a manner that added to Jessica's irritation,
Emily bustled about the large kitchen, setting the lem-
onade-filled glasses on the table before walking to the
icebox to remove ice chips for the drinks and two thick
beefsteaks.

Eric, seated opposite Ben, pushed back his chair and
stood. A wide grin tilted his lips. "Wipe that sour look
off your face and come over here and give me a hug and
hello." Stepping away from the table, he held out his
arms.

Despite her annoyance, Jessica laughed and walked
into his enfolding embrace. "Hello, Eric." She gave
him the hug he'd demanded, then leaned back to smile
up at him. "How are you?" Before he could reply, she
went on, "And what in hell are you doing here, at this
time of the day?"

"I could say I came acourtin'," Eric drawled, sliding
a sparkling glance at the somber-faced man observing
their display of mutual affection.

"You could even tell the truth," Jessica retorted, removing her arms from around his neck.

Eric pulled an injured expression. "I'm bleeding,
Ben," he appealed to the older man. "Your daughter

has cut me to the quick with her sharp tongue. She doesn't believe me."

"She doesn't believe any man." Ben snorted.

"Perhaps because she considers herself one of them."

Her silver eyes flashing a warning, Jessica wheeled around to face her tormentor. "You had better explain what you mean by that remark, Mr. Se-gun-do."

"Calm down, Jessica," Eric murmured, obviously fighting to suppress a bout of laughter.

"Just look at yourself." Segundo ran a slow, narrow-eyed, insulting glance the length of her rigid body. "You dress like a man. You act like a man. You swear like a man." A disdainful smile kicked up the corners of his mouth. "What is a real man supposed to think?"

An uneasy silence blanketed the room.

Eric's booted feet scraped the floor in an uncertain shift, but a grin tugged at his compressed lips.

Ben cleared his throat.

Emily concentrated on the steaks she had just put into a large black cast-iron frying pan.

Jessica was incensed, as much by the fact that neither her father nor Eric had rushed to her defense as by the *segundo*'s scathing answer. She turned to ice in the baking-hot room. "Presupposing, of course, that a man, real or otherwise, is capable of thought," she retaliated, indicting her father and friend with a slicing, cold-eyed glance.

"Now, Jessica," Emily said in a soothing voice. "Please, don't get your father riled up with your blue-stocking, women's suffrage attitude."

"It's not an attitude, Mother." Jessica whipped around to confront this new attack. "And it's not blue-stocking. There are women from all walks of life, from all over this country, working for the suffrage movement."

Ben grimaced. "Damn foolishness."

Jessica swung back to her father. "It isn't foolishness, and you know it." The light of challenge glittered in her eyes. "Do you consider Mother beneath you?"

"Of course not!"

"There you go." Her smile was smug, superior, and lasted all of a few seconds.

"But I feel certain your mother would be the first to admit that, though equal to your father, she is still a woman, different from a man, but content with her natural role." Segundo met her glittering gaze with a stone-eyed stare.

"Hogwash." Jessica glared at Segundo. "Natural role, indeed. By whose decree, God's or man's?" He opened his mouth to respond. She didn't give him the time. "Never mind. I'll tell you. Since God made women every bit as intelligent as men, I suggest that this traditional-role business came into effect more by human than by divine design."

"Oh, Jessica, no!" Emily looked shocked. "The Good Book says that the Lord created woman as a helpmate for man."

"But does it define in what capacity?" Jessica arched her eyebrows. "Does it really read, chapter and verse, that women are by nature fit only to handle the dull, boring chores, while men get to do all the interesting and exciting things?"

Emily blinked. "But, dear, I don't consider my chores dull and boring. I enjoy doing for my family."

Jessica heaved a tired-sounding sigh. "I know,

Mother. And that's fine, as long as you derive enjoyment from it." She swept the faces around her with a shrewd look. "But what about the women like me, the countless number of women who don't enjoy those household pursuits? What about the women who want more from life than caring for a man?"

"Let 'em have a bunch of babies," Ben growled. "That'll keep 'em busy and out of trouble."

Jessica threw her hands into the air. "That's always a man's answer! Keep them pregnant."

"Jessica!"

"Mother!" Jessica mimicked. "Really, shocking as it may be, I am conversant with the word pregnant."

"Perhaps," Segundo drawled, "you'd be better employed if you were conversant with the condition."

An image sprang into Jessica's mind, bringing with it feelings and sensations. Her pulses raced with the memory feel of him, arching his body into hers. Heat flooded her cheeks and her breath became lodged in her throat. She wanted to scream at him. Her hands itched to lash out at him. Her fingers clenched around the . . . damn! She had forgotten her whip, left it looped around the saddle horn.

The realization shook Jessica; she never forgot her whip! She opened her mouth—no suitably damning words materialized on her tongue. It didn't matter, she wouldn't have been heard above the sound of her father's and Eric's raucous laughter.

"You tell 'er, boy!" Ben gasped through his laughter.

"Yeah, that's a real good one, Segundo!" Holding his sides, Eric dropped into his chair, as if too weakened by merriment to remain upright.

In disgust, Jessica gazed into the suspiciously innocent expression on her mother's face. "It doesn't take a great deal of wit to amuse men . . . does it?"

"Aw, Jessica, don't take it to heart." Reaching out, Eric caught her hand and drew her onto the chair next to his. "The *segundo* was only funnin' you."

Jessica's suspicions grew, but not in regard to the expression on her mother's face. There was a familiarity in Eric's voice that bothered her. "You know the *segundo?*" She jerked her head at the man.

"Well, sure." Eric appeared surprised at her question. Then he went on, too quickly. "I mean, I met him yesterday morning, when we separated the herd. And then again early this morning, when he helped us out with the rustlers."

She was instantly alert. "Rustlers?"

"Uh . . . yeah." Looking uncomfortable, Eric shot a look for help between Ben and the *segundo*. "Didn't you know?"

Jessica's sharpened gaze trailed his. "No, I didn't know, but I intend to find out." Her pointed look landed on Ben. "What's it about, Dad?"

"Just like Eric said." Ben moved his shoulders in a shrug. "The Circle-F was hit last night." His face was grim. "Muldoon was wounded."

Jessica jolted. "There was an exchange of gunfire!" Her wide-eyed gaze swung to Eric.

"Yeah." Eric grimaced. "First time."

Jessica's head swung once more, homing in on the *segundo*. "And you were there?"

"Yes."

"Why were you there?"

Segundo stretched out his legs and made himself comfortable. "I couldn't sleep, so I took a ride."

Jessica was becoming more suspicious by the second. "And you just happened to ride out in the direction of the rustlers?" Her tone was heavily laced with skepticism.

"*Sí.*"

"Uh-huh." She gave him an arch look.

"Lucky for us that he did too," Eric said . . . again too quickly. "They had us pinned beneath that stand of trees near the property line. Segundo's sudden arrival flushed them out and sent them running."

"How fortuitous." Jessica's voice was dust dry.

Ben frowned at her. "There could have been some serious injuries here, Jessica," he scolded. "Instead of being sarcastic, you oughta be grateful the *segundo* was there."

Jessica was less than impressed, and let her feelings show. "In other words, never look a gift horse in the mouth?"

"Unless it's wearing a Trojan brand on its rump," Segundo inserted in a soft drawl.

Jessica started. There it was again, a revelation of his knowledge. First literature, now history. A *segundo*? A common working cowboy? Unusual? She dismissed the thought out of hand, substituting unbelievable as closer to the target.

"You *are* well read," she observed, watching for the smallest change in his expression. Her diligence proved unnecessary, for he flashed a blatant grin at her.

"Like you, *señorita*, I have been to school."

Her eyes narrowed. "Mexico City?"

Ben saved his *segundo* from her inquisition. "What difference does it make, girl? Where he went to school hasn't a damn thing to do with these damned rustlers."

Frustrated but forced to agree, Jessica relented . . . silently promising herself another time. "You're right, of course." Unlocking her drilling stare from her quarry, she turned to Eric. "How many were there?"

"Four."

"I don't suppose you got a good look at any of them?"

"Nah." Eric shook his head. "It was too dark, and when Segundo scattered 'em, they came out from under the trees like a shot, bent low in the saddle."

It was the same old story; not one positive identification had been made since the rustlings began. Jessica sighed. "So we still have nothing to go on."

"Not quite."

Jessica whipped around to stare at Segundo, but before she had the chance to demand an explanation, she was compelled to shift her gaze back to Eric.

"Segundo winged one of them."

Elated by the information, she shoved her chair back and jumped to her feet, nearly knocking her mother off of hers as, at that moment, Emily approached the table carrying two plates, filled to overflowing with the steaks and mounds of home-fried potatoes.

"Jessica!"

Even as Emily yelped the warning, Segundo was up and moving, swift and silent as smoke, steadying the older woman while rescuing his belated luncheon meal.

"Good God, girl!" Ben shouted. "Where in hell do you think you're going?"

Jessica felt embarrassed, awkward, and gauche . . . and not for the first time in front of the *segundo*. She was getting pretty tired of the humiliating feelings. "I'm sorry. I got a little excited." She came close to choking on the apology. "But this is the first lead we've had, and I guess I was going to dash into Sandy Wash and investigate."

"I've been."

Her gaze skipped to Eric. "You have? When?"

"This morning."

"Well?" Impatience nudged her voice up a notch. "What did you find out?"

Ben glared across the table at her. "Maybe if you'd sit down and shut up, he could tell you."

"And me," Segundo murmured.

Chastened, Jessica sank onto her chair without further demur, although she did fix a prompting stare on Eric.

"Pickin's were slim," Eric said with disgust. "They're shy one hard case at the Sawdust, and"—he smirked—"fortuitously, Metcalf has been out of town for two days. The story is that he had business in South Pass."

"Fortuitous, indeed," Segundo observed.

"Bull." Jessica's observation wasn't quite so genteel, but more to the point.

Eric nodded agreement. "Yeah."

"But there is a hired gun among the missing?" Segundo raised his eyebrows in time with the fork-speared piece of steak he raised to his mouth. He chewed, swallowed, and angled a pleased smile at Emily. "Excellent, *señora.*"

"*Gracias.*" Emily chuckled. "*Señor.*"

Suspicion flared anew inside Jessica. Eating her food without tasting it, she skimmed the faces around her with a speculative glance. A niggling sensation was telling her that something was going on and that she was being excluded from some secret understanding between her father, her mother, Eric, and the stranger—Segundo.

Eric and the *segundo*. Jessica slid a glance from one man to the other. The niggling feeling intensified inside her. What was it about the two men?

The thought intrigued her. The men continued to talk, but their voices faded and grew faint. Absently making inroads into the food on her plate, while unaware of a bite she consumed, Jessica lowered her eyelids and unobtrusively studied the men seated on either side of her.

They were both extremely attractive men—both tall, slim but muscular, sharp-featured. The strong similarities struck Jessica as rather odd. Of course, their heritages could explain the likenesses. They both had the blood of darker-skinned races flowing in their veins—in Eric's case, Shoshone Indian, and in Segundo's, Latino. Still . . .

". . . South Pass."

The sound of the place name snagged Jessica's attention. Her confused musings fractured, to reform in a concrete demand. "What did you say about South Pass?"

Eric looked at her empty plate, then gave her an indulgent smile. "We were talking about one of us visiting South Pass to nosy around a mite, see if we can learn something about Metcalf's urgent business."

Excitement bubbled up in her. "I'll go."

"I think not." Segundo's cool voice burst the bubbles . . . and fired her temper.

"Think again."

"Jessica!" Ben's voice was rough, his scowl fierce.

"Climb down off your high horse. The *segundo*'s right. You can't go to South Pass."

Can't? Jessica despised the word can't. Why couldn't she go to South Pass? Because she was a woman?

Why else?

Her conclusion brought with it a bristling sense of injustice. Anger overrode the small amount of prudence she possessed. Shaking with indignation, Jessica lashed out at the men with unthinking vehemence.

"Why can't I?" she demanded of her father, but for the benefit of the other two men as well. "I can take care of myself, and you know it." Her glittering gaze shot to Eric. "And so do you. I can ride as well, shoot as well, and, if necessary, fight as well as any man on this ranch, and you both know that too." She paused to draw a shuddering breath. "So, you tell me, why the hell can't I go to South Pass?"

Taken aback by the depth of angry passion in her attack, Ben and Eric sat staring at her in mute surprise. The *segundo* did not suffer a like reaction.

"You would learn nothing."

The very calm, very softness of the *segundo*'s voice tore through Jessica with the freezing force of a mid-January blizzard. The chill was reflected in her eyes. "Why wouldn't I?" Her voice was icy, and arrogant.

"Who would you question . . . a barkeep? The blacksmith?" Segundo's smile was faint, derisive.

Jessica went him one better. Her smile was superior. "A woman?"

He frowned. "What woman?"

She contrived to look innocent. "A whore?"

"Jessica!" Emily was scandalized.

"Touché." The *segundo* was amused. "You obviously know your Mr. Metcalf."

"He's not my Mr. Metcalf!"

"But, even assuming Metcalf indulged"—Segundo continued as if she hadn't exclaimed the denial—"would a . . . eh"—he shot a glance at Emily—"one of those women be willing to discuss a customer with you?"

His point was valid and deflating. On reflection, Jessica was forced to admit that it would very likely be bad for business if a whore had a loose tongue. Conceding defeat, she slumped back in her chair. She felt ridiculous, and that made her feel mean. Losing face was bad enough, but losing to the *segundo* was intolerable.

Fortunately, for him, Segundo was gracious enough, or wise enough, not to bask in the warmth of his minor victory. Instead, he posed a question none of the others had as yet considered. "What sort of business meeting would Metcalf have had to take care of in South Pass?"

"Beats the hell outta me," Eric said, quickly adding to Emily, "beggin' your pardon, ma'am." He shrugged. "I figure the story about a business meeting was just an excuse for being out of town for the rustling."

"Hell, there ain't much business in South Pass anymore." Ben didn't add a quick apology to his wife. "The place is practically a ghost town."

"I see." Segundo was quiet a moment, contemplative, then he continued, "Nevertheless, I think I'll take a ride tomorrow." He flashed a grin at Ben. "I've never seen a ghost town, not even one that's just practically one."

Ben shrugged. "Suit yourself."

Suit yourself? Jessica couldn't believe what she'd

heard. Pondering her father's curious response, she looked from one man to the other. Who was in control here? She knew without doubt that had their foreman Frank ever as much as suggested taking ranch matters into his own hands, her father would have reined him in with a roar. Yet he had agreed to Segundo's decision with a casual "Suit yourself."

Again Jessica felt a distinct sensation of missing something. What was going on? That niggling feeling crept through her once more, but she couldn't put her finger on the reason for the feeling.

There was something . . . some element she was missing, but . . .

". . . and you can have them delivered from there." The tail end of Emily's comment snagged Jessica's attention.

"Have what delivered from where?"

Her face flushed from the heat of the cook stove, Emily planted her hands on her waist and gave Jessica an impatient look. "The party invitations, what else? While he's there, Segundo can have them put into the mail sack that goes to Cheyenne out of South Pass."

"Are they finished?"

"Not yet, but they will be." Emily's satisfied smile set off warning bells in Jessica's mind. "You and I are going to finish them if it takes us all night."

Smothering the protest that sprang into her throat, Jessica glared at her benign-faced adversary. He was enjoying her discomfort. She knew it, just as surely as she had known he was laughing at her when she had run, galloped away from him, after he had awakened her body to a sensuous awareness of him.

A tingle trickled down her back and pooled at the

base of her spine. Jessica shifted position on the hard wood chair. She was still unbearably aware of him.

To make matters worse, not only was she facing a long evening laboring over the dratted invitations, he was going to South Pass, and she wasn't.

And he was still laughing at her.

Jessica's teeth ground together.

God, she detested this, this . . . Segundo!

9

"Ain't much of a town, is it?"

"I've seen worse." Duncan slanted a dry smile at the big man resting in the saddle on the horse next to him. He hadn't wanted or asked for a guide to accompany him to South Pass, but Eric had sent Muldoon along just the same. They had brought their mounts to a stop outside the cluster of sorry-looking buildings that had once comprised the booming town. Sweltering beneath the unrelenting rays from the late-afternoon sun, South Pass looked deserted, and justly so.

"Seen better too. Mostly all that's left are the dregs, the folks that are fresh out of hope . . . and the

whores. I'm afraid this place is not long for this world."
Sean grinned. "You were right, this is no place for a
lady."

Duncan cocked a brow. "A lady?"

"Yeah." Sean laughed. "Eric told me that Jessica
wanted to come and play Pinkerton agent. He said she
got a little upset when you threw a hobbling line on her
idea."

"It appears Eric said a lot," Duncan said in a tight
voice, annoyed by the idea of Eric discussing Jessica
with the other man, and who knew who else? Controlling an urge to question Muldoon, he kneed his horse
into motion.

"Hey, Segundo! Hold up. What are you so riled
about all of a sudden?" Nudging his own horse into
motion, Muldoon frowned as he came up beside
Duncan. "What did I say anyway to set you off like
that?"

Duncan's expression was grim. "Does Eric talk
about Miss Jessica often and with anybody?" he coun-
tered.

"Hell, no!" Sean looked both amazed and confused.
"Why, that'd be like talking about his own sister."

"But he talks to you?" Duncan persisted.

"Now and again. We're friends and, well, I suppose
Eric thought the story was too good to keep to himself." Sean's expression sharpened with interest. "Why
should anything Eric says bother you?"

Duncan appeared a lot cooler than he was feeling.
"Miss Jessica is my employer's daughter. I won't stand
by while her name is bandied about."

"Bandied about? My, my, ain't we the high-class
one?" Though Sean smiled, he fixed a drilling stare on

Duncan. "Let me tell you something, *amigo*. Eric would be the first in line to put a stop to any bandying about of Jessica's good name. He's been watchin' out for that little lady for a long time now. Like I said, he loves her like a sister."

Just so that's the only way he loves her. Keeping the thought to himself, Duncan forced himself to relax. He was feeling edgy and frustrated because of the lady in question. He hadn't slept well and had writhed and sweated through wild, erotic dreams concerning Miss Jessica. The lady filled his mind, waking and sleeping. She was driving him crazy with desire.

Duncan was impatient with this tangle about the cattle rustlings. He wanted the mystery solved, finished, so he could concentrate on bringing the imperious Jessica to heel by dragging her beneath him, naked and vulnerable.

But it wasn't Muldoon's fault that Duncan found himself riding into a dead-end town he had no earthly wish to be in, Duncan chided himself. Relenting, he offered the big Irishman a faint smile.

"I suspect that Eric is not the only man on the Circle-F who looks after Miss Jessica like a little sister."

"Ya got that right." Sean visibly relaxed. "We all kinda look after her, from David-Chill Wind right down to the youngest cow hand, on both the Circle-F and the B-Bar-R." He paused to emit a soft chuckle. "Even though we all know just how well Jessica can take care of herself."

They had entered the town and were walking their horses along the rutted, desolate central street. While Duncan's keen gaze missed nothing of his surroundings, his attention remained on the subject at hand.

"So she claims," he replied wryly.

"And rightly so." Sean's chuckle expanded into a full laugh. "Hell, I've seen that girl in action, and I ain't hankerin' to be on the receiving end of it."

"Action?" Duncan was instantly alert, and deeply concerned. "What sort of action?" Following the other man's lead, he turned his horse into the hitching rail in front of a dilapidated building. A rough board sign with the faded word SALOON scrawled on it dangled from one rusty hook.

Sean stepped down from his horse, slow and stiff-legged, and squinted over the saddle at Duncan. "I've seen her use that whip she's never without." A broad grin lit his handsome face. "More'n one of the B-Bar-R hands have been heard to brag in the Sawdust that, with only the tiniest flick of her dainty wrist, Miss Jessica can knock the balls off a fly with the tip of that whip of hers." His blue eyes danced with laughter. "Come to that, the brag isn't much of an exaggeration, neither."

The mental picture Duncan received drew a burst of laughter from him. And he didn't doubt the implication behind the cowboys embellished boast—he had seen Jessica in action with that black, lethal-looking weapon.

Yes, he mused, trailing Sean to the entrance to the saloon, Jessica Randall was ripe for taming. A thrill of anticipation shot through Duncan, momentarily cooling the heat sheening his body with sweat.

Damn this rustling business. And damn this Josh Metcalf for whatever game he was playing. Duncan's lips flattened into a straight, grim line. He had to clear this mess up, posthaste. He didn't have time to waste on some two-bit swindler. He had a job of seduction work to do.

His purpose set, Duncan turned to Sean. "Do you think we will learn anything in here?"

The Irishman shrugged. "Don't know. Maybe." His white teeth gleamed in a wide grin. "But it was a long ride, after a long, dry spell, *amigo,* and right now, this minute, more than information, all I'm lookin' for is a cool beer"—his grin grew wolfish—"and a hot woman."

Being a normal, healthy man, Duncan understood Muldoon's physical plight. Extremely thirsty himself, he homed in on the first of Sean's objectives. "They have cool beer?" He indicated the bar with a head movement.

"Nah." Sean made a face. "More'n likely the beer is warm as piss, but it's wet." He grimaced. "Come to that, it's unlikely the woman'll be much warmer. But I'm so damn horny, I'll settle for wet."

Duncan couldn't help but laugh; he couldn't help but like the easygoing Irishman either. He pushed against the sagging swing doors. "Well, then, shall we?"

"Lead on, Macduff."

Duncan paused in midstride to stare at Sean, unconsciously echoing Jessica's remark to him the day before. "You are well read."

Sean sent a furtive glance around the saloon's dim interior. "My mother force-fed us kids the classics, but don't let it get around, will ya?" Noting the absence of patrons in the bar, he grinned. "I wouldn't want to tarnish my rough-and-ready cowboy image."

"I'm as silent as the sphinx," Duncan vowed, moving into the narrow room.

The bar was unprepossessing in the extreme. It was dim and dank and dirty. It was also empty. Duncan was immediately reminded of the hovels in Asia, North Africa, and the Orient in which he had enjoyed many libations, the contents of which he had never questioned.

"Two beers."

The sound of Sean's voice drew Duncan's attention from his memory-stirring inspection of the crude building. The man behind the bar was as unprepossessing as the establishment. He was dim and dank and dirty. His head looked to be as empty as the room. Nevertheless, Duncan tried a testing query.

"I'm looking for a friend of mine," he began then, recalling the role he was playing, tacked on, *"señor.* I wonder if, perhaps, you've seen him in here?"

From his closed expression, it was obvious that the bartender was anything but green. "Don't know," he muttered. "I see a lot of folks. Does your friend have a name?"

"Metcalf," Duncan said. "Josiah Metcalf."

The bartender took on a leery expression. "He wanted somewhere . . . for somethin'?"

"Nah," Sean responded, setting his black curls jumping with a shake of his head. "We just heard Josh was here in town to do some business and thought we'd say howdy." With a show of casualness that didn't fool Duncan—or very likely the bartender either—he raised his glass and gulped down over half the foam-topped amber contents. "Warm as piss," he muttered, slanting a pointed glance at Duncan as he wiped the foam from his lips with the back of his hand.

"Hell, where do ya think ya are?" The bartender sneered. "The Cheyenne Cattlemen's club?"

"Cheyenne has a cattlemen's club?" Duncan arched his brows in patent disbelief.

"Damned straight!" the bartender exclaimed.

"Right elegant joint," Sean drawled. "You oughta mosey on down there some time, have yourself a look-see."

Reminding himself of the reason he was in South Pass, Duncan pointedly steered the conversation back to his original intent. "I might do that . . . some day, after I've taken care of more pressing matters."

"Yeah . . . ah, talking about pressing matters," Sean piped in, wiggling his eyebrows and grinning lasciviously. "Now that I've wet my whistle, I need to dip my wick." He turned to the bartender. "I've been hearing of late 'bout a certain woman here, a pretty little redhead. You happen to know any gal who fits that description?"

"That'd be Meg," the bartender said in a bored tone.

"Yeah, Meg, that's the name." An excited gleam sprang into Sean's blue eyes. "Know where I can find her?"

"Mister, around here it ain't hard to find anyone," the bartender said in disgust. "Hardly anybody left."

"Yeah, I noticed." Muldoon's voice was rife with impatience. "But where do I find this Meg gal?"

"Down the street and turn left." The bartender jerked his thumb in the direction. "It's a small place, sits all by its lonesome. Ya can't miss it lessen ya try."

"I ain't plannin' on trying." Sean downed his beer and swung away from the bar. "Ya comin', Segundo?"

Duncan smiled and shook his head. "No, I'll pass
this time. You go ahead. I'll see if I can find our friend."

"You mean that Metcalf fella you was askin' after?"
Not waiting for a reply, the bartender continued, "He
was in here a day or two ago." He smirked. "I told him
how to get to Meg's place too. Haven't seen him
since."

Duncan and Sean exchanged looks, then moved as
one toward the swing doors, tossing thanks over their
shoulders.

"Gracias, amigo."

"Much obliged, Mister."

"Do you think he's still there?" Duncan murmured
as they stepped outside.

"Could be." Muldoon flashed a grin. "Especially if
this Meg's as good as I've heard. Only one way to find
out." Turning right, he shot Duncan a devilish look and
started down the dusty street. "Goddamn, this snoopin'
work is tough on a man."

The house was small, but in excellent repair.
Duncan's steps slowed as they approached it. "I'll
wander about for a while," he said, coming to a stop.
"Perhaps I can pick up some information from the few
remaining merchants."

"You're not coming in?" Sean was so surprised he
forgot his practiced speech pattern.

Duncan's smile was dry. "Not in anyone today."

Sean threw back his head and roared with laughter.
"That's very funny," he exclaimed between gasps for
breath. "You're all right, Segundo."

"Gracias, you're all right also." Duncan inclined his
head at the house. "You go on. Have a good time, but
remember there is purpose to your plunder."

Muldoon laughed right up to the discreetly painted door of the whorehouse.

Meg watched the two men walk toward the house from behind the ecru lace curtains at her bedroom window. Customers? Or just curious? A tired smile played at the edges of her soft lips. It didn't matter either way. Though every quick roll on the bed added coffers to her war chest, Meg was in a mood, an unusual depression of the spirit, and she simply did not care. Tomorrow, maybe, she'd care. Today? She sighed. What the hell?

She was about to turn away from the window when one of the men came to a halt, recapturing her attention. The men exchanged words—not, as far as she could tell, an argument, but just a conversation.

Well, are you coming in or not? Meg thought, moving closer to the window for a better look. What little of them that she could see brought a catch to her breath and an unheard-of flutter of trepidation to her chest.

Both the men were tall and trimly muscular. Their faces were shadowed by their wide hat brims, but in the bright sunlight she could see enough to realize they were handsome men, if in diverse, compelling ways.

The one man's complexion was ruddy, earthy, and had a sheen of good health. Meg knew instinctively that she would have no difficulty in accommodating him as a customer.

The other man, the one who had stopped in the middle of the road, was a different breed of cat. Not a lap tabby to be paraded around on a leading line, Meg reflected, giving in to a delicate shiver. Oh, no, not that dark-visaged one. That one was a prowler, a predator, a mountain animal at home in the dark. Meg feared having that man in her house, let alone her body.

Unwilling to examine the whys or wherefores of her odd fear, Meg observed the men, unaware that her own mouth smiled when the ruddy-faced man burst into laughter. A sigh of relief whispered through her slightly parted lips when the laughing man turned toward the house—and the cold-looking one turned to stroll back down the road.

With her spirits amazingly revived, Meg hurried from her room and down the narrow stairway when an impatient-sounding knock rattled against the front door. Before reaching for the faceted glass doorknob, she smoothed a hand over the fine cotton wrapper tightly belted around her slender waist.

He was even better to look at up close. His eyes were as blue as a snow-fed mountain lake and sparkled like sunlight dancing over the waters. His ruddy skin was smooth and clear, and the teeth he bared in a wide smile were gleaming white and clean—an almost unseen phenomenon in the West.

"Afternoon, ma'am." He raised his hand and touched his fingers to his hat brim in a respectful gesture—an unheard-of phenomenon as applied to a whore.

Did the man know where he was? Was he lost? The thought caused an unprecedented twinge of disappointment inside Meg. She wasn't in the mood . . . still, he was appealing.

"Yes?" Meg said in a low, prompting voice.

The man looked both eager and unsure. "Is this Meg's place of business?"

"Yes." Rather shocked by the wave of anticipation

she experienced, Meg smiled and stepped back, swinging the door wide as she went.

"You wouldn't happen to be Meg . . . would you now?" Hope shimmered on his pleasant voice. Desire deepened the blue of the eyes that fixed an intense gaze on her flame-colored hair.

Irish. She should have known, Meg told herself, tilting her head to look up at him.

"Yes, I'm Meg," she said, somewhat stunned by the excited quiver in her voice. "What can I do for you?"

He laughed; the sound of it was oddly comforting. "I got a powerful hunger for a woman, ma'am, and a pocket full of payday money. I'd be obliged if you'd be willing to take care of the first for a part of the second."

It was the nicest proposition Meg had ever received. She wasn't in the mood . . . but . . .

"I'd be delighted." The wide sleeves of her wrapper gently swayed as she indicated the stairway with a sweeping movement of her arm. "This way."

He didn't say anything. He didn't crowd her. Keeping a two-step distance between them, he followed her up the shallow staircase, then through the open doorway into the bedroom. Meg quietly shut the door after him.

"Hey, this is real nice," he said, glancing around before turning to smile at her. Lifting his hand, he removed his hat to reveal a full head of shiny black curls. "By the way, the name's Muldoon . . . Sean Muldoon."

Irish. She knew it. Meg returned his smile with a request. "Would you mind if I called you Irish?"

"Hell, no!" He laughed. "I am that. Would you mind if I called you Red?"

"Hell, no." Raising her hand to her hair, Meg speared her fingers into the strands and shook out the flaming mass. "I am that."

"Hot damn," Sean said, flinging his hat into a corner. "You and I are going to get along just fine, Red."

"Yes, I think we are." With a sense of wonder expanding inside her, Meg untied the belt at her waist and shrugged out of the wrapper as she crossed the floor to him. She still wasn't in the mood . . . but . . .

Sean's eyes glowed a deep sapphire as he watched Meg disrobe, revealing softly rounded, creamy skin. She thought she could actually feel his glance as it skimmed down her body, and she heard his indrawn breath as his gaze came to rest on the bush of tight red curls at the apex of her smooth thighs.

"Goddamn, you are one pretty lady," he said in tones of hushed awe.

"Thank you." Meg's voice held laughter. "I'd be happy to return the compliment . . . if I could see you." Moving to him, she raised her hands to his shirt buttons. "Would you like some help getting out of your clothes?"

He swallowed and grinned. "Love it."

The process required a few concentrated minutes, the majority of them removing his boots. When, at last, Sean stood before her in his unadorned male glory, Meg felt a tremor of trepidation. The man was hung like a stud stallion. He could hurt her, make her . . . Meg's protesting mind flashed an image of Josh Metcalf, pounding, pounding away at her until she . . .

Meg shook her head to dislodge the image. Stiff, tense, she backed to the bed. "You're"—she swallowed to moisten her parched throat—"you're quite a man."

He took her statement for a compliment. A rakish grin tipped his lips as he looked at the object of her seeming fascination. "Yeah, that soldier's stood firm through many a battle."

Battle! Panic uncurled in Meg's stomach. He *was* going to hurt her! Employing every trick of the trade she had ever learned, she exerted every ounce of control she possessed to keep her growing sense of revulsion from showing on her face. Cold, freezing, she lay on the bed and shimmied to the side to make room for him. Her stomach clenched in time with the creaking of the bedsprings as he lowered his big frame onto the mattress beside her.

His hands were big but gentle as he stroked her, gentle and soothing. Meg lay still, unable to respond to the teasing inducement of his hands, afraid, afraid of the certainty of her own loss of control should his gentleness give way to brutality during the heat of passion.

Against her determined will, her nipples closed into tight buds of pleasure at the light caress of his blunt fingertip. Her breath grew shallow, her mind grew frantic.

"What's wrong?" Sean's voice was soft but laced with puzzled concern.

Meg was dry as dust all over. She could barely speak. "Wrong? What do you mean?"

"Ahhh, Red." Propping himself up on one elbow, he stared into her fear-widened eyes. "I'm not a yearling. I can tell when a woman doesn't want . . . what I want."

"It's . . . ah," Meg swallowed again. "I . . . oh, damn. I've been cranky the last couple days. Not in the mood." She flicked a look at him. "You understand?"

"Sure." He sighed. "You're due for the flow."

"No." Meg echoed his sigh. "It's not that." Grasping his wrist, she brought his hand to rest on her breast. "You go on. I promise, I'll give you a good ride."

Sean's long fingers stroked the satiny skin of the flattened mound, played with the quivering nipple. He exhaled a longing sigh. Then he shrugged. Then he smiled. "No. It's okay, we don't have to do anything if you're not in the mood."

Meg felt like wailing. Dammit! She never cried. She had given up on crying as a lost cause the night she ran away from that bastard who'd fast-talked her mother into marriage. This big Irishman was so nice now. Denying the need to weep, Meg smiled instead.

"Tell that to your soldier," she said, shifting a pointed look at his rigid manhood. "He's standing at attention, quivering to go into battle."

Following her line of vision, Sean gazed at himself with a wry expression. "Yeah, well." He exhaled a harsh breath. "He's risen to the call to arms many times without a chance in hell of getting into any action. He'll quiver at attention for a spell, then he'll stand at ease. I can take it." He gave a brief laugh that had the sound of a groan. "I have before."

"So have I." Reaching for him, Meg stroked the thick member. "I can take it too." Her voice was droll. "I'm not a virgin, you know."

"I figured." Sean grinned and flopped onto his back. "No, Red. If your heart isn't in it, I wouldn't be enjoying myself being in you."

He was lying. Knowing he was lying, to spare her, brought a film of tears to Meg's eyes. Obeying a sudden impulse, she scrambled up, positioning herself between his legs before he could grasp what she intended.

"What are you doing?" He hoisted his torso up to stare at her, eyes widening as she slowly lowered her head.

"You may not believe this," she murmured, tasting him with a flick of her tongue. "But I haven't performed this service for a man in over ten years. In a way, it kinda makes my mouth virgin territory. I'm going to let your soldier explore."

"Red! Are you sure? You don't hav—Oh, God!" Sean cried out in an agony of pleasure as her wet mouth encased him.

Excitement raced through Meg, bringing a strange moist tightness between her legs. She had always hated it, gagging at the feel of a man inside her mouth. Why didn't she now? Why wasn't she gagging?

Because she was enjoying it. The truth slammed into Meg with such force she nearly bit him. And that would be a shame, she mused, drawing on him with delicate persistence. Inflicting injury on the most vulnerable part of Sean, when she was deriving such never-before-experienced pleasure from ministering to him, would be a crying shame.

Irish was moaning, heaving his body into her mouth, but with such gentle thrusts, it made Meg wonder how it would feel to have those carefully controlled thrusts speared between the other pair of lips on her body.

Curiosity got the better of her. She had to know. There was some something, some intuition, teasing the edges of her consciousness. She had to know!

Easing her mouth away from him, Meg crawled up the length of his sweat-sheened body.

"Oh, Jesus, Red, that was so good." Sean's chest expanded in a deep breath. "Thank you."

Meg laughed into his passion-strained face. He was still as hard as sun-baked earth, yet he thanked her. In that instant, Meg decided she liked this big, handsome Irishman.

"Your soldier's still at attention," she said, teasing him with words and the feel of her legs straddling his taut thighs. "Let's show him some real action," she went on, shivering as she impaled herself on his pike.

"Are you sure, Red?" The lines of strain deepened in his face as Sean fought to keep his body still.

Smiling for him, Meg slid her body up and down on him. "I'm sure." She arched her strawberry-hued brows. "Are you going to make me do all the work?"

"Glory, no!" Sean shouted in glee. "You'll see. This soldier of mine is a first-rate charger."

His was not an empty boast. With rigidly controlled ferocity and tear-inducing care, Sean repeatedly thrust into Meg's womb, and somehow touched her heart. Without feeling a shred of pain or humiliation or hate, Meg's body opened to him, blossomed for him, shattered with him. Stupefied by the experience, Meg later lay beside him as the sense of euphoria slowly dissolved.

She was free! The knowledge that her intuition had been hinting at swept over Meg, bringing with it a different kind of euphoria. She was free! She had responded to a man without suffering the degrading impetus of brutally goading pain. No! She had not only responded, she had exalted in the sheer joy of coupling her body with a man's flesh.

Never, never again would she fear the feelings natural to a woman. Meg didn't know how she knew her intuition was true, but know she did. And with the knowing came a determination that never, never again would she perform for any man other than one of her own choosing.

A weight borne for too many years melted away. A sting of tears rushed to her eyes. Blinking, Meg turned her head to gaze into the relaxed countenance of her savior.

She loved him. He smiled. Meg smiled back. She was not in love with Sean Muldoon, but she did love him. She loved him and she owed him. She would owe him for every day that remained of her life. Meg gratefully accepted the debt.

"You're pretty special, you know that?" Sean's voice was rich with satisfaction.

"You're pretty special yourself, Irish."

Sean grinned. "For a lady who wasn't in the mood . . ." He broke off to laugh. "I can't imagine what being with you would be like when you are in the mood."

Meg's mouth curved into an enticing smile. "You could stick around until the soldier's rested and find out."

"Can't." Sean moved his head back and forth on the sweat-dampened pillow. "Got a friend waitin' for me."

A chill feathered Meg's spine. The dark-visaged man. Yet, even as the image of him cooled her passion-heated skin, the thought of why he hadn't come to the

house with Sean nagged at her mind and pride. She had
to ask.

"Why wait? Why didn't he come in with you?" Her
smile twisted. "Or does he prefer boys to women?"

"Segundo?" Sean bolted upright, shaking the brass
bed with his abrupt move. But he frowned, mulling
over her startling question. "Not the *segundo*." The
curls pasted to his slick scalp didn't move as he gave
one sharp shake of his head. "That hombre is one hundred percent pure male."

"Hmm." Meg let the noncommittal murmur suffice
for whatever he wanted to make of it.

Sean gave her an aggrieved look. "Segundo didn't
want to waste time. He's looking for a man."

"Uh-huh." Her expression said reams, and none of it
savory or complimentary.

He rolled his eyes. "Not for *that*! For a fact, he's
looking more for information about a man."

Meg wasn't surprised, or interested. There was always some man, a lawman or a bounty hunter or an
outlaw, looking for some other man. Their hunt-and-
kill games sickened her. Still, Sean was with this particular stalker, and she owed Sean.

"This man your friend's looking for, is he from
around South Pass?"

"No." Sean shook his head and stretched his arms
up over his head. Muscles corded his arms and rippled
across his shoulders. Body dew matted the black hair in
his armpits. "He's lately been staying up around Sandy
Wash."

"What's his name?" Meg asked, since she had been
visited by some of the cowboys and a few of the merchants from that area. "I might have run across him."

"Metcalf. Josiah Metcalf."

Meg froze on the surface and began a slow burn on the inside. Metcalf. That bastard. Run across him? She yearned to run across him—with a team of enraged stallions.

"Ever heard of him?"

Meg looked Sean straight in the eyes. "Oh, yes, I've heard of him." Bitter gall tinged her voice, malice glittered in her eyes. "I gave him a ride the night before last."

Sean was alert immediately. "You don't sound too almighty happy about the fact or the man."

"He's a dandified sidewinder," Meg said with a sneer.

"That's our man." With a quick heave, Sean leapt from the bed. "He didn't happen to talk about anything personal, did he?" His expression was heart-catchingly hopeful. "I mean, under those . . . er, conditions, men do sometimes."

"Sometimes," she agreed wryly. "Under those . . . . er, conditions. Only Metcalf didn't."

"Shit."

"It's that important?"

Sean moved his shoulders in a way that tugged at her. "Yeah, it's pretty important."

Meg hesitated, but only for a moment. "I did learn a few things about him. Don't ask how."

He brightened. She had to smile.

"Honey, Red, I don't give one solid damn how you got your information. All I need to know is, will you tell whatever it is to Segundo?"

Segundo. Meg suppressed a shiver. Even his name filled her with a sense of dread. She had known, in-

stinctively, from the first look she had of him, that that
dark-visaged man was walking trouble.

"Well?" Sean paused in the act of pulling on his
pants, waiting, one leg in, one leg out, for her reply.

"I . . ." Meg wet her lips. "I don't know. What is
your friend, this Segundo, after? Does he mean to harm
Metcalf?"

Sean grimaced and took the time to finish yanking
his pants over his tight butt before answering. "Hell,
Red, I don't know. And I don't care. He might. I'm
sure as hell certain he could. All I know is that he's
after findin' out whatever he can about some rustling
up our way."

Unconcerned with her nudity, Meg slid her shapely
legs over the side of the bed and stood up. "Metcalf's
into rustling?" she asked, slipping her arms into the
crumpled wrapper.

"Maybe not personally." Sean shrugged into his
shirt. "But we suspect he's behind it." He looked at
her with obvious appeal. "Will you talk to him?"

"Put on your boots." She sighed and pulled the belt
tight around her waist.

"Red?"

Meg hesitated a moment longer, watching him stamp
into his boots. She didn't want to meet the man, let
alone talk to him. But she owed Sean.

"Go get your Segundo."

10

❧

"What does she know?"

"Hell, Segundo, I don't know. She didn't tell me a blessed thing." Sean paced his steps to the long stride of the man beside him. "Asked me not to question how she got her information . . . as if I give a damn."

"I'd hazard a guess that she didn't get it from the merchants who are left here in town."

Sean frowned. "Nothing, huh?"

"No, other than that Metcalf was in town for a few days." Duncan shrugged. About all he had accomplished in the time he'd roamed around the withering town had been to dispatch Emily's party invitations. "If

he did have any business here, it certainly wasn't with
any of the merchants."

"Except the flesh merchant." Sean grimaced.

"Yes." Duncan murmured absently, recalling Jessica's stated intention of talking to a whore. Jessica. An
image of her, defiant and proud, formed to torment his
mind and body. Jessica. He should have heeded her
intuition, he mused. A grim, derisive smile twisted his
lips, a smile that his companion misunderstood.

"She's not what you expect," Sean said, coming to
an abrupt halt at the door of the small house.

"What?"

Sean studied Duncan's expression and shook his
head. "Meg, she's . . . well, she's all right."

"I gathered that from the satisfied look you were
wearing when you searched me out," Duncan drawled,
concealing the twinge of envy he was experiencing for
the obvious physical release Sean had enjoyed.

"I don't mean in that way." Sean made a face. "I
mean as a person, Meg's all right. She's a straight
shooter." A softness eased his tight expression. "Even
though she's all right in the other way too." His smile
was lazy-looking. "Fact is, she's a deal more than all
right."

"I'll take your word for it."

Sean's eyes narrowed at the wry sound of Duncan's
tone. "I don't want you treating her like . . .
like . . ."

"Like what?" Duncan said in challenge.

"Well, like she was beneath you or somethin'."

Duncan started in surprise. "Why would you think
I'd do that?"

Sean shrugged. "Because, for a minute there, you looked, I don't know, kinda mean."

He felt kinda mean. Horny mean. But his sights weren't set on a whore, or even some "good" woman of the town, any town. No, every cell and molecule in his body was screaming a demand to know, in every way, the joy of joining with the arrogant, aggravating, wildly arousing Jessica Randall. Impatience clawed at Duncan. He wanted to be long gone from this deteriorating excuse for a town. Mean? Damn right he felt mean, but not for the reason Sean had assumed.

"I was thinking about something else." Scowling, Duncan sent a narrowed gaze up and down the dusty, rutted road. "I want to get back to the B-Bar-R. I'm hot and dirty and hungry." He shifted his gaze to Sean. "Did you know that there isn't a decent eating establishment left to be found in this bloody, godforsaken town?"

"Er . . . no." Sean shook his head. "I had other things on my mind besides my stomach."

Duncan exhaled a short snort of laughter. "Yeah, I know." He motioned at the door with a nod of his head. "Let's get this over with, then make some tracks."

Even with Sean's warning, Meg was an unexpected surprise for Duncan. She wasn't anything like what he might have envisioned. She wasn't blowsy or overblown or rough-looking. Though not beautiful in a classic way, like Jessica, Meg was attractive in a well-scrubbed, wholesome-looking way.

To Duncan's concealed astonishment, Meg's startling appearance struck him as farm-maid fresh. Her flame-red hair gleamed with good health. Her eyes

were bright with humor and intelligence. Her voice was
sultry.

"Irish here tells me you're after Josh Metcalf," Meg
said, coming directly to the point as soon as Sean had
finished the introductions.

"Yes." Duncan matched her bluntness.

Her shrewd eyes searched his closed expression.
"Why? What for? Are you going to hurt him?"

Ignoring her first two questions, Duncan responded
to the third with a question of his own. "Would it
bother you if I did hurt him?"

"Bother me?" Meg laughed; it was not a pleasant
sound. "I'd pay to watch while you did it."

"You have a grudge?"

"You might say that."

"I might say, or do, anything." Duncan smiled; it was
not a pleasant sight. "To get the information I want."

"If you're trying to frighten me," Meg said baldly, "I
will admit that you're succeeding."

Duncan flashed a genuine smile of appreciation of
her honesty. "I'm not trying to frighten you, Meg. I
have never deliberately hurt a woman. I wasn't planning to begin here and now. But I am prepared to pay
generously for useful information," he added.

She went stiff. "I don't have my hand out."

"I know," he said, appreciating her pride as well as
her honesty. "That's why I made the offer."

"I was wrong."

Seeming to come out of nowhere, her remark confused Duncan. "Wrong? Wrong about what?"

"You." Meg had kept the men standing in the tiny
foyer throughout the brief discussion. Now she invited
them into the small parlor with a wave of her hand.

"Have a seat," she said, motioning to the cluster of delicate chairs and a striped settee. "Can I get you a drink, or something to eat?"

"Yes," Sean accepted with a grin.

"Later perhaps," Duncan declined gently. "In what way were you wrong about me?"

Meg seated herself on a curved-legged chair and modestly drew her wrapper over her knees before answering. "I saw you from the window earlier and thought you were a hard case, a bounty hunter, a lawman, or an outlaw," she explained. "But you're none of those, are you?"

"No, Meg, I'm none of those. I'm the *segundo* on the B-Bar-R ranch up near Sandy Wash." For some inexplicable reason, deceiving Meg bothered Duncan. "We've been troubled with rustling lately and suspect that Metcalf's behind it."

"Has he been trying to buy up property?"

Duncan and Sean exchanged glances. Duncan replied. "Yes, and a few of the small owners have sold out to him." He stared at her with probing intent. "Why?"

"I thought as much." Meg's smile was bland. "I . . . happened upon a telegram in his pocket."

"And?" Duncan prompted, unconcerned about how or why she just *happened* upon the information.

"It was sent from Chicago. It seems the railroad is planning to build a spur line into Sandy Wash." Her voice was wry. "Work's to begin next spring."

"Well, goddamn," Sean murmured. "The bastard's figurin' to make a killing."

The look Meg turned on the big Irishman was soft; her voice was hard. "That's the way I see it."

Duncan was quiet a moment, digesting the information. Then he shot a thoughtful look at Meg. "There's a telegraph office here in town?" He hadn't noticed one before.

Meg nodded. "Not an official office, but the telegraph desk is in the freight line office, on the edge of town."

He was up and moving toward the door before she had finished speaking. "I'll be back," he said, glancing at Sean. "You see if you can find out what we can do to reward the lady."

"I told you I don't—"

Duncan shut the door on Meg's protesting voice.

"You learn anything at the freight office?" Sean shifted in his saddle to look at Duncan. His expression betrayed the curiosity he'd been suppressing since Duncan's return to Meg's house some time ago.

The cloud of dust their trotting horses kicked up behind them obscured the sight of the town they had left moments before. It didn't matter, for neither man had turned to glance back.

"I wasn't trying to learn anything there." Grunting, Duncan settled into his saddle for the long ride ahead. "That was a good meal Meg prepared for us," he said, commenting on the surprising quality of the meal the woman had placed in front of them in short order. "You paid her well for it, I hope."

"No." Sean sighed and shrugged. "Meg refused to take anything for it from me, just as she refused to take anything from you for the information she gave us about Metcalf."

Duncan frowned. He didn't like feeling indebted to

anyone. "We'll have to think of some way to reward her."

"Yeah, I was thinkin' the same." Sean grinned. "So, I suppose that means I'll need to visit her again."

Duncan slanted a look at him. "I have a hunch that won't be too much of a hardship for you."

"Yeaah." Sean drew the single word out with meaning. He had a faraway look for a while, then his eyes cleared, the blue becoming bright and incisive. "You planning to tell me what you did do at that freight office?"

Duncan laughed, liking the sharp, intelligent Irishman more as the day progressed. "I sent a telegram to a contact I have in Chicago, asking him to check out our friend."

"Friend! That son of a bitch's no friend of mine." Sean looked capable of eating nails. "I can't help but wonder what he did to Meg to make her hate him so much."

"I dunno, partner," Duncan drawled. "But maybe, if you work it right, you could wrangle that information out of her . . . while you're looking for a way to reward her."

Sean brightened. "Yeah!" A wide smile lit his handsome face. "You know what, partner, damned if you're not okay to ride the river with."

Not wanting to reveal his ignorance about the meaning of Muldoon's declaration, but concluding by the man's tone that it was complimentary, Duncan replied with a simple "Thanks." Then urging his horse into a canter, he called, "I feel the same about you. Now let's go home."

* * *

The whip sang through the air and cracked a kiss on the rump of the calf hidden in the brush. The animal let out a startled bawl and plunged from beneath the cover and through the ragged break in the line fence.

Jessica tipped back her hat and swiped her sleeve across her damp forehead. Tilting her head, she shot a narrowed glance at the cobalt-blue sky. The intense heat of waning summer rose in shimmering waves from the parched earth. She was hot, thirsty, and tired. The base of her spine ached, radiating sharp-nailed fingers of pain throughout her body, and the day wasn't over. Sighing, she sent her horse after the calf. Then she dismounted and set to work mending the fence.

It turned out to be the longest day Jessica had ever lived through. She checked the position of the sun at regular intervals; in between, she asked Parker to check the time on his pocket watch. By the time she made her third request, Parker was giving her the leery eye.

"You feeling all right, Sis?"

"Hot." Jessica exhaled a harsh breath.

"It's summer." Parker stated the obvious. "The heat never bothered you before. You love summer."

That was before Segundo came. Confining the unpalatable thought to her head, Jessica nudged her horse into motion. "I guess I'm just tired of looking for these stupid strays and mending this damn fence."

Her brother laughed. "No shit! And here all this time I thought you were enjoyin' yoreself." His voice was bone dry, his drawl pronounced. "I'm damned."

Jessica slid him a glittering look. "You and the cows. What time is it?"

"I just told you!"

"So tell me again."

The day slowly unwound; Jessica's nerves and thoughts unwound with it.

What was he doing in South Pass?

She gave an impatient toss of her head.

Who was he talking to?

She shifted in the saddle.

Who was he with?

Jessica gritted her teeth and told herself she didn't care what Segundo was doing or who he was doing it with.

It was a weak attempt at self-deception, a bald-faced lie. She cared . . . too much. The very intensity of the caring infuriated Jessica. He meant nothing to her, nothing. Repeating the assurance like a litany proved ineffective. Her mind persisted in wandering away from her work. Her imagination took flight, soaring to the shabby town of South Pass.

There were whores in that cursed town, as there were whores in every town with a population of more than a dozen or so. And men were men, regardless of nationality or station.

And the *segundo* was most definitely a man.

Querida.

The endearment, and the echo of his soft voice, slithered through her mind like a poisonous viper.

Was Segundo saying that same word, in that same beguiling tone, to some eager and willing "soiled dove"?

Jessica shivered and cursed the heat. It made a change from cursing the *segundo.*

He had told her father he would be back before sunset.

Would this blasted day never end?

* * *

The animals were lathered from the hard ride when Duncan and Sean cantered into the Circle-F yard. The brazen sun was playing hide and seek with the tips of the distant mountain spears. It was hot as blazes. A normal late-summer day.

Duncan gave a silent groan of relief as he stepped stiff-legged from the saddle. The mesh-screened kitchen door was thrown open and Eric called a greeting as he crossed the threshold onto the veranda.

"How'd it go?"

Duncan grunted and dredged up a smile for his cousin. "Better than I expected." He slanted a droll glance at Sean. "And even better for Muldoon."

"Yeah?" Eric raised his brows. "How so?"

Sean laughed, shook his head, and reached for the reins of Duncan's horse. "You tell him," he said, grinning in sly self-satisfaction. "I'll cool Spirit Walker down for you." Chuckling, he turned away to lead the horses to the barn.

"What was that all about?" Eric switched his frowning gaze from Sean to Duncan.

"He visited a house of ill repute in South Pass."

"No!" Eric feigned shock.

" 'Fraid so," Duncan drawled, mounting the steps to the veranda, and the sweet shade it provided. "Good thing he did too."

"He was in that bad a shape, was he?"

Duncan swept the flat-brimmed hat from his head and raked his fingers through his sweat-matted hair. "That also." His urbane-sophisticate expression contrasted sharply with his working-cowboy appearance. "But of even more importance than Muldoon's physical relief was the fact that this particular 'lady' was the only person in town with any useful information. And, thanks to Muldoon, she passed it along to us."

"Are you saying that this whore has some proof that Metcalf is behind the rustlings?"

"Not proof." Duncan shook his head. "But she did have some rather interesting information to impart." Briefly but concisely, he related the day's events to Eric, ending with the tidbit Meg had given as he and Sean were leaving. "She also said that, though Metcalf appears to go unarmed, he carries a derringer concealed beneath his coat."

"That sneaky son of a bitch!"

"Precisely," Duncan concurred.

Grim-faced, Eric turned to the kitchen door. "Come on in, there's fresh coffee," he said, swinging the door wide. "How long do you think it'll take till you hear from this contact of yours in Chicago?"

Duncan shrugged in answer as he entered the spacious room. The heat from the cooking stove hit him with the force of a physical blow. Wondering how his aunt or any other woman could bear spending so much time working in the intense heat in the room, he greeted the flush-faced Inga before responding to Eric's question.

"Since I noticed Josiah Metcalf's name on Emily's invitation list," he drawled in a tone of voice that said his notice was deliberate, "and since I assume he will attend the gathering, I hope I'll receive a report before Ben's annual preroundup shindig."

"From Chicago?" Eric frowned. "That fast?"

"By special courier, yes." Duncan took a tentative

sip from the steaming cup Inga handed to him, then asked, "Where is Uncle David?"

"Resting." Inga heaved a despairing sigh. "The pain's getting worse for him by the day." She shook her head, as if trying to shake off her worry, then she worked up a smile for Duncan. "You'll stay for supper?"

"Can't," he said, setting the cup on the table and moving to the door. "Another time. I told Ben I'd be back by sundown." He gazed through the screened door at the mountains. "I had better make tracks or I won't make it."

"Oh, Duncan, I almost forgot!" Eric called, following him onto the veranda. "A wagon loaded with your belongings pulled in soon after you and Sean left this morning."

"Good. I was wondering when it would arrive." He grinned at Eric. "I could use a change of clothes."

"Do you want me to send the stuff over?"

"No, I'll come back tomorrow for a few things." He hesitated, then, grinning, went on, "I'll make it late tomorrow, so I can stay for supper."

With a final wave, Duncan loped toward the barn. He was in a hurry to get back to the B-Bar-R, and not because he had told Ben he'd return by sunset.

Jessica.

Her name whispered through Duncan's mind. Memories of her had tormented him throughout the day, teasing memories, erotic memories of the moments spent with his body pressed against hers. The taste of her was in his mouth, in his gut, in his loins. He felt a powerful need to see her, to just look at her.

Murmuring an apology to the tired horse, Duncan pushed Spirit Walker into a gallop.

He was back.

It was past sundown, almost dark. Bathed and dressed for the evening meal in a cool cotton blouse and skirt and soft house slippers, and refusing to recognize the questions nagging at her of where he was and whom he was with, Jessica started down the enclosed back stairway. She was three steps from the bottom when the distinct, unmistakable sound of his voice brought her to an abrupt halt.

Segundo was back.

Blaming the sudden weakness washing through her on the heat in the enclosed space, she paused to take a deep restorative breath, only to have the breath lodge in her throat as the content of what he was saying slammed into her.

". . . yes, Meg's a prostitute. Strange, isn't it, that the information should come from a whore, after Jessica had mentioned talking to one?"

He *had* been with a whore!

The tightness in her throat expanded. Her stomach churned. Gripping the stair rail with one hand, Jessica raised the other to her mouth.

On an intellectual level, Jessica understood the importance of the role the prostitutes played anywhere, but most especially in the West, where the men far outnumbered the women. On one occasion, she had even defended the position of some of the "soiled doves" as the only means available to earn a living for the women who, for various reasons, found themselves alone in the world, without male protection. But, at that moment, Jessica was not thinking on an intellectual level. Her emotions were in conflict and running rampant.

He had been with a whore.

Less than twenty-four hours after kissing her, touching her, Segundo had coolly ridden away, into South Pass, to take his pleasure with another woman. And not just with any other woman, but an experienced woman who sold her favors to any man who could meet her price.

Jessica felt sick.

Then she got mad.

A red haze of outraged fury clouded her mind. The murmur of voices wafting to the stairway from the kitchen were drowned out by the buzzing of angry voices inside her head.

What did she care if he wallowed in the sweat of a whore? He meant nothing to her. Jessica shook her head and swallowed the taste of bile. Revulsion diminished the sense of weakness. Strength born of disgust flowed into her limbs. Her chin lifted. Pride sent steel into her spine. Her shoulders squared. Her eyes blazed like sun-struck silver.

Who was he, anyway? Jessica chided herself in a scathing tone. The *segundo*. Bah! He was nothing more than a hired hand, a wrangler—a peasant who had had the temerity to inflict his attentions on the *patrón*'s daughter.

If he ever touched her again she would kill him, Jessica vowed. And she would take her own pleasure from inflicting just punishment on him. She would show him that she wasn't a simpering miss to be trifled with.

Her purpose set, Jessica focused her attention on the

discussion in the kitchen. What were they talking about? She frowned. Had her father just asked Segundo something about a contact in Chicago? Her curiosity aroused, Jessica descended the three steps into the room. Her quiet entrance went unnoticed by the three people seated around the table.

"I assume he will use the Pinkerton Agency to gather the information."

Jessica's frown deepened. Pinkerton Agency! What was Segundo talking about? Who was the "he" he was talking about? Deciding to have some answers, she made her presence known.

"Who needs the services of the Pinkerton Agency . . . someone we know?"

Her question produced the strangest effect. The three people at the table started, their heads jerking around, eyes staring at her as if she had materialized out of thin air.

"Where did you come from?" Ben growled, looking at her in an odd, almost guilty way.

"Er . . . Jessica, dear, we didn't hear you come down the stairs," Emily said, obviously flustered.

Strange indeed. Her suspicions aroused, Jessica looked at Segundo, waiting to reply to her parents to hear whatever inane remark he might make.

"Miss Jessica." Segundo confounded and irritated her by rising and giving her a half bow.

She should have reacted adversely to the sweaty, trail-weary sight of him. To her chagrin, she didn't. He was dirty. A dark stubble of beard shadowed his face. He looked exhausted. This last observation succeeded in stirring her ire. Of course he was exhausted, she reminded herself. He had probably spent a good portion

of the day engaged in vigorous physical activity with a
whore. Jessica controlled the impulse to curl her lip in a
disdainful sneer.

"Segundo." Her voice was cool, distant, dismissive.
At her tone, a light seemed to dim in his eyes, turning
them to cold and hard stones. Refusing to acknowledge
a sudden twist of pain inside her, Jessica hardened her
heart and her resolve. "You mentioned the Pinkerton
Agency?"

"*Sí.*" His tone was noncommittal.

"Why?"

Segundo looked to her father, as if for instructions.
"*Señor?*"

"You may as well tell her." Ben sighed. "She won't
give us a moment's rest unless you do."

"What won't she give you a moment's rest about
unless you tell her?" Standing just inside the doorway
to the wash shed, Parker glanced from his father to the
segundo.

Ben rolled his eyes and threw his hands into the air.
"Get it over with, Segundo."

"Meanwhile," Emily chirped in, jumping up, "I'll
get supper on the table."

In a low, inflectionless voice, Segundo launched into
a recitation of the day's events. To Jessica's surprise—
and a sense of hurt disappointment—he didn't even
gloss over the fact that he had garnered his information
from a prostitute. When he was finished, he sat back
and stared into her eyes with confusing, unnerving intent.

What was he expecting of her? Jessica wondered,
maintaining his stare with some difficulty. Had
Segundo believed she'd be shocked by his blatant ad-

mission of visiting a whore? Had he hoped she'd reveal outrage or, even worse, injury?

Querida.

Jessica fought against an inner need to give in to the expanding twist of pain inside. Segundo hadn't said the word, yet she could hear the soft, beguiling sound of his voice, whispering the endearment. She wanted to scream her fury at him. She yearned to claw at his face with her nails. She longed for the whip laying where she'd tossed it atop her dresser.

Womanizing bastard! Jessica didn't give voice to the scathing accusation, but in her imagination the whip cracked, searing the flesh on his broad back. Segundo didn't flinch with pain. Jessica did. His eyes flickered and searched her expression. Feeling exposed, she turned away.

"Is there anything I can do to help, Mother?"

Emily gave her a distracted smile, while continuing to stir the brown gravy bubbling in the large black frying pan. "The table needs setting."

"All right." Jessica gritted her teeth. The last thing she wanted to do was return to the table and the dark-visaged man seated there, watching her. Avoiding eye contact with him, she did as she was bidden, listening to the men talk as she prepared the table for the meal.

"So we're finally going to get a spur line into Sandy Rush," Parker said, grunting with relief as he dropped onto a chair. "And ol' Josiah's planning on getting rich from it." His lips flattened into a grim, hard line. "I think we oughta string the crook up."

"We have no proof, *señor.*"

"The *segundo*'s right, Parker." Ben scowled. "You

can't go hangin' a man because he received a telegram
. . . much as it'd give me pleasure to do just that."

"Ben Randall!" Emily spun around, brandishing a
wooden spoon. "Don't you be talking about taking the
law into your own hands! We didn't work for statehood
for Wyoming just to continue in the old ways."

Ben grumbled.

Parker made a face.

Segundo remained detached and impassive.

"Mother's right, Dad." Jessica absently pleated the
napkin she was holding. "And you know it, Parker,"
she chastised her brother. "We're only eight years away
from a new century and should be past the days of
solving our problems with a rope slung over a tree
branch."

"It worked," Parker muttered.

"Your sister is right, *señor*." Segundo stood to relieve
Emily of the heavy meat platter she was bringing to the
table. "If my contact can ferret out any evidence
against Metcalf, we must present it to the proper au-
thorities."

A sensation of warmth suffused Jessica. Segundo's
support of her principle was a small thing . . . and yet,
reject it as she would, the warmth spread to every corner of her being. Afraid he'd see, know, she sat down
next to him at the table, lowered her eyes, and
smoothed her napkin over her lap. Only she was aware
of the tremor in her fingers.

"I don't suppose you have any idea how long it'll
take to get a report from this contact of yours?" Ben
raised his bushy eyebrows and popped a chunk of beef
into his mouth.

"No." Segundo's smile was faint, yet strong enough to steal Jessica's breath. "But I am hoping to hear from him before the day of your party."

"You thinking of confronting Metcalf here, right in front of everybody and his brother?" Parker grinned in obvious appreciation of the idea.

Segundo's smile grew; Jessica's breath shortened. "I've been considering the possibility," he said. "In the event my contact cannot find any usable proof."

"The party's only two weeks away," Ben said. "Not a whole hell of a lot of time for your man to come up with anything, let alone get it to you in time."

"We'll see." Segundo shrugged.

Emily frowned. "I'm not at all sure I want you to get the report before then."

"Emily!"

"Well, I don't." Emily stood her ground despite her husband's displeasure. "Folks from as far away as hundreds of miles look forward to your yearly shindig, and you know it, Ben. They come here to let loose a little, to relax and socialize, to eat, drink, and even dance."

Dance. Jessica slid a sidelong glance at Segundo. What would it be like to dance with him? An anticipatory shiver skipped along her spine. Would he ask her onto the broad plank dance floor the hands erected on the day of the party? The shiver intensified, bringing her to her senses.

She didn't care, Jessica assured herself. She had been escorted onto ballroom dance floors by the scions of wealthy men and had felt nothing. She certainly wasn't excited about the possibility of being squired into a waltz by one of her father's employees.

The party meant nothing to her.
He meant nothing to her.
She'd show him.
Jessica couldn't wait for the day to arrive.

11

The extended heat wave broke three days before the party. Dark clouds began massing in the northwest early in the morning, shrouding the mountain spires in a gray mist. The front was slow-moving, billowing forth lightning-speared clouds at a snail's pace. Thunder rumbled over the hushed, expectant land, its deep voice carrying the promise of relief to the parched earth and every living thing on it.

Throughout the day the atmosphere grew steadily more oppressive. A prestorm stillness blanketed the land. By sundown the sky was the greenish color of bronze patina, edged by the advancing, rain-swollen black clouds.

Jessica greeted the end of the work day with a sigh of relief. Her clothes were pasted to her skin. Sweat beaded her body and ran in a trickle between the valley of her breasts. She felt drained and wilted. Slumping in the saddle, she gave Bath her head and allowed the horse to set its own quick pace back to the ranch.

She felt dispirited and irritable and yet, in all honesty, Jessica acknowledged that her low physical and mental state could not be blamed solely on the weather conditions.

During the previous week and a half, Segundo had been away from the ranch more than he'd been present. And, during the entire length of those days, Jessica had fought a bitter inner battle of conflicting considerations.

She barely noticed his absence.

Jessica's repeated self-assurance failed to convince her self.

She not only noticed, but missed the aggravating sight of him too intensely, the nagging voice of her inner self insisted with annoying persistence.

Nor did she mind that when he did deign to join them, either at work or at the table at mealtimes, Segundo appeared barely to notice her presence.

Jessica told herself she felt nothing but relief from no longer being the object of interest of those strange stonelike eyes of his.

The nagging inner voice laughed and called her a coward as well as a liar.

The silent battle with self raged on along the same lines day after endless day. Hoping to stifle the voice,

Jessica threw herself into her work, starting earlier and quitting later with each successive day. She slept little; she ate less. She lost weight; she took a tuck in the waistband of her pants and kept going, refusing to probe into the reasons for her mental and emotional discomfort. After nearly two weeks of endless internal warfare, Jessica was on the verge of tearing out either her own or the *segundo*'s hair.

The situation puzzled Jessica. She had never encountered or even heard of a ranch foreman—or *segundo* —who spent more time off the property than on it. Equally puzzling to her was her father's casual attitude. To all appearances, both her father and her mother seemed unconcerned by the *segundo*'s mysterious disappearances. It didn't make sense. It raised questions, some of which Jessica wasn't sure she wanted to hear answered. Questions like: Where had he gone every other day or so? What was he doing to keep him away so much of the time? And whom was he spending that time with?

Positive she already knew the answer, Jessica was loath to examine the last of her own questions. She had heard Segundo tell her father that he had received his information from a whore. To Jessica, that was a clear admission that he had been with the woman, which meant . . .

It was always at this point of her ruminations that Jessica slammed the door on her questing mind. She told herself that she neither cared nor wanted to know the answers. It was easier and safer than admitting she cared too much.

Meanwhile, the inner conflict was taking its toll on her body and disposition.

* * *

Duncan watched the approaching storm with a smile of satisfaction. But, although he was relieved by the prospect of having the heat wave at long last ended, the cause of his satisfied smile was not in the darkening sky but in the anxiously awaited report from his Chicago contact, now safely tucked under his waistband beneath his shirt.

The waiting would soon be over. The thought kicked Duncan's smile into a grin. The information contained in the report was just about what he had expected. To all intents and purposes, Josiah Metcalf was a petty thief and a manipulator who would take advantage of anyone or anything for his own personal and financial enrichment.

Resting easily in the saddle as Spirit Walker loped along at a comfortable pace, Duncan wasn't concerned with Josh Metcalf. He knew Metcalf's days of annoyance to the residents of the environs of Sandy Rush were numbered. The man would be dealt with at some point during Ben Randall's party.

It was the realization that the waiting and his self-enforced separation from Jessica was almost over that brought the smile to Duncan's lips and stirred the passion in his blood.

Jessica. How he had hungered for the sight of her, thirsted for the taste of her. Yet Duncan had deliberately kept his distance from her, not trusting in his own determination to wait until the business with Metcalf was finished before taking her, making her his.

And now the waiting would soon be over. The party was only three days away. And, after the party . . .

A white-gold streak of lightning pierced the roiling

black clouds overhead followed some thirty seconds later by the rumbling boom of thunder. Spirit Walker shuddered and danced sideways. Securing his grasp on the reins, Duncan studied the sky, judging his chances of outrunning the storm to the B-Bar-R. Lightning flashed and thunder roared, muffling the exuberant sound of Duncan's laughter as, leaning forward, he spoke into the twitching ear of the English-bred hunter. On command, the magnificent black animal leapt forward into a flat-out, mile-diminishing gallop.

Lathered and breathing heavily, the gallant horse dashed across the deserted ranch yard and into the barn, beating the deluge by a good three minutes.

The Randall family members were at the supper table when the storm unleashed its fury. Within seconds, the outside temperature dropped thirty degrees. Gusting wind swept through the screened door, cooling the hot, humid kitchen. Sheeting rain pounded against the veranda roof.

"Oh, that feels wonderful," Emily said, tugging the collar of her dress away from her throat while deeply inhaling the cool, moisture-laden air.

"Sure does." Ben heaved a sigh and smiled at his wife.

"Wouldn't be surprised if there ain't some hail in those cold clouds," Parker opined judiciously, continuing to shovel food into his mouth.

Jessica reacted to the urgent pounding of the rain as if to the summons of a long-awaited, much-loved visitor. And, in a sense, that's exactly what the storm was for her. Ever since she could remember, Jessica had run outside at the first drop of a summer downpour, eager to splash in the refreshing rain.

Forgetting the untouched food on her plate, she left the table and walked to the door, smiling as the misted wind bathed her heat-flushed face. Compelled by a sudden need to revel in the reviving water, she reached for the door handle.

"Jessica, don't you dare!" Emily cried. "You're not a little girl anymore. You can't go running around in the rain like a . . ." Her voice faded on a sigh as, without responding, Jessica pulled the door open and walked outside.

Unaware of the dark form in the shadows near the house, Jessica loosened her braid as she crossed the veranda and shook her hair free as she skipped down the steps. Within seconds, the silky silvery strands were soaked by the matching silver strands of rainfall.

It was glorious, cooling and delicious. Since the yard was deserted, with everyone taking shelter indoors, Jessica was tempted to tear the sweat-stiffened shirt from her body, but, to avoid scandalizing her mother, she prudently decided to enjoy herself while fully clothed.

Her delighted laughter blending with the keening wind, Jessica raised her face and arms in welcoming homage to the life giving, regenerating fall of water.

She was breathtaking.

Watching Jessica from the shadowed depths of the veranda, Duncan was overwhelmed by an emotion unlike any he had ever before experienced. There was tenderness, indulgent amusement, a touch of awe, and something else, some strange, exciting, but elusive element he couldn't quite define.

The childlike innocence of her laughter ran through him. Her pose of abandoned supplication aroused him with its ancient lure of bewitching seduction.

Aching for her with every particle of his being, Duncan imposed iron-willed control over the urge to leap from the veranda to her side to satisfy a need to know what it would feel like to make love to Jessica in the pouring rain.

Just three more days.

Repeating the phrase like a prayer, Duncan groaned, deep in his throat, as Jessica speared her fingers into her hair, shook out the sodden strands, and turned, presenting her profile for his inspection. Her clothes were plastered to her body, her pants girdling her slender woman's hips, her shirt outlining her upthrust firm breasts. His eyes feasting on her, Duncan wet his parched lips with the tip of his tongue and rubbed his tingling palms over the rough material encasing his thighs.

Jessica started when she noticed him, her eyes widening with surprise and . . . what? Before Duncan could identify the expression in her eyes it changed, becoming teasing and playful. Her lips curved into a taunting smile.

"Why are you hiding there on the porch?" she called over a loud boom of thunder. "Why don't you join me out here?"

Bemused by her expression and the bantering tone he had heard her use with others, but never with him, Duncan stared at her in mute surprise. From the day he arrived, Jessica had shown him nothing but haughty disdain. Being the recipient of her friendly teasing caught him off guard.

"Afraid you'll melt?" she called, laughing.

The free, exuberant sound of her laughter shot directly to Duncan's heart and took up permanent residence. Intuitively he knew that her laughter would beguile him for whatever remained of his life. A bolt of lightning struck again, this time inside his mind, clarifying his thoughts and tangled emotions.

He was in love with her.

Considering Jessica's treatment of him, Duncan was both startled and shocked by the revelation. She had not been sweet or accommodating or even kind—all of which he would have expected from the woman who succeeded in capturing his deepest affections. But there it was, the truth resounding in his head. For good or ill, he was in love with her.

Resigned to the inevitability of it, Duncan accepted his fate with a wry smile and a droll response. "I've been melting for weeks."

"Well, then, come on out," she invited, convincing him she had missed the admission within his answer. She spread her arms wide. "The rain feels wonderful."

Although Duncan was fully aware of her family gathered a few feet away inside the kitchen, he didn't hesitate any longer. After pushing away from the wall, he started for the steps. At that same moment, he heard the first hailstone strike with a ringing *ping* against the veranda roof.

"Get up here!" Alarm for her safety gave his voice a rough, commanding edge.

Jessica's expression changed from teasing to angry. Her chin rose to a defiant angle; her eyes narrowed. "What did you . . . ?" she began, only to break off, eyes widening, as a large hailstone struck her cheek.

She was moving, running, even as he reinforced his shouted order.

"Now, dammit!"

Duncan didn't know what to expect from her as she dashed up the steps and under the protective covering of the veranda roof, but it certainly was not the smiling face and laughing remark she presented to him.

"That stuff stings." Raising her hand, she rubbed her cheek. "Thanks for trying to warn me."

Duncan was well and truly undone. She was soaking wet and bedraggled. Her hair hung in dripping strings down her back. Still, to him, she was the most beautiful, appealing sight on earth. Her rain-glistened, laughing mouth had a special, irresistible allure. Unequal to the tempting sight of her wet lips, he pulled her into his arms and lowered his head to hers, crushing her moist mouth beneath his own.

As she had before, Jessica stiffened in his embrace. Her clothes were sodden, and she shivered. Tightening his hold, Duncan drew her closer to his hard warmth, absorbing the chill wetness into his own body heat. Her lips were as cold and delicious as mountain spring water, firing a raging thirst in his throat. Losing all sense of time and place, he groaned and drank deeply from her, needing more and still more of the sweet moisture of her mouth.

Jessica struggled with him, inciting his senses with the friction of her body rubbing over his. His passion flaring, Duncan slid his hands to her hips, dragging her to him, holding her tight and still against him, letting her feel the power of his thrusting manhood. She froze for a long moment, then slowly, her body and lips softened in response to his hard demand.

Wild elation tore through Duncan at her reluctant compliance. His desire ran rampant. Inserting a leg between hers, he nudged her thighs apart and stepped into the vee. She moaned and grasped his shoulders. He pressed into her and rotated his hips in abandoned sensuousness, his body seeking the honeyed haven of hers. He felt her shudder then, tentatively, begin to rotate her hips in time with his.

Beyond the veranda, the storm raged unabated, bringing a damp chill to the early-evening air. Beneath the protective roof, heated passion dominated. Tension spiraled inside Duncan. Surrendering thought to sensation, he tightened his grip on Jessica's hips and moved, backing her toward the shadowed wall. As her shoulders made contact with the surface, a loud call rang out from inside the kitchen.

"Jessica! Get in out of the rain before you catch your death from cold!"

Ben's disgruntled-sounding bark restored Duncan's sense. He released Jessica and stepped away an instant before the older man pushed open the door and strode onto the veranda.

"Oh, Segundo! I didn't know you were out here." Ben peered through the gloom. "Jessica? What are you doing, cowering there against the wall?"

"I am not cowering." Stepping away from the wall, Jessica boldly faced her father. "I . . . er, it started to hail and I ran up here, under the roof." She threw a quick glance at Duncan. "Segundo was here, watching the storm, and we were just talking about it."

"*Sí,*" Duncan said, endorsing her explanation, while sending a silent plea to his leaping senses to cease their torment to his body. "It is an awesome spectacle . . .

the storm." He caught Jessica's quick glance and knew she understood that his reference was to the inner, not the outer, storm. "Both surprising and overwhelming."

"Yeah." Ben stared out at the wind-tossed rain. "These late-summer storms can be beauties."

"Yes." Duncan stared into Jessica's emotion-tossed eyes. "Beautiful."

A flush tinged her pale cheeks, and she lowered her lashes to conceal the feverish glow in her eyes. Duncan was so intrigued by her reaction that he almost missed Ben's comment.

"Can be dangerous too."

Duncan smiled. "A little danger adds spice and excitement to every aspect of life."

"Maybe so, for you young folks." Ben turned a frowning look at Duncan. "But I can live without it."

Duncan's smile grew into a wolfish grin. "Strange, but suddenly I crave it." Though he spoke to Ben, Duncan knew by her indrawn breath that Jessica caught the secret meaning in his remark. He stared into her surprise widened eyes. "Don't you, Miss Jessica?"

"Ha!" Ben exclaimed, inadvertently sparing her the necessity of answering. "She's always craved danger and excitement."

Jessica's eyelids flickered and the color deepened along her cheekbones. "I-I think I'd better get out of these wet clothes." Spinning around, she escaped into the house.

"There's proof of it," Ben called after her. "Running out into a storm. Downright unladylike."

The scolding sound of her father's voice, and the soft sound of Segundo's laughter, trailed Jessica into the

kitchen, past her mother's exasperated sigh and her
brother's teasing grin, and all the way up the stairs to
her bedroom.

What had happened to her out there on the veranda?
she asked herself, shivering with the strength of the
memory of being crushed by Segundo's mouth and
body.

Heat flared inside her, in sharp contrast to the chill
bumps on the surface of her skin and her cold-numbed
fingers tearing at her wet garments.

Why had she responded so brazenly to him, instead
of pushing him away in rejection? She should have
slapped him, denounced him in tones of scathing disgust. Instead, she had kissed him back, arching into the
demanding hardness of his male body.

Why? She despised him—didn't she?

Despised?

The word echoed in Jessica's mind and she shook
her head in mute denial. As a wave of weakening trem-
ors washed through her, she groped for the bedpost to
steady herself. She felt fragile, uncertain, and scared. A
second wave washed through her, a wave carrying glaring self-knowledge. The force of the truth sent her to
her knees on the floor beside the bed.

She didn't despise him. She loved him.

No. No. Jessica cried in silent repudiation. She didn't
love him. She couldn't love him. Segundo had shown
her nothing but male arrogance, a tendency for male
dominance. And she would not be dominated by any
man.

Jessica's frantic mind scrambled for alternatives and
latched onto the obvious. She had spent most of her life
on the ranch, exposed to the basic and natural biologi-

cal urge to mate. That was it, of course, she rationalized. What she was feeling, experiencing, was the
emergence of physical needs too long suppressed.

A ragged breath escaped the tightness gripping Jessica's throat. What she was feeling wasn't love but the
natural physical response built into all living creatures
to couple and thus reproduce. And she could prove her
theory.

Willing strength into her trembling limbs, Jessica got
to her feet. Determination lifted her chin. She would
prove it, not only to herself but to Segundo as well.

If she was right, as she convinced herself she was,
she would react in the same physical manner to any
other physically attractive, virile man. And the perfect
opportunity to prove her theory was only two days
away.

There would be many attractive men at the party.

It wasn't working.

Stealing a moment in the shade of the tree beside
the house, Jessica patted the moisture from her brow
and glanced around at the boisterous activity in the
ranch yard.

The weather was perfect, warm but without the intense, energy-sapping heat of the previous weeks. It
was nearing sundown and a refreshing breeze had
sprung up, cooling the gathered mass of overheated
bodies and the occasional flare of tempers.

Laughing, chatting women rushed back and forth
from the kitchen to the long tables set in a line at one
end of the shaded veranda, replenishing the varied se-
lection of foods offered to the horde of hungry guests.

Children ran about the yard and outbuildings, playing all sorts of youthful games, calling to one another in voices raised with exuberance and excitement.

The upright piano had been moved from the parlor to the far end of the veranda, where the musicians Ben Randall had hired out of Cheyenne were working up a sweat earning their pay, playing loudly if not exactly melodically.

No one minded the sour notes. The dance platform the ranch hands had erected early that morning next to the veranda was packed solid with foot-stomping merrymakers.

Until a few moments ago, Jessica had been in the center of that enthusiastic crush of humanity, testing her theory for all she was worth with the strapping young son of a rancher from the Powder River basin.

And it wasn't working. Her body still burned with the impression of Segundo's hard contours, her lips still tingled with the memory of his searching mouth.

Sighing, Jessica sipped the lemonade she'd poured for herself from a large pitcher on the serving table after excusing herself from the rancher's son.

Why did she feel nothing? she mused, staring with brooding eyes at the makeshift dance platform. The tall, towheaded young man was not only handsome but intelligent and witty as well. And yet, other than a sense of fun and camaraderie, she hadn't felt the slightest of stirrings while in his company. Come to that, she hadn't felt much of anything to speak of with any of the men she'd conversed and danced with, including Josh Metcalf, who had outdone himself in charm and compliments.

She certainly hadn't felt anything even remotely similar to the excitement and confusion Segundo could stir inside her with the mildest of looks from his odd turquoise eyes.

Segundo. Merely thinking his name caused an expectant shiver inside Jessica. And, after the warm friendliness of his attitude toward her since the afternoon of their passionate interlude on the veranda, her heightened sense of expectancy had been rampant all day—rampant but unsatisfied.

Eyes narrowing, Jessica watched as Segundo led a prominent Cheyenne matron in a western version of the waltz. Jessica had expected him, waited for him to ask her to dance. But Segundo had avoided her throughout the day, his eyes becoming more distant and hard with each passing hour.

She didn't care, Jessica told herself, lifting her chin to an arrogant angle. Raising her hand, she absently brushed aside the wisps of silvery hair that had escaped the pins anchoring the fashionable knot on top of her head. The last thing she wanted was Segundo's attention, she assured herself, denying the ache of emptiness deep inside her.

She did not need him!

It was only a physical reaction, quite normal for a healthy young woman. Jessica clung with desperate insistence to her theory, even though she had been unsuccessful in her attempts to prove it. She simply hadn't run across a man with the right chemistry yet, a chemistry strong enough to spark her own, but when she did, she felt sure . . .

Jessica's introspection was distracted by the sight of her neighbor shouldering his way onto the dance floor and calling to the musicians to desist with the noise. Perplexed by Eric's actions, she was wondering what he was up to when he shouted to the crowd for their attention.

"If you'll all quiet down, I have an announcement to make that I'm sure you'll all be happy to hear!" Eric yelled over the loud babble of voices. He waited to continue until the din had subsided to a questioning murmur. "I have received word that, come next spring, the railroad is planning to build a spur line into Sandy Rush."

Eric's news was met with a moment of shocked surprise, then a roar of delighted approval swelled from the assemblage. Laughter and whoops of joys rang on the early-evening breeze wafting through the yard.

As surprised as the guests by the announcement—if not by its contents—Jessica stared for an instant into the expressionless faces of Eric and Segundo, then shifted her gaze, searching the crowd for Josh Metcalf. When she had him in sight, she took note of the smile he was wearing. Though wide and toothy, Metcalf's smile looked forced and strained.

Goddamn! How had that half-breed learned about the railroad company's plans to build a spur line? Josh raged inwardly, while careful to keep his smile in place.

Seeing his dreams of power and wealth dissolve into nothingness in the rejoicing of the local residents, Josh ground his back teeth and raked his mind for alternatives. Feeling trapped, he glanced around for an out, a way of salvaging something from the ashes of his dreams. His restless gaze came to an abrupt stop on Jessica Randall.

Renewed hoped leapt inside Josh's tight chest. Of course, the Randall bitch! On her marriage, Jessica would come into a sizable piece of land, property in a prime location in relation to the prospective spur line. And, instead of her usual attitude of cold disdain, Jessica had been exceptionally friendly during the two dances he had shared with her. If she had softened to his advances, maybe . . .

Josh began moving in her direction even as the speculative thoughts churned in his mind. He had charmed many concessions from as many women, he was an expert at charm and seduction, and Jessica was just another woman—to be used then discarded when he was through with her.

Josh Metcalf's smile underwent a subtle change as he approached the slender woman standing in the flickering shadows beneath the old tree.

Evening settled like a blessing on the land. Torches were lit and lamps brought out from the house to illuminate the scene as the party continued unabated.

Standing alone on the fringes of the happy crowd, Segundo stared with narrow-eyed intent at the laughing couple twirling around the dance platform. It was their third dance together, the third time Jessica had gone with what appeared to be eager willingness into Josh Metcalf's arms.

Segundo had been keeping a careful count of all the men she had danced with; he had also been keeping a tight rein on his temper. His control was crumbling in time with his count. Fury burned like acid in his mind and gut at the sight of Jessica in Metcalf's embrace.

Jessica was innocent—even if she was behaving more like an abandoned hussy. And Josh Metcalf had the look of a practiced rake. The longer Segundo was forced to watch them, the madder he became. His anger was nearing the explosive stage when, before the dance had ended, Metcalf drew Jessica from the platform and into the darkness at the back of the house.

Unobserved and as silent as a shadow, Segundo followed the retreating couple. Hearing the hushed sound of muted voices, he came to a stop at the corner of the building.

"Really, Mr. Metcalf, I will be missed. We must return to . . ." Segundo heard Jessica begin, only to be interrupted by Metcalf's pleading voice.

"Oh, Jessica, stay for a moment. Your hair is beautiful, like spun silver, in the moonlight."

"Thank you, but I can't stay. I must get back to . . ." Again he interrupted her.

"You can't imagine what being with you like this means to me. Please, let me hold you again in my arms. I promise, just one kiss and . . ."

"And you'll be a dead man," Segundo finished for him.

12

Startled, Jessica let out a muffled shriek and whirled around just as Segundo stepped away from the house, into the bright moonlight.

"What the devil!" Josh's body jerked and his hands fell away from Jessica's shoulders. "Who are you?"

Something in his measured pace as Segundo moved toward them sent a thrill of trepidation through Jessica.

"Segundo." His voice held a lethal softness. "Mr. Randall's right hand." He kept his gaze fixed on Metcalf but whispered a command to Jessica. "Go back to the party, Miss Randall. I have business with this man."

Jessica bristled at his dismissive tone. "What business? I know of no—"

"Go." Segundo sliced a look at her. Even with only the light from the moon, Jessica could see the terrible fury in his eyes. "At once."

Her pride and sense of outrage at his interference quailed before the look of him, the deadly sound of him. She wanted to argue, deny him the right to order her around, but her considerable courage failed her. Maintaining her façade, she tossed her head in a gesture of unconcern and walked away. But she didn't go far. In a dense pool of darkness beside the house, she stopped and turned to observe the confrontation.

"You're nothing but a hired hand," Josh said in a sneering tone. "I have no business with you." Casually slipping his hand into his right jacket pocket, he moved to walk around the man standing in his path.

His movement created a reaction so incredibly swift it brought a gasp of disbelief to Jessica's lips.

Moonlight glinted on a blade that appeared to leap into Segundo's right hand, while in the same instant his left hand snaked out to grasp Josh's wrist, caging his hand inside his pocket. There was a blur of movement, then the point of the blade was pressed against the soft underside of Josh Metcalf's left jaw. Metcalf froze in midstep.

"I'll have the derringer," Segundo said, easing Metcalf's hand from the pocket. Metcalf's fingers were wrapped around the butt of a small handgun. "Don't you know that playing with guns can be dangerous to your health?" After plucking the weapon from the other man's hand, Segundo tossed it aside.

"I'll kill you, you dirty greaser!" Metcalf's strained voice denied his bravado.

Jessica went rigid with shock on hearing the derogatory term, and held her breath, fully expecting Segundo to retaliate in a swift, forceful manner. She quickly realized that he didn't need to use physical force.

"There are ways of killing a man that are swift and painless." Segundo's whispery voice sent a horrifying coldness down her spine. "I know those ways."

Jessica was shivering with an unnamed fear and couldn't begin to imagine what Metcalf must be feeling.

"And then there are ways of killing a man that are slow and excruciatingly painful." Segundo's voice had acquired a note of anticipation. "I know those ways also."

Expecting to see the blade pressed home, into Josh Metcalf's throat, Jessica's mind went numb. Her heartbeat thundered in every pulse in her body.

"Wh-what do you want?" Metcalf's voice was little more than a quivery squeak. "I-I have some money. You . . ."

"Money gained from the sale of stolen cattle," Segundo cut him off with soft harshness. "You bastard. I wouldn't touch your tainted money."

"Then . . . what?" Metcalf sounded on the verge of tears.

"My woman."

"What? Who?"

"Jessica. She is mine."

Jessica's trembling body jolted. His woman! Her fear stunned mind flared with alerted alarm. His woman! She was no man's woman, would never be any man's possession! How dare he assume rights over her, as if she were a thing! How dare . . . Jessica's raving thoughts were scattered by the low, scary sound of Segundo's voice.

". . . and now there is nothing more left for you here, Metcalf," he was saying. "I think it would be healthier for you in another place—perhaps another state."

"You can't scare me off!" Metcalf blustered. "I'm not alone here. I have men, you know."

"Yes, your hired guns. There are many here with a longing to meet your men." Segundo's voice was even more frightening for the thread of satisfaction woven through it. "I have heard mentioned a kind of party for you and your men, a party with a rope and a tree branch."

In the watery light, Jessica could actually see Josh Metcalf swallow. She unconsciously mirrored his action.

"That's lynching!" Metcalf yelped. "They wouldn't!"

"No?" Segundo said silkily. "You and your men have two days to be gone from here. If you doubt my words, remain and find out if they wouldn't."

Jessica didn't see Segundo's hand move, but it must have, for she heard Metcalf whimper.

"You cut me!" he cried. "I'm bleeding."

"A scratch." Segundo's tone dismissed the wound as of no account. "But a taste of what will happen if you ever again lay your thieving hands on my woman."

Jessica had heard enough. Careful not to make a sound, she backed away several paces, then turned and fled to the veranda side of the house. Not for an instant did she doubt that Segundo would hesitate in carrying out his threats, and not for an instant did she doubt that Metcalf and his men would be long gone from the area within the two day time limit.

My woman.

The phrase reverberated inside her head. The problem of the hit-and-run rustlings had been neatly solved. But, for Jessica, her own personal problem had just begun.

The problem's name was Segundo.

She tore around the side of the house at a run, then came to a jarring halt, blinking against the glare from the torches and lamps after the dimness of the moonlight. Shaking with the combined reactions of fear and outrage, she forced herself to breathe slow and deep to calm her twanging nerves. When a measure of her composure returned, she noticed that the crowd was considerably diminished.

The party was ending. The dance platform was empty. The musicians were standing in a small group, having a much-deserved last drink. Wagons, buckboards, and buggies were lined up in the yard. Sleepy children were being loaded into the various conveyances for the ride home. Other families, those from more distant regions, who would spend the night on the ranch and get an early start home in the morning, were drifting off, to the foreman's house, the married cowboys' dwellings, or the makeshift quarters they had arranged for themselves. Babies whimpered. Dogs barked. Last-minute thoughts were being spoken. Good nights were being exchanged.

Viewing the chaotic scene reminded Jessica of her duties as the daughter of the house. She longed for the

privacy of her own room, to sort out her thoughts, un-
tangle her jangling emotions, but knew her place was
with her parents and brother, bidding farewell to their
friends. Squaring her shoulders, she crossed the yard to
the departing guests.

"Oh, there you are, dear." Looking tired but happy,
Emily held out her hand to her daughter. "We were all
wondering where you'd disappeared to."

Coming up beside her mother, Jessica grasped her
hand and managed a ghost of a smile. "I've been off by
myself for a while." Her voice was strained; Jessica
hated lying at any time, but most especially to her
mother. "I've developed a dreadful headache." That,
at least, was the truth. Her temples were pounding as if
a herd of crazed cattle were stampeding through her
head.

"That's too bad," Emily commiserated with her.
"Have you taken a headache powder?"

"No, I haven't been in the house," Jessica said,
glancing around for an excuse to change the subject.
She found it in the absence of their nearest neighbor.
"Have Eric and his men left already?"

"Yes, a little while ago." Emily sighed. "Eric said he
needed to look in on his father."

Feeling a pang of sadness, Jessica unconsciously echoed her mother's sigh. As she always had, Emily had
sent an invitation to the elder Robertsons. As they always had, knowing that most of the other guests would
resent their presence, David and Inga had sent their
regrets through Eric. Their son faced any opposition to
his presence at any gathering with stoic determination.

A feeling of despair settled on Jessica, despair and
compassion for the outrage of discrimination her friends

had suffered over the years. Bigotry sickened her, which was why she'd been so shocked to hear Metcalf call Segundo a dirty greaser. Not wanting to think of that ghastly scene, she pushed it from her mind.

"Is Mr. Robertson's condition getting worse?" she asked, genuinely concerned for the older man.

"I'm afraid so." Emily shook her head. "It's a pity. David was always such a robust man." She frowned, then literally shook herself out of the doldrums. "But, come," she said, tugging on Jessica's hand. "I see the Bensons' are about ready to pull out. We must say good-bye to them."

To Jessica the good-byes seemed to go on forever. Her headache was approaching the blinding stage by the time they waved the last wagon off. Segundo had not put in an appearance. She hadn't caught as much as a glimpse of him since she'd run from that awful scene at the back of the house.

Not that she wanted to see him, Jessica assured herself, shuddering in remembrance of the terrifying deadliness of him. She didn't. Now if she could only convince her traitorous body of her mind's decision.

It was after eleven o'clock. Jessica had been up since before dawn. And tomorrow was a working day. Smothering a yawn behind her hand, she said good night to her family and went to her room. She felt grimy, overtired, and emotionally drained, and longed for a soothing bath before crawling into bed.

A quick glance into the standing mirror brought a grimace to Jessica's lips. The puff-sleeved, white cotton blouse and navy umbrella-style skirt that had looked so crisp and pristine that morning were now wilted and soiled. Shifting her brooding gaze from her reflection, she peeled the garments in layers from her body and stared through her bedroom window.

The moonlit yard was quiet. Everyone had settled in for the night, the cowboys in the bunkhouse, the stay-over guests in their various accommodations, her parents and brother in their respective rooms.

Where was Segundo?

The thought induced a shiver inside Jessica. Turning away from the window, she pulled on her wrapper, lowered the wick on the lamp on her dresser, and quietly left the room.

Standing naked beside his bedroll beneath a tree some distance from the house, Duncan dumped a bucket of water over his head to sluice away the remaining flecks of soap suds clinging to his muscle-tautened body. The cold water drew goosebumps to the surface of his skin but was ineffectual against the hot fury raging unabated in his mind.

Dark and savage atavistic urges had begun emerging from deep within his subconscious mind with his first sight of Jessica dancing in another man's arms. For most of the long day, Duncan had fought the driving impulses, but he'd lost the battle when Metcalf drew her away from the crowd.

Duncan had promised himself he'd have Jessica after the business of Metcalf was completed.

And now Metcalf was finished. Duncan was as certain of that as he was his own name. Though no intellectual giant, Metcalf was wily, and smart enough to realize that when ranchers talked about a hanging, they weren't just flapping their gums in the breeze. Necks had been stretched before, and Metcalf knew that as well. His hired guns were outnumbered, and their necks were as precious to them as Metcalf's was to him. The hard cases would cut and run.

Metcalf was definitely finished.

Now the *segundo* was going after his woman.

Ignoring the cautioning voice of reason he had adopted after years of studying and assimilating knowledge, and the disciplines of control and precepts of nonviolence he had embraced, Duncan had been following the dictates of instinct when he'd trailed Metcalf and Jessica to the back of the house. Now, hours later, with intellect and knowledge consumed by blind anger, he continued along the path of pure instinct.

Still naked except for the breechcloth his uncle had ceremoniously presented to him the week before, Duncan stepped from the shadows into the moonlight, then moved as silent as the mild breeze wafting across the ranch yard.

Duncan knew that Jessica's bedroom was situated above the veranda, overlooking the yard. A soft glow from a lamp illuminated her bedroom window. After noiselessly scaling the veranda post, he climbed the sloping roof. The window was open a few inches. Through the lace curtains at the window, he could see that the room was empty.

Where was Jessica?

He slid the window up as far as it would go, slipped inside, then cast a quick glance around the room. All was quiet. The bedding was turned down. A long cotton nightdress lay along the foot end of the bed. But where was Jessica?

His tread soundless on the Aubusson carpet covering the planked floor, Duncan crossed the room to the open door. The lamp on the dresser by the doorway cast a dim light into the hallway. With his senses alert to the slightest noise, he picked up the muted sound of splashing water at the end of the hallway.

Jessica was taking a bath.

A memory scent of her soap permeated his senses. With his inner eye, Duncan visualized Jessica, luxuriating in the bath, her skin slick and rosy, her nipples tight and pouting.

A sensual shudder streaked through his body, intensifying his need, heightening his arousal.

Intrusion! the inner voice of reason cried, attempting to break through the fog of desire blanketing his mind. The voice gave Duncan pause . . . but only for an instant.

Intrusion? Duncan examined the word. In all decency, could he intrude on her privacy, her person?

The sound of another splash reached him. The vision of her, naked and wet, filled his mind, muffling the voice of reason. Hesitancy retreated before the overwhelming advance of passion and anticipation.

Yes! Duncan silenced the inner voice with savage intent. Jessica was his. He would have her.

His strong features set into unrelenting lines of determination, Duncan moved to position himself between the wall and the door. Still and poised, he waited with stoic patience for his prey.

A floorboard in the hallway creaked. A faint smile shadowed Duncan's lips. Jessica was coming.

Her body relaxed from the bath, and half asleep on her feet, Jessica entered her room and quietly shut the door. Yawning, she rose to her toes to blow out the lamp, then tugged free the slipknot in her belt and removed her wrapper as she walked to the bed. She was reaching for her nightdress when a broad hand curled around her throat, freezing her in place, arm outstretched, fingers spread.

Fear exploded inside Jessica. A scream rose in her throat, only to be trapped there by the slight pressure of a thumb against her windpipe and a warning whisper in her ear.

"Not a sound, Jessica."

Segundo! Jessica's mind whirled. It was late. Everyone else was asleep. What was Segundo doing in the house? In her bedroom! What did he want?

His woman. The answer slammed into her, leaving her cold and weak. Suddenly wide awake, and more frightened than she had ever been, Jessica fought to stem a rising tide of panic.

Forgetting his warning, she blurted out, "Wh-what . . . ?" Her voice and breath were cut off by a brief increase of pressure against her throat.

"Softly," he murmured, so close to her ear she could feel his lips brush her skin.

"What do you want?" Jessica's voice was so faint it was barely audible.

"You."

Hearing her fear confirmed had a strange effect on Jessica. Anger shot steel into her spine. She was still afraid, but now she was mad as well. She would not be violated! At least, not without a fight.

"No!" The denial leapt from her lips in a harsh whisper of determination.

"Yes." His voice was as soft, and as adamant.

"I'll fight you."

Segundo laughed softly and drew a shiver from her by gliding the tip of one finger down the length of her spine . . . her naked spine. "There are ways. . . ."

His voice of here and now faded, overshadowed inside Jessica's mind by the echo of his chilling voice of earlier that evening.

There are ways of killing a man . . .

Her father! Her brother! Breathing ceased. Her mother! Terror was a colder hand gripping Jessica's throat than the warm fingers of her assailant. But he wouldn't hurt Ben or Parker, and surely not her mother! Would he? Her memory flashed, and she could see, hear Metcalf's whimpering fear. Segundo was capable, more than capable, he was lethal.

Her anger was gone, banished by the fear expanding inside her. Only determination remained. Jessica knew she would do anything to spare her family—anything, even if that anything meant submitting to this man's lust.

Prepared to plead, beg if necessary, with him, Jessica turned to face him. Her voice died a soundless death as her body made contact with his.

Segundo was as naked as she!

The realization set off a chain reaction inside her. A tremor erupted in the depths of her being, growing steadily stronger as it worked its quaking way to the surface of her skin. A gasp broke free of her constricted throat when the hand hovering at the base of her spine flattened and drew her closer to the musky warmth of him.

"You tremble." His voice was hypnotic in its very softness. "Are you cold?" He didn't wait for a response, but gathered her into an intimate embrace. "Let me warm you."

Jessica couldn't think, couldn't speak, could only feel her soft feminine curves conforming to the hard, angular contours of his body. The strength of his maleness pressed against her, making her startlingly aware of the extent of his arousal, and the scrap of cloth covering him.

What was he wearing? The inanity of the thought struck Jessica, bringing a bubble of near-hysterical laughter to her trembling lips. What difference did it make? It wasn't enough, not nearly enough. She could feel the broad expanse of smooth skin on his muscle-ridged chest and the lightly haired roughness of his taut thighs.

The feel of him, his very maleness induced a strange weakness in Jessica. Seeking support, she reached out for something to cling to. That something happened to be his shoulders.

"Yes." Segundo's lips were close, too close to her own. "Hold on to me, *querida*. Hold on tight."

No! Made aware of her unconscious action, Jessica released her grip, then immediately clutched him again, fingers flexing, nails digging into his flesh, as he swept her up, into his arms, and carried her to her bed.

Jessica raked her mind, searching for a means of escape, as he settled her on the soft down mattress. He straightened to his full height to remove what she could now see was an Indian breechcloth. That wasn't all she could see. Her thoughts fragmented as she stared, wide-eyed and fearful, at the magnificence of his male form.

Jessica had never seen a completely naked man before, but even in her innocence she knew Segundo possessed a singular masculine perfection. Speckled moonlight played over his body, delineating his sharp facial features, defining the musculature of his tall, finely honed frame, revealing the sheer size, power, and strength of his thrusting manhood.

He moved toward her. A thrill pierced her trembling body. The bedsprings creaked as he slid onto the mattress beside her. Her thoughts went wild, scampering in a dozen different directions at once.

Without a murmur, he drew her into his arms.

She had to think of something, some way, to stop him! But what? How?

One hard thigh slid over hers, pinning her to the bed.

Jessica thought of forcefully raising her knee and started to move one leg, then she thought of her family. Her leg went limp. She couldn't take a chance on endangering her family—no matter what the cost to herself, her pride.

His mouth covered hers. His lips were hard, sensuous, frighteningly enticing.

Jessica tasted a different flavor of fear. A spark ignited in the core of her femininity, quickly spreading tongues of fire throughout her body. Her breath quickened, while her mind screamed a denial of the response she was feeling.

Her options reduced to one, Jessica forced a stillness into her treacherous, aroused body and lay stiff but passive in his embrace.

His passion mounting to the limits of his control, Duncan stroked the satin smoothness of Jessica's body as he deepened his kiss, teasing the inside of her mouth in an attempt to draw a response from her.

Jessica lay still as death beneath him.

Frustration sank its claws into him. Dammit! He raged in silent despair. Why didn't she fight him as she'd vowed she would? He could have handled her if she had. Resistance from her would have fueled the fury driving him. If she had struggled, grasped the whip laying useless on the bedside table, Duncan felt, believed, he could have taken her without a twinge of remorse. But this coldness, this stillness she maintained, was chipping away his determination.

Tearing his mouth from hers, Duncan raised his head to stare at Jessica. Moonlight played over her pale face, revealing the shadows of fear in the depths of her gray eyes.

Her fear of him was his undoing.

In that instant, Duncan knew he couldn't do it, couldn't force himself to take from her the satisfaction his clamoring body was demanding.

Duncan had never in his life used his superior strength against a woman. And, of all women, he knew he could not deliberately hurt Jessica and continue to live.

His body ached with his need of her, but more than release, he needed her response, the fire and passion she had revealed to him that day on the veranda.

He loved her. He would kill for her. He would die for her. He would not, could not be the instrument of her pain.

Lowering his head, Duncan took her trembling mouth with gentle care. One kiss, he thought, savoring the taste of her with tempered hunger. Just one more kiss, he vowed, and then he'd leave her in peace.

Jessica's lips were soft but cool. Hurting from a need that went much deeper than physical desire, Duncan was about to lift his mouth from hers when he felt her first tentative response. Excitement singing in his veins, he held his breath and deepened the kiss. There was a moment of nerve-stretching hesitation then, with a low moan, Jessica parted her lips and surrendered her mouth to him.

Murmuring soft inciting words in several languages, Duncan called on all his acquired expertise to fan the spark of her response into a blaze of passion.

Jessica's body was on fire. Her mind was consumed by the flames. Thought was suspended. Sensations dominated. And the sensations were delicious.

Never would Jessica have believed that a man could give her body and senses such exquisite pleasure. And yet, from the moment of her initial response, Segundo had proceeded to teach her the wonders of shared intimacy.

Segundo's touch was a wonder in itself. He did not attempt to overpower her with his masculine prowess, like a prancing stud stallion or snorting bull. He seemed to know that she would recoil from a blatant sexual assault.

Instead, his touch gentle, careful, Segundo seduced Jessica's mind and senses with the delicate caress of his hands and mouth and soft, exciting voice.

He whispered words both shocking and alluring, cajoling her to explore with him the ancient realm of erotic play and drenching sensual satisfaction.

Beguiled by his enticements, Jessica surrendered herself into his keeping for the journey into what was, for her, the uncharted territory of the senses.

For Jessica, the journey was an awakening of earth-shattering proportions.

Jessica had always believed that a kiss was merely the touching of two pairs of lips, pleasant perhaps, but not a momentous event. Segundo taught her the error in her innocent reasoning.

His mouth alone was an education in erotica.

How was it possible that one mouth, however attractive, could induce such delightful sensations? Jessica asked herself—while she still possessed the ability to question. The seeming contradictions contained in his kisses were a source of amazement to her.

Segundo's mouth felt hot against hers, yet caused a tingling chill inside Jessica. His mouth was wet, yet she felt a curious dry ache in her throat. His tongue probed the inside of her mouth with delicate care, yet she felt pierced to the depths of her being. His lips teased and played with hers, yet she felt strangely tormented.

Altogether, the conflicting qualities of a simple kiss were more than her detaching mind could assimilate, so she gave up the effort and gave in to the wonder of it all.

Like a student starved for knowledge, Jessica mirrored each successive action of her master teacher. When Segundo sensitized her skin with light strokes of his hands and fingertips, she reciprocated by smoothing her palms over his muscle-taut back and broad chest. When he glided his tongue down her arched throat to her breast, she returned the caress by tasting his salt-flavored skin. And, when he took the tight tip of her breast into his mouth and raked his teeth over it, she responded by sinking her teeth into his shoulder and arching into the pleasure-pain he inflicted on her.

Jessica's mind was long lost to her, and she was a quivering mass of tension, trepidation, and anticipation by the time Segundo slid his perspiration-slick body into the heated valley of her parted thighs. Holding his passion-tense body still at the portals of her femininity, his beautiful turquoise eyes stared intently into hers.

"Do you want this, *querida*?" Segundo's voice was soft, hoarse with strain.

Want it? Jessica blinked in surprise. Didn't he know? Couldn't he see that she felt she'd die if she didn't have it . . . have him? She stared at him in confusion.

"Do you?" he persisted. "I need an answer, Jessica. I need to hear you say it."

"Yes! I want it!" Jessica's voice was little more than a dry rasp. "I want you!" With a show of abandonment that would have shocked her an hour ago, she raised her hips to him in invitation and demand. "Now!"

"And I want you." Segundo moved to press his manhood against her. "Now."

Jessica felt a testing probe and then a quick, clean thrust, wrenching an involuntary cry from her as the hard extension of his body pierced her maidenhood. Her muscles contracted in automatic reaction to the sharp pain caused by his invasion. Segundo went still inside her.

"The discomfort will soon subside," he murmured, lowering his head to bestow a gentle kiss on her surprise-parted lips. "And your body will adjust to the fullness of mine."

Within minutes his reassurance was proved by the

easing of the tension in her muscles and the heightening spiral of tension inside Jessica. Suddenly she was desperate for some unnamed something, and grasping Segundo's flanks, she drew him closer, deeper into her body.

Segundo responded with swift effectiveness. With ever-increasing thrusts of his passion-taut body, he drove her to the brink of sensual madness, and then, his harshly drawn breaths echoed by her own, he tipped them both over the edge, into the explosive swirl of shuddering, pulsating release.

Shattered by the experience, Jessica lost consciousness for an instant. When she revived, Segundo lay sprawled on the rumpled bed beside her, drained and satiated.

Turning her head on the sweat-dampened pillow, Jessica stared at the beauty of his sharp features. His eyes were closed, his face free of tension. In relaxation, Segundo appeared vulnerable, not at all the arrogant, dominant male she knew him to be.

It was an illusion and not to be trusted, Jessica thought, shaking her head in denial of his benign appearance. As if he felt, sensed her thoughts, Segundo stirred and opened his eyes to stare at her.

"Come here to me." His whisper held more command than coaxing invitation.

Although Jessica's body and senses had been gloriously seduced, as the haze of physical satisfaction dissipated, her mind reasserted its authority. Recalling where she was, who she was, and who he was, she shook her head.

"No."

A smile twitched the corners of his lips. "Very well,

then, I shall come to you." Moving with lightning speed, he rolled to her, over her, caging her within the bars of his strong arms. Dipping his head, he captured her mouth beneath his. His hard kiss was a benediction and a punishment.

Jessica tried to withstand his sensual inducement but was quickly caught, consumed by the fire of arousal. This time Segundo's lovemaking was fierce and hot, his body a weapon used to bring her to sobbing defeat. His seed was still spilling into her when he stared down at her, his features set into harsh lines of determination.

"You are mine now." Segundo's voice held flat finality. "You belong to me."

"Never." Jessica glared at him, anger and defiance rising within, vanquishing the lethargic afterglow instilled by his lovemaking. "I will never *belong* to any man."

"No?" His expression sardonic, Segundo glanced down, to where their bodies were joined together. He was laughing softly when he raised his head to look at her. "You belong to me, are a part of me now. You will always belong to me."

"No!" Furious, with him and with herself for succumbing to him, Jessica pushed against his chest, dislodging him from her. "I said never, and I meant never." After rolling away from him, she scrambled from the bed and ran to the open window. "I'm a person, not a possession." Lifting her head, she stood naked and regal in the waning moonlight. "I don't need you or any man to validate my existence."

Segundo frowned. "I never said—"

"You've said enough." She cut him off ruthlessly. "I've heard enough." Jessica motioned at the window.

"Now, get out of here," she ordered in a raw voice. "Or I'll scream so loud the cowboys in the next county will hear me."

Expecting an argument or another sensual attack, Jessica was amazed when Segundo shrugged and rose from the bed. Narrow-eyed and suspicious, she watched as he fastened the breechcloth around his hips, then paced across the floor to her. She stiffened when he raised a hand to her face. Smiling, he grasped her chin, lowered his head, and brushed his mouth over hers.

"You are mine, Jess," he murmured against her lips.

Jessica opened her mouth to refute him; he forestalled her by kissing her again.

"It will soon be dawn," he murmured, releasing her. Moving with the silent swiftness of a shade, he stepped out the window, pausing to call back to her in a commanding whisper, "Don't come out to work today." The whisper grew faint as he moved away. "Stay here and sleep."

13

❧

The crack of the whip reverberated on the clear mountain air, and a wild-eyed cow bellowed and burst from its hiding place. Flicking the whip overhead to keep the animal moving, Jessica followed the cow out of the bush and into the meadow nestled in the mountain foothills.

It was the third day of the roundup, and Jessica was tired, but then, she had been tired since the day of the party. Sleeping on a bedroll on the ground had certainly not made her feel any better. Sleeping or, more accurately, trying to sleep on the ground with Segundo stretched out less than three feet away from her was hardly conducive to calming her rattled senses. Her mental condition didn't bear thinking about, and yet Jessica could think of little else.

After Segundo had faded into the darkness that disastrous morning, Jessica had paced the floor, railing at him and at herself in turn.

How dared he presume to order her not to work? she had seethed, glaring at the open window through which he had disappeared. Who did he think he was?

He was the man who had robbed her of her virginity! That's who he was.

The thought had brought Jessica up short, trembling with rage and resentment. The overbearing, arrogant bastard! He had forced her to yield to him, that son of a . . .

At that point, Jessica's conscience intruded, reminding her of her unbridled response to his lovemaking. Segundo had not forced her to do anything. She had given herself with shameful abandon.

The galling acknowledgment stole the thunder from Jessica's fury. Overwhelmed by despair and self-disgust, she had stared at the rumpled bed, hating herself for the pleasure she had derived from their encounter, even as her body tingled with remembered excitement.

Had she seriously considered that she was falling in love with him—a man she knew only as the *segundo*?

The question tormented Jessica with unrelenting persistence throughout every hour of every day. In response to the nagging memory of that afternoon when she had first pondered the ridiculous idea, she retaliated self-defensively by adroitly avoiding the issue.

Love him? Jessica reflected, shaking her head to dislodge the unpalatable notion. How could anyone love a

man who would invade her bedroom, and her person,
and make her enjoy it . . . against her will, of course.

Love him? She didn't even like him!

But, like him or not, Jessica knew she had to tolerate
him. He was still, after all, her father's *segundo.*

Segundo.

Merely thinking his name, or more precisely his title
—she didn't know his name—caused mental disrup-
tion. Ever since he had left her, naked and furious, that
predawn, Jessica had been fighting an inner war of
emotional conflict.

How could she ever face him again? How could she
face anyone? By surrendering to him, and to her own
sensuality, a sensuality Jessica had not as much as suspected she possessed, she had betrayed every principle
of independence she had fought so hard to maintain.

Jessica had longed to obey his whispered command,
but her pride had denied her the luxury of hiding in her
room, in her bed.

Her bed!

The thought had galvanized Jessica into action. Weariness fled as she lighted the lamp and walked to the
bed. She groaned in despair as she bent low to examine
the bedding. The sheet was stained with the proof of
her maidenhood.

She could not let her mother see that sheet! Muttering imprecations against the man who had initiated the
maiden flow, Jessica pulled the offending sheet from
the bed. Then, slipping into her wrapper, she'd tiptoed
from the bedroom to the bathroom.

Filling the tub with cold water, Jessica had submerged herself, scrubbing the sweat from her body and
the traces of semen-diluted blood from her inner

thighs. When she had finished, she dumped the sheet into the water.

It was not yet dawn when Jessica, dressed in her usual work day garb, crept from the house to pin the spot-free sheet to the wash line.

Tired but determined, Jessica had presented herself for the morning muster. Her father took her appearance as a matter of course. Segundo leveled a forbidding frown at her.

Her chin cocked at a defiant angle, Jessica had silently dared him to deny her the right to join the roundup. When he remained silent, she felt a tiny thrill of victory.

That was before she learned that Segundo would be bossing the roundup crew.

He watched over her like a fluttery mama hen with a newly hatched chick.

Jessica looked exhausted. Duncan felt a twinge of guilt for the extreme paleness of her skin and the purplish darkness under her eyes. She appeared about to cave in, and he was determined to be there to catch her if she did.

Although the business of the rustlings had been resolved and Josh Metcalf and his hired guns effectively ousted from the vicinity, to all intents and purposes Duncan was still the *segundo* of the B-Bar-R.

Duncan had wanted to reveal his true identity the morning after the party—and a more personal and intense, event—but had acquiesced to Ben Randall's request to continue the masquerade until the roundup was over or the real foreman, Frank, returned from Argentina.

Though at first he had derived amusement from playing the role, Duncan now chafed with impatience to have done with the farce. He wanted Jessica, physically and legally. He wanted to go home, taking her with him as his bride. But he had given Ben his word, and he would keep it. Duncan would play the role of *segundo* for a few more weeks.

With utterly supreme, masculine confidence, Duncan didn't doubt for an instant that Jessica would accept a proposal of marriage from him, once she was informed of his true identity and rank.

Weren't American women, at least the daughters of wealthy men, not merely eager but avid to marry a British title?

Like any other informed man of the times, Duncan was fully aware of the growing number of young, and not so young, American heiresses whose fathers were providing enormous dowries to arrange a union between their little darlings and some impoverished members of the British peerage.

Duncan Frazer, Lord Rayburne, was far from impoverished. Quite the opposite. With his vast estate holdings, both in England and Scotland, his lucrative shipping lines, and his seeming luck playing the stock market, Duncan was a very wealthy man,—even without counting the value of the sixty-thousand-acre Circle-F spread and the stock on it.

While he kept a narrowed eye on the slender back of his target, a cynical smile curved Duncan's thin lips. Oh yes, even with her defiant attitude and her show of resistance, Duncan was quite confident that Jessica would leap at the opportunity to accept a marriage proposal from him.

Anticipation of the nuptial event tingled through
Duncan, stirring his senses, arousing his passion. Thrilling to the memory of the intimacy they had shared, the
incredible sensations he had experienced while his
body was buried deeply within the moist, silken heat of
Jessica, Duncan shifted in the saddle and silently
cursed the necessity for deception and delay.

He was hurting for her, wanting her so badly he
could taste his need for her. One thought alone kept
him from shrugging off the responsibility he had accepted.

It was only a matter of time.

In the meantime, there was work to be done.

In his position of *segundo* and roundup boss, Duncan
was in charge of the operation. The work was hard and
demanding, but it was going well. Each day the herd
summer grazing in the small mountain meadow had
been increased by the strays rounded up by the crew of
nine plus Duncan, who worked as diligently as any of
the others.

They worked in pairs, scouring the bush and foothills
for strays. Duncan had paired himself with Jessica.

Now, watching her turn her cow pony back in the
direction of the hills after adding yet another wandering bovine to the herd, Duncan trailed along behind
her.

Thanking the talents of Shaky, the irascible wrangler, for her expertly trained cow pony, Jessica allowed
herself a few precious moments of rest while her horse
picked its way through the hills in search of more
strays. Made vulnerable by the weight of weariness
pressing into her, Jessica's shoulders slumped, and her

mind wandered, recalling the morning of the roundup
muster.

Poor Parker got stuck with the job of mending
fences. Jessica yawned through a rueful smile. This was
the first year since his fourteenth summer that her
brother was not with the roundup crew in the summer
pasture. She could still see the expressions that had
washed over her brother's face on hearing their father's
work instructions. Parker's initial reaction of shock had
swiftly changed to resentment toward the *segundo*, resentment that had been reflected on the faces of every
one of the hired hands.

That was five days ago. Since then Jessica had wit-
nessed the change in their crew. Slowly, as Segundo
proved himself, his worth in the eyes of the cowboys,
their resentment had changed from reluctant acceptance to full and unconditional respect.

The *segundo* knew what he was about.

He had earned Jessica's grudging respect as well
. . . at least as far as his competence was concerned.
Yet, while Segundo had managed to elicit her respect,
he had also reactivated the nagging sense of suspicion
Jessica had felt at odd moments ever since his sudden
and unexpected arrival on the scene.

Supposedly Segundo was a virtual stranger to Wyoming, and yet he appeared to know the contours and
vagaries of the terrain as well as, if indeed not better
than, the oldest hand in the outfit, and even Jessica
herself.

There was something she was missing, Jessica
mused, stifling another yawn. Something about the
segundo . . .

"Where are you going, Jess?" Segundo's soft call scattered her thoughts. "Do you know?"

Jessica stiffened with resentment unrelated to his efficiency as roundup boss. She resented his very presence, dogging her throughout every working hour. She resented his taunting voice, his knowing eyes, his too-familiar use of her name. But, however intrusive, his nudging question did bring to her a startling awareness of where she was.

"Yes," she called back, making a show of casually scanning the immediate area. What she saw instilled a deep feeling of chagrin. While stealing a few moments of rest and allowing her tired mind to wander, her horse had carried her steadily upward, into the less-accessible, higher foothills. Impatient with herself, Jessica naturally retaliated against him. "And don't call me Jess!"

Segundo responded with a maddeningly amused laugh and another blandly voiced question. "Exactly how many strays were you expecting to find up here?"

Disgruntled but trapped by her own inattention, Jessica was about to admit to being caught napping, when her horse stepped out of the trees and into a small, grassy clearing. As she reined in the horse, she saw a blur of brown movement among the trees on the other side of the clearing.

"That one hiding over there," Jessica said in tones of condescending superiority, indicating the area with the extended whip handle.

"Indeed?" Segundo's voice was dry with disbelief. After bringing his horse to a halt beside her, he dismounted and sent an idle glance across the clearing.

"Yes, indeed." Jessica made a face at his averted head. "I just saw—"

"Quiet." His voice was low, intent; his body was still, taut, alert. "Don't move, Jess." While he muttered the warning, Segundo slowly raised his hand and slid his Winchester from the saddle scabbard.

Mystified but alerted, Jessica glanced around her, looking for the cause of his sudden wariness. "What's the mat—" she began, frowning, as she swung her leg over the horse and jumped to the ground.

"Be quiet," he ordered in a harsh whisper.

Confused yet certain he had heard or sensed some impending danger, Jessica clamped her lips against the questions in her mind and waited for his next command. At that instant, all hell seemed to break loose. Both of the horses snorted, rolled their eyes, and danced backward. With a loud bellow of fear, the cow she had spotted came crashing out of the dense undergrowth beneath the trees. Loping behind the cow was the largest bear she had ever seen.

Jessica froze for a moment, staring in fascinated disbelief at the huge grizzly. Bawling in terror, the white-faced bovine lumbered into the clearing. Moving at incredible speed, the silver-tipped, yellow-haired bear swiftly overtook the cow. At first, intent on its prey, the beast didn't notice its two human observers.

As terrified as the cow, Jessica tore her gaze from the bear to look at the silent man by her side.

Segundo stood erect and alert, his long legs slightly parted, his arms hanging loose at his sides. His right hand confidently gripped the Winchester at midthigh.

The frozen scene was shattered by the frightened screams and prancing movements of the two horses. The grizzly lifted and swung its enormous head. Sight-ing them, it roared in rage at being interrupted and rose on its hind legs to its full height of nearly eight feet.

Jessica's throat went bone dry. Without conscious direction, her hand lifted to grasp the butt of her rifle protruding from the saddle scabbard.

The snarling grizzly started toward them.

In a slow, smooth movement, Segundo raised the Winchester to his shoulder. The cracking report from the rifle reverberated on the clear mountain air.

The grizzly kept coming at them.

More frightened than she had ever been before, Jessica settled the rifle butt against her shoulder, sighted, and gently squeezed the trigger.

Duncan felt as well as heard the shot fired a few inches from his right shoulder. He saw the enraged bear shudder. Even as he drew the trigger back on his own rifle, a sensation of deep satisfaction rippled through him, mingling with the fear churning in his gut.

The Winchester continued to speak as unformed and undefined feelings swirling inside him conveyed messages to Duncan.

He had caught a glimpse of Jessica's expression when the bear broke from the tree cover. She was frozen with terror. Still, she stood firm by his side, firing off shots in precise timing between his own.

This was a woman to live for—or die with.

As if impervious to the lethal doses of lead slamming into his eight-hundred-pound body, the bear remained upright and moving. Duncan's shirt was stuck to his back with sweat and the small hairs at his nape were raised and quivering, when he fired off a shot that went straight into the bear's brain.

The monstrous animal crashed to the ground less than two yards from Duncan's feet.

For long seconds silence held sway. The sweet mountain air was stained by the putrid stench of the dead animal.

Numbed by the experience, his breathing harsh and labored, Duncan stared at the felled beast. Then feeling returned in an exultant, euphoric rush, tingling through him, arousing him, impelling him to celebrate life in the face of death. From his right came the sound of wracking sobs of relief.

Jessica. Her name shuddered through him, intensifying the feelings rioting inside him. Duncan turned to look at her and had to bite back a reflexive groan. Never had he become so hard so quickly.

Stepping to her, he plucked the rifle from her unresisting fingers, then sheathed both weapons in their respective scabbards. He began unbuttoning his shirt as he turned back to face her.

"Take off your clothes."

"What?" Startled by Segundo's soft command, Jessica swallowed a final sob and stared at him in blank confusion. "What did you say?"

"I said, take off your clothes," he repeated, tossing his shirt aside. His hands moved to the buckle of the gunbelt riding his hips. "Now."

"But . . ." Jessica's voice cracked and she had to wet her lips before she could find the voice to continue. "Why?"

Segundo's lips curved in a smile; Jessica felt it in the core of her femininity.

"You don't mean . . . you can't mean . . ." Sputtering to a halt, Jessica glanced around her, shuddering as her gaze touched then shied away from the dead bear. Her eyes grew wide with surprise, even as a shocking burst of sensual excitement flared to life deep in her being. "Here?"

"Here." No longer smiling, Segundo set aside the gunbelt and went to work on the buttons on his pants, drawing her attention to the bulge straining against the material. "And now."

Fighting against a sudden, insidious desire to obey him, Jessica gulped and shook her head. "No." She straightened her spine and thrust out her chin. "I won't."

"You will." Segundo's pants slid down the length of his long muscular legs and bunched around the top of his boots. Crossing his ankles, he dropped smoothly to the cool grass and began tugging on his boots.

Jessica lowered her stormy gaze and felt her mouth go dry. Seated with his knees apart, Segundo's hard manhood was blatantly outlined by the soft cotton material of his underdrawers. Wetting her parched lips, she hastily shifted her gaze, and found herself staring into his shrewd turquoise eyes. Denying to herself the mounting excitement he had obviously seen reflected in her eyes, Jessica shook her head once more. "I will not," she said, beginning to tremble as he set one boot aside. "You can't make me do anything." Out of the corner of her eye, she saw him remove the other boot.

"Can't I?" In one swift, lithe move, Segundo was standing upright, stepping out of his bunched pants. The intense look of him sent a thrill skittering through her. The sensation splintered into thousands of shards of shimmering emotion when he casually flicked open his underdrawers and let them fall to the ground.

"Oh, my God!" The involuntary cry burst from Jessica's clogged throat at the sight of him. Against her will, she stared in wide-eyed fascination at his erect and thrusting sex. Seen in broad daylight, the sheer size of him was mind-bending and sent a fleeting thought searing through her mind: Had she actually sheathed this magnificently endowed man within her slender body?

Backing away, her nerves jangling, her trepidation warring with heightened sexual anticipation, Jessica glanced around to locate her horse. With the danger from the bear effectively removed, the animal was placidly grazing near the center of the sun-splashed clearing.

Deciding his nudity put Segundo at a distinct disadvantage, Jessica took off at a run. Upon reaching the horse, she grabbed the reins and leapt into the saddle. The startled horse reared, then shot forward, heading for the opposite side of the clearing. A disturbing pang of regret diminishing her feeling of elation for having outwitted him, she cast a quick glance over her shoulder and gasped in astonishment.

His red-tinged black hair streaming behind him, and laughing as if he were deriving immense enjoyment from the exercise, Segundo was sprinting after her, his long legs closing the distance between them. Within moments he was pacing alongside her horse. Grasping the reins, he brought the quivering animal to a shuddering halt.

"Get down, Jess." Segundo was no longer laughing. His eyes and voice were as hard as his body.

Stunned by his performance, Jessica sat staring at him in mute amazement. She couldn't move, but her mind spun crazily, shooting sparks of jumbled thoughts, all of which converged into two incredible, unbelievable ideas.

Segundo had the savage look of an Indian on the warpath . . . and he had outrun her horse!

Jessica's bemusement was ended abruptly, and she gave a strangled yelp, when he grasped her around the waist and hauled her from the saddle.

"I'm losing patience, Jess," Segundo growled, tightening his hold at her waist and giving her a light shake. "Get undressed at once—or I'll tear your clothes off of you."

His fierce, resolute look convinced Jessica that his threat was not an idle one. His sharply delineated features were set into harsh lines of determination. Positive the *segundo* would not hesitate to rip her clothing to shreds if she defied him, Jessica raised her hands to her shirt. Her trembling fingers fumbled with the buttons. Cursing with impatience at her ineptitude, Segundo slid his hands around to her waist to loosen her belt buckle and subsequently her trousers.

Within moments, harrowing and too few for Jessica's peace of mind, her clothing littered the ground, and she lay naked on her back in the sweet-smelling grass, the *segundo* kneeling between her parted thighs.

"No, I don't want this. I don't want you!" Jessica's dry-voiced protest was a mere token. She knew it, but, more harrowing and shattering to her peace of mind was the realization that she couldn't wait to have the emptiness inside her body filled by the fullness of him.

"No?" Segundo's eyes, his entire body seemed to shimmer with vibrant, joyous life. His strong white teeth flashed in a quick, chiding smile. "You don't want

this?" Lowering his head, he drew a gasp from her by
flicking his tongue against the tight crest of one breast.
"Or this?" With tormenting effect, he traced a slow,
swirling pattern with the wet tip of his tongue from her
breast to her quivering belly. "Or this?" His lips
cleaved a path through the protective cluster of curls on
her mound. "Or even this?" His tongue plunged with
unerring and devastating accuracy, then gently lashed
against the most erotically sensitive spot on her body,
wrenching a hoarse cry of unbearable pleasure from
Jessica's throat.

Her cry of pleasure changed to a moan of protest
when he raised his head.

"Ahh, you do want it?" Segundo taunted her.

"Yes! Yes!" Mindless, abandoned, Jessica arched her
sensitized, sensation-hungry body to assist him when,
relenting with a soft chuckle of satisfaction, he lifted
her legs to his shoulders.

"What do you want?" Teasing her, Segundo slid her
legs back and forth, heating the backs of her thighs by
rubbing them against the smooth warm skin of his
shoulders.

"All of you. Everything!" Driven to the edge of endurance by his teasing, Jessica wantonly reached out to
grasp his head to draw him to her.

"But first, my mouth," he murmured, driving her
wild with his tiny, stinging kisses. "Yes?"

"Yes!" Jessica admitted, then cried out as he jerked
his head back to stare at her.

"Then say it," he demanded.

"Damn you! Damn you!" Jessica shouted, as angry
with him as she was desperate for him. "I want your
mouth!"

"And I want your . . ." Segundo's voice was muffled by her mat of curls.

Jessica was caught in the undertow of sensation, drowning in the sea of pleasure Segundo was creating within her with his hot mouth and searing tongue. Her muscles were clenched around the tension coiling inside her. Writhing in response to the fiery passion consuming her mind and body, she sobbed a pleading demand for release.

"Segundo . . . please . . . please . . . I can't bear it!"

"Not yet," Segundo refused her in a strained whisper as, grasping her legs, he lowered them and clasped them around his waist. "But soon." Murmuring the promise, he thrust his body into the depths of hers.

Jessica wouldn't have believed it possible for the tension to heighten or the pleasure to expand inside her, and yet she felt both unbelievable sensations when Segundo drove the silky extension of his body into hers. Clinging to him, reveling in him, she arched into the steadily increasing rhythm of his pounding thrusts.

The inner tension spiraled higher and higher, scoring their faces with strain, sheening their bodies with passion-drawn perspiration, and then it snapped, unleashing its fury in a shimmering shower of cascading pulsations.

From a far distance, Jessica heard her own ragged cry of release echoed by Segundo's savage-sounding shout of masculine triumph.

Several long minutes passed before Jessica, feeling somewhat as if she herself had expired, came to her senses and to the realization of her less-than-ladylike position. Drained but replete, she lay sprawled out on the ground in a pose of utter abandon. His breathing harsh and uneven, Segundo lay spent and heavy on top of her, his mouth pressed to her throat, his fingers coiled in her wildly tangled hair.

When and how had her braid become undone?

Jessica was pondering the thought when Segundo freed his hands, placed the palms on the ground to the sides and directly below her temples, and lifted his chest from her flattened breasts. Then, as he had on the never-to-be-forgotten dawn following the pre-roundup party, he stared with glittering intent into her love-clouded eyes.

"Once again I have staked my claim of ownership upon and within you," he said in tones of blatant possessiveness. "You are mine, Jess, admit it."

And, as she had on that same morning, Jessica steeled herself against him and the unthinkable emotions she felt stirring inside her for him.

"Never," she said in flat denial. "I told you before that I will never be owned by any man."

"You will see," Segundo persisted. "You are mine. You belong to me, as surely as I—"

"No, *you* will see," Jessica interrupted him angrily. "I belong to myself."

"Indeed?" His lips slanting into a superior smile, Segundo moved his hips into position between her thighs, then thrust his quickening shaft into her body. "Strange," he murmured when she arched into his spear. "But it would appear that *yourself* craves being owned by the impaling claim of *myself.*"

"Go to hell, Segundo," Jessica snarled between breaths already shortened by rising passion.

"I'd much rather take you to heaven, my Jess," he retorted, smiling into her misty, silvery eyes.

Night was falling by the time Jessica and Segundo returned to the roundup camp at the edge of the mountain meadow. The chill of the evening air could not match the cold hauteur within which Jessica had belatedly but resolutely withdrawn.

Exhausted yet unable to sleep, Jessica spent the night, a blanket wrapped around her shivering body, flaying herself for what she considered as an act of her own self-betrayal. She had shamed and humiliated herself by not only giving in to the *segundo*, but by taking from him, feeding her own newly discovered appetites, hungrily, greedily, eagerly.

Stiff in her night-chilled muscles as well as her regrouped defenses, Jessica was up and gathering her gear together as the pearl gray of predawn outlined the ghostly shapes of the trees ringing the meadow.

A light glowed from the cook tent and she could see the shadowy silhouette of the cook as he moved around inside, preparing the morning meal. The aroma of fresh coffee wafted to her on the cold mountain breeze. Longing for a cup of the bracing brew, Jessica paused then, grim-lipped with purpose, she continued fastening her bedroll behind her saddle.

"Where do you think you're going?"

Starting in shocked surprise at the sound of Segundo's soft voice, Jessica raised her hand to her mouth to stifle a shriek and whipped around. The sight of him sent a thrill of warning through her. His form was sharply angled in the dim light of dawn. The tugged-down flat brim of his hat and the long flowing serape he wore at night instead of a blanket intensified the foreign, exciting, and dark look of him. He was too appealing, too attractive, too much for her to deal with after a night of self-doubt and despair. "You frightened me," she said on an indrawn shuddering breath.

"Sorry. Coffee?" Segundo held out a steaming cup, as if a peace offering. "The first cup in the morning always tastes best."

Wanting to be off, get away from him, Jessica hesitated. The tantalizing scent weakened her resolve. Giving in to temptation, she accepted. In her haste, she had forgotten her gloves, and her hands felt chilled to the bone. With a sigh of gratitude, she wrapped her fingers around the liquid-warmed tin cup.

Sharp-eyed as usual, Segundo noticed both her action and her sigh. His own impatient-sounding sigh echoed hers. "Here." After pulling his own scarred gloves from his hands, he shoved them at her.

"No, I—" she began, shaking her head.

"Put them on, dammit!" His fingers brushed the back of her hand. "Your skin feels like ice."

Shivering more from his touch than from the cold, Jessica stepped back, out of harm's way, and sent a swift glance around the camp to see if his raised voice had roused the sleeping cowboys. The huddled forms on the ground remained still. Segundo recaptured her attention by plucking the cup from her fingers.

"I said, put the gloves on."

Jessica bristled at the command but, choosing prudence over an audience of eight ranch hands, she clamped her lips against a retort and took the gloves. The warmth of his skin clung to the lining, enveloping her hands and fingers in heat unrelated to the softened buckskin, causing a tremor from her fingernails to the short hairs at her nape.

"I asked where you were going," he reminded her, handing the cup to her once more.

Jessica was so very cold inside and his body warmth was so very near, so very tempting. God! She had to get away! The tremor tracing her spine increased. Her teeth began to chatter. Becoming desperate, she gulped the coffee and muttered over the rim, "I'm tired. I'm going home."

Moving closer to her, Segundo peered into her face. Alarm, or some other emotion, flared to life in his turquoise eyes. "Your eyes are too bright, and your face is flushed," he murmured. After raising his hand, he touched his fingers to her cheek. "You feel hot, and yet you're shivering, as if with cold." His voice was edged. "Jesus Christ . . . are you coming down with something?"

His touch scattered the shiver, sending it deep to her bones and to the outer surface of her skin, causing a visible shake. "No, of course not!" Jessica said, taking another step back. She bumped into her horse and was trapped between the animal and Segundo's taut, alert body.

"Dammit!" Muttering the curse, Segundo whipped the serape over his head, then flung it over hers. "Take this, it'll keep you warm on the way . . ."

"No!" Jessica moved sideways to avoid him. Too late. The garment was draped over her shoulders, weighing her down with its lingering scent of him. His fingers trailed along her nape, searing her flesh, as he lifted her braid, freeing it from the material. His touch was brief but so gentle, so . . . tender, it pierced her soul. Shuddering in reaction, Jessica forced herself to breathless stillness and acceptance of his gift. Heat permeated her being. *His* heat. "Thank you." Speaking was an effort.

"You're welcome." His voice was a caress, abrading the tension shimmering inside her. He moved back a step, releasing the breath pent up in her tight chest.

"I-I'm going." Barely aware of what she was saying, Jessica groped for the saddle horn and the reins.

"Running away from me, Jess?" he asked, too softly, too accurately.

Jessica stiffened, in her body and in her resolve. A sense of self-preservation came to her defense. "I never run from any man, and I'm most assuredly not running from you, Se-gun-do." She drew his name out on a sneer.

"Good," he said smoothly, ignoring her dig. "I'll come for you when my work is finished."

A thrill combined of fear and anticipation shot through her. Repressing the confusing sensation, Jessica mounted her horse before deigning to reply. "Don't waste your time," she advised in a voice made hoarse by strain, as she pressed her heels to the horse to get it moving.

His hand flashed out to grasp the reins, holding the horse still. "I've claimed you, Jess." Segundo's soft voice was laced with steel. "I keep what is mine."

"And I told you to go to hell!" Sudden fury exploded inside her, fury born of stark terror.

What was happening to her? What had he done to her? Frightened, Jessica yanked the reins free and slapped them against her horse's rump. "And you can take your claim with you," she called as the animal shot away at a gallop.

The branding imprint of his touch burned Jessica's nape throughout her mindless dash back to the ranch.

14

"This town is the asshole of the world."

"I know." Meg smiled at Sean's reflection in her dresser mirror. He was reclining on her scandalously disheveled bed, propped lazily against a pile of pillows, grinning at her like a man sated with sexual satisfaction —which he was.

"So." Sean arched one black eyebrow. "Why do you stay here, Mary Margaret?"

Meg continued to apply a brush to her wildly tangled, bright-red hair and leveled a self-derisive look at his smiling, handsome image.

Somehow, and Meg still wasn't even sure how he

had managed it, Sean had coaxed her into telling him her Christian name, along with most of her sordid history. To her amazement, instead of recoiling from her as if she were tainted and unclean, thus beneath him, Sean had reacted with outrage for the degradation she had been forced to suffer and compassionate admiration for her tenacity and endurance.

Meg had long since lost count of the number of men she had known—in every way possible there was to know a man—but she had never known a man quite like Sean Muldoon. In her mind only one other man came any way near Sean's stature, and that was the man she knew only as Segundo.

In truth, Meg knew little of the impressive and still somewhat intimidating Segundo. And although he had made several visits to her home, relaxed in her parlor, eaten at her table, he had never visited her *house,* her workplace, her bed. And yet, though her actual knowledge of him was slight, Meg knew, intuitively and intellectually, that the silent, forbidding man called Segundo was a straight shooter, a man to be trusted, with her very life if warranted.

Meg had a bone-deep feeling that she would never really know Segundo—unlike Sean, whom she felt she knew and understood quite well.

In Meg's learned opinion, Sean was special, one of a kind. On reflection, that was probably the reason she had broken her tenet of silence about herself and her personal life. Even so, there remained one bit of information that she had not imparted to him.

"Mary Margaret," Sean called in a crooning voice. "Aye, and if it's not like you're staring right through me, lass." His Irish brogue was thick and overdone, a deliberate ploy to capture her wandering attention. "Have ya fallen asleep with your eyes open then?"

"You're a fool, Muldoon." Laughing, Meg tossed the brush on the organdy-flounced dressing table. "You know full well I haven't fallen asleep . . . then." Rising from the padded, striped satin vanity bench, she discarded her wrapper as she crossed to the bed. "I was thinking."

"About answering this fool's question . . . then?" Snaring her wrist, he pulled her onto the bed beside him.

"About you," Meg admitted, wriggling when his hand roamed from her wrist to her breast. "And your friend, Segundo."

"You're thinking about another man when you've got himself, Sean Muldoon, in your bed?" His scowl was dark and fierce, and a complete sham.

"Not just another man, Sean."

"Aye, that one. Segundo." Sean laughed. "Now, there's a man you'd want by your side in a brawl."

Meg laughed with him. "That's what I was thinking."

Sean gave her a droll look. "You were thinking about a brawl with him here in your bed?"

Meg smiled and shook her head. "No, Sean, I was thinking Segundo was a man to be trusted, like you."

"You trust me?"

"By now," Meg drawled, "you must know I do."

"Then why didn't you answer my question?"

She batted her eyelashes and looked innocent. "Did you ask a question?"

"You know damn well I did."

"What was it?"

"Mary Margaret." Sean growled in warning, but nevertheless, repeated his question. "I asked you why you stay here in this godawful place."

"I'm saving my money," Meg replied with slow and obvious reluctance.

"For what?" he persisted, undaunted. "There's not a damn thing here worth saving for."

"No, not here," she agreed.

Sean's lazy pose was belied by the light of shrewd interest in his blue eyes. "Where then?"

Sighing with acceptance of the realization that the big Irishman would keep after her until he wormed the information out of her, Meg gave in to the inevitable. "I'm saving to buy another house."

"Here?"

"Of course not!" Meg heaved another sigh and forged ahead. "I want to buy a house somewhere else . . . maybe Cheyenne."

"Where there are more paying customers?" Sean laughed, then continued before she could answer, "And thicker linings in their pockets?"

Meg looked him squarely in the eyes. "Yes."

Sean shook his head and laughed again. "You won't be adding to your savings by giving it away to me the way you've insisted on doing."

Meg shrugged. "It'll just take me a little longer."

"And you call me a fool?"

Turning, Meg smiled and snuggled into him. "I call you a friend, Muldoon."

"Hmm." Wrapping his arms around her, Sean pulled her on top of him. "Interesting."

Finally, the weeks Sean had spent riding hard and fast, back and forth between the Circle-F and Meg's place, had borne fruit. He could hardly wait to see Segundo and tell him he had learned of a way for the man to repay her.

Not that all his hard riding had been performed in the saddle. The chore Segundo had assigned to Sean had had delightful side benefits. Inhaling, Sean drew into his senses the intoxicating scent of Meg's soft skin. His lips curved into an enigmatic smile of satisfaction.

Jessica was quiet, withdrawn, pensive, moody. She was also scared. Over three weeks had passed since she had returned to the ranch house midway through the roundup. Three weeks, throughout which not a day, an hour had passed that she hadn't felt the burning imprint of Segundo's fingers at her nape.

It was a gesture, nothing more, Jessica told herself, an act of human compassion, holding little meaning other than normal concern of one person for another.

All Jessica's rationalization proved pointless; the back of her neck continued to tingle to the memory touch, hour after hour, day after day, week after week.

In all those weeks, Jessica had seen Segundo once, when he returned with the men after roundup was over. Recalling his promise to come to claim her, she had steeled herself for a confrontation that never came.

Segundo had remained at the house for less than twenty-four hours, then he was gone again, without a word, without a nod, without as much as a direct look at her.

Had she suspected a hint of caring? Jessica chided herself. Had she rationalized human compassion? Claim her? she thought, refusing to acknowledge the tight ball of pain in her chest. He behaved as if he didn't as much as know her.

Feeling strange, fragile, let down, but telling herself she was relieved, Jessica had questioned her father about the unusual and unorthodox comings and goings of his *segundo*.

"He said he had some important business to take care of," Ben answered vaguely, distracted by the pile of paperwork on his desk.

"Business? What business could he possibly have here?" Jessica probed, frowning.

"Dunno." Ben shrugged. "All he said was he had some business in South Pass."

Without another word, Jessica turned and left her father's office. The tightness expanded inside her chest, her throat was constricted. She wanted to scream.

South Pass. After all he'd said, claiming her as his, telling her she belonged to him, Segundo hadn't wasted any time in rushing away from her to visit his whore in South Pass.

That was over a week ago, the longest week of Jessica's life, during which she had swung from one extreme to another, raging in silent fury, weeping in utter dejection.

The final blow had struck her a few days ago, with the dawning realization that Segundo's seed had taken root in her body. Either on the night of her father's party, or during that abandoned encounter in the mountains, she had conceived Segundo's child.

At first, Jessica had denied and rejected the possibility. It was less than two full weeks since the expected time of her natural flow, and she had had some faint spotting. Nevertheless, intuitively and intellectually,

Jessica knew she was with child. The symptoms would not be denied.

Due to the detailed letters she received from the one close woman friend she had made while at school, a young woman by name of Matilda St. Claire of the prominent Boston St. Claires, Jessica was well versed in the symptoms of the entire process of pregnancy, from conception through confinement.

Ever the chatty one, Mattie had emptied her mind to Jessica from the first day of their friendship—which coincided with their first day together as roommates at the posh Boston boarding school—confiding everything from the most trivial thought inside her head, to her innermost secrets.

The bond of friendship that had immediately been established between Jessica and Mattie confounded all observers, from the teachers at the elite institution, to their classmates and their parents. To all surface appearances, Jessica and Mattie were complete opposites. In reality, inside, they were cast from the same mold. Their methods differed, but their respective values and goals were quite similar.

Both young women were fiercely independent, confident, and self-reliant. Both embraced the women's suffrage movement, espousing equality and the right to vote. And both considered their differences minor and a source of some amusement.

Mattie adored men, in all shapes and sizes, just as long as they were liberal thinking and agreed with her on all the important issues.

Whereas Jessica, on the other hand, while not actively disliking men, merely tolerated them and their attentions from time to time.

During their school years, Mattie had staunchly maintained that her two main goals in life were to marry and march, but not necessarily in that order. She wanted it all, a loving, understanding husband—preferably one who would happily march beside her—a family, and the eventual and unconditional success of the suffrage movement.

Jessica's goals were more select and, to her way of thinking, more practical. Beautiful, elegant, charming—when she chose to be—witty, if in a droll manner, she was much sought after by the scions of the Boston hierarchy. Jessica wasn't interested, for while she also wanted to live to witness the victory of the movement, what she wanted most was simply to return to her beloved home, the land, the mountains, the earthy ranch hands, and be allowed to do the work she loved to do. A particular man, and marriage, could wait—if they came at all. Jessica really didn't care.

But she did enjoy Mattie's letters, all of which overflowed with the varied and rich happenings of her life.

Mattie had found her loving and understanding man while attending a cotillion during her last year at school, and had married the bemused but delighted young lawyer two weeks after graduation. Jessica had remained in Boston to attend her ecstatic young friend. Almost exactly nine months to the night of the wedding, Mattie had been delivered of her first child, a son. Another son and a daughter had followed each successive year.

Therefore, Jessica knew, from Mattie's vivid accounts, all about the symptoms women were fated to suffer, to one degree or another, while in a delicate condition.

She was struck, at odd moments of the day and evening, with an overwhelming desire to sleep. Her breasts were tender to the touch, and the nipples were just a shade darker. But, for Jessica, the most telling of all the symptoms was the vague queasiness she was increasingly experiencing on arising each morning.

No, as fervently as she wished to see the evidence of a bright-red show of normal flow, Jessica knew her body was already nurturing Segundo's seed.

The knowledge induced a confounding and conflicting mixture of emotions within Jessica. While part of her thrilled to the idea of carrying, then cradling her own child, another part cringed at the prospect of being connected to, linked with, the arrogant, aloof, so-superior man who had fathered the babe . . . and had made her wild with pleasure during the act.

Segundo.

Did she love him?

Could she love him?

Jessica shuddered. How could she even consider loving a man like him? Except for the searing blaze of lustful passion he had revealed to her, Segundo appeared cold, formidable, calculating, and, on more than one occasion, deadly. In essence, the epitome of masculine supremacy.

How could she love a man such as he?

Since Jessica's acquaintance with love was all of the familial or dispassionate kind, she wasn't quite sure how to determine if what she was feeling was in fact the beginnings of romantic love or simply the response of flesh to flesh.

What she was absolutely certain of, however, was that she didn't want to be in love with him. Jessica didn't want to be in love with any man, but most especially not with the man known only as Segundo.

Because the *segundo* had discovered, and exploited, her hidden sensuality, he terrified her.

And so Jessica was scared, mind and soul-deep scared, thus not thinking in her normal, rational manner. Her frantic thinking process brought her to the conclusion that, should the *segundo* learn of her condition, he would attempt to take control of her, of her life, of her entire future.

Segundo would own her, body and soul.

Jessica had long since determined never to play the subservient role to any one individual, any man. The evidence of her condition underscored her determination. She had to think of a way to keep the *segundo* from learning about the child, his child, growing within her.

The question of how she could manage to keep the information from him tormented Jessica. She was slender, and the natural progression of her condition would be apparent to everyone before too long. Demands would be made upon her—conventional demands, parental demands, Segundo's demands.

Jessica knew she was strong enough to defy convention; she had been doing so all her life. She knew she was capable of defying her parents; she had done so, many times. However, the mere thought of defying the *segundo* filled her with dread; instinct warned her that he would not be defied. He would want his child . . . and her submission.

The realization of Segundo's more than probable reaction induced panic inside Jessica, panic that was not conducive to rational thought.

It was while in this frightened and confused frame of

mind that Jessica recalled the rumors she had heard of a method of termination, a method known by an old Shoshone shaman. Jessica had been friends with the shaman's granddaughter, Laughing Dove, ever since her free-running childhood days.

Repressing the urge to be sick to her stomach, Jessica crept from the house early one morning. Following an impulse born of desperation, she saddled her horse, loaded two others, and rode to the reservation to visit her friend.

Jessica did not approach the reservation empty-handed. As she had since her fourteenth summer, she led pack animals loaded down with blankets, bolts of material, and foodstuffs and drove a dozen head of cattle.

Jessica had always admired the Shoshone people, who had followed their great chief Washakie in his support of the white man. They were a proud people, and Jessica understood pride of race, even though there were times she despaired of her own stiff-necked people. Feared and shunned by most whites, the Shoshone lived apart, confined to a section of the vast land they had once roamed at will. Above all, she admired Washakie himself who, now well into his eighties, still remained actively involved with everything connected with the reservation, from the progress made in the schools to every facet of farming and irrigation.

Jessica was not surprised to find Laughing Dove waiting for her. Somehow, the young woman always knew when her friend was coming. Jessica no longer questioned the mystical knowledge of the Shoshone, she simply accepted it.

Nervous about what she was about to do and impatient to have done with it, Jessica forced herself to smile through the ritual of exchanging greetings and gifts with the members of her friend's large family. When at last the formality was over, she drew Laughing Dove aside for a private conversation.

"You are troubled, my sister." Dressed in a long skirt and a calico blouse made from the bolts of material Jessica had brought on her last visit, Laughing Dove stared at her from dark eyes liquid with compassion.

Accustomed to her friend's insight, Jessica smiled, sighed, and nodded. "Yes." Impulsively she grasped the other girl's hand. "I-I'm with child."

"And this makes you sad?"

Jessica closed her eyes, fighting pain. "Laughing Dove, please understand. I cannot bear this child." Opening her eyes, she looked into the face of sorrow.

"You wish to see my grandfather?"

No! The protest filled Jessica's mind. Tears filled her eyes. Her hand slid protectively over her flat belly. She couldn't. She couldn't. Jessica swallowed, then blinked back the tears. She must. Squaring her shoulders, she met and held Laughing Dove's sad-eyed stare and reluctantly nodded again.

"Yes."

"As you will it." Not a hint of reproach colored Laughing Dove's voice. Not a shadow of censure shaded her eyes. But a sadness seemed to settle over her slight form as she turned away. "Come with me. I believe Grandfather is expecting you."

Jessica felt a premonitory chill. The shaman was expecting her? Did he know? Would he help her? Her tread hesitant, uncertain, Jessica trailed her friend to the shaman's lodge. With a barely discernible hand movement, Laughing Dove indicated the darkness beyond the opening.

Fighting a sudden overwhelming impulse to flee, Jessica steeled herself for whatever was to come, gritted her teeth, and stepped into the dim interior of the lodge.

Looking small, fragile, ancient, the shaman sat, cross-legged, on the silver-gray pelt of a wolf. His white hair hung in lank tendrils over his bony shoulders. His black eyes gleamed like hot coals in his gaunt, expressionless face. "Speak."

Jessica's body jerked, recoiling as if from a physical blow from the low, scratchy sound of the old man's voice. Her heart thundered. Her stomach roiled.

"I-I seek . . . need your help," she said in choppy words pushed from her throat on uneven breaths.

"No, child." His eyes burned into hers, giving her the eerie feeling that they were peering into her soul.

"You . . . you will not help me?" Inexplicably more frightened of the old man than she'd been of the grizzly bear, Jessica inched back, toward the opening, the light.

"No need." The shaman's reedy voice held infinite sadness and compassion. "What is to be will be."

In her fear and upset, Jessica heard only refusal and her own self-condemnation for seeking his help in an act against God—the act of ending the life of her own child. And in that instant she knew she couldn't go through with her plan, even if the shaman agreed to help her. Shivering uncontrollably, she inched closer to the lodge opening. "I . . . forgive me for . . ."

"With the first heavy snowfall and the crack of the whip."

His fading voice didn't register on Jessica's guilt-ridden mind. Turning away, she bolted through the opening, into the warm autumn sunlight. Trembling, she stood still, staring inward in horror at the blackness of her own soul. How could she have even dreamt of committing such . . . Jessica flinched as Laughing Dove laid her small palm on her trembling arm.

"Jessica? Are you not well?"

"I must go!" Breaking free of her friend's hand, and her concern, Jessica ran to her horse. "I'm sorry," she called, scrambling into the saddle. "I . . ." A rising flood of tears choked her. Her face was wet, her vision blurred. Slapping the animal, she tore from the camp.

Jessica made it to just beyond the boundary of the reservation before, heaving, shuddering, moaning, she hung over to one side of her horse and emptied her stomach into the pungent, summer-dried grass.

Spirit Walker picked up his ears and pace as they drew near to the Circle-F yard. The ride had been long and wearying. His nostrils flared at the scent of home.

"Hungry, are you?" Duncan chuckled and shifted in the saddle. His back ached, his legs ached, his ass ached, but his spirits were high. "Or is there a filly you're hoping to cover?"

The horse snorted. Duncan laughed. There were times he felt positive the animal understood every word he said. "I know the feeling," he went on in a conversational tone. "Three weeks is three weeks too long, ol' buddy. I'm hankering to cover my own filly." He laughed again, amused at how quickly he had adopted the western speech patterns.

The horse responded with a head shake to the sound

of his master's voice. The bridle jingled. Duncan didn't see or hear the movement. He was lost in memory, reliving the events that had transpired since the last time he had seen Jessica.

Three weeks. Goddamn if it didn't seem more like three months. And then he had not touched her—had, in fact, hardly looked at her. He had known he could not, for if he had, neither looking nor touching would have satisfied; he'd have had to bury himself deep within her, then shackle her to him with the bonds of matrimony, in which case, the loose ends of his plans would not now be securely tied.

Duncan had returned to the B-Bar-R after the roundup to find a message from Sean Muldoon waiting for him. The note was brief and to the point. Muldoon had learned of a way in which Duncan could repay the whore Meg for her help in ending the nefarious machinations of Josiah Metcalf.

It had been the longest three weeks of Duncan's life, most of it spent on the back of his horse. Which, on reflection, had been to his advantage, considering the near-constant state of arousal his body was in and the fact that he probably could not have walked upright had he been out of the saddle.

Damn! The ache between his legs was close to unbearable, but the job was done. It had required a lot of travel, and even more money, but Meg was now the ecstatic owner of a rather large, elegantly appointed house in Cheyenne, situated quite close to the grand "town houses" the wealthier ranchers had built for themselves in the growing city.

One particular house had caught Duncan's fancy. Victorian in design, the house was large, roomy, deco-

rated with wide verandas and lacy gingerbread trim-
ming. He made arrangements to inspect the property
and, while wandering through the spacious interior, he
envisioned an elegantly gowned Jessica descending the
broad, curving staircase. In his vision, the gleaming ma-
hogany banister was festooned with draperies of deep-
green holly fastened by strategically placed bows of red
velvet.

He bought the house on the spot. The agent handling the property was young but astute. Favorably impressed by the man, Duncan followed up the sale by
offering the astounded young man the position of personal agent.

Young Charles Caulding was ambitious as well as astute. Having taken Duncan's measure as swiftly as
Duncan took his own, he had accepted the position
with alacrity.

Before taking his departure from Cheyenne, Duncan
charged his new personal agent with three instructions.
The first order of business was for Charles to set himself up in a small office. The second was for the young
man to dispatch a message to Scotland, inviting his employer's stepmother and half-sister to spend the approaching Christmas holidays with Duncan in his new
house in Cheyenne. And the third charge was for
Charles to see to all the necessary travel arrangements
in the event he received an acceptance from Deirdre
and Heather.

Well satisfied with the progress made, Duncan then
took his leave of the city.

Since Muldoon had opted to stay in Cheyenne for a
spell to help Meg get settled in, Duncan had had himself, and his erotic thoughts and hard body, for com-

pany on the long ride back to the Circle-F from Cheyenne.

Duncan didn't mind being, as Muldoon would have termed it, all on his lonesome. The long ride afforded him time to think and formulate his plans for the beautiful, exciting, infuriatingly independent Jessica Randall.

Memory surged of their time together in that hidden mountain dale the day they encountered the grizzly bear, reviving within Duncan's mind the scent and feel of Jessica writhing beneath the ministrations of his hands and mouth. His throat went dry, the palms of his hands grew slick, his shaft throbbed a demand for the silken sheath of her body.

Damn! Maybe he should have gone directly to the B-Bar-R, after all, instead of returning to the Circle-F. But, no. Duncan shook his head. He had a reason for returning to his home, a very important reason. He had locked the reason inside the bottom drawer of the desk in the ranch office.

Spirit Walker whinnied, ending Duncan's reverie. They were home. The weight of weariness lifting from his shoulders, he turned the horse over to the unfamiliar wrangler who appeared from the tack room. After admonishing the lanky handler to take exceptional care of the tired hunter, Duncan pivoted and headed at a loping stride for the house.

He was in an overriding, itching hurry, but affection demanded he acquiesce to a bit of fussing from his aunt. Inga plied him with pointed questions and well-cooked food. Duncan gratefully consumed the meal, while avoiding her questions by asking one of his own.

"Where's Uncle David?"

"Visiting the people." Inga's smile was sad and gentle. "There really isn't much real ranch work he can do anymore." She sighed. "Even the book work overtires him."

Duncan set his fork aside, no longer hungry. "Isn't there some sort of medical help available?"

"Here?"

She didn't need to elaborate. Duncan was well aware of the lack of innovative medicine in the West. "I don't suppose he would consider traveling to Chicago or New York City?"

Inga answered with a snort. "David? Never. He is with the shaman now. I know how your uncle's mind works. He believes that if the shaman can't help him, no one can."

Duncan was nothing if not a realist. Acceptance of his uncle's beliefs was difficult but unavoidable. "Then let's pray the shaman can help," he said, pushing away from the table. "I need a bath, then I'll be in the office, if you should need me for anything."

Opting for the cold water creek that meandered its way at the base of the incline behind the house over the necessity of lugging buckets of hot water up the stairs to the hip bath in the garderobe, Duncan collected soap, towel, and clean clothing from his bedroom, then left the house.

Less than an hour later, clean and once again attired in the rough but serviceable garb of the working ranch hand, he stood before his father's large solid oak desk, staring down at the reason for his return to the ranch house.

The ring was heavy, ornate, and outdated. But then, it was over a hundred years old. The thick gold was encrusted with diamonds, emeralds, and blood-red rubies, and had graced the delicate hand of Duncan's aristocratic English great-great-grandmother. It had been that lovely woman's marriage ring. Duncan had determined that the heirloom would be Jessica's marriage ring as well.

His fingers closed over his palm, and then he went still. There hadn't been a whisper of a sound, yet he knew his uncle was standing in the doorway.

"Come in, Chill Wind Blowing." Duncan's ready smile of welcome faded as he looked into his uncle's sober face. "Is there something wrong?"

"Yes." Bent, unsteady, David shuffled into the room. "I have just come from the reservation," he said in his precise manner. "I heard some disturbing information about Miss Jessica while I was there."

In the act of circling the desk to assist his uncle into a chair, Duncan came to a bone-jarring halt. "Jessica? What about her? What did you hear?"

David emitted a low grunt of discomfort as he eased his pain-wracked body into the leather chair. "She was on the reservation to visit the shaman."

"The shaman?" Duncan frowned. "Why would Jessica have need to visit him?"

"To beseech his help."

Duncan was thoroughly mystified. "But why? I mean, in what way could the shaman help Jessica?"

The old man's eyes were sad with wisdom. "Miss Jessica was seeking a method of ridding her body of the seed growing into a child in her womb."

For an instant, everything vital and alive inside Duncan froze in horrified reaction to David's explanation. His blood ran cold, icy fingers raked his nerves, his mind screamed in an agony of denial.

No! She would not! Not Jessica. Not his seed, his child, his heir! Could she? Duncan felt his stomach heave as a vision of her loomed in his mind, a vision of her, steadfast and determined in her defiance of him.

Would she? Could she?

The inner horror expanded as the truth slammed into him.

She could—and she would.

The instant was over. Cold horror melted in the advance of silent, flaming rage. The pampered, spoiled bitch! She dared contemplate ridding herself of his seed! His heir! He would kill her with his bare hands!

The time that had elapsed was mere seconds, during which not a hint of the blazing emotions rioting through Duncan was revealed on his chiseled face or in his flat, stone-eyed stare. And yet, like to like, Chill Wind Blowing correctly read sign on his nephew's expressionless face.

"The seed is yours, Stone Eyes?"

Duncan responded with a curt nod.

"I thought as much." David sighed. "All is not lost. The shaman refused to help her."

Hope flickered to life in Duncan's dead-looking eyes. "The seed is still safe in the womb?"

"It was when she left the reservation."

Whipping around, Duncan strode toward the doorway, his hand balled into a fist around the ring.

"Where do you go, Stone Eyes?"

"To insure the safety of my seed," Duncan growled, striding from the room.

* * *

Spirit Walker proved his lineage and his mettle on the hard, flat-out run from the Circle-F to the B-Bar-R. By the time they thundered into the Randall ranch yard, both horse and rider were lathered with sweat.

Duncan's teeth-jarring bath in the cold creek had been for naught. He didn't care. On the surface, he was hot and sweaty. Inside, he was as frigid as a snow-fed mountain lake.

After flinging himself from the shuddering horse, Duncan stormed into the house, startling Emily, who was at the cook stove preparing the evening meal.

"Well, hello! You're just in time for—"

"Where's Jessica?" he interrupted her in a bark.

Emily blinked in surprise but answered, "In her room, resting. I swear, that girl has done nothing lately but—"

"Where's Ben?" Duncan again cut her off, with such harshness she went wide-eyed with shock.

"He's in the office, but . . . Oh!" Emily exclaimed, as he crossed to her and grasped her by the arm.

"Come with me." Half running, half dragging her, Duncan propelled her along with him as he strode from the kitchen, through the dining room, and into the office.

Ben was hunched over the desk, and swung around, brows beetled, frowning at the interruption. A smile split his scowling face on sight of his visitor.

"Dun—I mean, Segundo, where in hell have you—"

"Duncan, not Segundo," Duncan said, slamming the door behind him. "From now on, it's Duncan."

"Good." Ben laughed. "It's not necessary anyway. Frank got back day before yes—"

Duncan silenced him with a slicing hand motion.

"You both may decide it isn't quite so good, after you've heard what I have to say to you." Stepping back, away from Emily, he drew himself up, facing them, not as their hired *segundo*, but as Duncan Frazer, the Earl of Rayburne.

Forewarned and wary, Ben heaved his bulk from the creaking desk chair. "What do you have to say to us?" He reached out to clasp his wife's hand, as if steadying her to withstand a sudden, forceful blow.

"I have it, on some authority, that Jessica is, in delicate terms, with child."

Emily staggered and, if not for her husband's support, would have fallen to the floor. Ben roared like a wounded bull.

"Lies!" he bellowed. "My Jessica has never been with a man! Where did you hear this slander?"

"No lies," Duncan said, meeting the older man's searing stare. "It is true. Call Jessica down, ask her. Demand she tell you the truth."

"But how can you know?" Emily whimpered.

"I fathered the child."

15

❧

"NO!"

Jessica stood at bay, just inside the office door, hands clenched, spine rigid, her jaw thrust forward in a show of angry defiance. Inside, she was a quivering mass of fear and uncertainty. Sheer willpower kept her erect, alert, and able to withstand the steady regard of the turquoise eyes watching her every move. How had he found out about her condition? How could he know so soon?

"But, Jessica, you must!" Emily looked stricken. "Think of the scandal!"

"I will not be forced into marriage with any man."

Her chin jutted a notch higher, and she glared down the length of her delicate nose at the man standing so at ease, so very casually at his ease, next to her father's desk. His lazy-looking stance infuriated her; his cool, superior smile insulted her. "And I most definitely will not be forced into a marriage of convenience with this . . . this"—she curled her lip in a tremor-concealing sneer and coldly elucidated—"Se-gun-do."

"Oh! Oh, of course not!" Giving a little trilling, nervous laugh, Emily turned a sparkling look on the two men. "We forgot, she doesn't know!"

The wave of relief washing over her mother's face, changing her expression from pinched to pleasant, baffled, deepened the confusion inside Jessica. At once wary and on guard, she skimmed a narrowed gaze over the faces of her tormentors. "Don't know?" she said, in demanding tones designed to disguise the trepidation coiling through her insides. "What exactly is it that I don't know?"

Jessica wasn't even sure she wanted to hear an answer to her question. What she was sure of was an overwhelming sense of urgency, a need to flee, as fast and as far as her horse, a buggy, a train would take her.

Run. Run. Run.

The inner command had begun ringing in her head when she had heard her mother call her to come down to her father's office. Instinctively Jessica had felt, had known, she would not like whatever it was she was going to hear.

Her instincts had proved infallible. She had felt under attack from the minute she entered the room. Her future had been decided, she had been informed. A wedding would take place, quickly, quietly, discreetly.

Convention demanded she be bound, legally, morally, righteously to the father of the child growing day by day inside her body.

"Convention be damned!" Jessica had responded, ruthlessly squashing a traitorous leap of expectant joy. He would own her. She would not be owned. It was then she had pulled herself together to make her stand. "No!"

Now, mere moments later, there appeared a new element she must deal with, an element of surprise. Jessica couldn't imagine what that new element could possibly be or, in fact, if she would be capable of dealing with it—since she was already fighting to deal with the sickness churning in her stomach. She only knew, from the sinking sensation pervading her being, that she wasn't going to like what she was about to be told.

Ben and Emily were exchanging telling glances with Segundo. He remained aloof, remote, apparently unconcerned, as if supremely confident of the eventual outcome.

His attitude worked like an abrasive on Jessica's nerves, emotions, and senses.

Damn him!

"Well?" Jessica had reached the end of her limited patience. If there was no escape, if she had to hear whatever it was they believed would change her mind, undermine her resistance to their marriage plans for her, she would listen, hear them out. Now. Then she would run . . . before she disgraced herself by being sick all over the carpet on the office floor.

"Er . . . Jessica, dear, please understand that we were not maliciously deceiving you but . . . er . . ."

Emily sputtered to a halt and sent a pleading look to Ben for help.

Jessica felt a crawly sensation on the surface of her skin. Her legs felt weak. Her breathing accelerated. A tightness invaded her chest. What could it be, she wondered, what manner of element could cause her mother to become so unsure, so tongue-tied, so flustered?

"Deceive me?" Jessica pounced on the expression. "In what way have you—not wanted—to deceive me?"

"The *segundo* is not who . . . what he seems." Ben's rough voice reverberated in the tense atmosphere in the small room.

Jessica shot a suspicious glance at the man under discussion. The beast had the gall to smile at her! The fine, taut rein on her patience snapped. So did she. "I suspected as much!" While speaking about him, not to him, Jessica stared directly into his odd, intriguing, damnably too attractive eyes. "If not Se-gun-do, who is he?"

His movement swift, lithe, smooth, he made her an exquisite, elegantly executed bow.

"Duncan Frazer, Earl of Rayburne, at your service, Miss Jessica."

Duncan!

The sound of his name pealed a mythical bell inside Jessica's stunned mind. She heard, felt the sweet chime to the depths of her soul.

Duncan. Duncan. Duncan.

Ever since Jessica was a little girl, for as long as she could remember, the name Duncan had embodied everything magical and wondrous. She had heard the name spoken in near reverence, too young to doubt or question the reason for such a depth of respect for what

was little more than a boy by the adults surrounding
her.

Duncan of the tender, gentle nature. Duncan of the
fierce, protective stance. Duncan of the adoring spirit.
Duncan of the land—her land. Duncan of the peoples
—her people, his father's people, his mother's people.

Duncan.

Her dream, her prince, her storybook knight.

Duncan.

Jessica had grown into a woman with an ideal se-
creted in the heart of her heart. She had looked on
other men, compared them with her ideal, and found
them wanting.

Struck into the very heart of her heart, Jessica stared
into the face of her ideal. She had met her dream, her
prince, her knight, and had not known him. She had
sheathed the ideal within her virgin body, taken his
seed into the nurturing warmth of her womb, and had
not recognized him.

Her dream was decimated. Her prince was a pre-
tender. Her knight was a nightmare.

Her ideal wore the name of Duncan . . . who wore
the name Segundo. And the *segundo* had revealed himself a man determined on a course of domination
through possession.

A tingle burned a certain spot on her nape, causing a
tremor to ripple through her, recalling the act.

A gentle gesture? A tender caress? Or a premedi-
tated, fiery brand of ownership?

Feeling bewildered, battered, betrayed . . . if by
herself more than him, Jessica tasted the bitter flavor of
defeat. If her secret ideal was a sham, she, her beliefs,

her principles, her life was a sham, a performance, a traveling medicine show, with empty medicine bottles.

Reeling, she stared into the depthless eyes of the medicine man, shuddering as the final, demoralizing blow registered on her stunned mind.

Duncan Frazer . . . Earl of Rayburne!

Dear God! And now she knew how he had learned of her plight; Duncan Frazer: Scot, Englishman, Shoshone.

Nausea sank its barbed claws into Jessica's stomach, tearing at the fabric of her flesh.

"No." A whisper, barely audible. Groping for the smooth wooden doorknob, she turned away from the dangerously enticing allure of turquoise.

"Jessica, dear, wait! We need to discuss . . ."

"No." Still a whisper, but a louder whisper. Blindly she twisted the knob and yanked open the door.

"You will stay right here, girl!" Ben's booming voice hammered against the back of her skull. "And you will do as you're told!"

"No!" No longer a whisper but a mournful, wrenching cry of disillusionment and defiance. "I will not!"

Jessica was running—not for her horse, not for a buggy, not for a train, but for the sanctity of the porcelain-enameled commode she had insisted on having installed in the second-floor guest room.

"Oh, Jessica, please wait." Emily rushed to the doorway; Duncan reached it first.

"I'll go." His smile was faint, apologetic, shadowed by acceptance. "She is my responsibility now."

Finding Jessica was easy; Duncan had merely to follow the unmistakable sounds of retching. He found her in the bathroom, her arms wrapped around her middle, her slender body doubled over the commode, her stomach heaving its contents into the gleaming white bowl.

"Ah, Jess," he said on a sigh. Crossing the room to her, he grasped her shoulders to support her shaking body. "Why didn't you tell us you were sick?"

"Go . . . away." Jessica blurted out the hoarse command between gasps for breath.

"No, you . . ." Duncan's voice faltered and his eyes flickered as the significance of her stomach weakness dawned on him.

Slowly the fury that had driven him to make that breakneck run from the Circle-F to her home drained from him. David had said only that she had sought the help of the shaman and that he had refused it. But the shaman's refusal had not precluded the possibility of Jessica having taken some headstrong and foolhardy action on her own. Relief quaked through him. Her very sickness was proof of her delicate condition. His heir was still safe, warm, protected inside her. His breath eased from his constricted chest.

Hidden from her averted sight, Duncan allowed a spasm of pained relief to fleetingly alter his set features.

His seed was secure.

The realization did not, by any means, exonerate Jessica. In Duncan's eyes she was guilty of intent. Jessica had meant to destroy the life they had conceived together. He would live with the knowledge of her intent, he had little choice in the matter. He wanted his child but, even more, he still wanted, still loved the mother of his child. That Jessica had given ample evidence to the fact that she did not return his feelings was just another form of rejection Duncan knew he would also have to live with.

So be it.

Duncan drew a slow breath. Perhaps, with time . . . with work . . . with tenderness . . .

Jessica's retching had subsided to irregular gasps and gulps. Standing erect, she shrugged to dislodge his hands from her shoulders and repeated her command. "Go away."

"I can't." Duncan flexed his fingers, then released her, but only to turn her to face him. Her face was pale, her lips paler still. Perspiration sheened her forehead, cheeks, and the dark hollows beneath her eyes. Her eyes. A pang of regret speared into his chest. Jessica's beautiful silver eyes had lost their shimmer to the tarnished dullness of misery. "I won't."

"I want you to leave me!"

"Never." Bending, he scooped her up, into his arms, and carried her from the bathroom to her bedroom.

"Let me go!" Jessica cried, struggling. She tried to fight him but, weakened by her bout of sickness, she was rendered helpless in his protective embrace.

"You need rest." Careful not to jar her, he lowered her to her bed. "You need your strength for the child."

"There will be no child!" She shouted the denial, glaring at him from eyes now wild and distraught.

The vehemence and certainty in her harsh voice gave him a moment's pause. Duncan stopped breathing. Her eyes betrayed her. Her eyes were wide, haunted by fear and doubt and shame. She had lied. He resumed breathing.

Without a word, Duncan turned and left the room. Silent as he, she watched him leave. A few minutes later, her eyes flickered in disbelief when he walked back into the room carrying an agate basin.

"What are you doing?" Looking wan and exhausted, Jessica was still lying on top of the bed. She jackknifed into a sitting position when he quietly shut the door. "This is my room! I don't want you in here!" There was a frantic edge to her voice, a hint of incipient panic.

Immediately Duncan was flung back in time, into this very room, into the night, *that* night. He could feel the sleek silkiness of Jessica's skin gliding along his own passion-slicked body. He could smell the permeating musky scent of unleashed desires. He could taste the heated headiness of splintering satiation.

Was that the night it had happened? Duncan speculated, staring at the pale, frightened woman on the bed and seeing an aroused wanton in her stead. Was that the night he had planted his seed in the fertile folds of her body?

Desire ripped into Duncan, stealing his breath, infusing steel into his shaft. Goddamn, he wanted her! Here. Now. Wan. Drawn. Frightened. Defiant. He wanted her so badly his back teeth ached.

"What are you thinking?"

Knowing his eyes would reveal his thoughts, his needs, his base desire, Duncan stared with bold deliberation into her wary, flickering gaze. "You know."

She shook her head and began inching back, away, toward the headboard. "No. You couldn't. You wouldn't."

"I could. I would." Forgetting the basin of water and the cloth he had fetched to bathe her face and soothe her spirit, Duncan took a step toward her.

"Are you mad!" Jessica cried, scrambling back to

press her trembling body against the headboard. "I will not have you! Do you hear? Not as lover! Not as husband!"

"You will have me, as both." His sense of propriety consumed by the voracious appetite of converging lust, Duncan set his fingers to work on his shirt buttons as he approached the bed and his woman. "In your room," he said in a raspy murmur. "In your bed," he continued, tossing the shirt aside and moving his hands to his pants. "In your body."

Jessica gasped at the muted clink of his belt buckle and shuddered as his fingers unfastened the small buttons on his pants. As if frozen with disbelief, she didn't move. As if fascinated against her will, her eyes remained riveted to his hands.

"No." Her voice held a catch, a moan, and the dangling threads of untangling desire.

A small smile played a sensuous game over Duncan's mouth as he watched her watch him slide the pants down the length of his passion-taut flanks, freeing the weapon of her destruction and delight.

"Yes." Tethered by the material pooled around his boot tops, Duncan dove onto the bed . . . and Jessica. "I told you before, you are mine."

Duncan had gone beyond the borders of thought and reason. Raging need released inherent traits of ancient Celt and Indian savagery. He was a Highland king, a Plains chieftain, a victorious warrior laying claim to his own.

His hands were rough and impatient, tearing the clothing from Jessica's quaking form without thought or care. She didn't scream or cry out for help. Staring into

her now-flushed face, Duncan knew why she made no
sound.

Her fine-boned features were tight, drawn, strained
by her own gathering excitement. Her eyes were wide,
the pupils dilated by desire.

Jessica wanted him!

The realization was as an aphrodisiac to Duncan's
mind. Hot blood surged into his loins. She lay naked
beneath him. Naked and vulnerable . . . and ready.
For him!

His eyes hungry with intent, Duncan feasted his
senses on Jessica's flattened white breasts. The puck-
ered buds were an appetizer too alluring to ignore. A
feral-sounding growl rumbling deep in his throat, he
lowered his head, shut his eyes, and enclosed the tight
flesh within his hot, greedy mouth. Her distinct flavor
was intoxicating, enticing, inflaming. He suckled once,
gently.

Jessica sucked in her breath, went still, then, with a
whimpered moan of surrender, she arched her back in a
silent demand for more.

Throbbing in response to her mute appeal, Duncan
made a meal of her satiny skin. Unaware of murmuring
in tongues, garbling the combined languages of the
Scot and the Shoshone, he told her of his need—of her
body, of her heart, of her soul.

She did not understand, nor seem to care. Neither
did he. He was lost, adrift on a fiery sea of boiling
waves of passion and ever-mounting crests of desire.

Now. Now. Now.

The cresting waves beat an increasing drumroll inside his head, his blood, his loins. Duncan clenched his
teeth to retain control, waiting, waiting for a sign from

her. It came in a harsh whisper and slim hands clutching at his hips.

"Now."

Obeying Jessica's plea induced not merely pleasure but excruciating relief. Duncan thrust into the moist heat of her, again and again, deep, deeper, and deeper still.

It was everything . . . and not enough, not nearly enough, for either one of them.

Jessica arched her hips, high. He captured them within his clasping hands. Holding her arched body free of the bed, he bowed his spine and loosed his pulsating quiver, spearing into her with all the force of his powerful body.

Jessica's teeth dug into her lip, strangling her cry of intense pleasure. She bucked, higher, seeking more. The tendons in Duncan's neck bulged into cords of steel as he strained to grant her release before his own.

The cresting wave crashed. They exploded as one. Duncan felt as if the top of his head had been blown away in the blast. Pleasure, so intense it was akin to pain, shuddered through the length of his body, robbing him of breath.

A like sensation robbed Jessica of consciousness.

"Jessica?" Raising his head from her breasts, Duncan stared into her relaxed face. "Jess?" Alarm streaked through him when she failed to respond. Her very stillness shot cold terror into his heart. Why was she so still? Had he hurt her? Jesus Christ! What had he done?

"Jess." Fear gripping him by the throat, Duncan lowered his head to press his lips to the pulse in her throat. The beat was a trifle rapid, but not erratic. Pulling back, he took a longer, closer look at her face.

Jessica's breathing pattern was steady, even, normal. She was sleeping. A tender smile touched his lips. Bending to her, he bestowed it on her sleep-softened mouth.

"I love you, Jessica Randall," he whispered, blending his life's breath with hers. "And not despite the fact that you are spoiled, arrogant, headstrong, and swear like a cockney street urchin, but because of all that you are, or reveal, and all the good, gentle, and magnificence that I sense you are, which you conceal."

Careful not to disturb his sleeping love, Duncan withdrew from her, from the bed. Then, hobbling within the confines of his bunched pants, he moved to the table where he had set the agate basin of water.

The water was cold. Duncan didn't mind. After soaking the cloth, he sluiced the sheen of perspiration from his face, neck, and chest. After dipping the cloth once more, he applied it to the most recently active part of his body. When he drew the cloth away, shock froze his gaze to the white material.

It was stained with blood. Jessica's blood.

God damn his black soul! He *had* hurt her!

"Jessica!" Though not loud, Duncan's raw voice pierced the haze of sleep clouding her mind. Muttering curses of self-condemnation, he tossed the cloth into the basin, yanked up his pants, and fastened the buttons.

"Jess!" His repeated call startled her into full wakefulness.

"What?" Jessica's eyes were wide open, filled with confused disorientation. "What is—"

"Are you injured?" he snapped, cutting her off. "Are you in pain?" Without taking his eyes from her,

Duncan swished the cloth around in the water, pulled it out, then, unmindful of the water dripping onto the carpet, carried it to the bedside. "Answer me!" he ordered, kneeling on the mattress next to her thighs.

"No. What are you talking about?" Jessica blinked, then yelped and squirmed as he gently drew her thighs apart. "What are you doing?"

"I've hurt you." Taking great care, Duncan pressed the cold, wet cloth to her mound.

Jessica jolted and yelped again, louder this time. "Damn you, that's cold! Will you stop? I tell you, I am not hurt!"

"No? Explain this." He lifted the cloth for her inspection. Water-diluted blood streaked the material.

Jessica frowned and peered at the cloth. "It's blood," she said on an expelled sigh.

"Dammit, woman, I know what it is!" Duncan's harsh voice revealed his inner agitation. "I'm asking why it is."

"Why?" Jessica blinked.

"Is . . . the . . . babe . . . in . . . jeopardy?" he demanded, pushing each spaced word through gritted teeth.

"No. I've had some spotting before and . . ." Obviously intimidated by his fierceness, Jessica answered quickly, too quickly, unwittingly admitting to the condition she had so vehemently denied.

Duncan pounced. "Spotting? Nothing more? No flow? No gush? No large clotting?"

"No, just the spotting, but—"

"But, hell, woman! And just spotting, my ass!" He was suddenly incensed, and frightened, which was why he was incensed. Planting his hands on the mattress on either side of her, he loomed over her, speaking slowly, succinctly, in a lethal tone of voice that forbade argument. "From this instant on, you will not ride, you will not run, you will not rush. You will rest, and eat well, and take extreme care of yourself and of our babe. Do you understand me?"

"Go to hell."

"Jessica." His voice was a soft, strained rasp.

"I don't take orders from you." Lying flat on her back, Jessica glared up at him, proud and unafraid. "My body belongs to me, to do with as I please."

"You are with my child. You are mine."

Her chin jutted into the air to scrape his rock-hard jaw. "I belong to no man. I will not be owned!"

Duncan smiled into her anger sparked eyes. "You will be my wife, *querida*." His unthinking use of the endearment spurred her memory and set a flame to her anger.

"*Querida!*" she breathed, baring her teeth and raising her hands to shove him back, away from the bed, and her. "Lies! Deception! Bah! You expect me to marry a charade?"

"Jess, listen. It was only done to—"

"I'd have welcomed you, damn you!" she shouted. "I'd have welcomed Duncan Frazer with joy in his homecoming. Why lie? Why pretend? Why deceive?"

Duncan recognized a time of reckoning and peacemaking when he saw it. Sighing, he gave a detailed explanation, beginning with the letter he had received from his cousin, Eric, and ending with her father's request for him to continue with the disguise until after the roundup or until the foreman, Frank, returned from Argentina.

"My father knew all this time?" she demanded in shock and outrage.

"Yes."

"And my mother?" Her voice had lost some of its sting.

"Yes."

"And Parker?" There was now a tiny forlorn, left-out, deserted note shading her tone.

"No."

Jessica closed her eyes. "You could have told us," she said in a hurt whisper. "We can be trusted, you know, Parker and I. You could have told us."

Duncan felt torn. He wanted to hold her, comfort her, reassure her. He stood firm. Prepared for whatever anger, invective, or understanding she might offer him. "I thought it best, wiser, not to."

Her lip curled. "You thought it best? Wiser?" Her voice rose. "Wiser to lie? Wiser to deceive?"

Duncan was unused to being brought to task by anyone, most especially a woman. Still, he held a tight rein on his temper and waning patience. "Jessica, I meant no meaningful deception. I merely sought an edge against Metcalf."

"Meaningful?" Jessica laughed; it was not a joyous sound. "Does deception come packaged in degrees? You lied. Segundo, indeed! You may call it meaningful. I'd call it something closer to the target. I'd call it the worse kind of betrayal of former friends, Duncan Frazer . . . my lord . . . Se-gun-do."

Duncan felt the shock of the word betrayal like a physical blow. Spinning around, he walked away from her, to stand staring out the window, into his own soul.

Her accusation was true. He had betrayed his

friends. Not only had he deceived Parker with his damnable disguise, but Jessica as well. Jessica, the adored child of his youth. Yet more damning still was his betrayal of Ben and Emily Randall. They had welcomed him with open arms and overflowing hearts. He had reciprocated by not only taking their daughter's virginity and planting his seed within her, but perpetrating the act of betrayal while under their own roof.

If Jessica was guilty of intent, Duncan accepted his own guilt of commitment.

So be it.

His eyes and visage free of expression, Duncan turned to face his accuser and his fate. "What's done is done," he said in a voice devoid of inflection. "And what is . . . is. My seed grows even now inside your body. I will have my child, Jessica, my heir. And my heir will bear my name."

Pulling the tangled bedspread around her nude body, Jessica rose and walked to stand less than two feet from him. Her head held high, she met his piercing stare. "You cannot force me to marry you."

"Not I," he readily agreed.

"Then who?" she retorted in tones of contempt.

Duncan smiled.

Jessica was unsuccessful in repressing a shiver. "Who, damn you?"

"I don't suppose that," he drawled, "while you were in your father's office, so thoroughly consumed by your own show of temper and bad manners, you happened to notice the look on your gentle mother's face . . . did you?"

Her face grew pale, her eyes dark. "My . . . mother?"

"Precisely." Duncan repaid her insult of a curled lip. "Have you considered what your reckless and fool-hardy determination will do to your mother?"

Jessica wet her lips. "I . . . I . . ."

"I thought as much," he finished for her, ruthlessly seizing upon her obvious love for her parents. "If you refuse to marry me, and as soon as possible, thereby allowing a reasonable doubt in the minds of everyone in the vicinity, you will be condemning your mother, as well as your father, to the roles of grandparents to a quarter-breed bastard."

She reeled back, as if he had actually struck her. Duncan moved, then paused, forcing himself to remain still, denying her the luxury of his protective, soothing embrace. He ached for her with every particle of his being, but he had to make her see reason, or face a future of emptiness and regret.

"You display all the grace and charm of a true, relent-less nobleman bent on having his way."

"At your service," Duncan repeated his earlier pledge, and his elegant bow.

16

The deed was done.

The chill in Jessica's fingers owed nothing to the howling wind sweeping across the flat land from the mountains, swaying trees, buffeting the house.

It was past mid-October, the wind was expected.

The marriage ceremony that had been completed moments ago had come as a surprise to the small assembly of guests.

Mere minutes before, Jessica had appeared at the head of the staircase, looking pale and too slender in the dated, yellowed silk and lace wedding gown in which her mother had taken her marriage vows over twenty-six years ago.

The cynosure of all the gathered witnesses, Jessica had descended the stairs to the off-key strains of the wedding march being pounded out of the upright piano in the Randall parlor by, of all people, Sean Muldoon.

Now, cold, trembling, and paler still, Jessica stood by her new husband's side, her left hand resting on his right forearm, her third finger weighted by the jewel-encrusted ornate antique ring he had recently, possessively, slid into place.

The initial stage of her ordeal was over. She was no longer Miss Jessica Randall of the B-Bar-R outfit. She was Lady Jessica Frazer, wife of Duncan Frazer . . . Lord Rayburne.

For the obvious reason of the bride's delicate condition, the guest list had been limited to include family members and employees of the bride and groom. Their numbers filled the spacious Randall parlor and overflowed into the wide foyer and large dining room.

Emily's eyes were bright, sparkling with tears of happiness. Ben's jovial voice boomed with pride and satisfaction. Parker stood at his mother's shoulder, a bemused smile on his lips, a puzzled look on his face. Seated comfortably near to the huge stone fireplace that had been converted into a makeshift altar, David-Chill Wind observed the proceedings through dark eyes lighted from within by joy. By his side, Inga smiled a blessing on the united couple. The hired hands of both the B-Bar-R and the Circle-F were ready to laugh and celebrate, if in a suitably subdued manner.

Standing tall and handsome beside his cousin, a grin

displaying his strong white teeth, Eric gave evidence of pride and pleasure in his role of best man to the groom.

The groom was impressive.

Sartorially correct, attired in the latest London fashion, Duncan looked the epitome of every woman's fantasy and every man's idea of the fabled English aristocrat. His behavior was peerless. He was charming, gallant, congenial.

When he addressed his pale bride, Lord Rayburne smiled and spoke in tones of gentle caring.

Jessica returned his smiles with stiff lips and fought an urgent need to be sick to her stomach.

The golden rays of early-afternoon October sunlight streamed through the long windows, dancing a sparkling path over the assemblage, gleaming on Emily's best china plates set out in readiness on the dining-room table, glinting on the silver flatware fanned out above the plates.

Laughing and chatting, Emily, Inga, and the wives of the married hands on the two properties bustled about, dashing back and forth between the kitchen and the dining room. Within minutes of the ritual of kissing the bride, the table was covered with an assortment of foods, both hot and cold.

It was time for the reception, time to celebrate the nuptials linking the two families.

Toasts were raised; Jessica's stomach murmured a protest. A plate of food was shoved into her cold hand; Jessica's stomach gave a lurch. The cowboys bantered about a shivaree; Jessica's stomach rebelled.

Declaring the need to change clothing, she took flight, if in a dignified manner. Jessica made it to just inside the bathroom door before her stomach spewed its contents onto the freshly scrubbed floor. It didn't amount to much, the weak tea she had sipped prior to the ceremony, the few swallows of wine she had imbibed during the toasts, the tiny piece of wedding cake her bridegroom had slipped between her trembling lips.

Nevertheless, Jessica was appalled by the small puddle at her silk-slipper-clad feet. A wave of defeat washed over her as she stared at the bile through silver eyes darkened and dimmed by utter despair.

"Are you all right?"

The quiet, concerned sound of Duncan's voice struck Jessica with the force of the flicking tip of her own whip. She gasped and went rigid. His hand touched her shoulder. She moaned and flinched.

"For God's sake, Jess!" Duncan's soft tone took on a serrated edge. "What's the matter with you?"

"I-I didn't make it." Jessica shut her eyes in dismay at the wailing sound of her voice.

"What are you talking about?" Duncan stepped to her side. "What didn't you make?"

"Careful!" She cautioned him, waving a limp hand at the spot. "I soiled the floor."

He came to a halt, his gleaming boot tips at the very edge of the watery puddle. "Is that all?" He shot a wry look at her. "Hardly cause for hysteria."

Tears filled Jessica's eyes. She was so tired, so very tired. "You don't understand!" she cried. "Mother scrubbed the floor this morning!"

Alarm flickered in his strange, beautiful eyes. Beginning to scowl, Duncan peered into her wan face. "Christ, Jess! It's nothing to cry about." Taking a gentle hold on her upper arm, he drew her around the mess and to the commode. "Sit down," he ordered, lowering her trembling body to the wooden seat. "I'll see to the floor."

Sniffling, and hating herself for her betrayal of weakness, Jessica sat on the receptacle her brother called "the throne" and watched in amazement as Lord Rayburne, resplendent in exquisitely tailored garb, filled the agate basin with water in preparation of mopping up the evidence of her queasy stomach.

A protest rose to her lips as he sank to one knee beside the puddle. Contrary to the surge of vindictive glee she would have expected to experience, Jessica felt a sharp sensation of consternation regarding the inappropriateness of the labor he was willing to perform.

"No!" she blurted out without thinking. "You can't!"

Duncan cast a haughty look and an arched brow at her. "I beg your pardon?"

Caught in the cleft of her own impulsive tongue, Jessica gave him a helpless look and a vague hand motion. "That . . . mess," she explained. "You can't clean it up."

A frown line drew his brows together. "No?" Duncan inquired with cool disdain. "And why can't I?"

Jessica's strength was returning, and with it her normal common sense. The situation was becoming ludicrous. The *segundo* might well set his hand to the task of mopping up after her bout of sickness, but Duncan was not in reality the *segundo*, even if her mind persisted in thinking of him as such. Duncan was, in fact, a peer of the British realm, and to her admittedly limited understanding of the matter, peers of the realm did not go about cleaning up after anybody—with the possible exception of the reigning monarch.

"It's unseemly," she said, blindly following the course of impulsiveness. "Give me a few moments more rest and I'll do it myself, or call Mother or one of the other women, but leave it. You'll ruin your beautiful clothes."

A fleeting expression of sheer astonishment swept across his patrician features, then vanished, blown away by the blast of his burst of laughter.

The free, buoyant sound of Duncan's unfettered laughter contained every element every one of Jessica's secret dreams and expectations were made of. In that instant, if only within that secret place deep inside her, Jessica acknowledged the depth and breadth of the love she felt for Duncan, this arrogant lord, who would to her always remain her own Segundo.

A bud of promise sprouted in the earthy substance of her acknowledgment, pushing its way forward into the nurturing light of acceptance. Maybe, with time . . . with perseverance . . . with mutual endeavor . . .

"I mean it!" Uncomfortable with her strange, startling, disquieting introspection, Jessica reacted by snapping at him. "Leave it!"

"It's nothing." Proving his point, Duncan made quick, neat work of the cleaning chore. "You see?" A slow smile tiptoed across his quirked mouth. "If you will recall," he said in a chiding voice, "I am a working rancher. Wiping up this little stomach spill was negligible, in comparison to wearing my rear to the nub chasing into the brush after strays."

Feeling put in her place, and not liking the feeling, Jessica stubbornly maintained her position . . . and his. "But that was before. You were dressed for the job."

"And will be again, presently," Duncan drawled, slanting a quick glance at the window, ablaze with midafternoon sunlight. "The day is on the wane. We both need to change. If we are to get home before nightfall, we must make a move soon to start for the Circle-F. The night air will be too chill for David."

Since Jessica viewed with uneasy trepidation the prospect of moving from the known safety of her home to the unknown future inside his house, she was not loath to delay their departure. But the mention of David's name propelled her to her feet. Not for any reason would she have that ill, proud but silent old man suffer discomfort because of her.

"It will only take me a few minutes to change." She skirted around him on her way to the door, but hesitated on the threshold to offer her gratitude. "Thank you for cleaning up. I promise the need will not arise again."

"You're welcome." Standing, Duncan studied her with somber regard. "You are feeling better?"

"Yes." Jessica added emphasis to her claim with a nod of her head. Then, since he appeared less lordly, more approachable, she made a bid to avoid being confined to the buggy on the trip to the Circle-F. "I feel well enough to ride."

"I think not." Though Duncan smiled, his voice was hard, flat, unyielding. The relentless lord was back, in all his commanding arrogance.

I think not.
The phrase echoed through the seething canyons of

Jessica's mind throughout the long bumpy ride to the Circle-F ranch. The friendly, loquacious young cowboy named Randy, who had been assigned the driver's seat next to her, had finally fallen silent, affording her the opportunity to nurture her feelings of self-righteous vexation.

Resentment burning brighter inside her with each successive jolt of the buggy, she gritted her teeth and railed against her bridegroom in silent rage and frustration.

Overbearing son of a . . . Jessica clamped her mind lid down on the insult to the gentle woman who had borne the maddening object of her ire and present predicament.

Just who did he think he was, anyway? she fumed, groaning as the right front wheel found yet another rock to climb over. Well, of course, he knew exactly who he was, she fumed, grimacing as the back wheel followed its predecessor.

Duncan Malcolm Frazer . . . Earl of Rayburne . . . Laird of—Jessica frowned. What was the title? Unable to dredge up the designation, she shrugged. Laird of Whatever . . . ranch owner.

The earl.

The laird.

The big boss.

Her lip curled above the curselike sibilant sound that whispered through her lips.

"Se-gun-do."

"*Sí?*"

Jessica started in surprise at the soft-voiced response. Her tender rump sprang a good two inches off the leather-covered buggy seat. The top of her head made thumping contact with the matching leather canopy.

"Dammit, man!" she yelped, clutching at the canopy supports to steady herself. "Where did you come from?"

"Up ahead." Duncan indicated the lead wagon, in which Inga and David were being transported. Because of the trail of dust behind the wagon, and her distraction, Jessica had failed to notice his presence.

"You startled me!"

"Sorry."

Jessica narrowed her eyes against the red glare from the setting sun swimming in the dark sky behind the mountains and fixed a baleful stare on the somber visage of her recently acquired *lord and master*. Though his expression conveyed regret, an underlying thread of amusement skeining his low tone ruined the effect. A stinging retort leapt from her mind to her tongue, only to be held at bay by another voice.

"Howdy, boss." Young Randy greeted his employer with easy familiarity. "How's it goin'?"

"Can't complain." Duncan's drawled, stock response elicited a wry expression and eye-roll from Jessica. His lips losing a fight against a grin, he continued, "I'm sorry I can't say the same for Inga. She claims her old bones are too brittle to handle the pace we've been setting."

Reminded of the rigors of the trip for the older couple, Jessica was at once concerned for their welfare. "How is your uncle? Is the trip proving too arduous for him?"

"Who knows?" Duncan's shrug was fatalistic. "Other

than an occasional low grunt, I haven't heard a sound from David since we rode away from the B-Bar-R."

Too many hours ago. Jessica kept the thought to herself, repressed a desire to rub her posterior to restore feeling to her travel-numbed muscles and slid an irritated, sidelong glance at the tireless man, seated correctly, and with seeming comfort, on the huge horse, Spirit Walker, trotting alongside the buggy.

"How are you holding up to the trip?"

Jessica shot a glance at his face. His eyes were also narrowed, trained on her expressive features. Collecting herself, she offered him a syrupy smile. "Me? Why I've hardly noticed the ride or passage of time," she lied, straight-faced.

"Uh-huh." Duncan gave her a droll look.

"Your lady's doin' jest fine, boss," innocent Randy piped in, obviously unaware of the undertow of tension rippling between the boss and his "lady" wife. " 'Sides which," he went happily on, peering at the outline of buildings in the distance, "we're almost home now."

"Yes, we are almost home," Duncan concurred in a low, contemplative tone that set Jessica's nerves jangling.

Home. Jessica's reluctant gaze was drawn to the structures growing steadily larger on the horizon. Duncan's home. His bastion of male dominance. She'd be alone there, on her own, unsupported by either her parents or her brother. Though she knew she was firmly embedded in the affections of his people, Jessica also knew that not a single one of them would defy his wishes in regard to her.

For all apparent intents and purposes, she would be owned. As much a possession of the "boss" as his land,

his holdings, his herds. Convention decreed that he, as
husband, provide for her. In return, she, as wife, was
duty bound to share her self, her life, her body . . .
with him.

The prospect was both daunting and enraging. The
promising bud that had sprung to life too many hours
ago wilted in the stifling fumes of her fury and fear.
Suppressing a shudder, Jessica stared with bold defiance into his hooded, watchful, blasted turquoise eyes.

"I will need a bath," she said with cool hauteur.

"A bath!" Randy blanched. "Ya mean . . . all
over?" Letting the reins go slack, he whipped around
to stare bug-eyed at her. "Git your whole self in water!"

"Yes." Jessica's lips twitched. "My entire body."

"Well, damnation, if'n that don't beat all!"

"You should try it sometime," Duncan advised,
choking on a bout of swallowed laughter. "It is really
quite an enjoyable experience."

"Me? No, sir!" Randy shook his head, setting his
long, straggly hair swinging, and resumed his grip on
the leather. "I ain't never dunked my nekked body in
any water in nineteen years, and I ain't fixin' to start
now."

Jessica fought the laughter bubbling in her throat
and might have won the battle if she hadn't caught the
grin Duncan tossed at her. Surrendering to the moment, she released the merriment tickling her tongue.

The buggy rolled into the ranch yard and into the
midst of the wagon and riders gathered there, to the
accompaniment of the blending sounds of mutual
laughter trilling from the throats of the boss and his
bride.

* * *

Their compatible laughter had struck the proper note on which to end the long day of celebration.

Grinning and sending them sly looks of encouragement for the wedding night awaiting them, the hired hands called their good nights to Jessica and Duncan and, joking among themselves, took off for the stable, and from there to the bunkhouse and their own private celebration with the beer and grub that had been provided by the boss.

Randy brought the buggy to a halt beside the wagon near the hitching rail. Before Jessica as much as stirred, a command from Duncan rang on the cool evening air.

"Stay where you are, Jess," he ordered, bringing Spirit Walker up close to the vehicle before dismounting. "I will help you down."

Jessica obeyed, but reluctantly, and only because she did not wish to create a scene or upset the elder Robertsons. Rigid with tension, she watched him approach and raise his hands.

Duncan's touch was light, gentle, impersonal. He released her the moment her feet were steady upon the ground. He turned away at once, striding to the wagon to assist Eric in helping Inga and David alight from the high-seated conveyance.

Stiff-legged but determined, Inga made straight for the house. "I'll have coffee and supper on the table inside a half hour," she announced, bustling, if slower than usual, to the kitchen door.

Hurrying after the older woman, Jessica made her own preference known. "You don't need to bother about anything for me, Inga. All I want is a bath and a bed." She wished the last words back into her mouth

the instant they were said, when she caught the muffled sound of Eric's laughter.

Bed. Good Lord, what a fool word to mention on this
of all nights! Chiding herself for her careless tongue,
Jessica slipped into the house on Inga's heels.

"I-I . . ." She, what? Jessica broke off to ask herself.
Feeling much younger than her twenty-two years, Jessica stood in the center of the large room, flushed with
embarrassment, staring helplessly into the compassion-
softened eyes of her husband's aunt.

"Sit down, Jessica," Inga said, smiling as she slid a
chair from beneath the table, "before you fall down."

A swell of emotion, unnamed, unfathomable,
clutched at Jessica's throat. "I . . . feel so odd, mis-
placed, strange," she confided in a strained whisper.

Her element-roughened face growing softer still,
Inga walked around the table to Jessica and reached out
to grasp her trembling hands. "It's only natural," she
said, imprinting the feel of her calluses into Jessica's
palms with a tight squeeze. "It's all so new to you, even
though you've had the run of this house all your life.
The strangeness will soon wear off. You'll see. You're
the mistress here now."

Oh, God, no! The protest streaked through Jessica's
mind, leaving a trail of gathering panic. She was one of
the hands, an outside worker. She knew little about the
day-to-day running of a household. She could, when
pressed, turn her hand to a little cooking, cleaning,
even sewing. Housekeeping tasks had been included in
the courses she had at school. But Jessica had never
excelled in them, as she had in the academic studies.

Her expression was as an open book to Inga. Chuckling, the older woman patted Jessica on the shoulder

and turned away. "It's not nearly as difficult as you're
thinking," she said, moving about collecting the essen-
tials for a quick meal. "I'm not going anywhere. I'll be
here to help."

"Thank you. I'm afraid I'll need all—" Jessica began, but broke off as the back door was swept open.
Bent and in obvious pain, David shuffled into the room,
flanked by his son and his nephew, who were both tot-
ing rimful buckets of water. Her face softening with
compassionate concern, she jumped up and circled the
table. "Can I help?"

David grunted and muttered three words. Since he
spoke low, and in the Shoshone tongue, Jessica had no
idea what his reply had been. She sent a puzzled look
at Duncan.

"Er . . . he said no, but thank you," Duncan translated, incorrectly, Jessica knew, by the twitch of his lip
and the choking laughter Eric couldn't suppress.
"We've brought your bath water," he continued,
changing the subject. "It will be hot by the time you've
finished your supper."

"I really don't want anything," Jessica repeated her
assertion. "All I want is a bath and—" She paused,
catching herself before uttering the word *bed* again. It
wouldn't have mattered; Duncan interrupted.

"Jessica, you will eat something." The order given,
he turned away to carry the bucket to the side of the
stove and pour the water into the heating reservoir attached to the side.

Anger and resentment resurged in Jessica. Damn his
orders! she railed, glaring at his curved back. Hot words
of protest singed her tongue. Jessica caught them back
before they could spring to life. Prudence held her still

and silent. She could not, would not expose her feelings in front of these good people who were both her friends and his family.

Simmering with repressed anger, Jessica forced herself to eat a portion of the meal of steak, eggs, and home-fried potatoes Inga placed on the table in a surprisingly short time.

They had all just settled around the table when a quick rap rattled the door. Muttering a tired-sounding "Now what?" Eric pushed his chair back and strode to the door.

"A rider out of Cheyenne brought this message for the boss from that agent fella of his'n while you were all over to the Randall place," the bunkhouse cook said, thrusting a packet into Eric's hand. "I'd'a brought it sooner but I was busy dishin' up the grub the boss sent over for that hungry bunch of cow punchers."

Agent? Jessica frowned. Duncan retained an agent in Cheyenne? Intrigued, she toyed with her food and observed her husband as he read the brief message. Curiosity consumed her as his eyes brightened and a smile tugged on his mouth.

"Heather is coming to spend the Christmas holidays with us in Cheyenne," he said to the room at large, his eyes scanning the note a second time.

Heather? Jessica drew a blank. "Heather?" she asked in a polite, prodding tone.

Duncan looked up to reveal a smile of obvious delight with the message received. "Yes, Heather. My half-sister. I sent an invitation to both her and my stepmother, but Deirdre has declined." He shrugged. "It appears she has other plans."

His explanation jogged Jessica's memory, and she recalled hearing about Malcolm Frazer's second marriage and the subsequent birth of a daughter. At the same instant that memory stirred, another bit of Duncan's information settled in her mind. "Did you say that Heather was coming to spend the holidays with us in Cheyenne?" She emphasized the last word. "But . . . why Cheyenne? I mean, won't we be here?"

Duncan's smile was mysterious, enigmatic. "No, Jess. We will celebrate the holidays in Cheyenne."

Jessica was now thoroughly confused and even more intrigued. "But where in Cheyenne?"

Cradling his coffee cup in his hands, Duncan sat back in his chair and gave her a teasing smile. "You'll see, when the time comes. Until then, it will remain a surprise."

Jessica felt an acute sense of frustration as well as impatience. Duncan was deliberately teasing her curiosity. She would have loved to badger him with questions but, as she also loved surprises, she somehow managed to refrain.

"I see" was all she said in reply. "And when can we expect your sister, Heather?"

Duncan frowned and cast a quick glance at the note. "There is no date indicated here, but I'm positive there will be a follow-up letter." His eyes took on a faraway look. "Heather is a lovely girl. I hope you'll like her."

"I hope so too," Jessica said, meaning it, instinctively feeling that by Christmas, she would be needing the support of a female friend closer to her own age.

The bath water was hot by the time supper was over. Nearly unconscious on her feet, Jessica gratefully followed Duncan and Eric up the back stairs and along the hall to the master bedroom. Eric said a soft good night and slipped from the room immediately after dumping the contents of his bucket into the slipper-shaped metal bathtub in the small dressing room.

While the men filled the tub, Jessica stood, staring in stunned surprise at the dimensions of the master bedroom suite. The sleeping room was more than spacious, easily accommodating a large, masculine-looking chair and a long, striped silk chaise longue positioned near a wide stone fireplace, in addition to two heavy, intricately carved bureaus, a tallboy for hanging clothing, and, taking up most of one wall, a huge posted bed with a flat-topped canopy, hung with closing draperies.

When the men exited, Jessica crossed the richly carpeted floor to gaze into the room. There was, of course, no toilet, but a sigh of relief whispered through her lips as her gaze came to rest on a straight wooden chair with an enclosed base and a lidded seat. At least she would not have to use an exposed commode or trek outside to the outhouse.

Jessica had felt pangs of dismay at having to give up the luxury of the bathroom in her father's house, which she had herself planned by incorporating ideas used in the design of the bathroom acquired by George Vanderbilt in 1855. But, as she stared into the room, she realized she had gained the advantage of at least a measure of privacy, since the dressing/bathing room connected only to the master bedroom.

"Would you like my assistance?" Duncan drawled from his near-lounging position at the bedroom door, impressing upon her the dubiousness of the privacy afforded by the small room—since she would be expected to share it with him.

Jessica went stiff as a board. "Certainly not!"

"Then . . . enjoy . . . my lady." Laughing, he gave her a sweeping bow and backed from the room.

Heathen! Jessica fumed, setting her fingers to work on the tiny buttons of her blouse. Barbarian! she ranted, dropping her hands to the waistband of her skirt. The invectives rolled through her mind, interspersed with each discarded piece of her clothing.

The water temperature was perfect, hot and soothing. As she slid into the water, Jessica gave a long, blissful sigh and immediately fell asleep.

The giddying sensation of sweeping motion startled her awake. "Oh! What . . . ?" she exclaimed, blinking against the dizzying sight of the ceiling swirling overhead.

"The water has grown cold."

Duncan's soft voice registered on her sleep-fogged mind at the same instant she became aware of his hard arms around her dripping wet body.

"Put me down!" she commanded, if unsteadily.

He laughed, low in his throat. The sound of his laughter sent chills chasing down her spine and a jolt of cold reason to her disoriented mind.

He was headed for the bedroom, for the bed! She would be lost if he . . .

Jessica's thoughts were sent scattering as Duncan set her down, on her feet, in front of the cheery fire leaping in the fireplace. Before she could sputter a word, or even catch her breath, he was briskly applying a drying towel to her body . . . her nude body!

"Stop that!" she cried, swatting at his hands. "I can dry myself."

Neither her actions nor her protests had any effect.

Ignoring her, Duncan continued to press and pat the moisture beaded skin of her arms, her breasts, her legs, her . . .

"Segundo!" Jessica's voice was sharp with command.

The towel-covered hand hovered above the sparkling wet curls on her mound, then slowly dropped to his side. There was something in the way Duncan's hand fell away, some odd nuance that nagged for her attention and consideration. Jessica's mind groped for a descriptive word. It teased the fringes of her awareness, then fled, routed by his sudden movement of withdrawal.

A strange ache pierced Jessica's chest as she watched him turn to pick up something draped over the arm of the chair. When he turned back to her, she saw that he was holding her best flannel nightdress.

"Put this on before you get chilled." Without waiting for her to comply, he drew the material together with his fingers, then slipped the garment over her head.

Feeling safer, more confident, enclosed within the voluminous folds of the gown, Jessica brushed away the fingers he raised to the tiny buttons at her neck. "I will do that," she said, fumbling with the small buttonholes.

Making her more nervous by the second, he watched her every move until the last of the fourteen buttons was fastened. "Now, into bed," he ordered.

Jessica wet her suddenly parched lips and shivered as his eyes monitored the glide of her tongue. "I . . . ah . . ." she began, raking her mind for an excuse to prolong the inevitable moment when she would have to share his bed, and her body, with him. "I think I'd rather . . ."

"Spare yourself the protestations, Jessica," he interrupted impatiently. "I want this child. And I am not altogether ignorant about the process. I will not be sharing the bed with you . . . at least not until the spotting has ceased completely. So you can get into bed without fear of me forcing myself upon you." A faint, mocking smile twisted his lips. "Not that I have ever needed to use force with you."

The sting of his truth brought a flush of embarrassed, and angry, color to Jessica's pale cheeks. "As I suspected, you are no gentleman," she retaliated, sneering. "My lord."

He arched one dark brow. "Would you recognize one?" he drawled, turning to saunter to the door. "I should think it would take a real lady to recognize a true gentleman."

"I never claimed nor aspired to be a helpless and useless lady!" Jessica retorted. "I'm a person. My own person!"

"Nevertheless, you are now a countess. Lady Rayburne." He mocked her with another sweeping bow. When he faced her once more, he was cold, serious. "And, lest you forget again, my name is Duncan."

Defying him, Jessica drew herself up to her full height and gave him her most condescending look. Her voice as frigid as his, she said distinctly, "Never, my lord Se-gun-do."

17

Chill Wind Blowing was dying.

Duncan resisted, fought against the intuitive truth, but the irrefutable evidence of impending death stared him in the face whenever he looked into David's eyes. Death lurked there, dimming the dark-brown depths to shadowy black.

Duncan knew as well that his uncle wanted to die. He could read the longing in David's eyes, the anguished yearning to be set free of the crippling confines of his painful muscles and twisted bones.

Eric also knew the truth. In unspoken understanding, the cousins communicated their sorrowful knowledge of the difficult days approaching. They made a silent pact to keep the knowledge from Inga, who, with unflagging optimism, continued to hope for a miraculous change in her husband's worsening physical condition.

An unfamiliar weight rode Duncan's shoulders. His uncle's physical condition wasn't the only thing worsening. The situation between Duncan and his bride was deteriorating with each passing day. He had hoped that he and Jessica might come to a workable agreement—and perhaps even a mutual caring—with understanding, and tenderness, and time. But he had tried understanding and been misunderstood; had attempted tenderness and been rebuffed. Now, over a month since he had slipped his marriage ring onto her cold finger, time was all he had, too much time, to think, to doubt, to regret.

"Bloody hell!" Flinging his pen onto the accounts ledger he had been working on, Duncan shoved back his desk chair and sprang to his feet. Muttering curses and obscenities in several languages, he paced the length and width of the large, book-lined office where he had spent so many happy boyhood hours with his father.

Duncan's hours were not happy now. He could count on one hand the hours of happiness he had experienced during the previous month.

To begin with, he spent his nights alone on the narrow cot in the small room connected to the master bedroom, the room his father had set up as a nursery, in which Duncan had slept from infancy until the day he and Malcolm departed the ranch for Scotland. In addition, he had left the running of the ranch in Eric's ex-

pert hands, and confined himself to the office paperwork and the duties of attending his wife. Wanting
Jessica to continue to enjoy the privacy she was used to,
he had taken on the roles of upstairs maid, personal
servant, and general dogsbody. He did not consider the
work beneath him; nor was he averse to applying himself to menial labor.

Because he insisted on personally caring for Jessica,
Duncan knew firsthand that she was still spotting. Unknown to Jessica, he and not Inga, or the ranch hand's
wife who came in three times a week to help with the
heavy work, changed the bedding on the huge bed. He
noticed the occasional faint smears of blood staining
the sheets. Also, he alone emptied her bathroom commode, and he had noted the droplets of blood in the
waste.

The fact that Jessica was still spotting was as much of
a concern to him as the realization that David-Chill
Wind was dying. The spotting indicated that Jessica
could be in jeopardy, not only of losing their child but
of suffering ill consequences as well. And, though the
thought of losing his uncle grieved him, and the idea of
losing his seed tormented him, the idea of losing Jessica terrified him.

Duncan had enjoyed a full and varied twenty years
with his father, roaming the world, learning of other
cultures, customs, and concepts. Yet, throughout every
one of those years, he had carried a small, empty place
within him, a place that could only be filled by the
sight of his true homeland and the companionship of
his own people.

At the end of the cattle drive from San Antonio,
Duncan had believed the empty place was finally filled.

He had been wrong. The emptiness remained. Duncan was very much afraid that if he was unsuccessful in gaining Jessica's love, he would carry the empty place within him into eternity.

How to proceed? How to begin closing the widening gap between them? The questions plagued Duncan. If he could have the nights with her, that quiet intimate time, to talk, to reflect, to learn of each other, their hopes, their dreams . . .

Duncan exhaled a harsh sigh and a harsher-sounding curse. While he lay, night after endless night, alone, aching to be with her, to hold her, comfort her, join with her, his marriage remained unconsummated. His wife was a wife in name only.

In all fairness, Duncan acknowledged the effort Jessica was making to adjust to the sudden and drastic change in her mode of living. Accustomed to roaming at will on her father's property, she had accepted without obvious rancor the strictures he had felt imperative. Jessica had not once challenged his authority. She did not ride; she did not run; she did not rush . . . not even into speech. At least, not to him.

She called him Segundo.

A rough sound rumbled deep in Duncan's throat. Not once during the preceding weeks had Jessica used his Christian name. When around others—the family, the hired hands—she spoke at him, never directly to him, and then without using any form of address. On the few occasions when they had been alone, either in the house or the privacy of the bedroom, she addressed him as my lord or Se-gun-do . . . and then in tones of contempt.

Duncan had grown to detest the very sound of the name.

"Dammit!" Jessica yelped. She dropped the long-handled cooking fork and, sticking her finger into her mouth, laved the stinging burn with her tongue.

"Spit at you, did it?" Inga came to stand beside Jessica at the stove. "Let me see."

Jessica withdrew her hand to display the reddened finger. "It's nothing." She dismissed the bacon-fat burn with a shrug and reached out to pick up the fork. A teasing smile curved her lips. "It blends in with all the others." She ran a quick glance over the assortment of nicks, scrapes, and minor burns scattered across her hands and fingers.

"And each one marking a milestone," Inga observed in a praising tone of voice. "You're learning right well, Jessica. I vow that batch of dried apple turnovers you baked yesterday were every bit as good as mine."

Fine praise indeed! Jessica stared at the older woman in pleased amazement. Coming from Inga, who was justly hailed for her culinary skill, the compliment was an accolade, if not entirely warranted.

"I wouldn't go quite that far," Jessica demurred, savoring the compliment nonetheless.

"Well, I would," Inga said, gently shoving the girl aside and plucking the fork from her fingers to take over at the stove. "But then, I was here last night and you weren't."

"Last night?" Frowning, Jessica paused in the act of breaking the third of a dozen eggs into a mixing bowl. There wasn't time to stand by doing nothing while indulging in idle conversation. It was past five on a bleak and rainswept November morning. The men would soon be coming into the house, demanding breakfast. "Why? I mean, what happened last night?"

Inga chuckled. "Why, that husband of yours wolfed down three of those turnovers before going to bed, and then told me they were the best I'd ever made," she reported with feigned insult. "That's what happened."

Jessica was not only stunned by the information, she was beguiled by it. Duncan had praised her cooking! Of course, he hadn't known *she* had made the pastries. The reflection deflated some of the heady steam from her senses. Chiding herself for her too-eager hunger for his approval, Jessica contrived a bland expression and a casual tone. "Did you tell him that I had baked the turnovers?"

"Well, of course I did!" Inga exclaimed, managing to look affronted and proud at the same time. "I taught you how to do it, didn't I?"

"Yes, you did." Acting on impulse, Jessica turned to hug the older woman and plant a soft kiss on her cheek. "You've taught me so many things in the five weeks I've been here, and been so patient with me, I can't thank you enough."

"Go on with you." Flushed with pleasure, Inga briefly returned the hug before stepping away. "It's been a joy having you here. A woman gets lonely for the company of one of her kind, another woman to talk to."

"I've enjoyed it too," Jessica admitted, shocked by the sudden realization that she had spoken the truth. She actually had enjoyed learning the day-by-day running of a household. Would wonders never cease? She, Jessica Randall, the suffragette of independent thought and action, the working ranch hand, content in her enforced role of homemaker!

Content? The word clung to Jessica's mind, splintering her enjoyment of the moment. No, while she was not as miserable as she had expected to be, she was far from content. Contentment was beyond her reach, because, for her, contentment demanded communion with one particular person.

Duncan.

Jessica swallowed a sigh that had more the feel of a tight sob of anguish. The Duncan of her dreams would have exceeded her expectations. The *segundo* did not indulge in communion; he commanded, he demanded, he set down rules.

Jessica knew that the day would arrive when she would rebel; her very nature dictated defiance of him and his arrogant, arbitrary authority. But, for now, for a limited time, she would play the role imposed upon her, as he had played the role of *segundo*. Her reason for compliance was at once rational, emotional, and a source of expanding wonderment. Her reason was the new life growing inside her womb. With each successive day, the burgeoning life within Jessica became more precious to her. From the beginning, she had thought of the seed as Segundo's. Now Jessica possessively thought of the child as *hers*. And she wanted her child with every fiber of her being.

But Jessica wanted her child's father as well. And therein lay the cause of her discontent. For, while she knew Segundo wanted her, she feared and rejected his stated ownership. And Jessica had vowed never to be owned.

"Are you beating those eggs for scrambling or meringue?"

Inga's dryly voiced question drew Jessica from her disquieting reverie. Her face blank, she stared into the bowl at the frothy egg mixture. She didn't even remember breaking the last couple eggs!

"I . . . er, I was lost in thought," she confessed.

"So I noticed." Inga took the bowl from her. "Must have been some pretty deep thinking."

Jessica offered a weak smile and a practical explanation. "I was wondering what he said when you told him that I had baked the apple turnovers."

"Duncan?"

"Yes."

Inga opened her mouth to reply, but the voice that answered was low and masculine.

"I said they were the best turnovers I have ever eaten."

Jessica spun around. Duncan was standing just inside the kitchen door. He was wearing a rain-spattered, sheepskin-lined heavy jacket, his straight-brimmed, flat-crowned hat, rough wool work pants, well-worn boots, and a wry smile. The sight of him caused a near-painful yearning deep inside of her. For a moment Jessica could do nothing more than stare at him.

"Where's Eric?" Inga filled the brief silence with the question. "Breakfast is almost ready."

"He'll be here in a second." Duncan spoke to his aunt but kept his gaze squarely on Jessica. "Do you want me to bring Uncle David down from the bedroom?"

"No." Shaking her head, Inga walked away from the stove. "You get washed up. I can get David."

Duncan was quiet until Inga disappeared up the enclosed back staircase. "I meant it," he murmured when
the sound of her tread faded. "The turnovers were very
good."

Jessica felt a thrill of pleasure, a thrill she considered
out of proportion to his compliment. In a bid to regain
her balance, she overcompensated with a toss-away reply. "Thank you, my lord."

The change in him was immediate and dismaying.
Duncan's eyes flared with annoyance. A muscle
twitched along the side of his hard jaw. "Dammit,
Jess," he ground out, taking a step toward her. "I told
you my name is—"

"Duncan!" The shrill sound of Inga's voice cut
across his threatening tone. "Have you seen David?"
she called above the clattering sound of her rushed de-
scent down the stairs. "He's not in the bedroom!"

The anger flaring in Duncan's eyes flickered into
sharp concern. "No, I haven't seen . . ."

"What's going on?" Eric demanded, pushing into the
house. "I heard you shouting outside," he said to Inga.

"I can't find your father!"

Eric seemed to freeze in place. "Can't find him?
What do you mean? Where have you looked?"

"He wouldn't have gone outside," Duncan said in a
calming tone. "It's wet and freezing. He's here somewhere." With that, he strode from the room.

Within minutes a thorough search of the spacious
house was made; David was nowhere to be found.
When the four searchers returned to the kitchen, Inga
was frantic with worry.

"He must have gone out, but where?" she cried,
shifting a wild-eyed glance from her son to Duncan.

The men exchanged meaningful looks, then moved as one toward the door. In the tense silence following their exit, Jessica and Inga stared at each other in cold dread. Neither one noticed the smell of burning bacon wafting from the stove.

Instinct and intuition drew Duncan and Eric toward the Shoshone reservation. After more than a three-hour bone-chilling, skin-numbing ride through the freezing rain, they found David on a desolate, windswept section of Shoshone land.

He was dressed in only a fringed buckskin shirt, pants, and knee moccasins; he wore no coat, no hat, no gloves. He was seated cross-legged, facing his beloved mountains. His palms lay flat on his thighs, his arms were straight and stiff, supporting his curved spine. His head was tilted at a proud but awkward angle. His eyes were wide open, staring sightlessly at the mist-shrouded spires, so near yet forever far away.

Chill Wind Blowing was dead.

18

❦

The silence was pervasive and oppressive.

Seated on a hard, straight-backed chair next to her husband, her clasped hands laying on her black-clad lap, Jessica sat in absolute stillness, her pain-filled gaze fixed to the parlor wall, two feet above the handmade casket cradling the earthly remains of David-Chill Wind Robertson.

Unshed tears stung the backs of her eyelids. Bitterness burned the back of her throat. Her heart ached for the three surviving members of David's family.

Except for the Circle-F crew, Jessica's own family, their entire complement of hired hands, the preacher from Sandy Rush, and the silent Shoshone people, no one—not friend, neighbor, or acquaintance—had bothered to journey to the Circle-F to pay his last respects to the departed. To a man, Jessica knew they felt they had no respect to pay.

David-Chill Wind was only one more dead Indian—wasn't he?

The knowledge was disheartening and infuriating for Jessica, and she could see the effects of that knowledge on the three people who were now her legal family.

Jessica didn't need to disengage her stare from the opposite wall to view the evidence of the effects on their countenances; it was imprinted on her memory.

Inga's eyes had a haunted look, and her appearance had aged by ten years. Eric's soft brown eyes had grown hard and his face had lost all previous signs of fun-loving good nature. But, by far, the worst visage of all to look upon was that of her husband. Duncan's sharply defined features were set into an expression both formidable and frightening; his frigid manner was remote and unapproachable.

In her need to give as well as receive comforting and succor to relieve her searing grief, Jessica had braved Duncan's cold detachment late in the night of the day of David's death. He had turned on her with a snarl.

"Take your pity to your cold bed, white woman," he said in a raw whisper. "And take with you also the certainty that our quarter-breed issue will grow up subjected to the same intolerance given to my people." His voice grew stronger, hard with purpose. "But this land belongs to my people, and to me, and to my heir, more than to any other white man, and grow up on it he will."

Two days had passed since his slashing attack. Cut to the quick, Jessica had not had the courage to offer him as much as a word of sympathy or compassion. While his scathing remarks had deeply hurt her, she understood why he had made them. She had caught a glimpse of the agony revealed in his beautiful eyes before he had turned away and left her to grieve alone. Because she understood, she felt his pain as well as her own. And her own pain was great, because it was twofold.

The strain that had existed between Jessica and Duncan before had now expanded into a wide breach. She felt shut out, locked out, rejected. Being normal, and female, and pregnant, Jessica reacted to the atmosphere of strain in the most normal and female manner. She withdrew into herself.

Hurting, for David's family, for her own family, who were all his friends, for the hired hands of both outfits, and for his people, silent and stoic, who had begun drifting into the ranch yard early that morning, but mostly for her Segundo and herself, Jessica stared through pain-filled eyes at the wall.

In compliance with Inga's wishes, David-Chill Wind was buried beside his sister, Duncan's mother, Mary-First Star, beneath the old tree on the gently sloping knoll a short distance from the Circle-F ranch house.

Granite-faced and dry-eyed, Duncan watched in grim silence as his beloved uncle was laid to rest next to the woman they had both adored.

His wife stood by his side.

His wife.

Bitterness rose like a living entity to burn Duncan's

throat and ate like an acid inside his mind. Bitterness two-fanged, like the strike of a poisonous serpent, inflicting festering holes of resentment and remorse.

In his grief, Duncan had wrongly lashed out at his wife, when she had made the first tentative move toward healing the chasm separating them. In his fury aroused by the careless attitude of supposed "good" neighbors, Duncan had punished the one person who mattered the most to him and least deserved his antipathy. In his self-righteous stupidity, Duncan had slashed the string of her offer of sympathy into writhing ribbons of fraying misapprehension.

Cut off by the rapier edge of his tongue, Jessica had understandably drawn the cloak of self-protective composure around her emotions and responses.

Watching his hopes for a future for them curl up and die like the dry leaves swirling around his feet, Duncan accepted as earned the blame for the impasse in which he found himself. But, though the damage was done, he had never ascribed to the theory of letting go, and he was not without resources.

While his grief was real and deep, Duncan held firm to the shining promise of two diverse but solid factors to help pave the way for him into Jessica's good graces. The first of those factors was the expected arrival of his sweet-natured half-sister, Heather. The second was the wedding gift he had yet to present to his wife—the house in Cheyenne.

December descended on the Wyoming landscape swathed in gloomy gray clouds. The wind had sharp-edged teeth, portending harsher conditions to follow. During the two weeks since David's funeral, there had

been seemingly endless days of driving rain mixed with
sleet but, other than a few light dustings, there had
been no appreciable snowfall. But the snow would
come, swept by lashing wind, blanketing the earth,
freezing stock in their tracks, confining the human in-
habitants to their shelters.

Time was of the essence, and Duncan knew it.

"Supper's ready," Inga announced at the close of an
unseasonably mild and sun-splashed day. "I'll go get
Dav—" Catching herself, she came to an abrupt halt
midway between the stove and the kitchen staircase.
An expression of pain-filled consternation flickered
over her drawn face. She shut her eyes and bit her lip.
"Two weeks," she said, swallowing with obvious difficulty. "Two weeks and I'm still . . ." She broke off
again, shaking her head. "I'm an old fool."

"No! No, you are not." After crossing to the older
woman, Jessica drew her into her arms. "You are anything but a fool, and you're not at all old. It takes time,
Aunt Inga," she said, using the address without conscious thought, thus revealing the bond of affection
that had developed between them. "Two weeks is a
short amount of time, after all. You need—"

"You need a change of scene," Duncan declared,
drowning out the softer tones of his wife's voice.

Startled by his silent entry into the room, Jessica
gasped and spun around to glare at him. "Must you
forever sneak up on people?" she demanded, re-
fraining, as usual, from using any form of address with
him.

"Sneak?" he prompted, arching one dark brow.

Choosing to ignore his prod and his superior expression, Jessica homed in on his stark statement. "And what do you mean, she needs a change of scene?"

"I mean precisely what I said." Shifting his gaze to Inga, Duncan continued, "There are too many memories here, too many reminders of the past. I think it would be beneficial for you to distance yourself for a time."

Looking stricken, Inga shot a glance in the direction of the knoll. "You want me to go away from here . . . from him?" Her voice was hollow with disbelief.

"He's not there, Aunt Inga." Duncan's voice was soft with compassion. "He's here." He tapped a finger against his temple. "And here." His finger dropped to his chest, above his heart. "Wherever you go, you'll take him with you. I will too, just like I always have my parents with me."

"But where do you want me to go?" Inga cried, suddenly frightened, as if afraid of being banished.

"Where?" Duncan smiled. "Why, with Jess and me to Cheyenne. Where else?"

Jessica jolted with shock. "We're going to Cheyenne?"

Duncan favored her with a stern look. "I distinctly remember telling you that Heather would be coming to Cheyenne to spend the holidays with us, Jess. Have you forgotten?"

Jessica had, and admitted as much. "But when were you planning to leave? It's already the sixth of the month, and we could have heavy snow at any time," she went on. "It takes days to get from here to Cheyenne riding hard under the best of conditions, and—"

"I plan an early departure the day after tomorrow,"

he inserted when she paused to draw a quick breath. "I expect the both of you to be ready by then."

"The day after tomorrow!" Wearing like expressions of stunned disbelief, the two women spoke simultaneously.

"Yes." His tone was adamant.

"But, Duncan, I can't be ready that soon!" Inga said, throwing a glance at Jessica for confirmation.

Catching the glance, Jessica tossed it to Duncan. "Aunt Inga's right, we can't possibly—"

"You can, and will," he said, once again cutting her off. "I have received word that Heather will be arriving in Cheyenne on or about the fifteenth." His voice took on a hard note of purpose. "We will be there to receive her."

Tired and chilled to the bone by the frigid wind, the Frazer entourage pulled into Cheyenne late in the afternoon of December 12. It was snowing, but only in fits and starts that caused minor discomfort to the trail-weary travelers.

Numbed by tiredness, Jessica sat shivering beside Randy, as she had on the day of her wedding, except that now she was bundled inside blankets to ward off the biting wind.

"Boy, ain't this somethin'!" Randy exclaimed, his head swiveling back and forth as he tried to look at both sides of the street at once. "I ain't never been in a city this big."

Wondering what the young man would think of the city of Boston, Jessica smiled, murmured an appropriate, if vague, response, and set her own sights along the street. Vehicles of all shapes and sizes jammed the road.

Horses danced in and out around one another. Buildings of one, two, and three stories lined the telegraph-pole-dotted boardwalk. It was noisy, smelly, and dirty —an expanding western town.

Jessica saw but registered little of the activity. Her intent gaze was riveted to the hotel in the next block. She was tired, hungry, and cold. All she wanted was a hot meal and an even hotter bath, followed by a solid night's sleep.

A frown drew her eyebrows together when Muldoon, handling the reins in the lead wagon, drove right by the hotel. Jessica shot a puzzled look at Randy.

"Why didn't Sean stop at the hotel? It's the best Cheyenne has to offer. Where is he going?"

"Dunno, ma'am." Randy shrugged. "Nobody told me nothin'. I'm jest trailin' the leader."

The leader, of course, was Duncan. Astride Spirit Walker, Duncan had ridden point throughout the entire trip, doubling back at odd moments during the day to inquire about the comfort and condition of his aunt and Jessica. Eric had volunteered to ride drag, bringing up the rear of the entourage and eating the dust kicked up by the two wagons and the buggy.

Envying both men their freedom, Jessica was hard put to answer Duncan in a civil manner when he drew alongside the buggy to ask how she was faring. Throughout the long trip, her gritted reply had been the same, and always sent him wheeling away in anger.

"I am fine . . . my lord."

Now, close to the very end of her physical resources and her patience, Jessica strained to keep Duncan's distinctive black hat and his ramrod-straight spine in view.

An irritated outcry escaped her guard when she saw
him turn onto a cross street at an intersection.

"Where *is* he going?"

"Dunno, ma'am," Randy repeated. "But I reckon
we'll find out by and by."

A truism for certain, Jessica reflected a short time
later, as Randy tooled the buggy onto a tree-lined street
in the newer, residential section of the city. The buildings here were grand by any standards, private, elaborate mansions, owned by the wealthier men of business
in the city and the cattlemen from the surrounding
area.

Having been a guest in several of the homes, Jessica
was familiar with them. She was not, however, familiar
with the large residence that proved to be their destination, or the young man waiting for them on the
wrap-around veranda of the house facing the curving
driveway.

Asking herself whom it could be that Duncan knew
well enough to impose his family upon, Jessica's puz-
zlement deepened as, to her amazement, everyone remained in their respective positions, in the wagons and
astride, until Randy drew the buggy to a halt parallel to
the veranda steps. Then Duncan dismounted and
walked to the passenger side of the buggy.

"We're here, Jessica," he said, raising a hand to assist
her from the vehicle.

Yes, but where is here? Jessica asked herself, tossing
back the enfolding blankets. Her curiosity was heightened by the expectant expressions on the faces of her
observers. What was going on here?

An unexpected, odd curl of excitement flared to life
inside Jessica as she slid to the end of the seat and

reached for Duncan's extended hand. In a swift, surprising move, he brought up his other hand, grasped her around the waist and, as if she weighed nothing, swung her from the buggy and deposited her on the bottom veranda step. Then, his hand clasping her elbow, he drew her up the steps to the waiting, grinning young man.

"Jessica, I'd like you to meet Charles Caulding, my agent here in Cheyenne," Duncan said. "Charles, my wife, Jessica Frazer."

So, this was her husband's man of business. More than curious about the reason for the attractive young man's grin and look of avid anticipation, Jessica stepped forward and extended her gloved hand. "How do you do, Mr. Caulding? I'm pleased to finally make your acquaintance."

"I'm fine, thank you, ma'am." He cast a sly, intriguing, conspiratorial glance at Duncan. "And I hope you're still pleased an hour from now."

What a strange response, Jessica mused, beginning to frown. "I'm afraid I don't understand what you mean, Mr. Caulding. Why wouldn't I be—"

"You will understand in a moment," Duncan broke in to assure her. "The key, Charles," he went on, holding out his hand, palm up, in front of the younger man.

"Yes, sir!" His anticipatory grin growing still wider, Charles extended a closed hand, opened it, and dropped a door key into Duncan's palm.

There was a sudden tension in the air, a hushed expectancy gripping the group of people waiting behind her. Jessica experienced an unaccountable thrill tingle through her.

What *was* going on here?

Even as the thought formed in her mind, Duncan placed the shiny new key in her hand.

"Your castle awaits," he murmured, indicating the door with a sweeping motion of his arm. "At any rate," he continued, urging her forward, "the Wyoming equivalent of it."

A glimmering of understanding struck her. Feeling a sudden sense of anxious excitement, Jessica inserted the key into the lock with trembling fingers then, grasping the faceted crystal doorknob, she turned it and pushed the door open. The sight that met her startled gaze drew a gasp of surprise from her.

There were four strangers standing in a line inside the spacious entrance hall, three of them attired in black-and-white uniforms of house servants. The other one, little more than a boy, was dressed in the garb of a stable groom. As Jessica stepped over the threshold, the two women dipped into informal curtsies and the man and boy executed brief bows.

"Welcome home, Mrs. Frazer," they said in chorus.

Home? Jessica whipped around to stare at Duncan. "Home?" she murmured her thought loud enough to be clearly heard by Eric, Inga, and the men crowding around the open door.

"Yours," Duncan said, repeating the sweeping arm movement to encompass the house. "The deed, Charles." Holding her shocked stare, he held out his hand to the other man. As if prepared for the command, Charles smartly slapped a folded document into his employer's palm.

Her throat dry, her heart pounding, and a sensation of unexpected delight radiating through her, Jessica could only choke out a single word. "Mine?"

"My belated wedding gift to you . . . my bride," Duncan said, transferring the document to her hand. "As you will note, yours is the sole name on the deed of ownership."

Her very own house! Jessica was more than surprised, she was absolutely stunned. Her fatigue and hunger momentarily banished by dazed wonderment, she accepted the cheerful congratulations of Inga, Eric, and their men. Then, gathering her wits, she managed to respond graciously as Duncan introduced the recently installed servants.

"Gertrude Menger, your cook." He began with the older, plumper of the women. As the pleasant-looking, apple-cheeked woman stepped forward, a teasing, disarming smile played over his lips. "But she prefers to be called Trudy."

"Then Trudy it shall be," Jessica declared, smiling as she shook the woman's hand. "How do you do, Trudy?"

"Wery vell, tank you, Frau Frazer," Trudy replied in a strong voice with an equally strong German accent. "It vill be a pleasure to cook for such a pretty, skinny mistress." She gave a hearty laugh. "Ja, I soon fatten you up."

Laughing with the cook, Jessica turned to the amused sound of Duncan's voice presenting the younger of the women. "And this is Sarah Ramsey, your housekeeper."

"Sarah." Jessica smiled as she repeated her name. "I hope you will be happy here."

"I'm sure I will, ma'am," Sarah said, returning the smile. "It's such a beautiful house."

"And this is McCrea," Duncan forged on. "Your butler."

Butler! Jessica turned just as the staid-looking man bowed, low from the waist.

"Your Grace," he intoned in a British accent even heavier than Trudy's German inflection.

"Not your Grace, not here," Jessica corrected him. "Here I am simply Mrs. Frazer."

"As you wish, ma'am," McCrea agreed, although his tone left little doubt about his disappointment with her instruction.

"And this urchin bears the exalted name of Duke," Duncan went on, ruffling the shaggy hair of the boy who was boldly stepping out around the butler. "He will help Randy take care of the horses." He sent a wry glance at the young cowboy. "You'd do well to ride herd on this one, Randy," he advised in droll tones. "He is something of a renegade."

The boy grinned, revealing crooked but clean teeth.

"I'll keep the maverick corraled, boss," Randy said, winking at the boy.

"And I'll keep my eye on the two of them," Sean inserted in a dry-voiced drawl.

Reminded of the group hovering at the doorway, Jessica turned and waved them into the house. "Don't stand outside in the cold, come in where it's warm."

While Inga and Eric stepped inside the large foyer, Sean and Randy moved back, shaking their heads.

"No, thank you, ma'am, we have to see to the wagons and horses," Sean said, motioning to the boy. "Come along, Duke, you can show us where we're to bunk."

"Yes, sir!" Touching his cap in a gesture of respect

for his new mistress, the boy scurried around the group
and out through the door.

Taking command, as usual, Duncan began issuing orders. "Sarah, show my aunt and Mr. Robertson to their
rooms. McCrea, you look after the baggage. Charles,
wait for me in my office." He indicated a closed door
beyond the open, curved staircase. "I'll join you there
after I've shown my wife through the house." He
turned to Jessica. "Unless you'd rather rest first?"

"No!" Jessica shook her head. "I want to see the
house at once. And the stables. And the—"

"Very well." Duncan smiled.

"And I'll haf a meal ready for you vhen you've finished." Looking like a woman with a sacred mission,
Trudy bustled from the foyer. Her action galvanized
the others. Following suit, the group split to move off
in different directions.

Left alone with her husband in the entranceway that
suddenly seemed much larger than before, Jessica sent
him a sidelong glance. "Where shall we begin?"

"Why not right here?" Grasping her elbow, Duncan
led her to wide double sliding doors to the left of the
entrance. "Your sitting room." He smiled. "Or, as you
call it in this country, your parlor."

The reserve that Jessica had maintained since
David's death dissipated in the warmth of pleasure she
was feeling. Without conscious thought, she turned to
him, eagerly voicing her appreciation of the beautiful
room. "It's perfect!" she exclaimed, crossing the room
to examine every detail.

"You are pleased?"

Discerning an underlying note of anxiety in
Duncan's tone, Jessica shot him a startled look.

"Pleased? I'm . . . I'm overwhelmed by it all." She waved her arm in an encompassing gesture, indicating the velvet-covered settee and high-backed chairs, the plush carpeting, the delicate Meissen porcelain figurines set on the mantelpiece, and the carved, inlaid tables. Everything, down to the smallest detail, was exactly as she would have chosen for herself. "Who did this?"

"I did."

"You?" Jessica frowned, confused and rather shaken by his admission. "But . . . when? How?"

"Oh, Charles did the actual work," Duncan said, skimming the room with a critical gaze. "But I am gratified to see that he followed my instructions to the letter."

When had he come to know her, her tastes, so well? Jessica asked herself, pulling off her gloves as she moved around the room to enjoy the rich texture of the velvet, the smooth glide of fingertips against the cool porcelain. They had had so little contact or discourse. How had he learned so very much about her, her likes and dislikes?

Pondering the puzzle of the enigmatic man who was her husband, Jessica drifted into the connecting dining room. It seemed impossible, yet here also she found everything as she would have selected for herself.

"Beautiful," she murmured, smoothing her palm over the gleaming dining-room table. "I saw a table similar to this one in a friend's home in Boston." She smiled in remembrance of the occasion, and the envy she had felt for Mattie's mother for owning the lovely piece. "I recall promising myself one like it . . . some day."

"Indeed!" Duncan looked startled. "What an odd coincidence. I also saw a similar table in the home of a friend, and decided there and then that I should like one of my own."

The link, tenuous as it was, arrested them in silent communication for long seconds. His eyes, now soft as well as beautiful, spoke to her of possibilities beyond any she had previously dared to dream about.

Feeling her resistance to him, their situation, losing strength, Jessica took a cautious step back, away from him, the allure of his eloquent eyes.

Go slow, she advised herself, inching back yet another step. He was still the same man. The *segundo* had seduced her body, Jessica reflected. Was he now intent on seducing her mind? Could her mental seduction be one of the possibilities lurking in the depths of his eyes?

Suddenly afraid, of her own weakening more than of him, Jessica took flight, covering her retreat with the excuse of seeing the rest of the house.

"I must see the kitchen!"

The kitchen proved to be a homemaker's dream come true. Her cheeks flushed with pleasure, Trudy pointed out each and every convenience to Jessica. Here, once again, Jessica had the uncanny sensation that someone had read her mind.

It was the same, room after room, throughout the large house. By the time they arrived at the master bedroom suite, Jessica was feeling decidedly strange.

By itself, the bedroom appeared as an accurate reflection of Jessica's innermost person. The decor lent an aura of comfort and relaxation, a sanctuary of rest after a busy work day. The bed alone was an alluring oasis, long and wide with four tall posts supporting a flat canopy, not in the least fussy or frilly but elegant in its simplicity. The other pieces of furniture were constructed of solid oak, rubbed to a glossy finish. The carpet on the floor was wool, hand woven in the rich colors and designs distinctly Navajo Indian, beautifully blending two diverse countries and cultures.

The effect was not lost on Jessica. A niggling idea wormed its way into her mind. Quite like the mixture of furnishings in the room, she and Duncan appeared as different as day and night. And yet . . .

Jessica slid a hooded glance at him. The room reflected him, the man, as accurately as it mirrored her own personality. Even dressed in rough working garb, as Duncan now was, he fit, belonged in the picture of his surroundings. On consideration, she realized that the entire house seemed to have been made to order for either one of them—or both of them.

The startling realization struck Jessica with a sudden burst of insight. When had she come to know *him* so well? Her heart pounding from the strange combination of elation and apprehension, Jessica stared at his sharp profile.

She did know him! She knew his arrogance and his compassion, his remoteness and his warmth, his ruthlessness and his sensitivity, his strength and his weaknesses. She knew him, recognized his qualities, good and bad, simply because they were the same as she herself possessed! They were not opposites at all, as she had believed, but as alike as two people of opposite sexes could possibly be!

Jessica was no longer shaken, she was completely undone. Stunned by her unexpected enlightenment, she stumbled across the room and sank onto the edge of the bed.

"What is it?" Drawn by her action from his intent survey of the room, Duncan rushed to her side. "Jessica, tell me, what's wrong? Are you feeling sick?"

"No." Jessica's voice was scarcely more than a croak. "I . . . I'm a little tired, that's all." She needed time, to be alone, to think, to work out this tangle of illumination of seeming differences that were in fact the same. "If I could, I'd like to rest awhile before dinner."

Duncan's concern-darkened gaze probed her expression, her pale cheeks, her haunted eyes. "Charles highly recommends a young physician here in Cheyenne," he said, turning to stride toward the door. "I'll send Randy for him."

"That won't be necessary," she hastened to assure him. "I'm just tired." Jessica was hesitant to admit, even to herself, that since her bouts of spotting had not abated, she was frightened of what a physician might tell her. "The trip was so long, followed by the excitement of this house . . ." Her voice faded to a whisper. "I have nothing to give you in return."

"Nothing?" Duncan's tread was feather light as he retraced his steps back to the bed. His voice was low, his eyes soft, the touch of his fingertips a gentle stroke against her cheek. "You are carrying a gift beyond price inside your body. I have given you a house, a structure. You are giving me an heir."

Please God, Jessica prayed in silent desperation, feeling a dreaded trickle of wetness seep from her body.

19

"There's been a halt in the hostilities."

Meg glanced up with sharp interest at the big Irishman lying by her side. "They are talking to each other?"

Sean managed a prone-position shrug. "Well, Jessica and Duncan are exchanging words, but I can't tell if they are doing any real palaverin'."

"The house did the trick?"

"Seems like." Sean grinned. "Jessica sure makes no bones about how she feels about that house."

Meg sent a slow look around the bedroom. "I understand how she feels. Any woman would. Owning property gives a woman a sense of herself, and her security."

"And it just so happens that you two women in particular have the same man to thank."

"Yes." A touch of awe entered Meg's expression. "The same man, and a genuine lord, no less!"

"Jesus, don't ever let him hear you call him that!" Sean exclaimed.

"Why not?" Meg frowned. "You said he really was an earl, or whatever it is he is."

"An earl," Sean said. "But he told all of the Circle-F hands, everyone, that in this country he is just Duncan Frazer." He grimaced. "Even so, Jessica calls him 'my lord' . . . either that or Segundo."

Meg looked stunned. "I don't believe it. You say that Jessica is a smart lady yet, for a smart lady, I'd say she isn't acting any too bright in this instance."

"Yeah," Sean agreed, shaking his head. "But what can you expect from a woman in love and too proud to admit it?"

"I think it needs more of a drape."

Perched at the top of a ladder propped against the staircase railing, Duncan twisted around to give Jessica a glowering look. "A moment ago it had too much of a drape," he pointedly reminded her, flicking the holly garland he had just refastened to the banister.

"Well, I don't know." Jessica peered at the greenery and pursed her lips. "I want the house to look perfect when Heather arrives."

Duncan exhaled a deep, loud, sigh. "If you soon don't decide, I will still be on this ladder when Heather arrives." Risking a fall, he leaned away from the ladder to stare at the garland. "I think it looks perfect as it now is," he said in tones of aristocratic asperity.

Standing to one side in the spacious foyer to get the full effects of the decorations of looped green holly garland fastened with huge red velvet bows, Jessica shot him an arched look. "Very well, if you insist. Leave it as it is . . . my lord."

"Dammit, Jess!" Endangering life and limb, Duncan clung to the banister with one hand and turned on his precarious perch to glare at her. "How long are you . . ." His voice trailed away when he saw the expression on her face, the shimmering sparkle in her silvery eyes.

She was laughing at him! No. Duncan corrected himself, taking a closer look at her. She was teasing him! Hope burst like a bright summer dawn inside of him, hope that had been sprouting, like a struggling new plant, ever since he had presented her with the house three days ago.

"Are you making light of my title, madam?" he inquired in a droll drawl.

"I am doing my level best, sir," Jessica replied, dipping into a maidenly curtsy.

With a riot of emotions, all of them exhilarating, clamoring through him, Duncan carefully descended the ladder. "In that case, I feel I must ask if you are prepared to pay the consequences for your outrageous disrespect for my station . . . my lady?" Attaining the parquet foyer floor, he smiled and sauntered toward her.

Jessica held her position, and her teasing expression, and tilted her chin at him. "Really, sir, must I remind you that you are an English gentleman?" she retaliated.

A newfound excitement pounding in his blood-stream, Duncan allowed his smile to grow into a wolfish grin. "Ahh, yes, but we are not in England . . . are we? And here, in Wyoming, I am not the gentleman but the savage."

"No! Never that!" Jessica protested, instilling a deep sense of gratification in Duncan. That gratification swiftly changed to amusement when she went on, tauntingly, "A beast, perhaps, but never a savage."

"The beast has been known to bite cheeky young wives," he said in a warning murmur, lowering his gleaming eyes to her exposed arched throat. Duncan reached for her, needing to hold her, crush her against his yearning heart. His fingertips brushed the stiff material of her sleeves, then his hands stilled as the front door was flung open.

"Biggest coach I ever did see jest turned into the driveway, boss!" Randy informed Duncan in an excited rush.

Swallowing a string of frustrated curses, Duncan gazed for a moment into what he prayed was a look of disappointment in the depths of Jessica's eyes. Then, encouraged for a future, more private encounter between them, he turned to respond to the flushed and fidgety cowboy.

"It must be Heather."

Damn! Jessica was hard put not to cry her chagrin aloud at the inopportune interruption. As eager as she was to meet Duncan's sister, Jessica would have happily postponed the occasion forever for the thrill of just one moment of bliss in her husband's arms.

Barely able to believe that they had actually been

bantering in such a playful manner, Jessica paused to draw a shawl around her shoulders to ward off the cold before stepping outside onto the veranda.

It was late afternoon and the wind cut to the bone. Warmed by expectations aroused by those few teasing moments with Duncan, Jessica didn't feel the chill.

Maybe. Maybe. The hopeful word revolved inside her mind in time with the revolutions of the wheels of the coach lumbering along the driveway.

"Ain't that a sight to behold?" Randy asked, staring bug-eyed at the large coach with its retinue consisting of four mounted guards and another on the box beside the driver, all of whom were armed to the teeth.

His expression wry, Eric cast an over-the-shoulder glance at his cousin. "Where'd Charles hire the hard cases?"

"Pinkerton Agency," Duncan replied, studying the riders through narrowed eyes.

Standing hip-shot against the veranda rail, Sean listened to the exchange between the two men, while observing the vehicle come to a shuddering halt. The horses stamped, shook their heads, and blew billows of frosty clouds into the air. The riders sat motionless, waiting for orders from the tall man striding toward the coach.

"Randy, take the guards to the kitchen for a meal," Duncan said, reaching for the handle on the coach door. "Then show them where they can bed down for the night." He paused, hand grasping the handle, to skim the dust-streaked faces of the hired guards. "I'll be around to pay you and thank you, after I've greeted my sister."

Even knowing Duncan as Sean now did, he was impressed by the care his employer had taken in safeguarding his young sister's journey to Cheyenne.

Memorizing every detail of the girl's arrival to relate to Meg, Sean kept his gaze fastened onto the coach door. Duncan swung the door open, thrust his hand inside, then stepped back, drawing with him what appeared to be a small bundle of fur.

Heather Frazer emerged from the coach swathed in Russian sable. Her face was the single visible part of her body. Transfixed, Sean lost all awareness of his surroundings and the family members and hired help crowding forward to meet the awaited guest.

His breath trapped inside his chest, his heart hammering, his blood rushing through his veins, Sean stared, instantly infatuated, with the most exquisitely beautiful creature he had ever laid eyes upon. Without conscious direction, his lips parted; without substance, his voice whispered inside his mind.

"Jesus, Mary, and Joseph!"

"Oh, but I enjoyed every moment of it!" Heather exclaimed, responding to Duncan's inquiry about her long journey.

His features set into lines of disapproval. "You should have brought your maid with you," he said sternly, and not for the first time.

"Oh, Duncan, really, I was perfectly safe." Her soft, delightful laughter danced on the parlor air as she shifted her incredible violet eyes from her brother to Jessica. "I fully expected to enjoy it," she went on, as if he hadn't reintroduced the issue. She switched her sparkling gaze back to him. "That is why I requested

your agent to arrange a coach rather than book passage
on the train." Long, sooty black lashes framed her widened eyes. "Duncan, this country is so vast!"

Enthralled by the vivacious young woman, Jessica
barely heard Duncan's response. Less than an hour had
elapsed since Heather's arrival, and yet, from all appearances, the girl had captivated every member of the
Frazer family and crew.

Within mere minutes of being introduced to her,
Jessica had taken the girl's measure, and been both
satisfied and pleased with her conclusions. In Jessica's
estimation, Heather was more than a physically lovely
fifteen-year-old girl. Small and delicate, with an unbe-
lievably beautiful face, crowned by a mass of gleaming
black hair, she was a well-bred, well-educated, charming, and genuinely sweet-natured young woman.

Jessica had taken to the girl at once. Fortunately,
from all indications, Heather appeared to experience a
like response to her new sister-in-law.

"I love this house. When may I see the rest of it?"

Her attention snagged by the girl's enthusiastic request, Jessica smiled and answered, "Whenever you
like. But wouldn't you rather rest a bit first?"

"Oh, no!" Heather said, setting her teacup aside and
springing to her dainty feet. "I'm not at all tired."

Rising, Duncan headed for the doorway. "I must see
to the guards." He hesitated at the open double doors
to slant a quizzing look at Heather. "Are you positive
you would not prefer to rest awhile?"

Heather made a face at him. "Yes, I'm positive. Run
along, Duncan, please." She waved her small hand in a
gesture of dismissal and smiled at Jessica. "I want to
get better acquainted with my new sister."

Obviously suppressing laughter, Duncan accorded his sibling a deep, sweeping bow, looking not in the least incongruous, even in work clothes and scuffed boots. "Your wish is my command, my lady imp," he said, giving way to the laughter as he strode from the room.

"I adore that man," Heather murmured, her eyes and smile growing misty.

So do I, Jessica confessed, but only to herself. Feeling excluded and a disturbing sense of being the intruder in her own home, she stared at the empty doorway with naked longing.

"You love him very much, don't you?"

Startled by the girl's perception and forthrightness, Jessica jolted around to face her. How to answer? What to say? Jessica felt exposed, and suddenly very vulnerable. "Yes," she whispered, startled at how good it felt to finally give voice to her feelings for him.

Crossing to her, Heather grasped her hands. "I know it was dreadfully rude of me to ask that question," she admitted. "Duncan is always telling me that I have a decided penchant for poking my nose into things that are none of my concern." Her smile reflected the impishness of her brother's accusation, while her eyes revealed a maturity beyond her young years. "But I had to know, you see. He is so very dear to me, and I desire only the very best for him." She stared at Jessica with serious intent. "I am already convinced he has found the very best in you."

Struck speechless, Jessica stared back in astonishment at the smiling girl. Where had this incredible child sprung from? she asked herself. And what act of grace had she performed to earn Heather as a reward?

"But mind," Heather went on in a laughing tone, dissolving Jessica's bemusement. "Duncan has his annoying moments. He can be arrogant in the extreme, and altogether too superior and full of himself. I expect you to train him to heel."

Jessica burst into laughter, she couldn't contain it. The very idea of anyone training Duncan, the stern-faced Segundo, to heel was riotously funny by itself. But to have the order to do so come from his own sister, and a child-woman, at that, was beyond Jessica's powers of self-control. This child, this engaging scamp was like a breath of fresh air on a sultry summer day. "Your brother was right in his assessment, you know," she observed as her laughter subsided. "You are an imp."

"Of course." Tossing her head, Heather turned and sashayed to the doorway. "Now, may I have my tour of the house, please?"

Shaking her head in sheer wonder of the exquisite creature, Jessica followed in the girl's delicate footsteps.

A bond had been forged between the two women, a bond that strengthened with each succeeding tidbit of conversation, however trivial, they shared. In Heather's company, Jessica felt as young and free of restraint as she had during her school years and her close friendship with Mattie.

They ended the tour of the house at Heather's room. "I'll leave you to get settled in," Jessica said, stepping into the hallway. "Please don't hesitate to ask if there is anything you need."

"There is one thing," Heather said, giving Jessica a sidelong glance from beneath the feathery fringe of her long black eyelashes. "When I arrived, there was a devil-take-the-hindmost-looking man lounging against the veranda railing. A very handsome man, with striking blue eyes and dark hair curling from beneath his wide hat brim." Her lashes fluttered demurely. "What is his name?"

"You must be referring to Sean Muldoon," Jessica responded, amused by the girl's accurate description of the big Irishman. "Why do you want to know his name?"

Heather smiled, and answered with simple candor. "Because he is the man I am going to marry someday."

Reminded of her friend, Mattie, who had made almost the exact same statement about the man who was now her husband, Jessica laughed with indulgent affection. "Oh, I see," she said, arching her brows. "Were you planning to tell him first?"

"Eventually." Heather grinned. "Sean Muldoon," she repeated his name. "Yes, it will do."

Repressing an urge to laugh at the utter confidence of the very young, Jessica exited the room, leaving Heather to her schoolgirl dreams.

Heather's advent changed the entire routine of the household. No one seemed to mind in the least. Laughter rang throughout the rooms, as the young woman proceeded to charm and beguile every member of the family and staff. Young Duke followed at the girl's heels like an eager puppy whenever Heather ventured from the house. Eric obligingly escorted her on a walking tour of the city. Even Inga gave way to the girl's gentle prodding and emerged from her mourning to bustle about once more.

Sean Muldoon proved the only exception to the mass surrender to Heather's winning ways. Unusually quiet and remote, he absented himself from the house with increasing frequency.

Jessica noticed the signs of withdrawal in Sean and guessed at the reason for his restlessness. Sean was obviously attracted to Heather and concerned by the attraction. She was only fifteen, after all, and Sean was a mature man, over ten years Heather's senior.

But, although she noticed, Jessica could give no more than passing consideration to what was, in truth, Sean's problem. She had other considerations to contemplate. First and foremost of these was the sudden cessation of her spotting. Relief, hope, and joy vied for supremacy inside her with each successive hour that elapsed without a sign of a spot or even a smear of blood.

Then, of equal importance to Jessica, were the expectations shimmering inside her in regards to Duncan. The easing of tensions between them, which had begun on the day of their arrival in Cheyenne, had accelerated with the arrival of his half-sister, the effervescent Heather.

Duncan's new manner and attitude led Jessica to speculate that they might yet create the only kind of marriage she could or would tolerate, that of a partnership of two distinct individuals, each possessing equal status, willing to give as well as take, discuss rather than command, sharing both responsibility and afforded pleasures.

With a long, fervent sigh of gratitude for the well-appointed bathroom adjoining the master bedroom, Jessica sank into the steamy warmth of the oversize bathtub and rested her head against the metal rim.

Yes, by all indications, her situation was improving day by day, Jessica mused, raising a dripping hand to cover a yawn. She was tired—but then, shopping had always tired her, simply because she had always detested the chore. At least, she had always detested shopping before—before she had discovered the enjoyment of Heather's companionship and before she had become a homeowner.

Incredible as it seemed, Jessica was house proud. And she and Heather had spent the major part of the day shopping, not for themselves but for the house. The Christmas spirit was upon them, and, laughing together, they had searched the shops for items to decorate the house for the approaching holiday.

There were only four days remaining until Christmas, and there was still so much to do. Inga, quite like her normal self since Heather's appearance on the scene, had appointed herself assistant to the cook. The kitchen was redolent with the spicy scents of the season. Duke, Sarah, and even McCrea were busily employed on their off hours stringing shiny red holly berries. Heather was planning to prepare a traditional English plum pudding in honor of Jessica's parents and Parker, who were expected to arrive on the twenty-third to spend the holidays in Cheyenne. And Duncan and Eric had promised to find the perfect tree for the occasion.

A soft smile curved Jessica's lips as she recalled the lengths of red, gold, and green ribbon and the painted glass tree ornaments she and Heather had pondered over before finally deciding to purchase. Recalling the long-suffering expression of the clerk at the mercantile store brought a burst of laughter from Jessica's throat.

"Do you always laugh in your bath?"

Duncan's soft voice shattered Jessica's reverie; the

sensuality woven through his tone shattered her composure. Shivering, she sank lower into the water, hiding
her nakedness beneath the mound of bubbles bobbing
on the surface. "I . . . er, was thinking," she said, despairing at the breathy sound of her own voice.

"Amusing thoughts?" His noiseless tread followed
his question across the room to her.

Jessica swallowed and sank even lower into the water. "Yes. The clerk at the mercantile, he . . . what
are you doing?" She broke off to exclaim, her eyes
widening as he dropped to his knees alongside the tub.

Duncan's smile had the power to heat her blood
while chilling her spine. "Saving you the effort of
crinking your neck to look up at me while we talked,"
he answered smoothly, soothingly. "You were saying?"

"Saying?" Jessica blinked. "Oh! Yes. The clerk!
Well, he was polite and respectful, of course, but I'm
afraid Heather and I tried his patience somewhat."

"I've noticed the tendency in both of you," he observed wryly, flicking a finger against a fat bubble. The
bubble popped; Jessica jumped. Duncan laughed. "It's
enchanting and infuriating, in turn, depending on the
circumstances."

Bristling, Jessica started to pull herself up straight,
but quickly changed her mind when her full, sparsely
lathered breasts emerged from the water. Feeling hot
and cold and excited, she began to submerge. She
wasn't fast enough. Duncan's finger flicked again, this
time against the tightening crest of one creamy warm
breast. A low sound, part protest, but more moan, escaped her surprise-parted lips.

"Don't do that!" Even Jessica could hear the lack of

command in her tremulous voice, the absence of conviction in her tone.

Duncan heard it too. "But I like doing *that*," he murmured, stroking the bud once more. "And it's been so long since I've touched you." Then, unmindful of his shirt sleeve, he plunged his hand into the water to capture the breast. "Oh, Lord." He groaned, gliding his hand down the length of her body. "You're so soft and silky and wet."

And weak, Jessica silently acknowledged, thrilling to the gentle caress of his long fingers. A cry of pleasure burst from her throat when those fingers speared through the tight curls protecting her mound, causing a melting warmth in the depths of her femininity.

Surging up and over her, Duncan crushed her parted lips beneath his hunger-heated mouth. His kiss was hard and demanding, tasting of desperation. Jessica recognized the flavor, and returned it to him. His tongue plunged into her mouth, over and over again, delving deeper with each evocative thrust.

Heat unrelated to the still-steaming water seared through her. Her mind began to whirl. She yearned for his deeper touch, for his . . . Fear broke the grip of sensuality. The child! She couldn't take a chance on endangering his child!

"No . . . no." Whispering her denial, she tore her mouth from his and cringed back, away from his searching fingers.

"Jess, you are my wife, my woman. I need you." His voice was raw, his breath ragged. "I'd give anything, anything, to join with you in there."

His wife! His *woman!* Shock slammed into Jessica, swiftly followed by a blaze of fury. His! His! Nothing had changed, nothing. All the hopes and expectations she had been hugging to her heart had no more substance than Heather's schoolgirl dreams of romance.

Goddamn him! He had nearly succeeded in seducing her mind! Enraged, Jessica struck back at him in the one way she was certain would repulse him.

"Anything?" Jessica lashed out at him with disdain. "Even your precious heir . . . Se-gun-do?"

The expression that transformed his features from sensuous to stark sent a bolt of cold fear to Jessica's heart. The very look of him was menacing. Pulling back, away from her, Duncan stared at her from eyes as flat-looking and hard as the stone they resembled. His withdrawal, physically and figuratively, sent a rush of relief shivering through her.

"I'm sorry." With those two words the *segundo* returned, in control, cold, remote, the antithesis of the man Duncan had been since their arrival in Cheyenne. Standing, he pivoted and strode to the door. "I came to tell you that we found the tree you requested. Enjoy your bath, and your solitude."

As the door closed behind him, tears flooded Jessica's eyes and streamed down her flushed cheeks, tears of shame, and humiliation, and the broken promise of possibilities.

Over an hour later, dressed in a smooth wool skirt and high-collared blouse but wrapped in an impenetrable mantle of detached composure, Jessica went downstairs for dinner uncertain of what, or whom, to expect to find standing at the head of the table. To her surprise, she discovered Duncan there, his manner again easy, his stance relaxed.

"Have you inspected your tree, madam?" His voice was soft, teasing, and as free of strain as it had been before that shattering scene in her bathroom.

Convinced he was once again playing a role, this time for the benefit of his family and servants, Jessica bit back the stinging retort she longed to fling at him—along with the hardest object closest to hand—and drew a glaring bead on him instead.

"No, my lord," she managed to respond without a hint of sarcasm. "I'm saving that treat for dessert."

Their barbed exchange went undetected by everyone present, and the evening commenced with nary a person aware of the tension crackling between them.

The tree was magnificent. The pungent aroma of pine permeated the house. The atmosphere was festive. Everyone, family and staff alike, had been invited to gather in the parlor after dinner to decorate the evergreen symbol of the season. Sean Muldoon was the only one absent.

"No, no, that string of berries near the bottom has too much of a drape," Heather decided, directing Eric in his tree-trimming endeavors.

"Why does that remark have a familiar ring to it?" Duncan mused aloud, slanting a speaking glance at Jessica.

"Why, I have no idea . . . my lord," she returned, offering him a narrow-eyed glare and an innocent smile.

"We'll have to get a ladder to fasten the star on top," Inga opined, frowning as she measured the height of the tree.

Duncan stiffened.

Jessica turned away.

"I'll fetch the ladder," McCrea offered, just as the

door knocker sounded against the door. "After I have tended to my duties," he added, tugging his jacket into place as he walked into the foyer.

"Were you expecting visitors, Duncan?" Heather inquired, brightening as an idea obviously struck her. "Or could it be that Mr. Muldoon has decided to join us, after all?"

"No, I am not expecting guests," Duncan said. "Perhaps Jessica invited someone to join us this evening." He gave Jessica an arched-brow, haughty look.

Itching to give him a smack in his arrogant-looking face, Jessica drew forth her most insipid and blatantly false ladylike tone. "Why, no, I wouldn't have dreamed of it. When we are en famille? Not at the best of times," she paraphrased wryly, "or even the worst . . ."

"Jess . . ." Duncan said in warning, only to be interrupted by McCrea's return to the parlor.

"A boy has just delivered this message for you, my— Mr. Frazer," he announced, catching back the formal address as he crossed to Duncan with the missive.

"A Christmas greeting?" Heather wondered aloud, rising on tiptoe to peek over Duncan's shoulder.

"I seriously doubt it," he drawled, a bitter smile quirking his lips as he withdrew a folded sheet of paper from the thick, creamy envelope. A fleeting expression of surprise swept the bitter look from his set mouth as he scanned the note.

"Well, what is it?" Heather demanded, craning her neck to get a glimpse of the letter.

Jessica was curious as well, but wild stallions couldn't have torn a question from her compressed lips.

"It appears a party of our compatriots is staying here

in Cheyenne," he said to his sister. Then, his cool glance bypassing Jessica, he looked at Eric. "They have been the guests since fall at the hunting lodge of a rancher by name of Henderson." He raised his brows.

"Know of him." Eric answered the silent query. "One of the ranchin' tycoons. Has a big spread up in Platte County. I've heard about that hunting lodge of his too. Story is, ol' John Henderson was so taken with a lodge he was invited to while on a visit to England, he had a replica of the place built here for himself when he got back."

Jessica was simmering with indignation and resentment. She could have given his lordship the information he sought. Of course, she probably wouldn't have —but she could have. In defiance of his deliberate snub, she favored him with her most deadly, vapid smile.

Duncan ignored her. "Well, from this account," he said, again to Eric, "Henderson brought his party to his home here in Cheyenne for the holidays." He smiled faintly, but in a way that brought a shiver to Jessica's spine. "I have a passing acquaintance with two of his guests, whom, I gather, have just learned of my residency here."

"Really?" Heather piped in. "Who are they?"

Duncan gave her a quelling look but answered nonetheless. "Reginald Kirkland and his widowed sister-in-law, the lady Charlotte."

"Lord Wexton," Heather informed the others with a grin. "Reggie of the roving eye and bawdy wit, and the incomparable Charlotte, the maneater."

"Behave yourself, imp," Duncan ordered, before continuing. "Henderson is giving a small reception

Christmas night." He gave the paper a languid wave.
"Jessica, Heather, and I are invited to attend."

"Oh, how marvelous, a party!" Heather exclaimed.
"We will go, Duncan, won't we? Oh, please say we
will!"

Jessica was on the reluctant point of dashing
Heather's exuberance with a resounding no when, as if
reading her mind, and choosing to exert his authority,
Duncan stole the impetus and the moment from her.

"If it will amuse you," he replied to his sister, while
looking down his aristocratic nose to smile with maddening superiority at his wife. "Yes, we shall attend."

20

The snow began to fall in earnest midmorning Christmas Day, and by early evening the accumulation on the ground measured some five or six inches.

Her soft mouth set in a mutinous pout, Jessica stared at her reflection in the standing beveled mirror. Though not new, her flounced, watered taffeta gown was still elegantly fashionable, the deep-ruby color perfect for the occasion.

A lace-trimmed corset lay crumpled on the floor near Jessica's feet, where she had flung it in angry defiance of a lady's proper mode of dress.

She didn't give a bull's hindquarter what his lordship's tony British friends thought, Jessica decided, giving the undergarment a sharp kick. Her babe was more important than the bawdy-witted Lord Wexton, his maneating widowed sister-in-law, and the cream of the local Cheyenne society, and she refused to tie herself into the dratted thing.

Damn the reception, anyway! Jessica railed in silent, impotent frustration. And damn Duncan for telling Heather they would attend.

Jessica was definitely not in the mood for a party. After a long day spent playing the role of the gracious hostess for her parents, brother, and Heather, in addition to exchanging politely worded barbs with her arrogant, honey-tongued husband, Jessica felt more inclined to tear the stiffened silk gown from her body, crawl into her lonely bed, and indulge herself in a bout of weeping self-pity.

The very idea of her, Jessica Randall, succumbing to the detested state of weeping femininity startled Jessica out of her temperamental reverie. Leveling a final glare at the perfectly turned out, perfectly lovely mirrored image glaring back at her, she swung away and marched to the door.

Like it or not, Jessica determined to grit her teeth and accompany her husband and his sister to the Henderson's Christmas reception. Heather was so very excited about going, and Jessica didn't have the heart to see the girl disappointed.

As she descended the stairs, Jessica could hear the muted conversation and laughter from the dining room, where her parents, Parker, Inga, and Eric were enjoying their Christmas supper.

Disgruntled, and not in the best frame of mind to

partake of their merriment, she turned in the opposite
direction at the foot of the staircase, heading for the
kitchen and a cool glass of water to ease her anger-
parched throat.

Her soft, beaded, curved-heeled evening slippers
making a mere whisper of sound on the parquet floor,
Jessica moved listlessly along the hallway. The door to
Duncan's office stood slightly ajar, and as she approached, she caught the familiar sound of Sean Muldoon's voice.

Since Sean had failed to put in an appearance that
day, Jessica came to a halt and raised her hand to tap
against the door, thinking to wish Sean greetings of the
season.

"I must go, Duncan, and you know it."

Go? Jessica's hand wavered a breath away from the
door panel. Where must Sean go? And why? she wondered, stepping closer to the doorway to catch
Duncan's reply.

"The choice is yours, of course."

"I have no choice, and you know that as well."
Sean's voice was raw from strain. "Dammit, man, I
know it's wrong! She's too young, too sweet, too innocent. But I want Heather, want her so bad it's tearing
my guts apart. And if I stay, I'll take her and run with
her."

Surprise jolted through Jessica. So Sean wasn't indifferent to Heather as he had appeared to be! She felt an
aching sadness for the ill-fated attraction between the
pair. If only there was some . . . Her thought shattered as Duncan's voice penetrated her consciousness.

". . . and I would track you down," he said in a tone
devoid of inflection. "And I would kill you."

"Or I'd kill you, and, either way, I'd lose." Sean's tone was flat with resignation.

"Yes. I'm sorry, my friend." Duncan sighed. "When are you leaving?"

"Here? Tonight. I'll spend the night in town and pull out at first light."

"Does Meg know?"

Meg? Jessica frowned, puzzled by the unfamiliar name. Who was this Meg, and what did she have to do with the situation? The answer to her question was swift in coming and devastating in effect.

"Yeah, and she agrees with me about going. She asked me to give you this door key, along with a message from her."

"Thank you, and I'm listening."

"You always do," Sean drawled, sounding amused despite his tangled predicament. "Anyway, Meg said to tell you that, since you paid for her house, she wants you to feel free to come and go as you please. That's the reason she sent the key. She also said to remind you that you're always welcome, in the house as well as in her boudoir."

Jessica didn't hear Duncan's reply. Stunned by the shocking information she had overheard, she stood stock still, numb and barely breathing.

Slowly, as the content of Sean's inadvertent disclosure filtered through her sense of shock and disbelief, Jessica backed away from the door, distancing herself from the room and the man inside who had never ceased playing a role.

Dear God! No!

Pain close to agony ripped through her. Jessica clapped a hand to her mouth to stifle an outcry. Without conscious thought, she lowered her other hand to her abdomen in a gesture of protection.

What a fool she was, she thought, swallowing against a rising swell of bile. What an utter, utter fool! House proud! Idiot! Dupe! Gullible greenhorn!

Pressed back against the stairway wall, Jessica shuddered as wild and disjointed thoughts, impressions, and memories bombarded her mind.

She had known Duncan had made contact with a whore. She had learned about the woman from his own lips that day she had innocently overheard the conversation between him and her father. And she had suspected him of visiting the woman during his many long absences from the B-Bar-R but . . .

She had felt singularly honored by his gift of the house, and she was so proud of it, so very . . .

All the while she had gone along, happily believing Duncan had honored her, his wife, he had already paid a like compliment to a common prostitute!

In precisely the same time-honored and accepted manner of the titled gentlemen, Duncan had quietly arranged two convenient establishments for himself, one—who knew where?—for his mistress, and another, in the most respectable section of the city, for his brood mare!

Damn his faithless soul to hell!

Her stomach churning in time with her wildly racing mind, Jessica pushed away from the wall and rushed for the stairs, only to come to a sliding halt to avoid crashing into the girl skipping down the treads.

"Oh, there you are, Jessica!" Heather exclaimed. "I was looking for you. It's seven-fifty, and Duncan or-

dered the carriage brought round to the covered side
entrance at eight. Are you ready?"

"Ahh, no . . . I." Jessica paused to draw a calming
breath and search her mind for a plausible excuse for
remaining home to give to the girl.

"Well, no matter, apparently Duncan isn't ready as
yet either," Heather rattled on. "Will I do, do you
think?" she asked, twirling about to give Jessica an all-
around look at her gown. "And my hair," she chattered
on, not waiting for a reply. "I think Sarah did a
splendid job putting it up." She patted the glossy black
curls artfully fastened to the crown of her small head.

"Your gown is charming," Jessica said between measured breaths. "And the coiffure looks lovely, but—"

"You do know that, were I at home, I wouldn't be
allowed to attend this reception, don't you?" Heather
interrupted, smiling mischievously. "Mother is so old-
fashioned and tradition-oriented. She would absolutely
forbid it."

Distracted and not thinking too clearly, Jessica
frowned. "But why? It's not a grand affair, after all."

"Why?" Heather laughed. "Really, Jessica, are these
things so very different in this country? I won't make
my bow and have my season until I'm seventeen, and
until I do, I'm not supposed to put my hair up or attend
anything other than intimate family gatherings." Fairly
dancing, she came to Jessica to give her an impulsive
hug. "I can't tell you how excited I am," she said, filling the foyer with another trill of laughter. "Or how
delighted I am that Duncan appears to have forgotten
the boring old drill."

In truth, Jessica had forgotten, which wasn't unusual
since, considering it all silly convention, she had never

paid much attention to the strictures of correct social behavior. Now, so enthusiastically reminded, she felt a sinking, trapped sensation. Heather was so keen on going, so very ebullient, the idea of denying the girl the treat was unthinkable.

Jessica couldn't do it. Her sense of outrage and injury was intense and the pain was unbelievable, but Heather was not at fault, and Jessica still lacked the heart to deny the girl the promised outing, most especially now, knowing the effect Sean's departure would have on her.

Gathering her pride around herself like a shield, Jessica drew her dwindling reserves of strength together. She had not carved a niche for herself within a man's world to cave in to the crushing blow dealt to her by one arrogant, perfidious bastard in it, even if he was the father of her child.

Pulling her drooping shoulders upright and raising her chin, Jessica dredged up a faint smile for the girl.

"There you are, Cinderella," Duncan drawled, eliciting a startled yelp from his sister and a cringing response from Jessica with his silent entry into the foyer. A sardonic smile curved his lips as he sent a cursory gaze over his wife. "And I see you have your wicked sister-in-law in tow."

Struck speechless by his blatant audacity, Jessica glared at him in seething fury.

Heather giggled. "Jessica is not playing the wicked role in this Christmas performance, sir," she chastised him. "In this instance, she is the fairy godmother."

"Indeed?" Taking the pose of a posturing fop of an earlier period, Duncan raised an imaginary quizzing glass to one eye to peruse Jessica's entire form. "And have you finished the task of changing mice and a pumpkin into footman and a carriage, madam?" he inquired lazily.

"Oh, what fun!" Heather cried, laughing and clapping her hands. "It's your turn, Jessica."

Caught in the teasing byplay of the brother and sister, Jessica steeled herself against an urge to slap the former's smiling face and softened her tone for the latter.

"The metamorphosis is complete."

"Then let's away," Duncan ordered. "The carriage awaits, and midnight looms."

"Yes, let's away!" Heather caroled, dashing to the foyer coat closet. "I just know it will be a wonderful evening!"

It was a disaster.

From the moment she entered the Henderson mansion, Jessica knew the evening would be anything but wonderful. The house itself revealed the character of its owners. It was ostentatious, ornate, and overdecorated.

In their fifties, and obviously aspiring to be accepted, John and Clara Henderson were an embarrassment in their fawning over their British guests, the titled members in particular.

To Jessica's disdain, the older couple fairly gushed all over Duncan and Heather, while greeting Jessica politely but distantly, somewhat like a poor relation.

Lord Wexton immediately lived up to his reputation by ogling Heather's decolletage. The lady Charlotte did likewise by immediately attaching herself to Duncan.

The laughing group swept her husband and sister-in-law away, and Jessica found herself in the awkward and uncomfortable position of being excluded. The experience was not only unpleasant, it was disconcertingly enlightening.

For the first time in her life, Jessica fully understood the depth of rejection and isolation Duncan and his family had been subjected to because of their Shoshone connection.

Outraged by an overwhelming sense of injustice, for herself, for Duncan, for his family, and for every person who had ever suffered from mindless bigotry, Jessica again drew on her pride to sustain her.

Finding a quiet corner on the padded seat of an out-of-the-way window, she observed the artificial antics of her fellow guests and labeled them unworthy of a moment of her discomfort and embarrassment.

They were like peacocks, strutting about, speaking in studied droll tones, more impressed with themselves than with one another. Dismissing the group, she homed her sights on the admittedly beautiful Charlotte.

The elegantly figured and attired woman was acutely aware of Jessica's presence. She betrayed her awareness with calculating sidelong glances at the window seat from glittering blue eyes. After the third such glance, Jessica's sense of injustice gave way to the memory of Sean's disclosure, stirring to life her anger and resentment against Duncan.

What manner of man was he? Jessica asked herself, cringing inside as she watched him bend low over the touted beauty to catch whatever the woman was saying to him. Was he insatiable for a variety of women? Or

did his superior male image demand he conquer and
subdue every woman, be she titled, whore, or the defiant daughter of a Wyoming rancher?

"Duncan, darling." Charlotte's low, throaty voice intruded on Jessica's thoughts, drawing her full attention,
as she knew it was meant to do. "Do you recall that
divine night in Paris? The night you and I—" Her
voice trailed away to a suggestive murmur as she leaned
close to him to whisper in his ear.

The anger licking through Jessica's veins surged into
blind rage as she met another sly glance. Shaking with
fury, she rose and walked from the room. She felt sick
from disillusionment and defeat. Without a backward
glance, she retrieved her evening coat from the puz-
zled-looking maid and, unmindful of the inclement
weather, left the house.

Seeking only to be alone, Jessica trudged through the
deepening snow to her home. By the time she had tra-
versed the short distance separating the two properties,
her evening slippers and the bottom of her gown were
soaked.

After stealing into the house to avoid detection, and
resultant questions, Jessica went to her room. There,
behind the securely locked door, she gave vent to her
pain and fury.

Look at yourself! she demanded of her reflection in
the mirror. You are no better than any of the other
young American women who have bartered their bodies and souls for a foreign title!

Raising trembling hands, she yanked the pins from
her wet hair, blaming the tug at her scalp for the rush of
tears to her eyes, and shook the silver mane free.

You knew he was arrogant, ruthless, and deceitful,

she accused herself, sniffing as she kicked sodden shoes into a corner. And yet you allowed your traitorous body to betray you!

Lowering her hands to her bodice, she tore at the tiny row of pearl buttons. He is not worth a second of your pain, she instructed her image, brushing a tear from her cheek as she stepped out of the limp gown and flung it from her. He is not worth your spit!

He is with another woman!

But, damn him, he is mine!

The image froze inside the mirror. Jessica's mind stilled, then erupted with a sharp-edged memory. Wide-eyed yet sightless to the things around her, Jessica reviewed the scene enacted between Duncan and Josh Metcalf behind her father's house on the night of the party. Snatches of Duncan's voice assailed her inner ear.

"She is mine . . ."

"There are ways of killing a man . . ."

"My woman."

"*My* man." Jessica's emotion-roughened voice silenced the inner echo. "The father of *my* child."

Her chaotic mind now calmed, Jessica stood, staring into the eyes staring back at her, silvery eyes, narrowed and gleaming with purposeful intent.

There are ways. The errant phrase whispered through her mind and brought a cunning smile to her lips. Jessica had never been adept with a knife, but . . .

After spinning away from the mirror, she strode to the bureau in which she had placed her working clothes. Oh, yes, she mused, tossing her damp petticoat aside. There are ways of dealing with a thin-nosed, high-born, low-moraled maneater.

Jessica slipped out of the house less than twenty minutes later, dressed for war in wool pants and shirt, a sheepskin lined jacket, wide-brimmed hat, and sturdy boots. Crunching through the snow, she retraced her trail to the Henderson mansion.

The maid was away from her post in the reception hall. Not bothering to remove her thigh-length jacket, Jessica crossed the marble floor to the entrance to the near ballroom-size parlor. She took one step inside the room, and then another.

"Segundo."

The low-pitched but commanding sound of her tone cut through the chattering clatter of voices. Her steps measured, she advanced on the tall man and the clinging woman standing close together at the opposite end of the room.

Jessica heard several female gasps and a man's muttered curse as she advanced. Undeterred, she paced forward.

"Jessica, what do you think you're doing?" Duncan demanded, scowling as he ran a swift look over her attire.

"Step away from the bit—" Jessica curled her lip. "The lady Charlotte, Segundo." Moving the arm she held close to her side, Jessica revealed the whip coiled in her hand.

"Godawmighty!" John Henderson exclaimed.

"Oh, Jessica," Heather whimpered.

A faint-hearted woman screamed . . . and fainted. Jessica continued to advance.

"Jess, stop this at once," Duncan ordered, stepping

forward and half concealing the now pasty-faced lady Charlotte. "Go outside. I'll join you in a moment."

"I said step aside, Segundo." Loosening her fingers, Jessica shook the whip free of the coils. "I won't say it again." With a lightning flick of her wrist, the long strip of black leather cracked and snaked out to full length.

Duncan moved faster than the leather strand. His swiftness saved the lady Charlotte's beauty. The tip of the whip bit a chunk of flesh from a point high on his cheek. Blood spurted forth to trickle down his face. In an instant, the fashionably dressed gentleman changed into a cold-eyed, lethal-looking savage.

"Jess," he said in a deadly tone of voice, "I'm warning you . . ."

His warning went unfinished. Incensed by his defense of the other woman, Jessica flicked the whip again. Duncan's arm shot out and, as he had once before, he caught the leather, this time bare-handed. Then, as before, he started toward her, coiling it as he walked.

Jessica also reacted exactly as before. After flinging the whip at him, she turned and fled. Slipping, nearly falling, she ran all the way back to the house. She was gasping for breath as she stumbled onto the veranda.

Suddenly, with the sharp clarity of a gunshot fired in the stillness of night, the raspy, haunting echo of the shaman's voice reverberated inside her head.

"What is to come will come.

"With the first heavy snowfall and the crack of the whip."

"No! No!" Jessica moaned, fearful of the effects of her impetuous actions on her babe. Clutching her abdomen, she fumbled with the doorknob and shoved open the door.

Terrified, sobbing in anguish and remorse, she staggered inside and crumpled unconscious to the parquet floor.

Duncan was in a towering rage . . . and the grip of a crawling fear unlike anything he had ever before experienced.

Hearing nothing of the babble of assorted voices buzzing around him, seeing nothing, not even Heather's shocked expression, he pulled away from Charlotte's grasping hands and strode from the room in pursuit of his infuriating wife.

"Damned hellcat! Goddamn fool! Bloody damned situation!"

Cursing Jessica, himself, and the tense conditions of their tenuous union in turn, Duncan fingered the stinging gash on his cheek as he plunged into the snow-swirled night. His feet inside the elegant but useless evening shoes were wet before he reached the street. He didn't notice. Breaking into a run, he followed the skidding trail of Jessica's flight.

What in Christ's name had come over the woman to cause her to do such a damn fool thing? he asked himself, dashing the runnel of blood from his face. Did Jessica hate him so very much?

The conjecture turned Duncan's insides to ice. Until that instant, he had refused to speculate on whether she harbored hate for him. The inner fear wound into tight knots in his gut.

He loved her so very much. If she only knew . . .

The forward thrust of Duncan's body faltered, before resuming at an increased pace.

If Jessica knew!

They had spoken of lust, shared it, reveled in it, but never had the word love passed between them. The time, the circumstances had never seemed right for him to declare himself, his feelings, to her.

Maybe it was time, past time, for him to speak?

But what if she rejected him, repudiated his love? What in hell would he do then?

Duncan had too often suffered the soul-wounding pain of rejection. He had survived by learning to shrug his shoulders and go on. But now instinct warned that should Jessica reject him, there would be no shrug, possibly no survival.

Blast survival! Duncan thought, racing up the veranda steps to the house. If Jessica was safe and well, he would talk to her, and pray to Christ she was willing to listen.

Duncan found Jessica in a melted snow puddle on the foyer floor.

"McCrea!" His harsh call bounced back at him off the walls.

"Yes, sir, I'm com—Good heavens!" McCrea exclaimed at the sight that met his startled eyes. "What has happened?"

"I think she's fainted," Duncan said. "Go find that doctor Charles mentioned."

"At once, sir." Not wasting time by going for a coat, McCrea moved around Jessica to get to the door.

The door was closing behind the butler when Duncan remembered his sister. "McCrea!" he shouted.

"I left Miss Heather at the Henderson's. Send Randy for her."

"Immediately, sir."

Duncan didn't hear the man's reply. After scooping Jessica into his arms, he strode across the foyer and mounted the stairs, shouting at full voice power.

"Aunt Inga! Emily!"

21

"What are you doing out here at this time of the morning?" Sean slanted a glance at Meg over the saddle he had just settled onto the back of his horse.

"Came to see you off," Meg mumbled behind the hand she'd raised to cover a yawn. "And to give you the latest gossip making the rounds of saloons and cribs."

"Gossip?" Sean frowned. "What are you mumbling about?"

"There was a party last night at the Hendersons'."

"Yeah, I know. Duncan mentioned it." He shrugged and checked the saddle cinch. "So?"

"They had a bit of a to-do."

Something in her tone made him pause. "What sort of to-do?"

"Close to a brawl as you can come in polite society," Meg said, grinning at him. "Seems Duncan's wife took it into her head to take that whip of hers to one of Henderson's uppity guests. The way I heard it, the woman was crawling all over Duncan at the time. He took the strike on the face."

"No shit!" Sean's jaw dropped. "What happened then?"

"Jessica ran. Duncan ran after her."

"What about Heather?" Sean asked in anxious concern. "Did you hear?"

Meg nodded. "The customer passing the story retold all the details. Appears that little sister of Duncan's was cut out of the same tough cloth as him. She stood there in that house defending Jessica until Randy arrived to collect her." She smiled. "The girl has bottom sand, Muldoon. Maybe you ought to change your mind about leaving."

"No." Giving a rough shake of his head, Sean picked up his bedroll and tied it behind the saddle. "Sand or not, she's only fifteen."

"Lots of girls out here have one on the hip and another in the oven by the time they're fifteen," she reminded him.

"Not girls like Heather," Sean said, stepping into the stirrup, "Heather was raised in the lap of luxury. She'll be going home in a month or so, as planned. Duncan'll see to that." He sighed. "It's for the best."

"Your decision," Meg murmured, walking to him to place a hand on his thigh. "May the wind be at your back, Irishman."

"And yours, Mary Margaret," Sean returned the old Irish blessing to her. "Deal fair with Duncan," he added in unnecessary warning.

"Ah, laddie," Meg crooned, "I've a feelin' in me old bones that I won't be dealing atall any more with himself."

"Aye, lass," Sean echoed her croon. "I've the same kinda feelin'." Laughing softly, he nudged the horse into motion and rode into the snow swept dawn.

Jessica awoke to the stillness of a snow-laden morning. Her memory was fuzzy, but she vividly recalled the visit from the doctor at some point during the night, and his assurance to Duncan that both she and the child were safe and uninjured. It was only after his pronouncement that she had finally drifted into a deep, natural sleep.

Her baby was safe. Relief shivered through Jessica, dissipating the last lingering wisps of exhausted slumber. What had possessed her to act with such thoughtless disregard for the well-being of her child?

Rage and jealousy had possessed her. Jessica cringed at the thought, but could not deny the truth of it. Already simmering with anger over learning about the prostitute her husband had installed in a house in Cheyenne, she had been driven senseless with rage by the lady Charlotte's shameless behavior toward him, and consumed with jealousy because of Duncan's attendance on the brazen woman.

Duncan. She had struck him! In front of all those witnesses! He was such a proud man. Good Lord! What must he be thinking . . . feeling? The shiver inside

Jessica intensified into a shudder. She had to talk to him, explain, apologize.

Where was he now? Was he still here, in the house . . . or . . . Unable to bear the trend of her thoughts, Jessica turned her head to skim an anxious glance around the room. A sob lodged in her throat as her frantic gaze collided with the tall, solid reality of Duncan's figure.

He was standing with his back to the window, still dressed in the evening clothes he had worn to the party. The cloud-heavy morning light cast his profile in shadow, but even so, Jessica could see the harshly drawn lines of strain on his face, the paleness beneath his dark cheeks.

The sight of him brought a rush of warm tears to her eyes. She loved him so very much, more than she loved the land, more than her precious independence, more than her own life. She could no more deny her love for him than she could the love she felt for the child, his child, growing within her body.

Knowing Duncan had made a soiled dove his mistress cut her to the quick, but it didn't change how Jessica felt. She couldn't give him up. She loved him. The woman Meg couldn't have him. Duncan was hers, had been hers almost from the beginning, while he was still a stranger.

Staring at him through the mist of tears, Jessica saw a sudden mystical change in Duncan. Gone was the elegantly attired aristocrat, replaced by the *segundo*, looking tough and formidable in rough working garb, standing tall, rock solid, rifle braced to his shoulder as he coolly confronted a charging grizzly bear.

Segundo. Her Segundo.

"Segundo." Unaware of having whispered the name aloud, Jessica was startled by his sudden alertness, his silent swiftness as he moved to the side of the bed.

"Jessica?" Duncan bent over her, a concerned frown creasing his brow. "Are you all right?"

"Yes." Jessica blinked to clear the teary mist from her eyes, then gasped at the sight of the inflamed gash on his cheek.

"What is it?" he demanded, sitting down next to her. "Jess, tell me, what's wrong?"

"Oh, Duncan, your face!" she cried, impulsively raising her hand to his cheek. "I've hurt you!"

"What did you say?" He went still and tense, so tense Jessica could feel his tension in her fingertips.

"I said I hurt you," she repeated contritely. "I'm sorry. Can you ever forgiv—"

"Not that." He shook his head. "What did you call me?"

"Duncan?" Jessica frowned in confusion.

"Yes . . . Duncan," he said on a note of satisfaction. "Do you realize that is the first time you have ever called me by my Christian name?"

"Yes." Jessica lowered her eyes, suddenly feeling childish and ashamed of herself for the deliberate omission. "My conduct over the last months has been appalling, I know," she admitted, forcing herself to look at him. "But last night was the worst, and I want to apologize for the embarrassment I caused you and Heather."

Duncan looked more than startled by her chastised demeanor; he appeared thunderstruck. "Did you strike your head when you collapsed in the foyer last night?"

Though his tone was serious, a wry smile twitched the corners of his lips.

Wary of his intent, Jessica shook her head. "No, at least I don't think I did. Why?"

"Why?" His smile tested the bounds of his control. "I can hardly believe I'm hearing the Jessica I have come to know, the Jessica of angry defiance and the go-to-hell stance."

Jessica's eyes narrowed, and she tapped one finger-nail against his cheek. "Don't push your luck, cowboy. I'm offering you an apology. Take it or leave it."

"I'll take it," Duncan drawled, slipping into the speech pattern of the cowboys. "Seein' as how it's likely the only one I'll ever hear from you."

"Damned straight," Jessica allowed, wriggling into a sitting position to get a closer look at the gash. On examination, she could see the wound had been treated. "Did the doctor tend to that?"

"Yes." Duncan raised his hand to probe at the gash. "The stuff he applied burned like hell."

Jessica bit her lip. "I really am sorry, Duncan."

"No matter." He shrugged. "What bothers me is why you did it. What set you off?"

Jessica hesitated, then, tossing caution to the wind, she angled her chin and admitted, "I was mad, damn good and mad."

"I kinda figured that out all by myself," Duncan retorted. "But what riled you?"

Goaded by his persistence, Jessica let him have it . . . with both barrels. "You . . . and that friend of yours." She made a snorting sound of disgust. "I am sorry to have to tell you this, my lord, but the lady

Charlotte is no lady. She was all over you like flies on a rotting carcass."

Duncan grimaced at her unappealing description, then he went still, as if struck by a blow—or a thought. "Jessica, are you saying you were jealous of the lady Charlotte?" he asked, slowly, carefully.

"Yes!" she snapped, bristling anew with hot anger. "Yes, I was jealous. She had no right to drape herself on you like a Christmas ornament."

An expectant glow leaped to life in Duncan's turquoise eyes. "If you were jealous," he began, in a hesitant voice unusual to him, "I can't help but wonder if . . ."

Jessica didn't hear him, or the note of suppressed hope in his tone. Having given vent to a portion of her angry steam, she continued at full spate. "Also, whether or not it is a common practice of the aristocracy, I will not tolerate being subjected to the humiliation of living in the same city as your mistress. She will have to go."

An expression of incredulity swept over Duncan's face. "Mistress? What are you talking about?"

"Don't play dumb with me!" Jessica exclaimed. Thoroughly agitated, and needing freedom of motion, she pushed against his chest. Caught off guard, he sprang erect. "I overheard you and Sean in the office last night," she said, flinging the bedcovers off. "Step aside," she ordered, getting to her feet.

"The doctor said you were to remain in bed for a few days," Duncan said, reaching for her.

"I feel fine," she retorted, dodging around him. She paced to the opposite side of the room, then whirled to confront him. "I heard the message Sean gave to you from your whore, Meg."

"Meg! My whore?" Duncan roared. "Dammit, Jessica! Will you listen—"

"No!" she roared back at him. "You listen to me. I'm giving you fair warning. If you don't get rid of that woman you had the gall to install in a house right here under my nose, I will take my whip to the both of you." Her spine ramrod straight, she strode to within inches of his attention-tautened body. "Do you understand me?"

"God, I hope so," Duncan muttered fervently. "But, Jess, if you'll only listen—"

"Damn you, Segundo!" Jessica exploded. "Like it or not, as arrogant, overbearing, and bossy as you are, I love you! And you are mine!"

Duncan went absolutely still for an instant, then he too exploded, but not into speech, into action. Ignoring her yelp of surprise, he swept her into his arms, crushing her soft breasts against the solid hardness of his chest.

"Segundo!"

"You crazy woman," he murmured, lowering his head to hers. "Will you shut up?"

Her response was muffled by the press of his hungry mouth against her parted lips. His kiss was an accolade, a blessing, a commitment, sweet, stirring, infinitely satisfying. They were both gasping for breath when he lifted his head to stare into her shimmering gray eyes.

"Now will you listen?"

"Do I have a choice?" she asked breathlessly.

"No, you do not." Duncan scowled. "Yes, there is a woman named Meg, and I did pay for her house, but not for my private pleasure. I gave her the house as a reward, in gratitude for the information she gave me about Josh Metcalf. I have never been with her, never touched her. You are the only woman I have been with. You are the only woman I desire." He released her to bring his hands to her face, slide his fingers into her silky hair. "Now do you understand me?"

"I—I—"

"Dammit, Jessica! I love you! And you are mine!"

Speechless, quivering, hoping, Jessica stared at Duncan, her love for him at last unconcealed and shining from her eyes. "You love me?" she asked when she finally found her voice.

"Yes, I love you." A memory darkened his eyes. "Why else would I have forced you into marrying me, after learning that you had gone to the shaman to help you destroy my child?"

"You knew?" Jessica whispered, stricken, but then answered before he could respond, "Yes, of course you knew." Wincing at the pain exposed in his eyes, she drew a shuddering breath and confessed, "I—I . . . felt trapped. But I couldn't go through with it. I ran away from him, from the camp."

"Then you want this child?"

There was an uncertainty in his voice, a note of vulnerability that tore at Jessica's heart. Moved by the appeal in his question, she cupped his face in her hands and, for the very first time, kissed him of her own free will. "Yes, Segundo," she whispered against his mouth. "As God is my witness, I do want this child."

"Thank God. I was afraid you hated it . . . and me."

The moist breath from his sigh of relief bathed her lips; the audible catch in his voice pierced her soul.

"I love the baby already, and I love you, but—" Jessica hesitated, then, remaining true to her vow never to be owned, went on in warning, "I won't be a meek wife, Segundo. We'll clash . . . often."

He laughed. The exuberant sound of it was reassuring. "I wouldn't have you any way but as you are—defiant, challenging, magnificent. If you change, I'll beat you." He raised one brow in an arrogant arch. "Deal?"

Jessica laughed with him. "Deal. Do you want to shake on it?"

"I've got a better suggestion." Duncan's slow, sensuous smile sparked a flame of desire deep inside her. The flame flared out of control when he lifted her, gently deposited her on the bed, and slid onto the mattress beside her.

His kiss was warm, gentle, tender, the kiss of a man cherishing the woman he loved. Jessica was lost, and knew it. She didn't care. There would be future problems to weather, she knew that as well. It didn't worry her.

They were together, she and her Segundo, their strengths combined.

Together they could weather anything.

Epilogue

"Here is your grandson, Mother. And your great-nephew, Chill Wind Blowing." Standing before the two gravesites in the shade of the gnarled old tree, Duncan held his sleeping son in his arms and spoke softly into the hot July afternoon. "We are home . . . to stay."

An occasional murmur of conversation and burst of laughter wafted on the fitful breeze from the house at the base of the knoll, where the child had been christened Malcolm Benjamin Washakie Frazer less than an hour ago.

"Segundo."

A wry smile easing the solemn line of his lips,

Duncan turned at the soft call to watch Jessica make her way up the gentle slope to him. As always, the sight of her set his pulses hammering.

Jessica. His Jess. Lord, Duncan thought in near awe, though he would have believed it impossible, the love he felt for her grew deeper with every passing day.

Jessica had changed over the previous seven months, settled in to the role of being a wife and, during the last month, of being a mother. And, being Jessica, she excelled in both.

Truly content for the first time in his life, Duncan cradled his son in his arms, while worshipping his wife with his eyes.

"I knew I'd find you up here," Jessica said, smiling in tender understanding. "The food's been set out, and everyone's ready to eat."

Everyone meant the crews of the Circle-F and the B-Bar-R ranches, and the minister Duncan had collected in Sandy Rush late yesterday afternoon, when they had passed through on their way home from Cheyenne.

Jessica had wanted to return to the ranch after the holidays, so the baby would be born in their home. However, Duncan, wanting Jessica to have medical assistance with the delivery, opted for staying in Cheyenne, with the doctor at hand.

They had argued about it and Duncan had won. Jessica had conceded with good grace, but had refused to consider having the baby christened until they returned home. She'd allowed herself only two weeks of recovery before galvanizing everybody into action for the trip back to the ranch.

Now, home and happy, Duncan indulged himself by teasing his wife. "Still Segundo, hmm?"

"Did I call you that again?" A becoming pinkness tinged Jessica's naturally pale cheeks. "Oh, Duncan, I'm sorry. I don't even realize I'm saying it."

"It doesn't matter," he said, shrugging. And it really didn't matter to him anymore, not since the tone of her voice had changed from harsh to loving when she said it. "But I do wonder why the name keeps slipping out," he went on, holding the baby with one arm and sliding the other around her waist as he started down the incline.

"I don't know." Frowning in consternation, Jessica slid her arm around his waist. "I guess it's because that's the way I always think of you . . . as the *segundo*." Her voice lowered to a soft, enticing whisper. "My Segundo."

Later that night, when the house was quiet and the baby asleep in his cradle next to the big bed, Duncan held Jessica close to his yearning body, drinking deeply from her pliant, responsive mouth. When he could take no more of the sweet agony of wanting her, joining with her, he drew back, exhaled, and whispered a soft request.

"Would you do something for me?"

"Oh, Duncan." Jessica moaned. "I want to too. But you know we can't, not so soon after—"

"Not that, *querida*," he soothed. "I understand. I can wait. But I would like a favor."

"Yes, of course, anything, Duncan. What is it?"

"Call me Segundo."